MW00906537

"With *Shattering Glass*, Connor Coyne has fashioned a hypnotic tale that is at once universal and otherworldly, with writing that is as inventive as the plot."

— GORDON YOUNG

Author of *Teardown: Memoir of a Vanishing City*

"Don't be fooled by the playful tone and pastiche of Connor Coyne's second novel. *Shattering Glass* presents serious questions of identity and morality, posed by vivid characters of a strange and violent world."

— JEFFERY RENARD ALLEN

Author of *Rails Under My Back* and *Song of the Shank*

"It's the First Year Experience from Hell, yet in often gorgeous and startlingly original prose, Connor Coyne gets at something heartwrenching and heartwarming about coming of age in academia."

— JAN WORTH-NELSON

Author of *Night Blind*

SHATTERING GLASS

MORE BY CONNOR COYNE

Hungry Rats, a novel

CONNORCOYNE.COM
HUNGRY-RATS.COM
GOTHICFUNKPRESS.COM

A Manual on How to Survive Your First Year of College:
This First Reckoning to Address Matters
Pertinent to the Autumn Quarter
Most Concisely Summarized
by Issues Embodied
in the Observation of

SHATTERING GLASS

by the Robotic Cetacean Deep-Space Gospel Collective

Connor Coyne

GOTHIC FUNK PRESS

GOTHIC FUNK PRESS

www.gothicfunkpress.com

Flint, Michigan

SHATTERING GLASS

Copyright © 2011, 2012, 2013 by Connor Coyne

All rights reserved.

Edited by **Reinhardt Suarez** and **Jessica Coyne**

Reinhardt Suarez: theporkchopexpress.com/reinhardt-suarez

Designed and Illustrated by **Sam Perkins-Harbin**

forge22.com

ISBN-10: 0989920208

ISBN-13: 978-0-9899202-0-9

10 9 8 7 6 5 4 3 2

Second Edition

To the Mathewsniks.

Arkaic University

Arkaic, Michigan

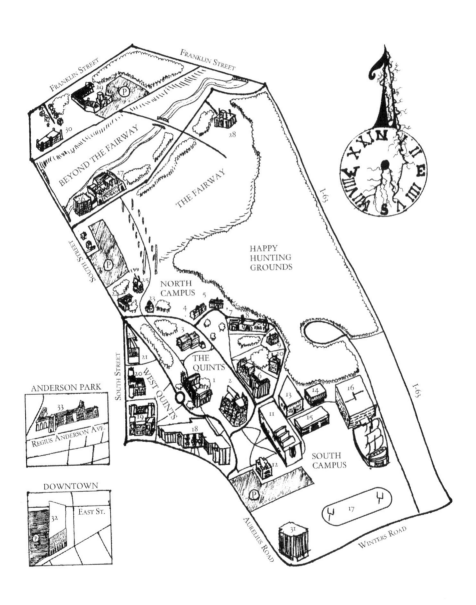

SPIRITUS GRAVIS
EST SOMNIARE

GRÜNDUNGHINTERGRUNDGESCHICHT

Be careful what you wish for.

Ten years after the calamity of Arkaen Spring, the city of Arkaic, Michigan was in dire straits. Blood ran in the gutters like wine. Houses lit up like candles on a birthday cake. The population had fallen by more than half, to just north of 100K. Property values had dropped just as quickly, a fact that was not overlooked by A. Olan, chair and president of the Olan Foundation and the wealthiest man in Arkaic.

Every respectable town has a benefactor, and Arkaic is no exception. For over one hundred years, the Olans have subsidized municipal projects, cultural events, and organizations, from block clubs to Rotary Clubs to the local Freemasons and the Knights of Columbus. The family has been a lifeline to the city in its direst need. They've also ensured that the commie elements in this left-leaning union town have stayed within their proper bounds; that is to say, in obscurity and tottering on an edge that drops off into oblivion. The Arkaen Spring brought everyone's dreams to fruition. What followed, however, was pure nightmare, and neither the pinkos nor the Olans could do much about the situation.

Until everything became as cheap as shit.

This was a rare moment, A. felt, a moment that hearkened back to the turn of the century (20th), when Christopher Olan came into town and bankrolled a few brick buildings called X Automotives. It was a smart move. X became one of the largest corporations in the world, and Christopher became a dangerously wealthy man. Of course, fortunes have diminished with time, both for X and for the Olans, and by 2006 the clan had been reduced to a modest existence as non-sub-billionaires and a common source of names for buildings and parks.

Yes, yes, a rare moment indeed, A. felt, elusive and precious. Soft veins in hard rock, deep underground. For the land had become so cheap, and tuition so high, that A. could buy up some dilapidated neo-gothic cathedralesque things in one corner of town, commit his funds to recruiting faculty and renovating, and still have enough left over for a healthy endowment. He had always wanted to be a father. Now he would be a father of minds, which is perhaps the best kind of father, in the end. He would build his school on the highest hill in Arkaic, in the vacant Arken County Lunatick Asylum, and power it with the raw memories of the ruined town. He would name it Arkaic University, and its color would be gold.

And so, in 2008, the old oak doors swung open to students for the first time, and they carried their tomes of Cervantes and Sterne and hundreds of sweaty Moleskine notebooks. They may have been the very first students, but the history of the place pressed down upon them. Pyrotherapy, cardiazol shock, and occasional stunning freedoms. The halls had all been freshly scrubbed and painted, but they smelled of the thickness of infinite dust. Even as the consciousness of earlier spectres made cobwebs in the students' brains, they started, through their own activities, to etch some inscriptions of their own. What fantasies would the students write? And how soon would this new mythology begin to intrude upon reality?

CHAPTER ONE
THE RAPID RISE AND FALL OF ADA SOMETHINGOROTHER

Don't let this happen to you.

September, 2011. Ada arrives late in the day, and the sparks leap from one serrated battlement to the next. Here it is, her new home, Calliope Cradle, her dormitory, and it looks more like a castle. Not a fairytale German palace, but a thick Slavic thing wearing a crumbling blanket of slate and dismay. She hauls her luggage up the ramp and through the vestibule to the courtyard. Her heavy-lidded eyes take in the wide, wide sky. She has an expressionless face that is always half-asleep (unless she's sleeping). It's hard to tell if she's listening or not. She yawns sometimes, which might mean that she's awake but dozy. Sometimes, she even picks up a pen and doodles some equations. Not especially lifeful, most days, but today she blinks. She blinks today, and those blinks, *shutter shutter*, are signs of startlement and discomprehension.

Shudder shudder. It's cool in there, among the tart cherry trees that flank the stone path. Cool, near the conspicuous gap where lay the alleged graves of Hobbes and Wallis, worm-dueling post death. There are seven houses in Calliope Cradle, and they all vie and compete with one another. It isn't like Hogwarts, though. None of these houses are virtuous; in fact, each is dedicated to a different deadly sin. Ada finds her tiny bedroom on the first floor of Acedia House, crushed between the lower rampart moat and the inner house lounge. It is a single. She'll have to watch how she dresses and undresses, as the curtains are dangerously diaphanous and the room is in good view of the courtyard. They say that cougars and lions hunt out there. Ada sees students reclining under the pear trees; they are the Orientation Designations. The brand new students are still too shocked and startled to lay at ease.

Touring the dorm, everything seems to be a flavorful extreme. Bits of sugar crust the knife-scarred doors, and some say a recruited descendent of the czar's daughter comes by to replenish them with dappled frosting flowers that she makes herself. In the basement, beneath the cafeteria, the floor has been graffitied with dangerous proofs, teaching earthbound hydrogen fusion, and, so doing, the solutions to the wounds of love. As George Clinton says, it's the balm. Calliope Cradle is not the largest dorm, though it is one of the most remote, sprawling on the edge of Seller's Creek. Students have to cross the Fairway to get to their classes, and while the firefly lanterns and xenon lamps flare all night long, Ada is a little nervous about the massive subterranean tunnels with whirring turbines and taut, tight mazes of chains. She's never heard of "chain power" before. She doesn't understand temporelectricity. She is a novitiate; here tread experts.

But she tries her best; that is to say, a little bit.

Ada leaves her luggage in her room and crosses the Fairway and the Quints to formally register at Olan Commons. She's been here before, as a twelfth grade prospective, but the room seems larger, now that it is filled with new students. They seem correspondingly small, because they are nervous and don't know where to look or what to do with their hands.

"Hi," says the boy ahead of her in line.

She looks at him, peripherally. She looks away. She doesn't want to talk.

"I'm Sam," says the boy.

Okay, fine.

"...hello."

"What's your name?"

"...ada."

"Sorry, what?"

"...Ada."

"You just get here today?"

"...yeah."

"Coo'. Me too."

Sam is tall and slender, and, um, gangly, with knobby knees and elbows, and face a that looks almost triangular, like a praying mantis. He has dark black skin and short-cropped hair. He wears a bright orange T-shirt of a zombie dolphin's head exploding in a spatula print of blood. Sam seems way too confident for his awkward appearance. *Gregarious* would be a good word.

"Man, this place is *crazy*," he says. "I've been here a lot, but I never knew how crazy it was. Those lights and those gardens are wild. But there's so many little hidden places all over. My dorm has a secret passage to the law library. And there're bricks where the mortar is all crumbled apart, and it looks like there's a door behind that. I got a potato cannon–homemade, right–and I thought I might shoot some bricks out of it. I've never shot a brick before."

Go away, Ada thinks.

"You've been here a lot? As a prospie?" she says instead. *Why did I just say that?*

"Who, me?" *Who else?* "Oh, not as a prospective student, or whatever. I'm from Arkaic. I wanted to go to XAI–um, the X Automotives Institute–but my grades weren't good enough. So I'm here to study engineering. Aeronautics, I think. What about you, where you from?"

Shut up, Ada thinks, and is about to say, but then the question catches in her brain. Where *is* she from? Since she has arrived, the dorm, the moat, the tunnels and chains, and, yes, the lights and gardens–in all their pungent power–their pregnant presence–they all ride (is that the word?) past or slide (is that it?) by or–elide–anything weaker and less vivid than themselves. Like her memories of her home. Her own dull memories of her own apathetic home.

"I don't know," she says, "Iowa or Missouri or something." *Davenport!* she thinks. *It's Davenport*, with relief.

"Huh," says Sam. "Well, it looks like I'm up," and he steps up to a desk and starts filling out forms.

Ada meets her parents back at the Cradle, and they spend the rest of the day in the vast dining hall with poop deck and barrel-vaulted ceilings. She then attends the Scholars' Designations Address, where a suited vagrant projects the aspirations of the University in Latin-cadenced words. "Lorem ipsum" and all that. As the sun sets, Ada stands with her parents, trying to recall their names. She awkwardly says goodbye. She makes herself give them a hug, but she's not accustomed to this, and it feels strange. Her arms are almost limp around their waists.

Back at the dorm, Ada goes to the bathroom to take a quick shower, to awaken her brain, always tired, always bored, and there she runs into–Sam!

"Hey!" he says, "You didn't tell me you were in Acedia House."

Blink blink. Startled. "Did ...did you tell me?"

"Yeah, I did!"

"Oh," she says. "Well. I don't remember."

"Oh, well anyway –"

"What are you doing in the girls' bathroom?"

"This isn't the girls' bathroom. The bathrooms are all coed!"

"They are?"

"Yeah, but you should look out that there," and he points to an interior window of dull black glass. "It's for ventilation, but it funnels lightning from the chain tunnels. I stood there for ten minutes earlier, and I saw a big ol' bolt!"

"...Oh."

"Anyway, I'm off to the house meeting. I'll see you soon?"

He leaves.

What's his name?

Ada decides to skip the house meeting. She's too confused, too bedazzled, to take on anything new. She wants refuge in her boredom and memories, such as they are. She wants to cultivate her nostalgia. She spends the rest of the evening unpacking and listening to her Black Eyed Peas–*The End, The Beginning, Blah Blah Blah*– and then she goes to sleep. She dreams her favorite dream. It's a dream about a time when she beat the computer at Hearts twice in a row.

While she dreams, things move just beyond her translucent curtain. Sam has gathered some other first-years in the courtyard, and they shoot old bricks at the moon from a potato cannon. On the Fairway, the fireflies have escaped their cages, and they swarm the gate and alight on autumn pansies and daffodils. It gets later, and most of the Orientees go inside to unpack or sleep. There aren't any Designations drinking out on the lawn at this hour, and if they are, then they certainly aren't drinking Old Krupnik. Leave that amber honey for the Poles.

The grass isn't green this September, but sharply emerald. It has turned purple in the nighttime, ultraviolet, as under a black light; yes, it is a black amethyst, like moonside shadows. The branches shake. The oak moans. Satyrs prance, and the Designations don't ride them. Satyrs kick when you do that. Bugs have sex on the peonies. Theresa Romanov licks her sugar flowers and belladonna buds. Pomegranate seeds that have the double bonus of prolonging life and acting as aphrodisiacs. Not that any naughtiness is happening here. Old Krupnik only bends Poles that way.

Meanwhile, high above, a late wash of the Perseids commences, and while most of the stones remain stone and fizzle in the atmosphere, a few of them spin and shift, dihydroxegenate and turn wet. They fall and hit the courtyard. The brambles and the trellises. The rambles and the turning pages of Descartes that ripple in the sourceless whisperless. Rain from a cloudless sky. The Designations don't kiss in the alcoves. They don't do more than kiss. The brighter and sharper of the new students don't step out into the dark to drink the wine of Histiaea and Lydia and, if they're feeling exotic, Kozol. The irregular stone walkway. The cobbled boards where parasites hide. Partisans' lances. Mumscores. Leaflets.

It's going to be a late fall this year. Balmy and barmy and strong. It isn't going to get cold at all. This September, September lasts forever. It isn't going to change, though the trees will grow and drop moon-shaped fruits to be eaten. The air is so thick you could suck it like a banana, and when you explode, your matter disappears.

Orientation is dangerous. It simply cannot be helped.

The RAs (Resident Advisers) have warned the Designations to pay special attention to listless students like Ada. After all, the things that are happening right outside her window flush with a passion and havoc that is absent from her very most cherished dreams. There's little hope not to dissolve into nothing. Even if she has one poignant last moment—a pale face, heaving chest, dry eyes, numb panic as she tries and fails to remember her parents' faces—she is simply too dull for this place. It forgets her, as it made her forget herself. The air goes thin and dusty and cool. The walls become as the air. Her mind is stretched and expanded to sleep. Her body has ceased to be. She fades away, erased from the universe.

The Designations do their best. They really do. Still, nobody bats a hundred, and every year a few students are elided. Professors notice that "Ada" is not coming to class. They either fail her or assume she has withdrawn.

Housing doesn't notice the decline and still sends bills to her parents.

"Ada?" they ask, "Who's Ada?"

And then, one day, several weeks in, Sam goes walking down the hall of the first floor of Acedia House. He stops when he feels something tug at him like a metal hook right behind his aorta. It's the plain wood door to his right. It leads to a bedroom. A single.

"Didn't someone used to live here?" he says aloud.

But the Tigers are on track for their twenty-eighth World Series win, and Sam doesn't want to miss the Game Four sweep.

He continues down the hall and gets on with his life.

CHAPTER TWO
ORIENTATION IS DANGEROUS

Pretty Hot

*Get your shit together **before** you go.*

"Pretty hot," says Sam.

For a dozen years–hundreds, it seemed–his Moms had driven him through the peaks and valleys of Elmwood Road on their way to the burbs to see his grandma. Each time, they passed Mallery's Storage. The hot and blazing white concrete brutalist pile accordioned out of the ground to a height of forty feet as if molded from the surplus mix of sand in gravel from the shattered street. On some floors, the folds flattened into slick fast panes of black glass, and on others, they prickled with ladders and antennae. "MALLERY'S STORAGE," solid block letters, plywood probably, had been cut with a jigsaw, painted brown, and drilled into the front of the concrete mass. Hot.

As a kid, at eight, Sam had imagined having a great job as an astronaut. He imagined the blue sky stripping darker and darker, as if he were peeling an onion from the inside out and watching for the enfolding night beyond. He didn't imagine the deafening sound, the throbbing in his eardrums, the insane shaking, no. Just that gradual shift in color. He saw the last layer fall away and there it all hung, vast and black and throbbing with matters and empties. There was something akin to the Apollos in Mallery's behemoth, and it gave Sam a thrill every time he saw it. This simple familiarity would be the first rung of his Jacob's Ladder, the first chance to touch with his eyes the power of human technology, four stories high. Sam would climb much higher.

September, 2011 found him suspended above a rift that defined opposite ledges.

"You're taking your sweaters," said Moms.

"No way Moms, too hot."

"You're taking them," and she carried a black garbage bag stuffed with woolly, warm things and dropped it into the trunk of the hatchback.

"I can just come get some if I need them!"

"I don't need you stomping through here at three in the morning because you didn't take any sweaters!"

On one ledge, all the sad and angry boys and girls from his neighborhood. A few of them were going to college and most of them weren't. Those that were went to Southern Michigan U or Arkaic Community. Those that didn't were holding down jobs, looking for jobs, having kids, or selling dope off corners. This ledge represented marginal houses on marginal streets, identical to Sam's house but more tired and run-down. Because mortgages are more important than lawn mowers. Because there wasn't a supermarket in three miles. Because education had never got no one nowhere, so why should it get going now? These were Sam's neighbors. They were his childhood friends.

"I'm going to pack these sweaters around your computer, Sam," said Kimmy, his little sister. She was in tenth grade. She sparkled because she was imagining college too.

"No, I got it."

"But this'll keep it from moving around in the back!"

"No, I got it, I got it!" he snapped, and pulled the monitor from the trunk, spilling sweaters everywhere.

On the other ledge, all the proud and tall boys and girls from the Southern High School Magnet. They were all going to college, every last one. They went to U of M or MSU, and farther, to strange names Sam had only heard once or twice: *Oberlin. Carlton. Macalester.* One kid had gone to Stanford. And yes, plenty went to XAI–the X Automotives Institute–right here in Arkaic. This ledge represented magical houses on magisterial streets, two or three times the size of Sam's house and yard. Because the gatekeepers of the past were the gatekeepers of the future. Because education had been a reliable skeleton key, and they had had the resources to afford it. These were Sam's classmates. They were his peers.

And then there was Sam. Hot. Overheated. Confused.

He was ten when Columbia disintegrated in the thermosphere. "Boom!" he had said, but he was secretly upset. *Brave people*, he thought. *Just like me*. He felt a silent terror. That Indian girl was pretty, he thought, in the still-too-young reptile part of his brain. And now they were all everywhere, all of them. Floating in the air he breathed.

"Do you still want to go to the moon?" his grandma asked that day.

"No. I want to go to Mars!"

"Bad idea, Sudzy." (As a little kid he had run around naked covered in soap suds.) "If God wanted us up there he wouldn'ta put us down here."

On the ride home, they passed Mallery's, and it looked bright, white, and high-tech. In his chest, Sam still wanted outer space, but his skull rattled with the knowledge that death up there was a sudden eclipse, a permanent extinguishing, and scattering all around the...everywhere. His skull hoped that his adventures would be both gentler and safer, but his chest argued that this was the most craven sort of settling. Either way, Sam felt too hot and looked out his window.

"You okay?" asked Moms.

"Your mom's okay," he said.

She stood in his bedroom doorway and tilted her head.

"You sure you're okay?"

He sighed.

"I'm not going to know...anybody there."

"There are plenty of kids from Arkaic at AU."

"Not that many," he said. "And they're all in arts and English." In the back yard, the leaves swayed in motion with *fin de siècle* resignation and astronaut dust. "I shoulda gone to XAI, at least."

"You're tellin' me," she said.

But his early, bold words had vaporized in the wake of furtive fears, a fatal concession. By the time Sam had re-upped his hopes, at seventeen, and started considering architecture, aeronautics, engineering—white lines on blue paper that arced skyward from the diagonal parts of Mallery's Storage—the moment had passed. It was far too late to craft an application for MIT or Caltech. It was even too late to make a play for Michigan Tech or XAI. He had a GPA of 2.X, and his SATs were nothing to brag about. He did, however, get accepted into AU, but only because they wanted enough science students to justify their state-of-the-art facilities. So Sam took out loans. A lot of loans. They were probably demolishing his future, too.

"Look," Moms said, "Where you're going is an unknown thing. No one knows what it'll be like. Now isn't the time to give up on yourself. You got there! You made it. So look around you and do something with it."

She gave him a hug. Sam farted. Moms frowned and stomped out of the room, while Sam laughed and laughed, and closed the windows and closed the door, letting the reek—beans and rank beef—settle into his bedding and shelves.

Moms and Pops and Kimmy got into the car, and Sam climbed in and held the computer and monitor on his knees, the mouse in his right hand, the keyboard in his left, crossed across his chest. His feet rested on his potato cannon.

"Sam!" said Pops. "Seat belt!"

"Um, okay," he said. He jiggled his shoulders, so they'd think he was taking the trouble—he couldn't reach the seatbelt without dropping everything. "Got it!"

Pops glared, but backed out of the driveway.

AU was a less-than-ten-minute drive away. They did not pass Mallery's. They swept in among the thick trees and cottagey homes on Elmwood Road, then turned off onto Old Benedict Street and plunged into the Arken River valley. There lay XAI, where the students wore starched, white-collared shirts or Greek sweatshirts and khakis, as the look of clean precision was essential to engineering a car or, God forbid, a rocket. Back up the hill on the other side, they arrived at the new old campus of Arkaic University, and it was a sight to see. Sharp. Serrated. Sweltering. Damaged. Dense. Fresh. Ruthless. Impassioned. Insane. Dark. All in all, pretty hot.

The next several hours were a storm-clouded rush from one scene to the next. Sam and his family unloaded his every earthly possession–there were a lot–into his basement dorm room at Calliope Cradle. It was a two-room suite, and while there was no sighting of his roommate–"Monty Valverde" from Springfield, MO– they did see two fine suitcases, black and sky blue, and a sharp looking silver laptop in the inner room.

"Looks like you missed out!" laughed Pops, and they unpacked in the windowless outer room. Not hot.

From there it was over the moat and through the gardens to the Olan Commons, where Sam registered in a big room with hundreds of other Orientees. They stopped at the campus bookstore so that Moms could buy an AU sweater, Pops an AU baseball cap, and Kimmy an AU flask. Then it was back across the Viaduct and Fairway to the Cradle for a wonderful lunch of mshikaki and Kashata. Pops had Nkonyagi. Then up to the dorm's master suite to meet Dr. Lawless, the Dungeon Master. Wine was had, and cheese sliced with smiling little knives and eaten on tiny little crackers. Bawdy poetry read. Then a solemn parade across the Fairway to the Elysium Chapel. Vijay Kumar Patodi delivered the keynote address, and Julian Beck the benediction.

"It is time to escort them to their cars," he said of the parents in the hall. "It is time to send them on their way." Icy cold, Sam thought with a smile.

So Sam and his family found their car parked on the grassy Fairway. He hugged each of them goodbye. Moms started crying.

"Moms, I'm like three miles from home!"

And away they went.

Now, he stands there for several long moments, taking in the city from above. Maybe it isn't much of a city anymore. Maybe it isn't much to look at. But from up here, the whole place, thick with streams and rivers, pockmarked with pits, pitted with hills, awash with the green of trees and overgrown parks, and the single strip of striking towers downtown...this is, at the very least, the best view in this neck of the woods. Behind him? Arkaic University. Density. Teeming life, too much life, too much energy. It can overwhelm him, he knows, and drown him out.

And then, before him, left of the skyline, just a bit, and the sun going down behind it, the accordion outline of Mallery's Storage. It chastises him with a crude cement middle finger: "You could have been so much more..." "You could have gone so very much further..." "But you were afraid." "AFRAID!"

Yet it is the university that stands tall on the highest hill and stretches its shadow over Arkaic to cover Mallery's each morning.

"Hi!" comes a ginger voice from somewhere behind Sam, and a new shadow slides in beside him. Sam sees a vaguely Latino boy, probably his own age but younger-seeming, with neat black hair, honeysuckle eyes, and carefully relaxed lips.

The boy appears to lean, slightly, although there isn't anything to lean against.

"Sam, right?" he says. "I'm your roommate, Monty Valverde." They shake hands. "And you're Sam O'Samuel."

"Yeah."

"So I was wondering if I could call you Samo. Since it's like your first name and your last, and I never got a nickname like that."

Your name is Monty Valverde and you never got a nickname?

"Um, sure," says Sam, I mean, Samo. "Hey, do you like potato cannons?"

"What's a potato cannon?"

"It's basically a bunch of PVC fixed together, and there's two kinds, combustion and pneumatic, but mine are mostly pneumatic, and they shoot potatoes and shit."

"Gross."

"I mean, potatoes and other stuff."

Silence.

"So..." says Monty. "How do you feel about all of this?"

And he sweeps his hand across the campus, over the Fairway and the Quints, from Calliope Cradle to the Commons.

"Pretty hot," says Samo.

Reinvention

You've only got one shot at reinvention, so get it right.

"So you're from around here?" says Monty, as they walk back to the dorm. "I know very little about Arkaic, Michigan."

Samo's face cycles through a number of expressions: confusion, perplexity, vexation, determination, and then an exaggerated gritty badassness.

"It's whack," he says.

"Oh," says Monty. He pauses. "Well, it does look pretty ravaged, now that you mention it."

"No doubt!" says Samo.

"What about you?"

"Huh?"

"I know even less about you than I do Arkaic."

"Oh," Samo says, his face cycling through expressions again. "I'm...normal."

"Yeah, but you're planning to reinvent yourself, aren't you?"

"Um...what does that mean?"

"You only get to do this a few times in your life...start over from almost nothing. And you look like that's what you want to do."

As disorienting as the day has been, Samo has put together a sort of plan to reinvent himself. The biggest advantage to being alone here—not knowing anyone else from high school—is that he can erase any personality traits he doesn't like and magnify his better qualities. No, he hasn't figured out the career stuff yet, but he'd like to be a sexy badass, and get laid a lot by various attractive/interesting/intelligent women. For starters, no Afros for Samo. He had done that in tenth grade, and his hygiene had not been sufficient to pull it off without looking like he had slept in a ditch somewhere. From now on, he'd keep it cut short and clean. Also, sunglasses, all the time, even indoors, even at night. Maybe not at night, but definitely indoors. He'd have to wear his old sneakers for now, but the first chance he got, he was buying some expensive ones and never looking back. He had to get rid of all those sweaters. Cosby sweaters.

"I don't know," Samo says. "Man, you're crazy!"

Monty smiles, because he has seen almost everything that Samo has tried to hide. That's okay. Monty does not judge, and has, in fact, planned a sort of reinvention of his own. It is much simpler: he won't speak a lot. In high school he was a sort of Margaret Farquhar, always talking, always asking questions. Asking weird questions. He knows that words can be interpreted as deviance, but silence is positively mysterious, especially when delivered by a not-too-heavy, not-too-slim vaguely Latino boy with honeysuckle eyes.

"Oh," says Monty. "Okay."

At any rate, AU is the perfect place for this strategy. Most of the students here are socially inept, and Monty just has to beat the pack. He's not hoping to be a sexy badass or to get laid...not as his primary goal, at least. He has his sights set on the fulfillment of destiny.

No I don't, he thinks. *I don't believe in destiny.* He believes in spiderwebs. He believes in connection. He believes that strands of intrigue don't ricochet off into the darkness at unrelated angles; the specific gravities of secrets are severe. When Monty folds his hands symmetrically behind his head and looks into the darkness-hidden white plane of his bedroom ceiling, he sees convergence. The convergence of the very small number of people that control the vast majority of the world's wealth. The simple observation that so many politicians and celebrities and wise men and women die such violent, untimely deaths. The absolute proof that the world is infiltrated by all manner of otherlings. These things must be understood and acknowledged by anyone who hopes to survive the drastic upheavals to come. Monty is no fan of David Icke–David Icke is antisemitic– but there's a disconcerting plausibility to his claims that the earth is ruled by shape-changing demoniac lizards from space. The truth will be Monty's fulfillment. He will learn the truth here. The illusions will collapse, and answers will slide into his hands.

Will they?

The gravel crunches under his feet. His feet are big, at least compared to the stones underfoot. But the universe is big, and suddenly Monty feels small and vulnerable. *What if I'm wrong?* he wonders. *Then I've given up everything...*

"Hey," says Samo.

It's the truth. Monty could've gone anywhere he wanted. He had a 4.4 in all the toughest classes and a 1560 on his SAT. But in ninth grade, he attended a (fellow weirdo's) birthday party, and there, the Ouija board told him to go to a school of insanity in Michigan. Monty had laughed. He didn't believe in Ouija boards, and anyway, there was no such school. His thoughts on the subject started to turn when he got a postcard from AU in his junior year, mentioning that it had been built on the site of a former insane asylum. *It has to be a coincidence*, Monty thought. *Ouija boards are a sham. Superstition.* And yet, he wrote the school back and accepted their offer to visit. They put him up with a Czolgosz scholar from Alpena, who introduced him to all the most eccentric geometers, and Monty started to wonder: *What if the Ouija wasn't a coincidence? What if it's just a part of the pattern I'm not allowed to see? What if it's the one irrational thing I'm supposed to trust?*

"Hey," says Samo.

And the irony struck him powerfully: as a starkly self-aware conspiracy theorist, Monty knew that Rule no. 1 is not to trust anyone, from the shadows to the graveyard. Still, as he had stood in the Quints that night and saw the bright blue trees ranging about him, their waves in the wind thrusting toothy spruce needles through the expansive sky like the velvety prongs of a fractal's edge, Monty trusted that this would be his home. That was in 2010. Almost one year later, he is passing those same trees. They look like simple trees now; ordinary, not Ancient Elders whispering their secrets like Meskwaki code talkers. Maybe he had been wrong to trust the message. Maybe he had just thrown away his chance to go to Harvard or Yale...maybe it's all wrong, and he's all alone in the –

But there! Thunder: the trees dance and whisper again. The sky reddens with a rust blood tint. The dorms and campus are set aflame. The wind turns, and somewhere deep below his feet, cold and burning magnets turn. The world is opening up and sharing its secrets...

"Hey!" says Samo.

"Hello?" says Monty.

"Are they going to feed us?"

"I don't know. Cheese maybe. And soda."

"Hah," says Samo. "You just said 'soda.'"

"So?"

"You're in Michigan, bitch, you don't drink soda here. 'Less you're going to some '50s diner or something. It's called pop."

The Orientees gather in the fourth floor lounge of Acedia House, a gloomy and cavernous room shaped like a hollowed-out kidney bean. At one end stands a massive stone hearth next to a sliver-thin window. At the other end were a Foosball table and a big box TV. In between was a card table with pop and pretzels. The House Masters–Ryder and Riley Maven–do a quick head count. There are fifteen students, but there will be three times that number when the upperclassmen return. "Okay," they say, "let's introduce ourselves." Let's let everyone know who we are and where we're from. Oh, and say something interesting about yourself.

There's the Texan, Argosy Jackknife, the most awkward-looking of the bunch. His clothes are expensive, probably; preppy, but way too big for him, and his shirt almost slides off his left shoulder. He's white with tangled blonde hair and glasses, and he bites off his fingernails, stacks them in a pile, and starts to make a little tower. His interesting fact is that he went to high school with Alexis Bledel's little sister, but she didn't want to date him.

And then there's Elaine Trotter from the South Side of Chicago. She has a sweet and open expression, warm but anxious, a broad nose, brown eyes, thick braids. She doesn't know what's interesting, she guesses, but everyone in her family plays a different kind of aerophone, and so she guesses that they're a sort of band, and that's kind of cool, she guesses, right?

And there's Esmeralda Prentice from New York City. Skinny and pale with feathery, dust-colored hair and terrified eyes. Samo is taken aback to see tangles of hair where her arms meet her shoulders. She has made glass explode just by looking at it. And Cassidy Antrim, who makes the perfect martini, just like Winston Churchill would like it (sans vermouth). And Brent Gatsby, who says something-or-other, but Samo doesn't care because he looks like a hipster, so how cool could it be, really? And a bunch of other people, too. None of them from Arkaic. Not remotely.

Then it's Samo's turn. He's up.

Be cool, dude. Be a player. "I'm Samo. I'm from Arkaic, yeah. It's whack. Um." Pause. Pause. "I been in a threesome, awwww yeahhhh!" *But I haven't, so, um, shit.* "I got a potato cannon and I like to shoot things out of it. Like potatoes." *Dammit! Regroup! Take two!* "Hey, what do you call ten dead babies in a blender?" Silence. "Nevermind...it's just a joke."

Now it's Monty's turn. He takes a drink of his Dr. Pepper, and the galangal burns his mouth. He refuses to burp. He lets his breath out slowly.

"I'm Monty Valverde, and I'm from Springfield, Missouri. I've spent some time studying this dorm of ours, Calliope Cradle, and I think we're definitely being watched by extraterrestrials."

Great, thinks Samo, *now they all think I'm a pervy pyro, and my roommate is a weirdo.*

I've said just enough, thinks Monty.

"Okaaaay then," says the RA, Monica. "We're going to let you get back to unpacking again pretty quickly, but we just wanted to give you a small bit of collected wisdom we've picked up here at the Cradle the last few years.

"First, seriously, guys, seriously, don't, don't go down by the tunnels, and don't fuck with the turbines. They can fuck your shit up. It's still new technology, and nobody fully understands the effects that it has. Think of it as radiation. If you live in a town with a nuclear reactor, you're going to get a higher dose, but nothing that can really hurt you, not just by living there. But you don't want to wander around the core, either. These things are drawing energy off of memories and experiences, and they can disorient you, or even kill you. The chain tunnels are off limits for a reason.

"Second, in a week you'll have a chance to see the different Student Organizations—we just call them SOs—and just be careful who you team up with. Some of them—like, not to name names, but maybe TOG—Theatre of Gold—or some sect of Artemis' Society—are under federal investigation. So keep that in mind."

"Thank you, Monica," say the Mavens. "Okay, goodnight to you all!" Everyone stands and scatters for their rooms.

"I think it's kind of weird that we're down in the basement. And then that shit about the turbines? What do you think about that? I think it's crazy! And that thing about those clubs?! What do you think about that?" asks Samo. "What do you think?"

"I think it's pretty hot," says Monty.

Shattering Glass

You'll always meet people when you play the music too loud.

The sun, it slips, slips, slips away on the very first day of Orientation.

"Ezzie!" comes that sharp, ringing voice from the outer room.

And just like that, it's gone. The day is done. Violetine shades paint the sawtooth grass. She's sure, because the lawn is at eye level through the thick and leaded glass. Esmeralda Prentice, a.k.a. Ezzie, has arrived in Arkaic, and anxiety sinks in her stomach like a cinder block in a sea of melted imitation butter. She's not thrilled to be here, but she stands in her small, bright yellow, basement room, and she is...well, she's here.

"What is it?" she calls.

"You don't mind if I play some Prince, do you?"

"What?"

"Prince! As in Rogers Nelson! I want to play him. Is that okay?"

"Um, sure."

"But I want to play him loudly! I mean, there really isn't any point if I can't play him loudly!"

Ezzie is a bit afraid of what "loudly" might mean to her suitemate, Dunya. The old oak door is closed, but it seems to shake with every word.

"Um, okay?" says Ezzie.

"Great! Thanks!"

Thunk clatter. Crash. Ezzie turns toward the door, her eyes carefully skirting the mirror to avoid her reflection. *Don't want to take any chances*, she thinks.

"Should I play *Controversy* or *Purple Rain*?"

"What?"

"I mean, I think that *Purple Rain* is good for this time of year, overall, but I kind of feel like *Controversy* is better for moving into a dorm room."

"I don't know. I don't know either of them. I think you should listen to whichever one you want."

"Okay, well I'm going to go with *Controversy* then, because it just sort of fits the mood tonight, doesn't it?"

"Sure."

Ezzie's known Dunya for all of one hour, but the girl makes her smile anyway. They're going to get along fine, or at least as well as Ezzie gets along with anyone. A feeling of familiarity and comfort. *Who is Prince Nelson, anyway?*

Ezzie turns away from the door and resumes hanging her fabulous shawls. She is a long way from New York, but she's brought her favorite accessories: rings and bracelets and necklaces and anklets and shawls and hats and slippers and gloves—they're not expensive, really, but they are opulent and expressive in a thoroughly Manhattan sort of way. It's hard enough to find such a particular density of eclecticism—with sequins and inner moonlight and eternal nothingness and fake fur—in Brooklyn, to say nothing of Arkaic, Michigan. Perhaps she won't wear them. She doesn't expect to be patient with the questions she'll hear, but her accessories do comfort her and remind her of home.

And then the sound descends, one of the most amazing things she's ever heard. Funky and thick, fast and slow, squashed fat beats tripping by with...with, what exactly? With a God Damn Swagger, that's what the fuck what! That voice, that beautiful masculine feminine voice swells in a pulse with far more attitude than staccato chants should be allowed to own. Ezzie's never heard of Prince Nelson before, but he also reminds her of home, and she aches again, deep down. That cinder block has entered the thermocline. Arbitrary magic has replaced silky destiny, and it makes her click her teeth together.

Through most of her childhood and teen years, Ezzie felt as though she stood in the amber cloud–the sepia warmth–of Fresnel lanterns. Their dusky protection. It was figuratively, and sometimes literally, true. Her mother, her father, her uncle, they had all raised her with meticulous care and sat up long after she had gone to sleep, deliberating on what paths to set. Without any unreasonable or unyielding pressure, they guided her, with smiles and suggestions, toward the bright colored blocks and autumn horse rides that the Bloombilt Private Academy Preschool offered on the misty banks of the Hudson. The 50s. From there it was an easy dance–Ezzie had loved dancing as a child–to enroll at the Vanderberg School on the clouded shores of the East River. The 30s. And one day when Ezzie was in sixth grade, her mother caught her moving her dolls across her bedroom and delivering their varying speeches into the purple infinity of the rippled stucco walls.

"Rocky the Reindeer doth bestride the narrow world

Like a brachiosaur, and we petty animals

Walk under his huge legs and peep about

To find ourselves a dishonorable place to forage

in the forest."

Clearly, her passion was the theatre, so Ezzie was enrolled in the St. Antipas School of the Arts, high above the messes of Wall Street. "If we'd given her a sledgehammer," her mother later joked, "she'd have smashed the fourth wall herself." Ezzie came to wonder if her writerly game had merely been a nod to her lack of friends.

Still, she had to enroll somewhere, and theatre was a good fit. Ezzie saw many plays, from Broadway bright to Williamsburg drab and, once, at a happening, she got to stand on a bidet next to Tony Kushner. She preferred writing to acting and tech. Her plays were an outlet for her driving emotions, her dramatic voice, that never, otherwise, found a listener.

(Carmen sits on the park bench, clutching her hems in her hands. Bright wash from DS. Craig enters UR. He shouts.)

CRAIG

(Horrified.) Don't look into the sun, Carmen. Don't–

CARMEN

The longer I look, the more I can see –

(He tries to pull her from the bench, shielding her eyes with his hands. She resists.)

CRAIG

You'll scar your eyes doing that. You'll never see right again!

CARMEN

Everyone is an angel. Halos surround them all. You, too, Craig! You too!

CRAIG

Look away, Carmen! I love you!

(She stands.)

CARMEN

You do. But it can't hurt me. It isn't the sun. It's just a stage light, and we're just actors standing on a stage.

(Alphonse runs on DL, and smashes through the fourth wall with a sledgehammer.)

ALPHONSE

Grahhhhhh!!!

Later, after the sudden blackout, a tiny Asian boy stood behind Ezzie's family and waited to shake her hand. "I–I–I," he said, "really liked your play." "Really?! Thank you!" And thus she took her first furtive steps into *actual* friendships and conversations with other humans.

From there, Ezzie's life started to arc in an upward direction. She was never "popular," but she had a circle of friends, and they liked her and shared her interests. She went to parties with her friends and danced unselfconsciously to the music. Once, she kissed a boy and was unimpressed, but on the walk home she kissed a girl and thought, *Hmm...this warrants further consideration.* She tried to write a play about the experience but it never quite came out right. She had amazing grades and stellar test scores (almost on par with Monty Valverde's) and she was ready to incinerate the world with her art.

Ezzie was determined not to let any of the fame and attention go to her head. With her millions of dollars and critical credentials, she'd buy a small, one-bedroom condo in Soho, and she'd go down to the corner deli to sip kosher soup and discuss the zeitgeist. This was after she'd go to college at Yale. The great playwrights all went to Yale.

Ezzie didn't go to Yale.

Her apotheosis was short lived. As her junior year turned toward her senior, her friends drifted away in an unacknowledged froth of sneers and whispered cruelty. Her mom and dad separated, and that calm guidance that had smoothed her every path vanished as her parents turned to tend their own raw wounds. After Yale rejected her, so did Harvard, Columbia, Cornell, Princeton, Dartmouth, UPenn, and Brown. That was all of her applications. On the tearful day when she received the last rejection, the headmaster called Ezzie to his office and urged her to consider Arkaic University.

"It's a new school–practically brand new," he said, "but they have an impressive faculty pedigree. I think it would be perfect for you."

Is there still light? she wondered. *An illuminated haze of hope? Will a Fresnel lantern guide me home to...Michigan?*

"Why?" she demanded. "Why do you think it's *perfect* for me?"

"Because," he stormed, "when A. Olan was having his second affair, his secret was safe with me, God dammit-all!"

And lo! The lights go out. So does the sound.

"Aw, shit," Ezzie hears through the door, and for the first time, Dunya's voice is quiet and subdued.

Ezzie sets her shawl down. Does she move to the door? Every choice, the most miniscule moment, always seems fraught with consequence. She doesn't want to step out and take too much initiative, like the boy upstairs blathering about potatoes and dead babies. But moving to the door to see what happened–that couldn't be such a drastic move, could it? *Of course not!* she thinks. *Why am I so slow here?*

Oh well, it doesn't matter, because Dunya has opened the door herself and stands there, tall and imposing, holding a small votive candle in her palm. Its glow perfectly halos her own soft and expressive face. Her short, light hair and warm brown eyes are set off by sharp, almost angry eyebrows.

"Oops," she says.

"What happened?" Ezzie asks.

"I think I blew a fuse."

"Should we go get Monica? I don't know where the fuse box is."

"Me neither."

"Let's go."

They open the door to the hall and, "Ahhhh!" there's a shadow there. The shadow of a man. Well, a slight and generally unintimidating man, but it is a shock nonetheless.

"Who is it?" asks the shadow.

"It's Dunya and Ezzie," says Dunya.

"Oh, hi. It's Monty."

"Monty?"

"I live across the hall from you. With Samo."

"The potato cannon guy?"

"Yeah, that's me," comes dimly from a room across the hall. Ezzie smiles.

Monty continues. "Do you know what happened to the lights?"

"I think I blew a fuse," says Dunya.

"With the funk?"

"With Prince!"

"Ahhhhh..."

"Where is the fuse —"

"The fuse box is in our room on this floor. But you guys have the fuses in a line on your window. I guess Monica didn't tell you. You can't keep the fuses too close to the fuse boxes unless they're plugged in, or the current causes them to explode."

Ezzie looks at the floor, even though nobody can see her face.

"Something about the chains building up too much vibe between them," Monty continues.

"I'll go in and get them," says Dunya.

"That's okay, I got it!" says Ezzie, and she scurries into the suite and back to her room. By now, the lawn has turned purple-black, and there's no turning back. Night has officially arrived. She finds the fuses and returns to the others.

A few minutes later, the lights are on again, much brighter than before. The four first-years stand in the hall: brick, dusty, cramped, dry. Winding stairs lead up to the rest of the house, and there are three doors visible. To each side of the stairs, a round, green, perfect door opens into each suite. The doors bear construction paper signs:

SAM O'SAMUEL

ARKAIC, MI

and

MONTY VALVERDE

SPRINGFIELD, MO

and

DUNYA BLAVATSKY

RICHMOND, CA

and

ESMERALDA PRENTICE

NEW YORK, NY

A third door lies straight across from the stairs in a dismal and cobwebby corner. It is thick and metal and corroded and rusted and practically welded shut. Even the right key in that lock might bend and snap, and it would take a very strong person to actually pull the door open. A furtive, faint clicking sound comes from the door, as if a small machine is embedded not in the room beyond, but within the door itself. This door leads to the chain mazes. It makes them all a bit nervous, so they retreat to Ezzie's room.

Why my room? she wonders. "So this is my room!" she says.

"Esmeralda from New York?" asks Samo.

"That's me!" Nervous laughter. *I'm meeting so many people so quickly. I shouldn't be nervous. Why am I so nervous? If I laugh like that, he's going to think I'm into him already.*

Samo looks at Ezzie in a particular sort of way.

Shit, he already thinks that.

"Aren't you the one who breaks glasses by looking at them?" Samo asks.

"Um, yeah."

"How does that work?"

"I don't know. I really have no idea. When my uncle parked the car, I just looked at the back window and it sort of fell apart. I thought something must have fallen on it, but then a window cracked in the cafeteria and a mirror in the bathroom. It's weird, but every time it was right as I was looking at it. I don't get it, and I don't like it. I shouldn't have mentioned it."

"And you just look at them?"

"If I look at them a certain *way.* I don't really understand it. I don't know how it happens."

"I'm starving," says Monty. "But I don't know if there's anywhere to eat around here."

"I've got some Hot Pockets," offers Dunya.

Ezzie turns to look out her window again. The grass is completely dark now.

"Hey!" says Samo loudly, expansively. "Anyone want to watch me shoot off my potato cannon?"

Ezzie winces, and her bedroom window explodes.

Samo fires off a Keanu-esque "whoa!" while Dunya pulls Ezzie back from the window. Monty stoops to pick up a shard of glass, looking unsurprised and almost pleased. For a moment, everyone is motionless in the shattered silence. Then the lights go off again, and Dunya's record resumes. The students gather the glass and dump it into paper bags. They string up a towel in front of the now cold-blowing window and Ezzie checks the fuses again. Prince tells her she should keep her eyes shut while he...you know. At last, everyone is together again and breathing deeply.

"We've got to look after each other," says Dunya. "We're the Basement People." She says it to be reassuring, but they have to pause and linger. The record needle hits the inner groove and resets itself with a click. Another, farther, fainter click confirms that somewhere behind the unopenable door the chains turn.

"I —" says Ezzie, stopping for breath. *What is happening to us here? This place is deranged!* "I —" she says, and they're all looking at her. *I what? Finish the sentence, idiot!* "I'm hungry too. I wouldn't mind a Hot Pocket. But really, I wouldn't mind getting out of this building for a bit, either."

"That sounds right," says Dunya. "Samo! Why don't you show us your potato cannon?"

"Okay!" says Samo.

He's been waiting all night for someone to ask him that.

Bricks as Mortars

Watch where you point that thing.

A full moon smiles down on the courtyard of Calliope Cradle. I mean, it really smiles down. Dunya has always thought that the man in the moon was the original inspiration of Munch's scream, but man, not this moon. The shapes are the same, but the glow splashes out like a massive lens, a grinning spotlight, saying, "hey you kids, this is your show, so go crazy!" *Our show. My show.* Dunya shakes her head precisely because it is all so crazy. Then she shivers and notices the goose bumps running along her arms. Arkaic is about as cool in September as Richmond is midwinter.

"Bricks!" says Samo, and sure enough, bricks randomly poke out of the soft soil like mushrooms around a rotting tree. It's strange because the dorm was built from Indiana limestone; bricks don't feature into its construction. Dunya stoops and pulls a brick from the earth.

"Can you shoot these?" She humors him.

"Never have, but I don't see why not."

Samo holds up a length of PVC, camouflaged with bands of black gaff tape, and drops the brick inside. It lands with a satisfying crunch.

"I got pneumatic ones," he says. "They're much cooler working. Air powered. But they don't have the kick that the combustible ones do!"

He empties half a can of hair spray into the thing.

Samo pushes a red button and fires the brick at a wall. It impacts with a clatter, leaving a chalky scar at the joint of two stones. "Whoa!"

They hear a groaning sound. The oak overhead sways, and its leaves rustle, but there isn't any wind, Dunya notices. *Wait, yes there is. My head's getting to me.* She shivers, and her hairs prickle on their goose bumps.

Samo loads another brick. He fires. This one flies into the shadows and makes a strange sound, as if it has crashed through a window. Again, the four students hold still and hold their breath. But all of the dorm room windows are dark, and the courtyard is apparently empty. The oak continues to rustle overhead, although now the wind has stopped. It's a bit warmer, but Dunya's goose bumps haven't gone away. *All in my head.*

"I'll aim better this time," Samo says, apologetically. "Can't get kicked out, haven't even gone to a class yet!"

The third brick strikes a wall in full view of the moonlight, makes a shattering sound, and leaves a wet streak on the stonework.

"What the fuckadoo?" says Samo, and Dunya steps forward to take a closer look. *Is it in my head?* That's what she had wondered when she got the letter of invitation from Dean Rochet, of the Arkaic University Department of Anthropology. "We have received a copy of your paper on 'Ghosting and Self-Germination in Black-Eyed Peas' and are most impressed. We would like to invite you to visit our fine school, and if you successfully complete the application process, we will advocate on your behalf."

At that point, Dunya was well into her last semester of high school, and she was only mostly sure she was going to graduate at all. She hadn't considered college to be an option at the time, though she was hoping to upgrade from her job as popcorn popper at the cineplex. How had they gotten her paper? And why were a bunch of *anthropologists* interested? She wasn't sure she understood anthropology, other than that it involved stealing ancient artifacts and murdering Nazis; she was less interested in them than they were in her.

Still, they were right to praise her science project. Her sole academic achievement in eighteen years of life *was* pretty damn amazing. She'd gotten the idea at a Pearl Jam concert, when Eddie Vedder was mumbling something about the "the seed inside your soul...make it grow." Actually, she had misheard him. He said "*I see* inside your soul," but the seed (such as it was) had been planted, and

Dunya moved on the idea at once. She spent long afternoons riding the BART from Richmond to Berkeley, grilling grad students on proper lab procedure and making off with lab equipment. If the trains had stopped running, she would steal a bike–don't worry, she only ever stole from douchebags–and ride it the last several miles home. She'd stay awake into the deeps of the night with a cup of coffee in her fist–half milk and a quarter cup of sugar–and the Ramones on her headphones. Each day, she slept through her first two classes, which was fine, as she was failing them anyway. Suddenly Dunya wasn't interested in urban exploring or pyromania anymore. She'd been possessed, and Dr. Frankenstein was her muse.

And then, on the day before St. Patrick's Day, it happened. "Ghosting," as she called it, "leads to self-germination." A black-eyed pea, placed, under the right circumstances, in the right soil, in the right humidity, at the right moment, and with the right intention, would ghost itself into a clone–a double–a white-eyed black pea. "The Teleological Ratio and the Theosophical Constant." She didn't know *exactly* how it worked–she hadn't developed a working theory–but she had predicted the event, and its implications were staggering. Properly developed, this could end global hunger, at least where legumes were involved. And yet the experiment had stalled. Each event produced a good seed and an evil seed, and the evil seed extended its shoots and runners and strangled the good, and they both died. Instead of one edible bean, Dunya was left with zero. She passed the class, largely on the quality of her presentation, but nobody took her work seriously until she had gotten Rochet's letter.

Now, Dunya is stranded in mid-Michigan, two thousand miles from her dad, from her friends, from that magnificent earthquake-imperiled city on the edge of world. *That's okay*, she thinks. She figures she's done everything worth doing out there anyway.

The brick has vanished, replaced by what looks like a broken bottle. Broken glass. Dunya finds a tattered label among the shattered mess in the leaves and grass: "Old Krupnik." And instead of impacted masonry on the stone wall, there's a wet streak. Dunya swipes her finger down and puts it in her mouth. It tastes like thin, rich honey with a little something extra.

"Whoa!" she says. "This tastes alcoholic!"

· · · · ·

The students spend the next quarter-hour pulling bricks from the earth and throwing them against the walls, to the apparent irritation of the oak. While some of the bricks dissolve into drinkable puddles, others don't, so the four assume they're hallucinating. Then, as the night hurries along into deeper darkness, a shadow passes overhead. Only Samo notices. It is STS-136, the final flight of the Space Shuttle program, and he knew it would be passing overhead at about ten o'clock p.m. (EDT). He recognizes the fast-moving star because he has trained himself. He was not, however, expecting the rain. Moments after the shuttle has passed, the meteors follow, shearing down toward the earth in sharp streaks, and then, with the stars and the moon and the aurora watching, it suddenly starts to pour.

"Shit!" the first-years scream, and scramble back inside. It's dry. It's stale and dark and calm now, even though the rain spears off the roofs in great sheets of translucent wetness, they can't hear a thing. As they had run inside, Samo could've sworn he'd seen something move on the periphery: a man with goat horns and woolly feet, perhaps. A gloomy girl wearing a white lace dress brocaded with diamonds. And then they are down the stairs, into the basement, next to their bedrooms and that big metal door.

The Orientees

Orientation is orientation.

It lasts for ten days.

Ten powerful days in the city and for the world at large. The Tigers move into one of their most decisively inspirational post-seasons ever, while Occupy Arkaic forms a mile-long chain of humans lying on their backs down the middle of East Street. Meanwhile, at AU, chains of another sort wind through their violet, phosphorus-coated tunnels deep beneath the jagged verdure.

Dunya, Ezzie, Monty, Samo. They will remember this week as a flood, a tsunami, a clear crush of action that rushes around their ankles–okay, unusual situation, but nothing unmanageable–then their thighs–better grab onto something!–their waists–a thought tornado that drives pencils through Prousts–and oh! their bodies–against the limestone cliffs of those insane crucibles of scriptifaction. Their conscious thoughts are pulverized, but although they emerge inexperienced, they change. It is undeniable. They are not what they formerly were.

They are college students.

Testing begins on the second day. Samo bombs his math placement test; not a good omen for an aspiring astronaut. Monty, on the other hand, aces his test and gets stuck in Honors Calculus. He's one step closer to his parents' goal that he become a doctor. One step further from his goal to become anything but. Dunya sweet talks her adviser into signing her up for the Classic Vampire class, because her dad wants her to have "the good time I couldn't have (mumble mumble) fucking longshoreman (mumble mumble) solar cantata." Ezzie visits the Roach Lounge of Theatre of Gold, and the upperclassmen there stare at her.

"You wrote that thing *Everquestion!*" one boy says.

"It wasn't a thing," she stammers. "It's a play."

"Yeah! Wow! Welcome!"

But then she doesn't know what else to say, and sits down on a broken-down La-Z-Boy. Her heel crushes a cockroach.

Dunya gets the call from her dad. "You better call the bank," he says. "They aren't covering that—the Arkaic University Department of Anthropology—and they said very nice things about you by the way—but they can't help out with the financial aid. And you know I can't. So what I mean is, sweetie, you gotta get some money."

At night, Samo swears he knows he's in a basement when he stares up at the ceiling. He knows that a ceiling is just a ceiling—it shouldn't make a difference—but he knows he can tell the difference and wishes that there were tree branches swirling on either side of his bed, swirling in a spiral wind. *I don't have any windows!* The confined space stresses him out, and this, too, does not bode well for a future in space travel.

One room deeper, Monty is chill. His days have not gone well; he's done fine in math and science, poorly in language and the humanities. But *everything is connected*, and if he has performed thus, then *there is a reason* and *it will reveal itself*. The air is dusty. The dust is thick with mystery. Therefore, he breathes clues.

And anyway, the tests are only one part of Orientation. Other things move as well: the next night, "Discover Arkaic!"

When Samo gets on the bus with his housemates—not just his Basement People, but *greasy!charming* Argosy and *witty!sweet* Elaine and that *slippery!awkward* fellow Giovanni Martini—to ride downtown for dinner and a movie, he expects his stupid *dead! factory* town to disappoint everyone and himself.

It isn't so.

The bus is so crowded that a bunch of boys and girls from Cain Tower are forced to stand in the margins, and an Indian girl is pressed on her feet at his side, awkwardly leaning into Samo's seat. "I can't even stand!" she complains. "You're too much!" she says, "You're too fat," to the boy in front of her, but he grins, and it's just a joke between them; he isn't fat, just large, and they tell him this a lot (evidently). "I'm going to fall on my ass on this guy..." (meaning Samo!), "and I don't even know him." *Should I say something?* Samo thinks.

"You can sit down," Samo says. "I don't mind –"

"Oh, what a gentleman."

"I mean, I'm not standing up," Samo says, laying thick implications about where she should sit.

"Yeah yeah, chivalry is dead," she says, and sits on his lap *just like that!*

Holy shit! Samo thinks. *Jeans on jeans, her ass, my crotch, damn!* It feels good, her ass. And then, telling himself that this is an experience some 90 percent of ninth graders have known, *don't get excited, nothing to be excited about here.* But maybe he gets just a little bit excited. After all, she's majoring in physics, she says. She's got perfect, perfect, silky silk hair. She has a vicious sense of humor, just like Samo. *Just like me!* "What do you call ten dead babies in a blender?" she asks. Her name is Candace Bhatt. *Damn!* Samo thinks, and he asks her for her phone number and *she totally just gave it to me!*

They get off the bus, and Samo eagerly hisses "Did you see that? Did you see that?!" to Monty and Argosy. They walk in mist to sit in plush booths in beach-bright incandescence at King Carol's #2 Coney Island. They sample all of the coney styles–Detroit, Flint, and Grand Rapids–in the core of Arkaic. Ezzie pulls them through grimy doors, over dirt-streaked black-and-white hex porcelain, into dingy closets with hundreds of awful outfits on sale for one dollar, and some transfiguring paisley nightgowns going for two. "Oh, it's wonderful! I am going to change as soon as I get back."

"I'm getting this!" says Samo, holding up a coonskin cap.

Dunya pulls them into a used CD and new T-shirt store, open late for the event, and Monty drags them into a gay metal bar. "They were playing Cannibal Corpse," he says with a shrug. "I didn't know they were gay."

There, in the thickening gloom and the thinning sidewalk crowds, the rain catches them again, *down with a shot!*, and draws grisly, rust-colored streaks down the cracked pavement. The golden light of the pyramid topping the Pyramid Bank Building washes over the wet in steady, solid lines. The warm wind carries heavy pollen and other aging weights from the reluctant-to-leave summer, and then, and *then*, just when they laugh and revel in the soak, the storm turns from the north and ripples the puddles with the promise of frost soon.

The real memories, the deeper ones, come later that night, when they're trying to get home, but they ride the bus for too long and end up far from the city, in the Arkadian Business District, near the mall, with fields and sprawl and broad lawns all around and overhead. The jagged scent of mowed grass and wet mulch. It is a four-mile walk back to campus.

"I don't know why I'm here," says Dunya.

They believe her.

"You have to make a play on that Candace Bhatt," Monty tells Samo. "I think you two should hook up."

"Thanks," says Samo. "Me too."

Ezzie doesn't say much, but she smiles.

When they get home, they all go to sleep.

The next day, the very next day, their house, Acedia House, it is the greatest house in the Cradle, *obviously*. Not like those other awful houses, and especially the adjacent close neighbors, Greed and Wrath. Wrath has a score to settle; no one knows why, but they write Acedia students up for nothing and report them to housing. Greed is just whiny, bitching about the cold wind that blows through their bathrooms when Acedian students climb through the shared fire escape as a shortcut to get to the dining hall. Monica shares the secrets of these wise transgressions, and the Orientees observe and obey.

It's all about learning, Orientation, and an Orientee is such as defined by how much he learns. Samo is determined to learn it all. He especially learns not to dump bleach onto his blue jeans and T-shirts as they whirl through the wash on a spin cycle at two or three in the morning. This, too, he will never forget.

44

The fourth day of Orientation is "Arkaic Service Day," and it wedges thoughts in Ezzie's brain that she will never dislodge. She only has to sign up for one shift but, not wanting to miss an opportunity, she chooses two. She rides a bus to an elementary school in a forgotten corner of the East Side, and there she helps sort donated books by age and subject matter. Then she rides to the West End Soup Kitchen to chop and boil eggplants and ladle them with chicken broth into deep foam bowls. The hood here is different from the hood in New York. Here, it's naked and open, bleak and hollow and vulnerable. Uncontested and unclaimed. She remembers it in fallen electrical cables and shattered glass block windows. Opaque houses, overgrown, shunning the light. It will soon be winter, and there isn't a lot of light here then, everyone says. Not so much from short days as from cloud cover. She doesn't forget it. The thoughts grow slowly, but they've taken seed deep in her brain.

Monty remembers another night: "College Day at Campus Arkaic," a complex of museums and art venues on the other side of downtown. As they sit in the planetarium, waiting for the show to start, the machine breaks, and it's twenty minutes before anyone has figured out the problem.

"Okay!" says Dunya, "Tell us an embarrassing secret!"

They've all gone, already, so now it's Monty's turn. "My favorite song, is, um, 'Paparazzi.' Lady Gaga." Not too impressive a secret, maybe, but a moment later, Samo gets up in front of all two hundred students and announces: "I am going to entertain you all, and dedicate this to my favorite Basement People, and my brothers and sisters from Acedia House." He starts singing. He gets through ten seconds–"It's so magical. We'd be so fantastical."–when the crowd starts booing, and Monty, Dunya, and Ezzie have sunk to the bottom of their seats. "What? What?" yells Samo. "Can't I get a DJ in here? Can't I get a DJ?" The other students start throwing their stiff programs at him, and he runs back to his seat.

"Cut a guy a break," yells Dunya, standing. She starts beat boxing.

She is, it turns out, really fucking good. She keeps waiting for someone to step up and start rapping, but none of those AU fools is up to it. When her high pitch static singe hugs the vinyl hairs on all those cheap red chairs–the hidden balance of salival 'plosives–half of the students spin in their seats, looking for the synthesizers.

"Did I annoy you?" asks Samo.

"Shhhh!" says Monty.

Then, agony, the seventh night, the deadline, deadlines–*oh Ezzie!*–and she pulls and pulls at her feathery hair. She half hopes that a clump will come off in her hands, so Dunya will notice her pain without Ezzie having to explain it. But all she gets for her trouble is a sore head.

It's the classes. Which classes will she take? At this point, they're mainly core requirements, and yet there are variables, things she cannot see, cannot control, and no one is here to offer their discerning advice. Case in point: hum, as in the humanities. Ezzie could take The Soul of Civic Duty, or she could take Escaping the Greeks. They both have exciting syllabi, and she's heard good things about the section leaders, but she knows it will really come down to the students, the quirks of the homework, the fluctuations in daily lives that lead to supernaturally pertinent points, to life-changing insights and observations, to the weather even, and, and, and, and, *and!*

A snapping sound.

A jagged crack roots down her computer screen.

"Fuck!" she says, with a hiss.

There's a tap at her door.

"Yes?"

Monty opens the door.

"I hope I am not bothering you."

"No, Monty, I'm just picking out classes."

"Oh." He looks at her computer screen. "Well, we're just going outside to play some Ultimate Buzkashi. Do you want to come?"

"Sure," she says, and even smiles. "I need a break."

She won't remember the moment when she chooses her classes. She will remember the moment when she launches herself through the air, snow shovel between her legs, and strikes the glow-in-the-dark stuffed Eeyore in the belly. He jumps up over the moon and comes down across the goal. Ezzie lands on her face, busting up her lip and scraping her head along the clumps of shag grass.

Speaking of the Fairway.

On the very last day of Orientation, when the upperclassmen move in and the halls of Acedia House rattle with the sound of trunks, the crinkle of Trojans, and the crashing hammers of awakened radiators, the university offers one last party for the Orientees. It starts at 9 p.m. in the Grand Hall of Olan Commons, and Samo won't miss anything, not a thing. But Monty is too tired, and Ezzie is getting ready for classes, and he can't find Dunya anywhere. So he goes on his own.

The party is off to a mediocre start, but then the lights shut out, and strobes begin to beat across the sullen faces in the AU trustees' portraits. Then Karl Hyde (himself an AU student) steps out of the crowd and takes the turntable, and things start moving for real. First, the bass tugs a beat boat through still waters made to ripple by the fast fury of the electronic beam machines. Second, said machines feel far more juice than they need, because the Commons get the choicest surges, the most succulent moments, seconds and instants fed through earthbound phosphorus to satiate thirsty cables and foam pads–cardboard, even!–coating ambitious speakers. And third–well God damn!–there she is, just like he hoped, that one, yeah, Candace Bhatt, shaking that thing and dancing to that beat. Samo decides to shake his own thing. Of course, he's long and gangly, and he can't dance. But Candace sees him and nods in his direction, and next thing they're dancing together. High up, in the treatment-plagued crags and crannies of the cavernous limestone room, gargoyles grin downward. They don't know anything. They're dumb stone. But the electricity is alive, because of what it *is*, which is to say, not mere electricity. The nevernormal.

So here's a hypothetical for you: if living electricity infuses limestone walls and the gargoyles therein, and said gargoyles grin down on college first-years who dance as if they know what they're doing, would the gargoyles, in fact, be alive? And if living, would they look down with lust and dark intentions? Because these aren't very friendly looking gargoyles.

Anyway, the party ends, and Samo walks Candace back to Cain Tower on the edge of campus. After ten days here, he figures he's learned the basic layout, and he turns with confidence back toward his dorm. He passes through the lush and willow-dripping hills and furrows of South Campus, where he can see distant cars wink by with a hushed mumble along I-63. And on through the inner reaches of the West Quints, where the remnants of the party remain—hanging Chinese lanterns with florid dragons twisting across their stretched tissue skin and the lingering scents of watermelon and lemon meringue pie. But when he turns up the path that must lead to the Fairway, he finds himself in the Quints instead. *This campus is bigger than it looks*, he thinks. No problem, though. The Quints, themselves, border the Fairway. He walks through the long shadows quickly, knowing that the empty windows, and worse, the gargoyles, are watching his every move. At the far edge, between Valentine and Peppington Halls, opens a path that he knows will take him home.

It doesn't.

Now he finds himself in another hollow space, with silent classroom buildings and libraries rising up on every side. Some of them are brutalist. Some of them are faceless. The tall trees frown down. More gargoyles glower. They're all everywhere, every all, every. Ever. Well, where the hell is he? And what are those red will 'o the wisps floating in the distance? Samo squints and tries to make them out. *Oh, those are Chinese lanterns.* "Huh," he says aloud. *I'm back at the West Quints.* "Did I pass the wrong buildings?"

Worried that he's either losing his mind, or that space is rearranging itself around him, Samo traces his way back to South Street and follows the edge of campus until he arrives at the Fairway. Farther on, Calliope Cradle swings into view. To his left are the distant blinking lights of downtown, shut down, forlorn, except for some crusty tents occupied by the Occupy crowd. Samo could follow South all the way back to the dorm, but that would take longer, and anyway, it feels like a silly and superstitious thing to do. Instead, he cuts directly across the Fairway. He hums a bit of techno. Then he realizes that he's humming too slowly, too deeply, and tries to speed the beat.

It sounds weird in his ears.

He speeds the tempo up anyway, but now he can't even keep the melody straight in his head. The notes get all tangled.

He stops walking and humming.

The wind curls along his head, putting its wraithlike fingers through his short hair, massaging his scalp. Stealing tears. Drawing his breath short.

"What?" he says aloud.

The streetlights, a few hundred feet away, are impossibly dim, and the Fairway is as bleak and empty as the wild. He can't hear the cars on I-63 anymore, and he can't see the lights from the Quints. He knows, however, that those gargoyles are still watching from their perches.

"Um," he says. "Problem."

He leans on one foot, then the other.

"Hypothesis? Solution?"

Nobody answers. Because, of course, he is ass alone out there.

"Okay."

He gets down on the ground, leans on the grass, and presses his naked ear tight against the cold, wet earth.

His hypothesis is correct. He distinctly hears the slow sonorous rhythm that kept correcting his own humming. It's deep, like a train moving down tracks a mile away, but its cadence is metallic-sharp and occlusive profound. It is the sound of subterraneous metal chains slipping down twisted corridors through extra-dimensional engines. It is, he knows, the same sound that ticks through the basement a few feet behind his bedroom walls.

CHAPTER THREE
RITES OF INDUCTION

Quasimodo's Metamorphosis

Don't be late. Oh, fuck it, be late.

Orientation may be dangerous, but it is only a dress rehearsal. The first week of college is another matter entirely.

As the upperclassmen return and move into the bigger, more desirable rooms throughout the dorm, Ezzie tries to keep a low profile. Oh, she meets them; they share the same dining hall, after all. They sip the same dishwater coffee and chew the same stringy rotisserie chicken. There's an acerbic football nut named Joe Newcomb and a saucy Detroiter named Krista Baroque. An opinionated second-year named Velma Brass warns Ezzie not to sleep through her first day of class. This is sweet but absurd advice; Ezzie is terrified and expects that her nervousness will probably wake her two hours early.

She's half right: she *is* awake two hours early. Anxiety has kept her eyes wide, as she imagines all those large, friendly, experienced, confident upperclassmen sauntering through their first day of the quarter for the fourth, seventh, tenth time. The moon shines too brightly, and its deathly light bleeds through the sheer curtains. But one hour before her class, Ezzie has fallen into a restless sleep, even as the light outside starts to grow.

Ezzie opens into that world on the stickiest summer afternoon, thickly steeped in unyielding gray air, and the light fragments through her swollen ocelli. Her legs twitch. Her wings have become dry from disuse. No, *no*, she says. *That's okay. I'm sick of being shy and impossible and alone. It's time to stop being this way.* So she molts.

Tsuku-tsuku boshi. Orientation was centuries ago. *And what do they know, anyway, that I should be stuck in the corner watching all and doing nothing?* Well, a kite goes sailing through the air, and *it must be the wind b'cuz there ain't no wind on a morning like this.* Ezzie flies away, sailing the thermals, her tail rippling in the teasing breeze—*it's nowhere! It's everywhere! It's not here!* Earthbound again. "Oh, stop, you!" she says. Students are running beneath her, far below, between her legs, the audacious ones, even, even, eew gross, *they're scurrying over my toes.* She stomps them, and their minuscule crushed little bodies bleed into the dust. Ezzie wakes up laughing and sitting up in bed.

Motes swirl in the horizontal morning.

Ezzie checks her alarm. 7:55 a.m. *I'm going to be late to class!* She doesn't care; this doesn't happen often—two or three times a year at most—and she can't let the moment escape. Ezzie hurries to her dresser and picks up her notebook. She sits down at her desk and begins writing, quickly but carefully, deliberately, forcing herself not to rush. She has to get all of the details right, or she won't be able to pick it up where she left off. Sometimes she feels that this is the only thing she does right, but she does it better than anyone else, so that's okay.

Finally, when Ezzie's filled a page and a half with some notes and ideas, she writes in the top center of the first page:

QUASIMODO'S METAMORPHOSIS

It is almost 8:30 when Ezzie arrives at Anderson Hall for Escaping the Greeks. She's been running, and didn't shower or put on deodorant, so she's wet with the sheen of sweat. She hasn't brushed her teeth or combed her hair, either. As Ezzie enters room 419, she sees Cassidy Antrim sitting in a corner, and he flashes her a cutting smile.

"Participation is non-negotiable," Professor Plumb is telling everyone, "and attendance is fundamental to participation. If you aren't here, then you are failing." He glares at Ezzie through silver sunglasses. "But back to Marat and Marat. Marat the martyr and Marat the cannibal."

Sticker Shock

Before you buy books, make sure your parents have refinanced their house and have good credit.

Also, make sure you can bench 40 or 50 pounds.

Monty gathers in the prosperity of a well-prepared Monday. He woke before dawn and downed a Red Bull before jogging through purple dew to Columbine Rec Center. After working out and showering, he stopped at the Strawberries Dining Hall for a couple fried eggs and hash browns before hitting Honors Calc. Calculus is calculus, which is to say, neither pleasant nor unpleasant. After an Echinacea coffee (you just put the tea bag right in your coffee with some honey) he heads down to the campus bookstore to get his books before the next class.

He is slightly surprised.

"When you get your books," his dad had said, "just use your credit card and send me the balance."

"I got it, dad, I've been mowing lawns all summer."

"Trust me. You'll thank me for this."

Monty will. The calculus book costs log10 what it should, and while the Humanities books are only about twenty dollars each, he has to buy ten of them. *It's okay*, he thinks. *One thing at a time. Get a basket. Put it on the card.* The calculus book alone, which for some reason features a bacterial bloom on its cover, is enough to make the basket start feeling heavy. The Generic Chemistry book is even heavier. The Spoken Latin class calls for some DVDs, and they aren't heavy, but they're going for forty bucks a pop, and he needs three. And then the weights of history and the arts start to pile on: Ovid, Milton, Molière, Melville, Makepeace, Millay, Miller, Morrison, Milton, Mistlethwaipe, and *My Life Among the Massholes* by I.P. Muhpanz. And then some. By now, the basket's plastic handle has bent into a horseshoe shape.

"What?" Monty asks it. "This is what you were built for."

He starts to stagger toward the checkout counter when he catches a glimpse of Dunya out of the corner of his eye. He's about to say "hi" when he sees her face, stark and stricken. Monty knows that look. Tightness around her typically relaxed lips. A dazed look in her typically sharp eyes. A slight slump of her shoulders, which nevertheless seem to be tensed. Muscles work about her mouth; she's clenching her teeth. She's only a few feet away, but she doesn't notice him. She's staring at the pricetag on the Generic Chemistry textbook and knows that she's defeated. It might be a long struggle, but Monty knows that expression, and knows that she knows she is bound to lose.

He slips away before she can see him.

When I'm wearing a look like that, he thinks, *I don't want anyone talking to me.*

Dénouement

Know your weaknesses. Know your strengths.

"Unacceptable!" thunders Plumb. "You've all had it so easy. You've had teachers who've wanted you to succeed. You'll have none of that here. I want you to fail. The humanities cost fools their careers and the successful their souls, and if you fail some classes now and figure that out sooner, then I've done you a favor."

Ezzie is stricken. "But I –"

"If you can't demonstrate punctuality for a simple college class, then you lack the discipline you'll need for this stupid roulette wheel."

"No, it, it –"

"Now your grade is 30 percent attendance, and I have you down as having missed the first of twenty classes. So you're already 0 for 1.5 percent, and it's only getting harder from here. You probably were out late at that techno party I heard from my house a mile away."

"I wasn't, I –"

"When did you get here?"

"What?"

"When during the lecture?"

"Um...Marat."

"See, you missed the Cardinal de Rohan. Good luck appraising revolutionary sentiment without *him*. Give me your notes."

"What?"

"Give me your notes, I'm going to write down some articles for you to look up."

"Oh...okay."

She hands her notes over. Plumb frowns.

"*Quasimodo's Metamorphosis?*" *Oh shit.* "Is this a joke? Is this what you were up to while you were missing my class?" He reads. His frown deepens.

"The cicada," he murmurs, "molts in a moment to become herself. From moths and magma to perplexed men, all things are born fresh."

All things are born flesh, and wherever we live, whatever farmstead or city, whenever the year or era, we are only sovereign of our own bodies and minds. Our skin is the most distant frontier, and no, we cannot travel. Some nations are untethered. Some nations revolt.

Plumb flips back through Ezzie's notes.

"I just want to say," he reads, "goodbye."

A small, flat tear slides down Plumb's cheek.

"I'm sorry," Ezzie says. "It has that effect sometimes." Looks at the floor. "I mean, my writing has that effect." She looks up.

Plumb removes his sunglasses with his right hand and wipes his eye with his left. He sniffs and looks out the window at the lazy, breeze-tickled ivy, still green, still imagining the summer. *Schlithick!* Ezzie starts. A jagged crack has cut the window where Professor Plumb is looking. He quickly puts his sunglasses on again.

"I want you to look up the Cardinal de Rohan and read as much as you can about him for Wednesday's class!" he yells. "And don't be late again. Do you hear me?!"

The Fruits of an Academic Life

Save money whenever you can. There is no jackpot to be won here.

On the first day of college, Samo saunters into calculus ready to learn the steep, straight angles that rockets follow en route to orbit. He's wrong...no rocket has ever followed such an angle. They all curve, mostly downward, and a few quite thoroughly so to disaster. So Samo spends eighty minutes listening to gibberish about unfathomable fractions (*If* d *is a variable and* x *is a variable, how can I figure out what either is? And isn't* d/dx *just the same as saying* 1/x*?*). Okay, okay, he's not that clueless. *But I might as well be. None of this makes any sense.*

When class ends, Samo walks back to the Cradle and has just sat down to a tuna melt when Kimmy calls on his cell phone.

"What can you tell me, sis?" he asks.

"So Tino says they're in a dumpster behind the new parking garage downtown, but Rico says they're in a crack house in the Os. Who's right, I don't know, but if it was me, I'd fail a class before I went poking around the Os."

"Thanks, Kimmy. I can handle myself."

Samo chugs his Vernors and heads out again, leaving his tray on the table. He walks downtown and finds the dumpster at the parking garage, but after digging around in foam peanuts and discarded banana peels for a half hour, he hasn't found a single discarded calc book. *That means they'll be in the Os.* Samo catches the next bus north. The Os are simultaneously Arkaic's most diverse and its most ravished neighborhood. The bus drops him at the corner of Owen and Orion, and he walks until he finds Outer Street. From there, it's just a couple blocks past abandoned and occupied houses–hell, they're all pretty much abandoned and burnt-out–to a chilly, sunken, hollow patch where a shotgun shack shank-leers its naked black windows into the shadowy afternoon, taunting him.

Samo walks right in and just about stumbles over the must-be-a-crackhead sleeping on the floor.

"Don't shoot!" Samo screams.

"Whaaaaaat?" says the man, face down on the floor.

"I said, 'don't shoot!'"

"Whaaaaaat?"

"I said, 'I said...' um, I'm just here for the calc books. I heard you got some."

"Yeah. What's in it for us?"

The man is still prone, with a kidney bean-shaped (and colored) wet patch on the back of his pants. Samo's pretty sure this is exactly what it smells like. For a minute, he considers ransacking the place without the squatter's permission.

"Um —"

Then again, these are the Os. You don't tempt fate in the Os.

"I got a twenty?"

"That'll do," says the man.

They share a quiet moment of mediation together.

"Just put your damn money in my damn hand!" The fingers of the man's upturned palm twitch eagerly. Samo puts the money in his hand before heading deeper into the house, and the shitty smell deepens. In the bathroom, Samo finds a claw-footed tub with a stack of liquor-stained textbooks, including several for calculus. The covers have all been ripped off, although the fuzz of mold half-captures the cover photo. Samo chooses one that smells slightly better than the others.

"What's with the covers?" he asks himself.

Another shit-stained man sits up from beneath the bathtub.

"It's the fucking bookstores," the man says. "Whatever they don't sell, they rip off the covers and send it back to the distributor. That cuts mighty close to the distributors and the publishers, and so they stiff the authors. It's a big, bright chain of 'fuck you' and 'eat a dick' that all ends at yours truly."

"You're a writer?"

"Why the fuck else would I be living in this shithole?"

Samo shrugs. "Selling dope?"

"That would be my colleague out there, the Renaissance Humanist. He got an F from P+, if you know what I mean. But if you want to do me a favor, when you're done with that book, just tape on the cover from another textbook and sell it back to the bookstore. It doesn't matter what cover. Anything'll do. They'll give you ten, maybe twenty bucks for it, then try to sell it to some dumb kid for a couple hundred. They don't care."

"Suckers!" says Samo, and laughs.

"Stick it to the man, man."

Samo leaves, stepping over the original crackhead on his way out the door.

"For your fuckformation," he says, "my dissertation was Rabelais."

Samo's waiting for the bus on Owen, but it doesn't come. He hails a cab and gives them the last of his cash. You don't tempt fate in the Os.

Everything Begins with a Ritual

Relax into the moment.

That night. Lights flicker overhead. Chicken in the cafeteria.

"Dunya, how you doin'?" Ezzie asks.

"Hunh?" Dunya lifts her heavy lids. "I'm doing great."

She looks awful, with big bags under her eyes and a slack, shadowed frown. She holds a spoon in her hand, half-full of chicken chowder.

"What are your plans tonight?"

"You ever notice the chicken around here? Day one we get rotisserie chicken. Next day, fried chicken breasts and legs. Day after that, chicken cutlet. Day after that, chicken soup. Day after that, chicken-flavored ice cream. Then it starts over." Her voice sounds strained and exhausted.

"They stock a lot of chicken?" Ezzie asks. Pauses. "Get it? Chicken stock?"

Dunya shrugs. Several seats down, Alyssa Carnival is bending her spoon and putting it in her bowl, like a little graveyard in her own November-gray chowder.

"Hey Dunya," Ezzie says, starting over.

"Huh?"

"Want to audition for some plays?"

"What?"

"I was hoping to have one of mine performed by TOG, but everyone's told me pretty much that everyone has to start out onstage. I don't really like acting, personally, but you have to do what you have to do."

"Guess so."

"Well? Will you come with me?"

"Come with you and audition?"

"Sure. Or if you liked you could do –"

"Hell yeah, I will!" Dunya says in a loud voice, and stabs at the chowder with the spoon. "I'll audition for those bitches."

• • • • •

At dusk, the auditionees are met in front of Elysium Chapel by Chris Conscription, the faculty adviser.

"And that's exactly what I am — your adviser," he says, wearing his self-effacing smile, running his palm through his self-effacing hair. "Theatre of Gold is a student-run enterprise, and you'll find that every play here is produced, directed, and performed by students. And we're not talking a couple plays in a black box somewhere. I mean dozens of plays per year. Maybe even hundreds."

"Student plays?" Ezzie mouths to Dunya. Dunya doesn't notice.

"Now I know that many of you are first-years, and I'm glad that you have come out to audition. Your first play can open all sorts of doors here. In later quarters you can do more acting or tech, maybe playwriting, maybe directing. But it all starts here." Chris waves at the white-crowned church and the shadows behind it.

"We are auditioning in the *chapel?*" asks a lanky boy from Suriname.

"Oh no," says Chris. "You're auditioning *behind* the chapel." When the students don't seem to understand, he goes on. "Your experience with TOG will begin with a ritual. I think you'll find that just about everything you do here at AU begins with a ritual. So behind me, behind the chapel, are the Happy Hunting Grounds. They're not expansive, but you can get lost in there. Tangled knots and all. That's where your directors are waiting to audition you. Any play you find, you can audition for. Auditions go on all night, so your chances correspond to your level of determination. Understand?"

Not really, most students seem to say with their feet and shoulders, but a few take reluctant steps forward. After three or four students have entered the Grounds, the spell snaps, and the mass of forty aspirants charges the darkened mass.

"Come on!" says Dunya, grabbing Ezzie by the wrist. "I'm not going to fuck this up."

The heavy trees rush upon them and over them. Silence and blackness engulf them.

The Happy Hunting Grounds of Arkaic University are not large. They are scarcely three thousand feet from Sellers Hollows near the Fairway to the mosquito fens on Winters Road, but to the uninitiated, a high wave of crushing trunks and branches draws them in, draws them down. Once submerged, the depths are both deeper and darker than what they have expected. Ezzie's feet stumble through the dirt, but Dunya has a tight grip on her hand and moves with feverish speed.

The dark is explicable; while winter is the darkest time of year, spring and summer bring the thick foliage and heavy vines and moss coats everything, living or dead, blotting out the sun. And yet, by late September, the days have already gotten short. Early autumn is the darkest time of year in the Happy Hunting Grounds.

The silence is more mysterious. *Where did they go?* Ezzie wonders. *Aren't another thirty plus students stomping around in here? Shouldn't they just be a few feet away from us? And aren't there a dozen directors out here, waiting with scripts and forms and pencils and card tables? Why is everything so still?*

Ezzie would like to ask Dunya these things, but Dunya doesn't seem to be in a listening mood. She clutches Ezzie's hand painfully tight and pulls her, quickly and deliberately, about the spear-like tree trunks. And then, something sticky. Ezzie has walked through a heavy spider web. She wrenches her hand away from Dunya.

"What?!" asks Dunya.

"Web!" Ezzie claws it away from her face. And thinking that she feels tiny, fast things scurrying across her face and down her throat, she screams.

"Stop screaming!" shouts Dunya.

Their voices are muffled, absorbed by the heavy messes all around.

"What's the matter?" asks Dunya.

"This place doesn't creep the hell out of you?"

"It's just a forest, Ezzie."

That was condescending! Ezzie thinks. *Still, what am I going to do? Go back alone? Get lost?*

"Fine," Ezzie says. "Let's keep going."

And they move through the hushed haze of evening, where green-black trunks up close fade to green-gray trunks at a distance, and things more silent than they ought to be flit and run the very peripheries. Dunya strides on; her voice is brisk and strong, jarring in the deep.

"The upperclassmen call this the Horrid Haunting Grounds," she says.

"Why is that?" asks Ezzie, panting as she walks, although she isn't sure she wants to know.

"It's like the Aokigahara—"

"The what?"

"Oh," says Dunya, "people go in there to kill themselves. Usually an overdose, or they hang themselves from the trees—more than a hundred every year."

A hundred? Really? I think we would've discovered one by now, Ezzie thinks.

Dunya continues. "Each year they get a bunch of volunteers and walk through the forest, and when they do, it's pretty much just one body after another. Tourists go there to see if they can find a body, and they usually do. And people also go in there to rob the bodies of money or even clothes. It's so thick, you see, that, the

64

bodies are picked apart by the animals, so even if the bodies are found in less than a year, they're pretty much nothing but bones. Also, a lot of the bodies are probably never found by anyone. They post a bunch of signs outside telling you not to go in, saying things like 'Life is worth living,' and 'Think about how sad your family will be if you die,' and things like that."

But I haven't seen any signs, Ezzie thinks.

"Also, the soil is volcanic, and there are strange metal deposits," says Dunya. "So compasses don't work. That's why a lot of people die even if they don't intend to kill themselves. They just get lost. It's too big, and they can't find their way out."

Ezzie stops, and Dunya turns around.

"Wait a minute," Ezzie says. "That's not possible. The whole campus isn't that big. You can't be more than, I don't know, ten minutes from the edge of this forest at any time."

"What, you mean here? This isn't even that big. I was talking about the Aokigahara."

"The..."

"The suicide woods of Japan?" says Dunya, annoyed. "At the bottom of Mount Fuji?"

"But what about the Happy Hunting Grounds?"

"What about them?"

"Why do the upperclassmen call them the Horrid Haunting Grounds?"

Dunya shrugs. "I don't know. Probably because they're dark and depressing. You know, like the Aokigahara."

They start moving again, and Ezzie hears a sound off to her right now—dim and faint, but clearly human voices, relaxed, relieved. *Some of the actors must have found the auditions. But we don't seem to be headed that way.* Indeed, it would be hard to move that way, at least directly. The trees are close together and choked with underbrush, and the air has gotten so thick that it is almost pitch black off to either side. Dunya seems to have found a rudimentary trail that winds between the few larger trees and curves steadily off to the left. They're heading downhill. After several more minutes in the darkness, Ezzie hears more voices, laughing somewhere, maybe singing, but these are much fainter than before, and definitely behind them. The path grows broader, firmer, less choked with roots, and in the distance ahead, Ezzie sees the indigo sheen of twilight grass, an opening, an escape. A wind rips the heavy air in two, and its weight is dispelled by the sounds of humming and a strange and gentle rippling.

Finally, the path opens into a small clearing and, beyond the clearing, the remote extent of the Fairway. Ezzie knows that this is correct because whenever she leaves Calliope Cradle, she sees the Temporelectrical Power Plant in the distance, and here it is in front of her, much closer. It looks like a cubical concrete mausoleum adorned with cooling spouts and time cells, with a tower that spikes up from the middle. The cells glow with a ghostly white light. The air thrums gentle around her. The light is steady, and so time passes with little variation. Little resistance.

Then, the clouds make way for the gibbous moon, and Ezzie sees the source of the rippling sound. Not leaves. Not animals. Not this time. Nooses. Dozens of them. New nooses. Old nooses. Wire nooses. Rope nooses. A noose made of neckties. A noose of electrical tape. Hanging from every tree, six or eight or twelve feet off the ground.

"Dunya," she says. "Look at that!"

"Huh," says Dunya. "Weird."

"What the fuck! This doesn't freak you out?!"

"A little. I'm from a kind of rough town, Ezzie. There's an abandoned hospital near my house, it's all covered with pentagrams and Satanic slang and so on. It's mostly just kids trying to be badass and scare people away. I'm sure this is probably like that. Like, what good is a noose made out of electrical tape? Anyway, we don't have to stay here. I mean, the auditions aren't here. I thought I heard some voices awhile back. I think we should go back the way we came."

66

"Oh no," says Ezzie. "I don't want to go back in there. It's dark out now, if you haven't noticed. We can just head back to the Cradle. If we walk down to the power plant, I'm sure there's a road."

"Ezzie," says Dunya. "I'm going to audition." Her voice is firm, non-negotiable. "And you are too. You want your plays performed, right? You don't want to give up on your dreams in the first week of college because you got afraid of the dark."

Again, that condescension. "It isn't just the dark," Ezzie says, "It's the nooses all around us."

"Okay fine," Dunya says. "We won't go back that way. If we follow the Fairway to our right, that'll take us down by the stream. We can follow the stream back into the Haunting–I mean, Hunting Grounds. I'm sure we'll hear someone and figure out where to go from there."

• • • • •

As it turns out, Dunya is completely right. They follow the shaded banks of the forest away from campus until they arrive at Sellers Creek, which curls south under the rush of I-63. A well-maintained path takes them away from the stream's banks, and into a younger, lighter part of the forest. After another several minutes, they hear a series of short, sharp screams and an enormous, guttural belch.

Then a light of garroting orange–or is it blue?–flashes from the base of the trees: Pele torches flare in this deep wilderness. A water cooler. A card table. A flaccid lizard lazing under the simpid moon.

"Simpering?" asks Ezzie.

"Welcome!" says a tall stereotype wearing a shamrock in his tweed cappie. "Are you interested in auditioning for us?"

"Yes," murmurs Ezzie, but Dunya bellows, "What play is this?"

"Well, lady, it is *The Night of the Iguana*, by Tennessee Williams."

The lizard belches.

"I don't know anything about that!" says Dunya, "But sure, let's audition."

Ezzie nods.

They fill out audition forms.

"#5. Are you willing to swear onstage?"

Yes, Ezzie writes.

"#6. Are you willing to appear partially/completely nude onstage?"

Ezzie sneaks a peak at Dunya's form. She can't get a good glimpse.

Um, Ezzie writes.

They're handed scripts. Dunya reads for Maxine and Ezzie for Hannah. No surprises there. But Ezzie fumbles her lines horribly. Dunya reads with the heavy momentum of a locomotive slowly building its speed. When the scene has finished, Dunya leans against a small maple and studies her lines. "You seem nervous," the director tells Ezzie. "Have some refreshment." He hands her a glass of water from the cooler. She takes a drink. It isn't water. It's Old Raj. It geysers out of her mouth. "No, no!" yells the stage manager, a bespectacled girl wearing–really really–a Catholic schoolgirl outfit. "That's expensive!"

"Holy shit!" Ezzie says. They're laughing at her.

"We're not laughing at you," the director says. Ezzie waits for the follow-up: *We're laughing with you.* But they don't say that either, and so she thinks: *Maybe they're being sincere.*

"I'm sorry," says Ezzie.

"We should be sorry," says the stage manager, awkwardly dabbing Ezzie's chin with a woolen muffler. "We didn't give you a warning." Dot dot dot. "But it *is* expensive."

Could've fooled me, Ezzie thinks. *It tastes awful. Like peppery, piney, celeryish rubbing alcohol smell.*

"Try again!" says the director. They read the scene again. Ezzie notices no improvement. The lizard screams. "Thanks!" says McDirector. "We'll post results on Friday."

"We're auditioning for all the plays," says Dunya. "Maybe you can tell us where to go next?" Pointing, pointing. "Okay."

Over the barrow and through the woods, to *Mad Forest's* house manager they go. "Welcome!" he swoons, with two audition forms in his hand. They stand in a large but shaggy clearing, and there is a much larger crowd here, and time-charged animatronics of Charles Olan and President Gerald Ford.

"Take stock in the situation!" booms Olanbot.

"Go to hell, New York!" roars Fordbot. "Go to hell!"

Clouds puff up over the stars like cotton candy. Torches lick the leaves. Deep in there, Ezzie recognizes a couple kids from the Cradle. Jason James is a boy from Wrath House, tall and friendly, 70s hair, like a cheerful teddy bear, and he reads with a cutting Romanian accent. Then there is Velma Brass.

"Hi, Velma!" cheers Ezzie, too ready, enthusiastically. But Velma is busy rehearsing her part and does not notice. Meanwhile, Dunya has finished her form and is looking at a script.

"I think," Dunya says, "I should read for the Vampire. Since I'm taking that class on the Classic Vampire. Do you mind that?"

"Okay," Ezzie says.

"See, I knew you were going to say 'Okay,' because some vampires know what you're going to say before you do. I know that from my Classic Vampire class."

Why am I so passive? This is theater! This is my thing. This is what I was born *for!* And so they read, and Ezzie is so-so, so-so, discouraged and downcast.

"You look stressed," says the house manager. "Have a sip, and relax a little." He hands her a mug of coffee. Except it isn't coffee. It's Templeton Rye. Ezzie sprays it all over the house manager, and he tries to catch the falling drops in his own mug. "What what!" he yells. "That's expensive, and...*very* hard to get around here!"

"I'm sorry?!" Ezzie says. A clear, clarion voice rings out in a Slavic-Romantic cadence. It is Dunya. Everyone starts to cry.

"Go to hell!" bellows Fordbot.

After that audition, Dunya and Ezzie move on to the next clearing, where students pollute the air with the sounds and smells of weed cutters and electric snow blowers. Auditions for *Hamletmachine*. Ezzie starts to relax a bit. She stumbles and stutters over half her lines, but it doesn't upset her; she's never been a good actor anyway. *This is part of a process*, she tells herself, and so her readings are comfortable if not transcendent. Dunya, on the other hand, transcends. Ezzie doesn't know what her suitemate has seen this week—what she's been through—but something has plugged her in and turned her volume up all the way. She does all the actorly things: enunciates clearly, speaks from the diaphragm, and projects, but it is really the passion that stands out.

"I want to be a machine," Dunya says. "No pain. No thoughts." Both pain and thought is evident. And so when that play's Canuck director hands Ezzie a glass of presumably expensive, piss-colored liquid, she knocks it back and heroically holds it down. "Herradura," says the director. "My name is Cara Klay, by the way. Nice to meet you, Esmeralda."

"Ezzie!" Ezzie says.

And then it's on to audition for a play about a handkerchief or something, but they're passing out Mount Gay, so that's pretty cool. The director asks the actors to dress up as furries before reading their parts.

"I don't want to see your faces!" says the director. "I want to hear your voices inhabiting the masks and those fuzzy bodies." The actors comply. Ezzie saddles into the world's saddest pony while Dunya assimilates herself as an ursine basilisk. Looking out through those lateral, dichromatic glass eyes, Ezzie finally relaxes into the role, content to read well and evoke a legitimate character: Emilia. But Dunya's Desdemona is a burning pyre, soaring and tearing

70

through the pages, incinerating them in her hands so that when she finishes her moment, the other auditionees get shy and slink back, and the director's assistant flips through her files to see if there's another script to replace the one that has been reduced to ashes.

One last saunter through the forest.

By now, it seems that most of the auditionees–twenty at least–have converged in a broad clearing with a leaping bonfire of green flames–*it's either chemical or the passage of time.* The director herself–Elizabeth Kraus, a fourth-year from Tokyo–walks around with an undisguised bottle of ÍS Vodka and pours a little cup for each newcomer.

"Okay, it smells kinda gross, but just a sip," says Ezzie, and Dunya smiles warmly.

"You're my sister," Dunya says, "and I will take care of you, always."

Ezzie knocks back her glass–pure crystal–and it does taste gross, but it warms her inside. Not the drink, but Dunya's words. "Thanks, Dunya. You're not going to be like those people I knew in New York. I can feel this. I know it." Dunya has no idea what Ezzie means, precisely. Ezzie can tell this at a glance. It doesn't matter. The emotion was felt. The sentiment expressed. An act of courage. Something that would have been easier if she had been drunk, but after all, she has spit out or declined almost all of the liquid courage she's been offered tonight. "What play is this, anyway?" Ezzie asks Elizabeth.

"It's my own adaptation of Jodorowsky's *The Holy Mountain.*"

They read again, and the congregation of stars and planets attend to Dunya's words, alighting upon her skin and stitching her with shining silver tattoos of the words-made-magic-through-her-speech. She supernovas through the script and becomes the brightest flame in that pale-dark night. All of the actors and technicians look on in awe.

"Jesus," says Elizabeth.

"That's my name!" answers Dunya with the dark energy trembling through her from head to toe.

"She's amazing," says a lighting designer, admiring the ample but atmospheric backlighting Dunya's reading has forged through freak of physics.

"I know," says Ezzie, fondly. "She's my roommate."

And then she has a thought.

"By the way...did you guys put up a bunch of nooses on the other side of the forest? As a prank or something?"

"Huh? Oh, us? TOG? No. No that's just part of the forest. It's like this dark dense forest, I mean, I'm sure you've already seen for yourself. Where compasses don't work, and you can get lost and die. Where all sorts of people despaired of their lives and went and hung themselves."

"I know, I know," Ezzie says. "Aokigahara."

"The what?" he asks. "What's that?"

Ezzie is disturbed again, but she doesn't want to be disturbed. It has taken her half of the night to relax. Instead, she asks about the location of the final play. "Oh," says the boy. "It's out there somewhere. I don't know. They're handing out Busch Light, if that's your thing. I don't remember the playwright, but the name of the play is *Elephants Sitting on Dildos.*"

Ezzie and Dunya decide to call it a night.

CHAPTER FOUR
ASPECTS OF SECRECY

Q.E.D.

Allies trump O-KE-DOKE.

And so, the week moves.

For some, it moves more painfully than for others.

The worst experience goes to Samo; he studies more this week than he has in most months of high school. He's only taking three courses: Basic Calculus I, Basic Physics I, and Introductory Kyrgyz I. So what's the problem? For starters, his calculus class, the *tutored* calculus class, assumes he already understands differentiation. Samo does not. His physics class makes the same assumption, except this is worse, because it isn't a tutored class, and most of the other students seem to be far ahead of him. And Kyrgyz, his fun class–the blow-off class–is a nightmare. Samo arrives on Tuesday, and the prof tells him that he'll have to know the Cyrillic Alphabet by Thursday.

"I like Cyrillic," Monty tells him in the dining hall that night.

"No way," says Samo. "The number three is a letter; 'nuff said."

He tries to transfer to a Spanish class, but **Кечирип коюнуз!** Every section is already full to the gills.

Compared to Samo, Dunya has a seemingly kick-ass week. Early on Wednesday, she finds out that she has been cast as THE STAR in *The Holy Mountain*, which has now been renamed *The Moldy Fountain*, pending thematic inversion in anticipation of legal challenges.

"That's too bad," Dunya tells Elizabeth Kraus over her phone.

"No it's not!" says Elizabeth. "It's *wonderful*. This play is going to be even better! Anyway, you are definitely the star in this show. I'm sure you've heard by now that you were the subject of quite a bidding war among the directors. There were directors that wanted to cast you in plays that you didn't audition for; in fact, the director of *Elephants Sitting on Dildos* was going to exchange his entire cast to just have you, but Chris put a stop to it. I won out in the end—this is the third-to-last show I'll be directing—but I had to give up a lot of my other top choices. You'd better deliver, Dunya Blavatsky."

But the cold, gray sun is a harsh change from the torchlit, moonlit forest. Dunya has to come up with $8K for tuition by the end of October, or her enrollment will be terminated, as well as any theatrical debuts. She spends the afternoon doing homework in the campus bookstore, because she cannot afford the books.

Ezzie envies Dunya's apparent success, but her own week has also started to improve. She isn't cast in a play, but Cara Klay shows up at the Cradle on Wednesday night and invites Ezzie to be the dramaturg for Müller's *Hamletmachine. Dramaturg! That isn't as good as acting; it's better!* Contemplating this during her second hum class with Professor Plumb, Ezzie looks out the window onto the Quints, where students mill about with their armfuls of books and Thermoses of coffee. She feels a sudden rush of hope and excitement and blows out the glass with her mind and eyes. Shards rain down. "Aw, jeez!" floats up from the pavement below, and Ezzie looks carefully down at her desk.

"You know," Plumb says as she's leaving the classroom, "I hear that a pair of sunglasses is sufficient to counteract miraculous happenings." His expression is blank as he speaks, and she can't see his eyes behind his own silver lenses. That night, she walks down to a gas station and buys a pair of cheap yellow shades.

Monty, at least, is thoroughly in his element. Each morning begins at six with jogging and weight training at the rec center, a fresh breakfast at Strawberries, and then his classes. He stops at the Commons for an Americano after finishing his first class and studies in the Olan Library until dinner. After dinner, he takes a walk around the South Side or catches one of the arty films on campus. If he's still got any homework, he does it in his dorm room. He's usually wrapped everything up by midnight.

It's his perfect schedule, and he foresees smooth sailing: academics, grades, no problems. He knows that midterms and term papers and finals will ratchet up the pressure, but he has planned his strategy meticulously. He has a margin of error and knows that he is in control.

Monty's favorite part of the day is the three or four hours he spends at the library. It's one of AU's more postcardable spots (but of course, there are dozens); it was originally used as a symposium hall for the various alienists in residence at the asylum. Given the gravity of their vocation, the space is appropriately grim. The many-arched, brick-planed ceiling swoops together on each side in slate grooves, smoothly gathered into stone gray urns. Between each of these, vast banks of vertical green windows look out on the grotesqueries of crumbling Arkaic. Limestone plank walls, granite columns, green marble floors, ebony tables, agarwood doors. The only expenses spared, evidently, are the lights. Narrow and dim incandescents hang too high for easy reading, and the shadows gather thick in every tapered corner. This, Monty thinks, is a room that hints at the magisterial expanse of secrecy in the world. It is an attitude so sullen and sober that it won't brook admiration even in broad daylight. All this reminds Monty of his desire to understand, to really know *something hidden*, and so he attacks his studies with a silent, laser-sharp intensity. He reads and reads, and is so focused that one page slides quietly into the next with hardly a ripple against his brain waves.

And yet, when Monty wakes up early each morning, he suspects that he is missing something significant. Certainly not the fast orbit of ideas that suggests possibility and convergence and keeps him restless and wakeful; *that* is going great. He worries that he's missing out a different sort of secret that flows through the air: implied conversations that he cannot hear. He has hardly spoken with any of the other students...*any* of them. Not his classmates. Not his housemates. Not even Samo, not much, even in passing.

Someone swears in the outer bedroom. *Samo isn't usually up this early.* Monty stands and dresses. He knocks on the door.

"Yeah?" comes Samo's tired answer.

Monty opens the door. Samo sits at his desk with his head in his hands. A halogen light is bright in his face, and his desk is littered with cans of Mountain Dew and O-KE-DOKE corn puff crumbs.

"You just get up?" Monty asks.

"No!" Angry, burdened.

"Then...what, you haven't been to bed?"

"I...suck at this problem set."

"You've been at it all night?"

"Yeah..."

"Mind if I take a look?"

Samo is silent for a moment, then half-grabs, half-crumples the half-written page and tosses it into Monty's hand. As Monty scans the problems, Samo continues to talk. "If it's so easy right now, what's it going to be like a few weeks from now? I've been staring at this thing all night. It doesn't even make sense. I mean, of course it makes sense. It's freaking obvious. I mean, first they're talking about x and a, okay, sure, makes sense, but then they're talking about d and ε, and how do they do that, just start talking about two totally different things. Whatever. And then there's that word–that one!" Samo slaps the paper. "*Implies*...implies! Then why are we doing a proof about all this? I thought that the point of math wasn't to imply but to prove!"

Monty has put on his glasses and tries to read the problem through Samo's chicken scratch. It's a simple one: prove the definition of a limit.

"You know," Monty says, "just because something is implied doesn't mean it isn't proven. You know proof by induction, right?"

"Not really," says Samo, pissed-off, hands in his pockets. "Tonight's a big night on campus. I wanted to go there. I wanted to stand in the light, man. But I've been up all night at this and now I'm fucking tired!"

"I can help you with this," says Monty, sitting down on the bed. "Come on, sit."

Samo sits.

"Look, so you're right, they are saying something obvious. You just have to say it in the language they like. Just pretend you're in your Kyrgyz class —"

"Don't you even mention that stupid class!"

"Okay, fine." Monty pauses. "Start with ε. It's bigger than zero. It tells you so. It has to be this way. Same thing for d. Also bigger than zero. If it isn't, then their definition won't work."

"Stupid limits."

But Monty has started to draw on a scrap of paper. His brain has seized upon a castaway statement Samo has made–a strange thing–but he won't get a good answer from his roommate until they've solved this problem.

"And in order for their definition to work..." he draws: $|f(x)-f(xo)| = |ax+b-(axo+b)|$. "You understand that, right? I mean, you know why."

Samo looks at the page for a long time. "Um...yeah."

"Okay."

"Like substitution, in algebra."

"Right, I get that."

Monty continues to draw.

It takes a while, about twenty minutes, before Samo can follow the progressive logic from given to □. Samo nods, gravely, reluctantly, and Monty perceives shame in those broad, tensed shoulders.

"Thanks," Samo says.

"Now just a second," Monty says. "What did you mean, something big is happening on campus tonight?"

"It's Friday of first week." As if this explained everything. "The SOs Fair is tonight."

"I don't follow."

"Oh hey, where have you been? I mean, everyone knows. After dinner tonight, the SOs–student organizations–they have a big party on the Commons where you sign up for their mailing lists and shit. I want to check out the pneumatic club, but they also have free pizza and beer."

"Beer?"

"Yeah nobody checks IDs. That's what Mossy Fairbanks says...um, third-year on the fourth floor."

"Samo," says Monty, shaking slightly. "If I help you finish your problem set, will you keep me company at the SOs Fair? I'm just a little uncertain, being the first –"

"Yeah, sure! You don't have to help me, either, if you don't want to. I'd like it if you did, though."

"I'll help you," says Monty, smiling. "I've just–big secret here, never told anyone–I just haven't ever had a drink before."

"Well I've never not sucked at math before. Never really tried, you know?"

Syzygy

Sometimes you cry, probably (most likely).

Hazard is Samo's eyeball when his two gloves dissolve onto his skin and he wears them without waning. It's a new moon, nearly, by now, and the glassy surface of Arkaic–electricity, barely bought for the city at large (municipal budgets are indeed *that* tight)–turns the lower slopes of each urban hill the pitchy color of happy hunting boughs. But up here, time turns when swift glimpses in furtive directions push the pendulum into a highly eccentric orbit. Where looking–nay, imagining!–is enough to make a difference. Back at Southern High School, the marching band blows fat sounds into brass mouthpieces, and *stomp, stomp, stomp* go football players, toward state-sponsored scholarships at the biggest Michigan schools. Back home in Arkaic, *brownout brownout,* the lights go out, and a single candle burns. Dunya aches on her nineteenth birthday quietly today–nobody knows, and she doesn't want anybody to know–because of all of the chaos back home in Richmond. Her father's humming Howlin' Wolf, and he'll get a second mortgage on the damn house, hell yes he will, he hasn't told her, but she knows. When she picks up the phone and nothing profound is said, Ezzie is next door, oblivious, because her own orbit is turning onto a new anxiety. *What is happening back home? Why did he call drunk?* Who called drunk? Her own father.

"There's things you don't know," he sobs. "Things we've never told you! I...I haven't seen your mother in years!"

And then hangs up.

He won't pick up when she calls him back.

And the sun is down, and the darkness is long, long, long, and early autumn cool, cool, cool, but there's so much scheduled to happen tonight. So much to happen tonight.

"What's the word?" asks Monty.

"The word," says Samo, "is that my high school has a kick-ass marching band, and a kick-ass football team, and I can hear them right now."

"That isn't a marching band," says Monty. "That's the chains behind the door over there."

"No it's not!" and Samo leaves his room, barefoot, in boxers and a wife-beater, with fake chains he got in NOLA swinging around his neck, because hey, why not? He's got a platinum one with an emerald scarab, a gold one with a ruby rose, and a silver one with a sapphire dragon.

Out on the hill, the same hill where he stood on the first day of Orientation, he can see the tottering, rottering city. At his right, as expected, are the Pyramid and the skyscrapers downtown. There's a bonfire somewhere; someone's burning leaves, and the air is singed with warm soot. Cold air tonight. Saltpeter skies. Starry cataracts. And then, at the center, is the faint-angled outline of Mallery's Storage. But off to the left, where he's really looking this time, past the naked white lights of XAI, and out on the West End, his family, his friends, all together at the football game. At Southern, where boys larger and stronger than Samo bash each other's brains in, where the sexy cheerleaders kick up their muscled thighs, and where the sexier trumpet players and timpani players wrap their taut-sharp and peat-dark palms around valves and drumsticks. Their cunning eyes, their wily minds. None of them have joined him here.

"You're right," Monty says, stepping up behind him. "I can hear it."

It's out there.

A soft soft *boom boom booming that* sails softly over the hills and is barely dispelled in the wind.

"I kind of wish I was there," Samo says.

Monty smiles. "Let's go to the SOs Fair, Samo."

SOs

You should gaze for long into an abyss.

Mossy has lied.

Many of the SOs have little trays of candy bars, bowls of popcorn, plastic cups of pop, or plastic plates of stale pizza, but there's no beer to be seen. In fact, the best offerings, food and drinkwise, are the huge tables of milk and cookies supplied by the Law School Council.

Samo is surprised, but Monty is floored. He's been in Olan Commons many times, but *Good Lord!* He hadn't expected this. How does a school of this size–less than seven thousand, including the grad students–manage such a large and diverse artillery of student organizations? Each organization has its own table, with its own plethora of videos, music, food, drink, email lists, fliers. There are hundreds of tables. The vast, dim, cavernous room is filled with the sound of delighted pens and pandemonium.

Samo wanders out into the morass, then stops when he realizes that Monty is standing in the entryway, staring.

"Monty!" he shouts.

Monty starts and walks over to Samo.

"This is big...–ger than I expected."

"No kidding? Let's go!"

On their left, the X-Ray Goggle Soup Kitchen (XRGSK) maintains two boxes, one filled with non-perishables and canned goods, and the other filled with Akiyoshi Kitaoka-vision glasses. A few tables down, a pyramid made entirely out of potatoes demarcates the space of the Idahoans in Arkaic Association, while the very existence thereof is noisily disputed by the ersatz Arkaic University Flat Earth Congress. A brassy performance by Horns and Pom Poms tries to satisfy Samo's nostalgia for his old high school, and he does crack a momentary smile. A bit further on, a stack of old literary journals with pull-out tabs primly advertises editorial participation in the Arkaen Review, and naturally, Amnesty International and Habitat for Humanity are well-represented. Less well-represented? The Arkaic Republicans. He sits alone in the middle of his Formica folding table with his hands clasped, stoically enduring the flagrant obscenity and debauch happening all around him. Most of this originates at the Cross-Stitchers Club, which appears to be utterly smashed and reeks of patchouli. A whole column of tables are dedicated to Baseball, Badminton, Handball, Rugby, and Bowling, and stunningly aerodynamic airplanes sail back and forth between the two mathematical societies: X Squared and The Cartesian Coordinates.

"Mossy! Mossy!" yells Samo.

"Samo!" Mossy has just finished signing up for the O! Catoblepas mailing list. He is as tall as Samo but mysteriously handsome. He has a motorcycle, but he ruined his Datsun on I-92 when he decided to drive the last three miles home on a flat. None of the native Arkaens were particularly sympathetic to the story.

"Yo! You told me there'd be beer here."

Mossy laughs. "I lied, Samo, but I didn't think you'd come otherwise. You're glad you came, right?"

"I don't know. It's loud."

"Ah shutup it's loud. You can get your drink on later."

"Okay okay."

"So who's this?"

"This is Monty."

"What house?"

"Acedia House," Monty says.

Mossy looks confused.

"Monty's my suitemate," says Samo.

"Oh," says Mossy. "I haven't seen you."

"I haven't been around much," says Monty with a shrug.

"Cool. Well make sure you get some of those cookies from the law school. They made them from scratch, from grandmothers."

"There are grandmas in those cookies?" screeches Samo.

Mossy doesn't laugh.

"Make sure you check out Artemis' Club," he says. "I'm telling you, they're the coolest SO on campus."

"Will do. Are there engineering clubs?"

"I only know one; the Fraternal Order of the Pneumatics," and Mossy points to a distant table, where a group of students in togas inspect an oversized airgun.

"Holy mama," says Samo. "I'm there." And he's off.

Monty could try to keep up with Samo, but it seems futile at the moment. Samo moves too quickly, and Monty is interested in different things anyway. He starts wandering an aisle where most of the tables are manned by students in costumes, or at least unusual hats.

"Greetings, comrade!" yells a boy in a Fechner beret at a table with an 8 1/2 x 11" paper proudly proclaiming, "Annoying Pinkos!" The salutation sets off a flurry of competitive singing from the Arkadian A Cappella, the Arkaen A Cappella, and Just Another A Cappella Group. At another table, a group of students stands in contorted poses before their own placard, which is so ornately drawn that it takes Monty several moments to recognize the single word title: "Calligraphy." *I can't get drawn in, Monty thinks. My schedule requires me to stick to my plan. I'm already short on sleep, and once I start getting involved in extracurriculars, I'm going to start slipping. I won't get into the deep research. I won't learn the true secrets. I won't have the time or the energy to uncover the other reality implied by the masked walls in the Olan Library.* Still, something seems false about this argument to Monty. He can't put his finger on it, but what if his studying isn't enough? What if he studies for four hard years here and it doesn't yield a single meaningful answer?

He finds himself standing in front of a table where a single soul—man or woman, faculty or student, he can't tell—sits in the lotus position wearing a shinobi shōzoku. The table is unadorned, except for several dozen fortune cookies.

"Who are you?" Monty asks.

The figure doesn't answer but gestures for him to choose a cookie. He picks it up, opens it, throws the pieces into his mouth, and as he eats, reads the message:

We are the Book Ninjas.

"You know that fortune cookies are Chinese and ninjas are from Japan, right?"

The figure gestures for Monty to take another cookie. He does so:

The origin of the fortune cookie is a contentious subject.
They may, perhaps, have originated in Japan.
But this is irrelevant, as the Book Ninjas are not bound
by tradition, region, or history.

"So what do you do?"

The figure gestures, and Monty takes another cookie:

Break the law.

"That's informative." Monty finds himself getting annoyed. "How do you break it? To what end? What do you accomplish?"

You may have noticed that school textbooks are very expensive here.

"Yes, I have noticed," Monty says ruefully.

This is an affluent school, but not all
of the students here are wealthy.
In the first degree, we liberate books for the benefit
of financially stressed students.

After Monty has finished reading this fortune, the masked figure takes it and eats it. Monty is stoic.

"Degrees?"

There are higher degrees. They are not revealed to the uninitiated.

"Oh." Monty hesitates. He's waiting for something. He isn't sure what. The figure becomes exasperated and gestures for Monty to take another cookie. "Okay, fine."

Forget about the higher degrees.
You must know someone who's having a hard time affording books.

"As a matter of fact, I do." His heart aches for Dunya.

You want to join us, don't you?

"I do."

Find out Dunya Blavatsky's class schedule
and get her the books she needs.
Do not alert her as to your activities.
When you do this, you will have joined the Book Ninjas

and we will reveal ourselves.

"How will you know when I've fulfilled my mission?"

We'll know.

The figure is evidently tired of "talking" and casually begins replacing the cookies that Monty has eaten. For his part, Monty has an upset stomach. He's nervous too; he's supposed to *steal* books to join this club? That sounds a lot more drastic than signing up for a mailing list. Given the vague conversation, he's not sure how participation will affect his schedule, either.

As Monty leaves the table, he bumps into Dunya herself.

"Hi Monty," she says.

"Oh! Hi Dunya."

"Have you joined up anywhere?"

"Um —" he looks back at the Book Ninjas. The silent figure stares at him. "Nope, not yet."

"It's hard to resist, isn't it? There're so many options."

"Yeah."

"I guess I'm in TOG, since I got cast in that play. And now I'm also signed up for the Saint Simon Socialists. It's the sort of thing my dad told me about growing up, so now I'm excited to learn more about it. And I guess I'm going to be an anthropology major, so I signed up for the Anthrostrology mailing list."

"Oh."

"You've got to sign up for something."

"I don't really have the time."

"Oh come on, we can find something for you!"

Dunya leads Monty back toward the center of the room, where the tables are clustered most densely.

"I've heard if you join the Kyrgyz Club you get to make some really delicious yogurt," she says.

"Samo warned me against them."

"Okay. What about Bueno Tango?"

"I have two left feet."

"Humane Secularists?"

"I'm not religious."

"You're not a vegan, are you?"

"No."

"Because I hear they get naked a lot at the Hunt of the Wild Tofurkey."

Monty stares at her.

"Yeah," she says. "Probably not a great fit. Well, there's huge participation at the Faux League of Nations. Let's take a look at that."

But Monty is distracted. "Hold on a minute," he says.

He steps up to a deeply scarred table where a frighteningly real looking skeleton is seated next to three students wearing toile neckties.

"By a continuing process of inflation," Monty says, "government can confiscate, secretly and unobserved –"

"– an important part of the wealth of their citizens," finishes the redheaded girl sitting at center.

Monty hesitates.

"Capitalism is the astounding belief," he says, "that the most wickedest of men will do the most wickedest of things –"

"– for the greatest good of everyone," she finishes.

Monty hesitates.

"Is that?" he asks, pointing to the skeleton.

"Yes."

"How did you –"

"– we swapped him for a fake."

"Oh. Wow."

Monty finds himself signing up for the mailing list and agreeing to be Secretary at the next meeting.

The name of the group is The Skeleton Keynes.

He turns around to rejoin Dunya, but she has left and is talking animatedly at a table for the D.I.Y.MFers.

So I've joined two clubs, he thinks, and sighs. Monty continues along the aisle. He passes the Finally Feminists, Student Government, the Furtive Democrats Association, The Middle-Eastern Students for Christ, Archaic Arkaic, and the Chess Club.

One table is loaded down with delicious-looking produce. Eggplants, sweet potatoes, sweet corn on the cob, broccoli, turnips, rutabagas, and more kinds of beans and peas than he can count.

"Wow!" he says. "What's this?"

A short, slightly chubby girl with thick ponytailed hair steps out from behind the table.

"Oh, I'm sorry!" she says in a chipper voice. "I think I misplaced our sign. This is the Order of the Eggplant."

"Is this a vegan thing?" he asks suspiciously.

Her expression darkens slightly. "No, although I am a vegan. We're a community service organization."

She explains, concisely and colorfully, that in a city with ten thousand abandoned houses and twenty thousand vacant parcels, silver linings have to be seized and smelted. "We partner with the Arkaic Farmers' Market, and local growers to use vacant land to plant gardens and build greenhouses. The food we grow on the parcels that we maintain, about two acres on the South Side here, we donate to the soup kitchens around town. Also, we volunteer at the soup kitchens several times a month."

"But do you keep any of that produce for yourself?" Monty asks.

"You can get great produce at the Farmers' Market."

Monty hesitates.

"Okay," he says. "Sign me up."

After leaving his name with the Eggplants, Monty decides he'd better head for the door and return to the Cradle. He's already joined up with three SOs in about a half hour, and this alone may irreparably damage his serene regimen of exercise, study, exploration, and sleep. But he has just turned around and bumps into Argosy.

"Monty!"

"Oh, hi there."

"What have you signed up for?"

Monty tells him, omitting the Book Ninjas.

"Well I just joined up with the vegans."

"You're not vegan."

"I know, but they're naked a lot over there."

Argosy scratches at his scalp. White flakes start to dust the floor.

"Where are you going next?" Monty asks.

"Everyone's telling me to check out Artemis' Club."

"That's one of the ones they've warned us about...I mean, during Orientation."

"Of course they warned you 'bout it!" Argosy says. "They're awesome!"

"What do they do, exactly?"

"I don't know. I mean, people have told me, but I didn't really understand. I was hoping that someone could explain it to me."

"I really don't think I should sign up for anything else. It's already going to cut into my study –"

"Everyone says that Artemis' Club is the oldest and most mysterious SO on campus."

"Let's go!" says Monty.

As they walk through the crowd, Argosy smiles and puts his hand fondly on Monty's shoulder.

"I want you to know, Monty, I'm really glad that I'm getting to know you," he says. *We've only had two conversations.* "I mean," Argosy goes on, "I don't really know you yet...but everyone here has had a story so far. And I need to hear yours. Have you noticed you never run into boring people here? Ugly people, yes. Weird people, yes. Mean and sad people, yeah, sure, but everyone's got a vision and a story."

It's a good point. And such wisdom is doubly appropriate coming from the boy who builds Towers of Babel out of his own fingernail clippings.

Mossy is wrong about one thing. There *is* beer at the SOs Fair, and it's all at the table for Artemis' Club. Their table is not visually remarkable, littered with scraps of a numbered list, crumpled up papers, and Coke bottles filled with hoppy brew.

"Don't mind if I do," says Argosy, reaching for a frothy bottle.

A girl at the table in a *Papierkrattler* mask slaps his hand with a fan. "That's not for you!" she says.

"Ow!" he yelps. "Alyssa?!"

She laughs and takes off her mask. Monty remembers Alyssa Carnival as an Orientation Designation a couple weeks back. She has the most ribald sense of humor of anyone in Acedia House. Also, she rocks out harder than anyone but Dunya (in Monty's opinion) and is the drummer in her own band, The Freak Show. He didn't know that she was a member of Artemis' Club, however.

"You don't sign up for Artemis' Club," she says.

Oh.

"You're a part of Artemis' Club when you participate in Artemis' Hunt."

"What's Artemis' Hunt?" Monty asks.

"It's only the second largest scavenger hunt in the Solar System."

"That's it?" Argosy asks. "That's what all the fuss is about?!"

"You know," she says, "A lot of people say that before they get involved. But Artemis' Hunt will change your life. People get engaged during Artemis' Hunt. People get married during Artemis' Hunt. People hook up at Artemis' Hunt, and nine months later, their babies are born and become little Artemis' Hunt babies."

"Wow," says Monty.

"Wait a minute." says Argosy. "What does that even mean?"

Alyssa shrugs. "It doesn't happen until May. Then you can decide for yourself."

"What's this?" Monty asks, picking up one of the lists:

17. A complete deck of Starr Chromeo Trading Cards. (18 pts.)

25. A fully functional battering ram. Must be able to breach the barricaded doors of Olan Commons (without getting the Hunt canceled next year). (64 pts.)

48. What is the significance of Owen Rd. and Orion St.? (5 pts.)

54. At 7h00 on Tuesday, a non-captain member of your team is present at South St. and Winters Rd. They may bring the following: $20 in quarters, a coconut, an unsharpened #2 pencil, a notepad, *Bosom Buddies: The Complete Series* for DVD, an Arkaen-style coney, a valid passport or state ID (not a drivers license), an expired pass for the ATS, and an AU transcript demonstrating a GPA of less than 2.5. That is all they may bring. They should bid their adieus to friends and family beforehand. (120 pts.)

72. TBA. (ψ pts.)

"That's part of last year's Hunt List." She smiles. "On the first Monday after May Day (which we call Thargelion), Via Positiva releases Artemis' List at three a.m. Members of Artemis' Club—which is pretty much a third of everyone on campus—form teams and compete for the Golden Bow and Arrow. These relics go to the team which has accrued the most points by the end of that Sunday. Items can be anything. They can be found objects, like a traditional scavenger hunt. Or information. Or performances. Or construction. There's a road trip involved; last year students went to Iqaluit, and the year before that, they went to Chernobyl. And each item has a point value."

"Oh," said Argosy. "So it's just a game."

The smile vanishes from Alyssa's face. "Once you do it, you'll understand."

"Doesn't it just sound like a game, Monty?"

"Who is Via Positiva?" Monty asks.

"They're the mysterious judges of Artemis' Hunt. These Cokes are for them."

"I don't understand. Why aren't they running this table?"

"Via Positiva doesn't do the SOs Fair," she says.

"So you're, um, promoting Artemis' Hunt for them?" Monty goes on. "Shouldn't they be doing that?"

"I'm spreading the word, so they'll look fondly on Acedia House when the Hunt rolls around."

"So you're just trying to get people involved?"

"Pretty much."

"But not for eight months."

"Pretty much..."

They stand there in silence, with the noise all around them.

"Well, that's weird," says Argosy, walking off.

"You'll be back!" yells Alyssa. "Trust me. *Trust* me!"

Monty isn't quite sure what to do with himself. "Thanks, Alyssa," he says.

"No problem, um..."

"Monty," he says. "I live in the basement. With Samo."

"Samo!" she laughs. "Tell Samo I say hi!"

For the next two hours, Monty stalks the long aisles, stopping at dozens of tables. He passes the Inebriated Writers and the African and African-Americans Students United. The Abstract Ballet and the AU Journal of Law. The Spiritualist Club and Let's Play Hearts! He isn't seduced by the Hellenistic Association or the Multicultural Club, or even the Pythag-Koreans. The Catholic Collective is meaningless to him, and he is repelled by the militant phalanx of the Elysians, the Elysium Asylum, the Elysium Club, and the Elysian League.

And yet, Monty's *secrets* have taken on an ever more expansive definition. He sees promise in any opportunity to *discover the undiscovered*, which is, of course, everywhere. Monty has only lived eighteen years on this earth. It reaches much deeper beneath the stony folds of the Olan Library two stories above than he had ever imagined.

And so, before the end of the SOs Fair, Monty has signed up for the Aaron Burr Society and We Seek the Illuminati! He will write university interest stories for the Gold Standard and will help promote the artists recorded by The Beat Hip-Hop Club. Monty is purely rank-and-file in the Dominican Student Association, and he's not even sure exactly where he'll start with the AU Juggling Society. But secrets are thick in the air about the Goa-trance dancing Psychedelic Association, and who can turn down a heartfelt invitation from the Students Against Un-Dead Incursions?

At the end of the night, Monty finds Samo waiting for him at the entrance to the Commons, anxious to walk home between the white-glowing xenon lamps of the Fairway.

"Did you join the Order of the Pneumatics?" Monty asks.

"Yeah, I did," says Samo. "And Crew. They want me to be coxswain."

"Aren't you a little tall to be coxswain?"

"Huh? Oh, I don't know. But I *am* kind of worried," Samo says. "I only meant to join one SO, and here I joined two. I'm worried it's going to cut into my homework too much. What do you think, Monty?"

Monty can't answer, doesn't want to answer, won't answer, and now he doesn't have to, because the air is rent by the explosive sound of heavy metal driving oak wood into concrete tiles. Screaming from the back of the Commons. A huge, spherical pendulum—*a piece of one of the turbines?*—has fallen from the depths of the rafters—*why was it up there?*—to instantly demolish the table of the Positivist Club. The sole positivist is squatting and screaming and crying in a corner with all sorts of messes spreading throughout his pants.

"Yeah, nobody saw that coming," says Samo.

"What do you mean?"

"Oh, well the word I hear is that Via Positiva was pissed off because the Positivist Club had a similar name. They told the Positivists to disband. The Positivists didn't. So I guess this is what happens when you piss off Via Positiva."

CHAPTER FIVE
SOMETHING UNREASONABLE THIS WAY COMES

Early Shadows

Just because they're smarmy doesn't mean they're wrong.

Amoral bean counters and number crunchers convene behind translucent screens.

Sociopathic, bedraggled professors rake their fingers across their keys.

The bureaucracy and the academics fight tooth and nail, and yet, among their divergent missions, find some surprising moments of agreement.

Arkaic University is young. It is non-coastal and uninitiated into the ranks of established and respected institutions. But it's a feral and ferocious place. With an infusion of the old Olan fang-to-jugular philosophy, faculty and trustees concur: we'll scrabble and claw our way to respectability.

Hours of study per student? We can flush that up. You can't make an omelet without squeezing a few eggs.

Number of dropouts and transfers? We can satisfy here as well. You can't make fois gras without...

A crescendoing wave of student suicides carried out by pill and blade and noose and bang!–*most of all in the forest–secondly in the libraries–icky. You can't assemble a utopian institution without the appropriate high modernist regime.* It's very sad (*naturally*).

After this academic Crock-Pot cooks for a generation, it will surely churn out Pulitzers, Nobels, hell, maybe even a Heisman or two, and then Olan's brainchild will take its rightful place alongside the finest of the Ivies.

And so, on the second week of Autumn Quarter, the upperclassmen start muttering a word in apprehension, although the first years are puzzled to be hearing it so soon: "midterms." They wonder, *Aren't midterms things that happen, you know, during the middle of the term?* They ask about this at cafeteria tables around their rotisserie chicken (it's a Monday). "No," answer the upperclassmen, "a midterm could happen any week that's not first week or tenth week."

"I once had a first week midterm!" yells Xerxes Trough, a third-year with a weasel's face and an infuriating ascot.

Dunya thinks it would be funny to tighten that thing and watch his face pop bright red.

But this isn't the time for violence.

It's time to start thinking about midterms.

In the Basement of Despair

Sometimes you need to be persistent.

Sometimes you need to give up.

At all times you need to discern the difference.

She stands before him, the sharp jut of her sinuous hips (the sinuous jut of her sharp hips?), her many curves and angles, and that black, black, black hair. He pretty much aches about it.

"I can compromise on many of my expectations," she says. "I'm not unreasonable. But some of my expectations, I just can't compromise."

Her fierce, dark eyes.

"But the one thing you won't compromise on is the one thing I can't do anything about!" says Samo.

She'll be wearing that candy cane blouse, but it's a little too tight, a little too small, so he imagines...*imagines?*

"Right. What am I going to do? I tell my dad I'm dating a guy, and he's naturally going to want to know your name. Sam O'Samuel? That isn't an Indian name."

"So tell him I'm Samdap Osamgupta or something!"

"Great, then he'll think you're Bengali, which is almost worse than a black guy from Arkaic. No, he wants me to bring home a nice Punjabi man. He might tolerate something else, but *you?*"

Candace Bhatt recedes in his mind. She floats backwards. It's easily accomplished. She isn't even here. He's having this conversation on his phone.

"Look, Samo," she says, "you're a great guy –" *Aw shit!* "– and I'm really glad we got to spend some time together during O-Week, but –" *I can't listen to this.* "– maybe it's best if we just –"

"Gotta go, Candace, sorry!" Samo says in a rough voice. He hangs up the phone.

Evening comes early to the basement bedrooms of Calliope Cradle. He has an eastward exposure onto the courtyard, and anyway, his window is so close to the ground that the shadows of the other dorms rise far above the rays of the setting sun. It's five o'clock and already dark in here. Samo feels the warmth fading from his chest. O-Week had seemed so flush and full of promise, and the first week had been steeped in challenge and density. The SOs Fair had given him a deceptive reprieve. In the three weeks that had followed, the Pneumatics and Crew had taken hours and hours, and he would need hours and hours before this week's midterms. The first of many.

Samo is conditioned to relax. He has liked riding through life in the passenger seat—rolling down the window (even if it's icy cold) and feeling the wind rip through his hair while his hand cuts waves through all that nitrogen. This intensity—this place at the driver's wheel—these high stakes—takes a lot more concentration. After a lot of coaching from Monty—*Who knows how long Monty will be able to help out like this?*—Samo has caught up on his calculus. But he's still way behind in physics, and he's thinking about dropping his Kyrgyz class. In exchange for what? He needs three classes to be a full-time student and keep his financial aid. *Aw, shit.* Candace was going to be a break from this stress and anxiety. She was going to be the one area of his life in which the anxieties were supposed to be less and better than those of high school. So much for that. So much for love and...baseball. *Punjab! Silkworms! Harmandir Sahib! Bhat!*

Samo sighs.

Well, it's a half hour before dinner, and at least now he won't feel guilty about looking at porn.

Samo flips on the computer. In this new, blue light, he makes out a small note, tightly written in Monty's neat script: "You have access to the physics lab? Can you get me some 'Precious Polymer?'"

Our Minds are Not an Appendix

Conspicuous inattention in class makes one more likely to be called upon.

Ezzie is sitting in Professor Plumb's Escaping the Greeks evening study session, thinking about her impending first midterm, when a familiar shadow falls across her desk. It's Monty. An exhausted-looking Monty.

"What are you doing here?" she asks.

"Nice shades," Monty says, and takes a seat.

Class has started. Ezzie pulls her sunglasses lower over her eyes.

"Page 7319, *Kritik der reinen Vernunft*," barks Plumb as he strides across the space and starts stabbing the board with chalk. White clouds of dust float up and coat his silver shades.

"A secret," whispers Monty, and starts scribbling on a photocopy he has brought in with him.

Plumb spins on his heel with a squeak and flings the chalk at Monty. It flashes an inch above his head and vanishes into a corner of the classroom.

"And who are you, whisperer?" thunders Plumb.

"I'm," says Monty, stunned, "an auditor."

"I never allow students to audit my class!" says Plumb. "Leave."

Monty gathers himself and his books, stands stoically, and leaves. As he passes Ezzie, he hands her his paper with his note in the margin.

Read this! c/o the Psychedelics Ass.

And so, as class goes on around her, Ezzie reads.

"Knowledge, as has been shown, consists in the perception of the agreement or disagreement of ideas," says Plumb.

"That's Hume," says Cassidy Antrim, with a cocksure smile. He crosses his legs under his kilt. "Kant thinks he's wrong."

As Plumb scribbles something on the chalkboard, Ezzie reads:

THE ARKADIAN ARCHIVE
June 30, 2009

ARKAIC UNIVERSITY PROFESSOR VANISHES DURING FACULTY
HAZING

Plumb continues: "Objects are given to us by means of sensibility, and it alone yields us intuitions; they are thought through the understanding, and from the understanding arise concepts. But all thought must, directly or indirectly, by way of certain characters relate ultimately to intuitions, and therefore, with us, to sensibility, because in no other way can an object be given to us."

"Does he define sensibility as a contained thing, or are its boundaries up for grabs?" asks Cassidy.

Detectives with the Arkaic Police Department said that they are investigating the whereabouts of missing person Dr. Lorraine Glass in response to statements by the Arkaic University Department of the Humanities.

Plumb: "If the receptivity of our mind, its power of receiving representations in so far as it is in any wise affected, is to be entitled sensibility, then the mind's power of producing representations from itself, the spontaneity of knowledge, should be called the understanding. Without sensibility no object would be given to us, without understanding no object would be thought. Thoughts without content are empty, intuitions without concepts are blind."

"But both concept and content are evolved within us to present an adaptable advantage," says Cassidy, stretching. "Even as abstractions, they are functional."

Dr. Glass, a candidate for tenure, went missing, says the APD, last Friday morning during a secret "initiation ceremony" held in the chain tunnels beneath the university. While University President Rachel Suffolk maintains that the event was part of an AU tradition, and that no laws were broken, she has accepted the resignation of Percival Plumb as Dean of the Department of Humanities. Professor Plumb will continue to teach at the university.

"Let us suppose that there is nothing antecedent to an event, upon which it must follow according to rule," says Plumb. "All succession of perception would then be only in the apprehension, that is, would be merely subjective, and would never enable us to determine objectively which perceptions are those that really precede and which are those that follow."

It is not known whether Ms. Glass's disappearance is connected to the recent shattering of window panes all over the West Side of Arkaic –

"Objectivity is over –" says Cassidy.

"Ms. Prentice!" says Plumb.

"Yes!" says Ezzie.

"How do you suppose that we know anything is?"

"Is what?"

"Is anything?"

She thinks. These are questions of connection. Any sort of connection is presumptive. But one has to muddle through.

So..."You don't know," she says. "You never know. But if you don't assume knowledge on any front, then you can't eat, can't find a place to sleep, can't find a mate."

"A fairly obvious line of thought, don't you think?" Plumb says, but Ezzie wants to keep going.

"I agree with what Cassidy is saying about the evolutionary function of our 'sensibilities.' It isn't a satisfying answer for Kant, which is fine, I guess, but it's a starting point we need to consider when we talk about these things. Just that there's isn't a way to talk about these things that isn't a thing itself. It's all...provisional."

"What is this starting point to which you refer?"

"That we're built to survive. And if our sensibilities are hopelessly subjective and unable to draw accurate conclusions based on actual phenomena, then we must empirically account for some other evolutionary function that they would fill. Distinct from accurate observation."

"Ah, but that could be called empiricism, along the lines of Hume. Perhaps even a Hume-esque atavism."

"Our minds have evolved for a purpose," Ezzie says.

"Perhaps our minds are an appendix," says Plumb.

"I'd like to Foucault some Kant," adds Cassidy.

October Girl

Be careful what you wish for.
What, we already offered that advice?
Um...Beware the Ginger.

When Samo gets hungry, he leaves the Basement of Despair to get some grub, something which usually improves his mood. But the Melancholy Morsels from the Dolorous Cafeteria are not what the doctor ordered. So Samo wanders out onto the Fairway. He picks up a stick. He pokes one of the strobing xenon lamps, aflame with the husks of dead fireflies. The resulting shock blasts him out of his shoes and knocks him out on the grass.

"Sweet!" he says when he wakes.

Rinse and repeat, rinse and repeat, but the fourth time out, he pees his pants.

"Samo?" says a pale boy with a smooth French accent.

"Hello, François."

François de Rivoli was born and bred in Marseilles and came to the U.S. with his father, who works at the Consulat Général de France à Houston. François' girlfriend is a Gupton-Jones girl named Erin, and she visits every weekend. She stands at François' side right now. Her strawberry blonde hair is bound up in spangly pigtails, all cheerleader-like.

"Um..." says Samo.

"Oh my God!" squeals Erin, "you peed your pants!"

"Oh, yeah," says Samo. "Oops."

He gets to his feet, noticing a third girl, a curvy redhead with napalm eyes, standing with the others.

"Well," he says, "you see, it happens when you do this."

He touches his stick to the xenon lamp. Stick in the air. Samo in the air. Samo's shoes left behind. Samo comes down on the ground, laughing.

The others murmur in surprise and appreciation. The redhead picks up the stick and thrusts it into the heart of the lamp. Smoke and sparks. Explosion. She sails through the air. Her eyes roll back in her head. She jerks and twitches. Her eyes open. She laughs. "Yup!" she says. "I peed myself, sure enough!"

After François and Erin have felt the charge a couple times, the four students dust themselves off.

"Samo!" says François. "Erin and I are going to Basque Film Night. Want to come along?"

"No," says Samo. "I'd better go change."

"Me too," says the redhead. "I'm tired."

They say goodbye and walk back to the Cradle.

"Your name is Samo?" she asks.

"Sam," Samo says, "but everyone calls me Samo."

"I like it!" she says and waits for him to ask her name. After about a minute, she says, "I'm Saturnia Dyson."

"Oh, that's a kinda cool name."

"Do you think so? A lot of people think it's a reference to the Roman festival, but actually it's not; my parents are lepidopterists. But I'm ready to come out of my chrysalis!" Her eyes narrow in a clever way, but Samo doesn't notice this. He's trying to figure out his keys. They've reached the Cradle, and the door is stuck.

"Here, let me get it for you," she says.

She takes out the right key and opens the door.

"Thanks!" says Samo.

"Well, I've got a brand new pair of roller skates, and you've got..."

"Phew!" says the doorwoman, "You two have made a wet mess of yourselves!"

Samo and Saturnia pass on through the vestibule and into the courtyard. The cherry trees have just started to go gold, and they're set aflame in the fire of the xenon floods. The floods are spaced along tubes that carry electrical time up from the tunnels and cycle it through the dorm. As Saturnia and Samo walk along the broken stone path, their shadows shoot upwards and widen before reaching for the stars.

"I haven't seen you before," says Samo.

"I've been here," says Saturnia. "I live in Lust House, so I'm on the other side of the courtyard from you."

Samo reaches the end of the path and enters Acedia House with Saturnia right behind him.

"It's getting cold out there," she says.

"It's October," Samo answers.

"I know," with a sigh. "October is going to be over too soon."

"It does have 31 days."

"I'm not used to these cold nights. Cool days, I can deal with. I'm from Miami, and yes, it's warm there year-round compared to here. Summer afternoons back home, we get a sea breeze, and it's a lot like those northern winds you get here. But there's nothing there like the Michigan cold at night. Strange. And menacing."

"I don't think so," Samo says. "I'm from Michigan. I'm from Arkaic."

"Good, then you know all about it!" says Saturnia. "Do you know how I can keep warm?"

"Well, I usually wear a jacket."

They've reached Samo's room. He opens the door and lets himself in.

"Oh," he says, "I didn't know you were following me here."

"I'm sorry," says Saturnia. "I didn't mean to."

"Well, I've got to take a shower and change my pants."

"Me too! Do you have a change of clothes I could borrow?"

"Um, sure. Just grab some jams and a T-shirt from my drawer."

Samo takes his towel and walks up to the first floor communal bathroom. He mentally traces the contours of integer signs, imagining the arcs and sinews they'll spell out on paper the next day. Then he imagines a xenon jolt and laughs. He's been standing under the hot rays of the shower lasers for several minutes when he hears one of the other showers click on and its curtain snap shut. Across the bathroom, Saturnia starts singing. She finishes first and leaves. Samo finds her in his room, sitting on his bed, her hair wet, wearing a pair of his jogging pants and a T-shirt. *She does look kind of sexy like that*, he thinks. Maybe it was the fuzz leftover from the jolts on the Fairway, but Samo's just now noticing that there's another girl–not Candace–sitting on his bed after sharing some hits of xenon with him.

"It's cold out," he says. "Why don't you wear this, too." He gives her a Cosby sweater.

"Thanks," Saturnia says. "I'll put it on later."

"So, you're from um, Florida?"

"Yes."

"Oh, okay. Guess you get a lot of hurricanes down there."

"Hurricane season is starting to wrap up right about now. A lot of the turbulence subsides, but that doesn't mean you still won't get hit by a pretty big impact sometimes."

"So you're still out of luck, even in October."

"Actually, October's my good luck month. Well, maybe not this year."

"Good luck?" Samo asks.

"Yeah," she says. "Do you ever find that there are times of year when things click for you, more than others?"

Samo thinks. He likes the summer for camping trips, but all that winter snowshoeing and sledding is pretty cool too.

"What do you mean?" he asks.

"Romantically, I mean. October's always been good to me."

"Oh?"

"Isn't there a time of year that's like that for you, too?"

Well, zero is zero is zero. "Not really."

"Yeah. I usually have a boyfriend in October. Even when I don't, something happens—a fling, a dalliance...something that keeps me warm at night. A couple of times..." She goes silent.

Samo is sure that there's something appropriate to say to this, but he can't begin to figure out what it is. It occurs to him that maybe—*maybe*—Saturnia is coming on to him. But he isn't sure, and if he flirted back, and was wrong, that would be embarrassing. After Candace's abrupt shutdown, he isn't ready for another diss on the same night. So he doesn't say anything.

"But this time," Saturnia resumes, "it's a lot less likely. I'm not from Arkaic like you, and I don't know anybody here. I don't know anybody in this town, and practically nobody even from the school. Just a few friends here and there, from class...dinner...whatever. You have to make conversation. But I don't think I've met anyone who could keep me warm through the night, you know, before October is over. I've only got one more week."

"Well," blurts Samo, "if Halloween rolls around, and you still haven't gotten lucky, you know where my room is."

Saturnia opens her eyes wide and smiles.

"Delighted!" she says. "I'll keep that in mind! I'll keep that in mind!"

They talk for a while after that, but Saturnia wants to talk about her wild life at her high school in Miami, while Samo has his mind on basic physics. Their conversation fuses, briefly, over the subject of the sea winds, how the cold air flushes from the sea to the land causing vast updrafts of cooling heat, huge banks of clouds that shift across the banks and sear the land and sea with lightning. But Samo has gotten tired and Saturnia impatient.

"So I'll see you in a week," she says.

"Yes, yes," says Samo, almost asleep on his bed.

She turns out the light and closes the door behind her.

Differentiating Shades

It is just as difficult to enforce forgetfulness as it is to deliberately remember.

After class, Ezzie isn't surprised to find Monty standing at a drinking fountain in the hallway of Anderson Hall.

"I read it," she says to him.

"I knew you would," he says, burbling through the water.

"He's watching us."

Sure enough, Professor Plumb stands in the classroom door, thirty feet away, his mirrored shades taking in the diminishing shapes of his students and Ezzie and Monty at the fountain.

"Then we'll split up," bubbles Monty's voice. "Meet me at the Barnes Library in two hours, okay?"

And they separate, walking different ways down the hall.

· · · · ·

Back at the Cradle, Ezzie bursts into her room: "Dunya, you'll never guess –" but Dunya isn't there.

"At rehearsal?" Ezzie wonders out loud. *I have rehearsal too,* she thinks, *tonight is going to be crazy busy.* She sits down at Dunya's desk to schedule her evening. A small, gentle, lacy object sits on the edge of the desk. It's a birthday card. For Dunya. From her father. It gives Ezzie an idea. Without stopping to think further, she runs up to the house lounge and talks to all of the students there, first years and upperclassmen, explaining her plan. She's doing it for herself as much as for Dunya, and the plan gives Ezzie animation and speed. Just as when she's writing a script, these forces overcome her nervousness.

"It will," she stammers, "make a big difference in everyone's day!" Then she runs up and down the stairs, along the brick corridors, banging on doors, and talking fast through the dazed stares. By and large, everyone is on board. Her last convert will be Monty, because he's the only one she hasn't told, other than Dunya herself. *Oh, but I've got to get to the library now! To talk with Monty about the other thing.*

. . . . .

The Barnes Library is the stark opposite of the Olan, but it contains the bulk of the books in the AU system. Sharp, stony concrete grooves shoot out of the grounds to a height of five stories, and deep in these cracks are lodged vertical slits of windows that open onto the bleak and unending stacks. A couple people have described the Barnes as a brutalist junior cousin to the Sagrada Família. Those people are crazy.

"How did you find out about that faculty disappearance?" Ezzie is asking, before she sees the tall and narrow boy, almost albino blonde, with a long ponytail hanging down his back.

"Ezzie," says Monty, "meet Jesse. Jesse is the Pony Pontiff of the Psychedelic Association."

"Nice to meet you," says Ezzie, shaking his hand.

"Pleasure mine," Jesse intones in a voice so deep that Barry White could have fallen into it. "Follow me."

They follow him into Special Collections, where illuminated medieval manuscripts and ancient papyrus scrolls dimly project their secrets through the foggy display glass. Or maybe it's the visitors doing the projecting. As they walk, Jesse talks.

"At our last meeting, Monty mentioned that he had met a student who could break glass by looking at it." Ezzie glares at Monty, but he doesn't notice. Jesse continues. "It reminded me of something that happened when I was a lowly first-year. One night, right after the end of the school year. A lot of students didn't hear about it because they were home for the summer, and the university managed to hush it up, surprisingly. But I was in an apartment just off campus with the Psychedelics. All of a sudden I heard a sonic boom, and all of the windows in my apartment blew in. Do you hear me? They didn't blow *out*, like something from the inside, or shatter like they had been rapped on too hard. The were broken in, all over the room. This happened all over campus, not a window left. It cost them millions of dollars to repair and probably a whole month to clean up. Everywhere, windows just broke. Even a mile from here, people were talking about cracks and splinters. *The Arkadian Archive* was covering it a bit, but then these Homeland Security trucks showed up and met with the editors, and there was no more reporting after that."

"What psychedelics were you exploring?" asks Ezzie.

"The very best of the very best!" says Jesse with a grin. "Brian Eno, David Bowie, and David Frum."

"When Jesse told me about all this," says Monty, "I knew there were secrets involved. So I dug up the old copies of the *Archive.* You see the newspaper itself had been purged...if you go and look at the records at the newspaper offices, they don't have anything about AU on those days. You have a lot more full-page ads, though."

"Same thing on the microfilms *here,*" says Jesse.

They're walking fast. The displays blur by. Ezzie struggles to keep up.

"Then I remembered the insulation," says Monty.

"The what?" asks Ezzie.

"I study at the Olan Library every night, and they have this display about the history of the building and how it's maintained. Olan is definitely the oldest building on campus. It costs a fortune to heat, and because of its Gothic construction, they can't really insulate it like a normal building. So they've gotten in the habit of crumpling up newspapers and wedging them into the cracks between the ceiling and the roof. They do a quarter of the roof every summer, so you would expect find four summers of newspaper history crammed up in there at any given time. I knew it wouldn't be easy to track it down, but I'm a member of the AU Juggling Society, and a lot of them are pretty good at heights and acrobatics. So we broke in last night and –"

"You broke into the library at night?"

"We got above the ceiling by a lighting grate, and after ripping a ton of insulation out, we found the article I showed you today."

"Wow, Monty. That's..." Ezzie took a deep breath. "So who knows about my glass thing? Because I don't want it getting around that –"

"Just Jesse here. And the AU Juggling Society."

"And you and Samo and Dunya. And Professor Plumb. And all the first-years in Acedia House, because I blurted it out during Orientation. Oh, this is a lot to take in!" Ezzie looks around. "Why are we here?" she asks.

They've come to the end of the hall, and Special Collections have fallen away for more mundane photos of departmental faculty, trustees, and donors.

Jesse leads them to a blown-up photograph of some of the most frizzy-haired, dreadlocked, dazed, and disheveled professors Ezzie has ever seen. They're standing in the Elysium Chapel in dim light.

"The Arkaic University tenured Humanities Department. Most of these profs are new," Jesse says. "Most of them came on after 2009. But a few of them were here when Lorraine Glass vanished in the chain tunnels. Like this guy. And this girl. And this girl. And this guy. And him, your own prof, Professor Plumb." Jesse pulls his finger from one grinning teacher to the next, five in total. They're all wearing sunglasses.

Live in Your Silence

Listen.

Two hours later, Dunya has finally caught a break. She stomps down the stairs to the basement and into the suite. Ezzie sits in the inner room, its door open, stark in the glare of a halogen lamp, taking notes on a notepad. Dunya closes the hall door and feels herself in the dark.

"So how are you?" asks Ezzie.

Is it time to tell someone? Dunya wonders. "Shitty," she says.

"You tired?"

"Hell yeah, I'm tired. Three classes today—that Classic Vampire class is killing me. And then I started as cashier in Proofs."

"What?"

"The basement snack shop. I spent most of the time chasing cockroaches."

"Yum."

"Then studying at the bookstore, and I just got a little to eat now. In a couple minutes I have to go to rehearsal."

"Me too!"

Should I tell her? wonders Dunya. *I should tell her. Ezzie has been good to me.* "Yeah, things are pretty bad for me right now –"

"Well, I've got a story for you. It involves sunglasses and time and secret cults and professors."

"Fascinating?"

"But first, something to cheer you up!" says Ezzie. She holds up the lacy birthday card.

Dunya is confused. "That's mine."

"I know!" says Ezzie. "It's a from your father."

"I forgot to put it away. My birthday was last week."

"That's what it says!"

"You read it?!" Dunya's voice goes up and her brows come together.

Ezzie doesn't notice. She's too excited to listen. "I did. And here you were trying to hide it from me!"

"Yeah, I was."

"Well I told Samo and Monty and all of the other first-years and all of the upperclassmen in the house, and everyone's excited. You've got a lot of friends here, Dunya, even in a short time. Everyone likes you. Everyone wants to throw you a party."

"What?!"

"I know! In no time at all! Friday! Saturday! Thursday! Not everyone can do it on the same day, but everyone is planning something cool for you." Ezzie swells into the expanse of friendship. This is how you're supposed to wear friendship, casual and close, like all of her calico coats and her silk scarves. This is the kind of friendship she has always wanted to wear like a fuzzy warm sweater.

"You fucking did this?!" says Dunya.

Ezzie stops.

A few moments pass.

"Come again?" Ezzie says.

"I can't believe you fucking did this!" snaps Dunya. "How am I going to go to parties? When am I going to have the time?! I, I, I, have to, do all this reading–this homework!–and memorize these lines and this fucking blocking and–on top of that–get how many thousands of dollars in three weeks on my own or I'm going to get sent home without a penny in my pocket!"

"What?" whispers Ezzie.

"You heard me!"

"I, I, I –"

"I didn't ask you for anything, Ezzie. My birthday was mine, and I chose to celebrate it on my own, in the dark, and that's the way I wanted it. Get a fucking clue!"

The door opens. There's Dunya's silhouette, for just a minute, poised and tight with rage. The door comes crashing shut. Dunya's feet tap angrily up the hard steps upstairs. Ezzie takes two sharp and shivering breaths.

Exodus

The desert welcomes students.

Rehearsal does not improve Dunya's mood.

She hasn't memorized her lines cold yet, and she stutters and pauses, and calling out "line!" grows more and more frequent until Elizabeth Kraus sets down her Moleskine and takes off her glasses. "We're almost a month into rehearsals, Dunya. We have to get these lines down."

By "we" she means "me," thinks Dunya. Then she remembers Ezzie's social charity and spits out the lines with such fire and contempt that the assistant director feels a heat on her face and moves back into the second row. But the rageflame sputters when Dunya hits a white wall in her memory and stumbles. "Line," she says. And again and again. By the time rehearsal is over, everyone is frustrated.

"Goodnight," says Elizabeth. "And work on those lines everybody."

She means me, thinks Dunya.

Faced with the prospect of walking back to the Cradle and having to either ignore or make up with Ezzie, Dunya shakes her head. She puts on her coat and heads out into the feral October. Tonight, the wind tumbles through the leaves, making the branches gape wide, like fanged jaws. She stares them down all the way to South Street, gets on the bus, and rides it downtown. Then, still not knowing Arkaic very well but wanting to get as far as she can from campus, she gets onto another bus that takes her deep into the North Side. She gets off the bus at Ash Highway. Vacant lots and ragged signs shivering in the chill range away to the west. To the east, things look a bit more promising, and she sets off along the highway. Even here, most of the buildings are vacant, with huge, stone-scattered parking lots. But then again...Dunya sees the traces of secret life among the desolations. Hidden treasures have ridden out the blizzard. She passes a used bookstore, a hole-in-the-wall bakery, a laundromat, a trophy factory, a used car dealership, and a Tiki-themed bar. They all hum with life, even though it's well past business hours. It warms her heart to know that some of Arkaic is alive, even on the edge of oblivion. It reminds her of home, of Richmond. Okay, so the differences are huge: culture, climate, health, and appearance. *Michigan is _no_ California.* But two down-and-out towns can share a common conversation across a few thousand miles, and Dunya hears it. She hears Richmond in the air. She recognizes its gravelly, staccato-rusted language.

She sees a Coney Island—the Atlantis Coney Island—and walks inside.

The Story of the Moon and the Stars

Let's talk.

Let's talk details. The man in the moon is a grimacing leper when you look at him the right way. *Isn't this state supposed to be smoke free?* Then why does the smoke hang in the air and remind Dunya of her dad's poker games back home? Well, what does she expect, a reprieve from the Michigan-ness of this place, this city?

Let's talk plot.

She enters the Atlantis at 10:11 p.m. and leaves at midnight sharp. She drinks four cups of coffee.

Let's talk perspective.

"What is going to happen to me?" Dunya asks.

She sits beneath her own set of rotating blades, air slicers, dull, luminous, glow balls.

"Why do I even try?"

Her very own ceiling fan.

"What is it, even? What about those stars? Could I see them? Are they out there?"

She splits a couple blinds open with her index and middle fingers, sees the stars, sees the moon, and wonders, and so what force that probes the field of a woman's heart, teasing sweat, faint heat, dimming eyes, swaying in the seat, in the booth, as if a fever, an ache, an itch to be scratched behind her navel or between *her lips...this man...the man in the moon...he's beautiful, what, with his soothing silent wail and all.*

"I worry about you," he says. "I worry about the world and I worry about you."

"Why do you worry about me?"

"I worry about you until I cry."

"Why?"

"You've touched the ocean, but have you touched the Great Lakes? They are broad and strange to human eyes, but their waters are stiller than you expect. They freeze in the winter. They're cool all summer long, and they get warm in the early autumn sunsets. They respond as the oceans do not. Clear water. Sand and stones. But I've never gotten to feel such things. Lake water never lay across my surface. Just pimples and sores. Have you touched them?"

"Touching is dangerous."

"But have you?"

"What if it's contagious?"

"Answer the question."

"Don't talk all condescending to me. Don't you dare."

"I spend all day, every day, just wishing for a drop, and I don't even see it."

So she asks the question. "What about the moon?" It's hard for her to answer, since she hasn't answered the question about the stars yet.

"Another cup of coffee, please?"

...

"Thank you."

...

"You're mad," she says. "Are you mad at me? What's wrong?"

"Sand in my eyes."

"Ha. So you do know about beaches."

"Not beaches. Sand. But not water."

"What about tears?"

"I don't know about them, either."

"You could tell me about sand and stars, though."

"Not stars. Not likely."

"Then what is the rough stuff at the bottom of the lake?"

"I'm not sure. I really don't know, but you are in a Coney Island, not a lost city. Not a treasure at the bottom of some big lake."

"I need you."

"Who said that?"

Let's talk conjugation.

"What do you think of those stars?" asks the cashier.

"What are they?"

"What are or will be stars?"

"What had been stars?"

"What is the being of stars?"

"Be a star!"

"How can I? I can't even describe it."

"How can't you be is the question?"

"Who said that?"

"Who are you? Who am I?"

"I'm the man in the moon."

"I'm a girl—a woman—who looks at the moon."

"Or vice versa?"

"Maybe."

"Well, we're both pretty young and fast, at least as far as this universe goes. But I'm older. I've swung down this orbit millions of times, and I've slowed that old blue stone through the years."

"Ha! And I've been alive for nineteen years."

"We are complete opposites."

"No, we aren't."

"How would you know? You're so young. So ignorant. All fat from water. You haven't even lived long enough to walk upright."

"And you're a cratered old desert of death."

"At least I'm not a horny little hallucination!"

"I'm not horny!"

"Yeah you are. You are and everybody else. All you ever think about is fucking."

"You were the one who mated with the earth, who penetrated her orbit and shattered her sanctity."

"We're all in heat all the time."

"Oh, I see. Me and everybody else includes you. So is that all there is to stars?"

"Everything."

"Nothing else to talk about?"

"Nothing but hormones and orbits."

"Where, most likely?"

"Who said that?"

Let's talk history.

The Atlantis Coney Island was built in 1959 and has changed names from Lucille's to SimSim's to Lulu's to Maxie's to Catflash to Roman's to Sam's to Sara's to Ashland to The Atlantis, and she's still buried in sand at the bottom of a Great Lake.

"I'm sorry...did you hear me? I'm sorry. It was my fault. You've left. The earth turns too fast. I'm getting dizzy. It's spinning too fast. Why are they even running the fans in October? I feel sick. I think I'm going to throw up. Won't you come back? I know it's hard to do, you know, with the earth turning, but...you are my moon man and I love you. See, I can say it now, and it's me saying it because I'm alone here, and there's no one else to say 'I love you' but me. Weird. When I don't talk, I hear things. The cars on the road. The other people eating here. That ceiling fan. Not much nothing. I mean. I miss you. I love you. I need you. I love you, I love you! Come back. It's...lonely."

Let's talk intermission.

Let's stop talking for a moment.

Ignore the mutter of the crusty auto workers. The sizzling, spitting steak. Stop straining your ears toward those groaning trains, those whistling winds and chipping sidewalks. Bow your head. Close your eyes. Pray or sleep. Dream awhile.

Let's talk setting.

Whishwhishwhishwhishwhishwhishwhishwhishwhishwhishw hishwhishwhishwhishwhishwhishwhishwhishwhishwhishwhish whishwhish.

"Hello, ceiling fan."

Whishwhishwhishwhishwhishwhishwhishwhish.

"You know it's already cold in here."

Whishwhishwhishwhishwhish.

"It's okay. Don't worry."

Whishwhishwhish.

"Do you know where the moon is?"

Whishwhishwhishwhishwhishwhishwhishwhish.

"I know, it's because the earth has turned. I turn too. Turn my back on you and look for the moon. I love him. I love him. I love him. I love him."

Let's talk.

What about those stars?

"I don't know," Dunya says, "but thanks for talking with me for a while."

The cashier smiles. "No problem."

"I didn't catch your name."

"Chris," he says.

"And you are –"

"Just a guy."

"And this is –"

"Just a place to be. To hide out sometimes."

Dunya nods, dazed, sleepy, but roses burst in her chest. It aches too much. Running water. Howling faces. Far away from home. Which home? Whatever home. Her head crowds with caffeine.

"Thanks," she says.

She heads toward the door.

"One last question," he says.

"What is it?"

"Where are you from?"

Now she could answer "Arkaic University," or she could answer "Richmond, California," but these don't feel like honest answers.

"Oh," she says, "nowhere really. Just under that ceiling fan. That's all."

CHAPTER SIX
SECOND CHANCES

Dunya's Crazy-Ass Party Week/End

Many of your best friends won't look or act much like you.

Those first midterms are inexorable, fated, fatal, a force of nature. They approach with glacial certainty, and they will not be slowed or stopped. Of course, the approach of Dunya's Crazy-Ass Party Week/End is almost as inexorable.

She avoids Ezzie as much as she can—it's easy to do, actually. Ezzie has the inner room, so Dunya just has to out-wake her roommate, then sneak in at night, sleep, and creep out in the morning. If this belies Dunya's *up-an-atem* attack on most of life's problems, well, she's got plenty of those. Another showdown with Ezzie is the last thing she needs. Besides, Dunya is usually either in the dorm lounge memorizing lines, in the library studying, attending meetings of the Saint Simons and the D.I.Y.MFers, or working in Proofs in between her other classes and rehearsals. It would be *harder* to find Ezzie than to avoid her. It works. Dunya doesn't see Ezzie that week. Not once.

Thursday rolls around, and Dunya's Crazy-Ass Party Week/End officially kicks off in the gentlest way possible. Three of the other girls from the house—Jenny Jenkins, Elaine Trotter, and Zena Milkinovich—have packed a basket dinner of sushi, wasabi, and petite oranges. They confront Dunya in the courtyard and invite her out for a picnic.

"Oh..." Dunya says, feigning ignorance. "What is this all about?"

"It's for your –" starts Elaine, but Jenny interrupts her.

"It's about the homecoming game this Sunday. We have to bless the football field with a companionable meal so that it will yield a victory."

They walk a mile, the full length of the campus, to Pierrot Field. They walk to the center of the track and sit down where the horizons are broken by trees instead of gutted houses and abandoned storefronts. It has gotten chilly out; in the morning, everything will be covered in a gray lace of dew, but tonight, the grass is still thick and green. Winter waits in the wings; it hasn't been given permission to enter just yet.

"Okay, surprise, Dunya!" says Elaine. "This is for your birthday."

"Thank you," Dunya says.

"Thank Ezzie," says Zena, with a secret smile.

"I didn't —" Dunya starts, and then realizes that she still doesn't know them well. These three girls are from her class. They're all her age. They went through Orientation with her. But somehow, in the month that had followed, the actual work had become overwhelming. It had crowded out most of the humans surrounding her each day. And that's a shame, because these are some remarkable humans.

Jenny is the consummate practical joker. It's hard to say whether she's a good student, whether she's wealthy, or where she's from, because her already-legendary reputation for pranks in Acedia House has eclipsed such details. Maybe she likes it that way. Maybe she has hidden such details as liabilities to enigma. Perhaps they even factor into some overarching plan to hold the whole University hostage to her hidden gnostic knowledge. When Monica, the RA, got congratulatory emails saying "I knew it! I *knew* it!" because she had finally come out after eighteen years in the closet, via her high school email listhost, everyone suspected Jenny. "But I'm not gay," Monica said, and while she wasn't, Jenny was, and that was the only reason the prank was funny. "Not that anyone was ever able to prove I did it," said Jenny.

Elaine Trotter could have tried to act hard, like Samo did, if she had wanted to. She hails from Morgan Park, Chicago, an area just dicey enough that she could go running with it. She doesn't. "I don't like the Lions or the Tigers," she says, "but I like you guys." She talks about how on June afternoons, with all kinds of seeds spiraling down through the sticky summer haze, her whole family migrates to their fenced-in backyard, overshadowed by Chicago's ubiquitous brick tenements, and they play their accordions and concertinas and harmonicas and sheng until the sun goes down and "the whole hood stops by to get they drink on!" "What do you all drink?" "We drink lemonade!"

Zena doesn't speak much. She's supposedly shy. Dunya doesn't buy this. Zena's from Dushanbe by way of Queens, but she has found matriculation to the Rust Belt to be more more of a jolt than emigration to the U.S.A. "When my sister and I got here, we explored by walking down West Street to the edge of the city and then back along Jefferson Street," Zena explains. "Those are some of the most dangerous neighborhoods in this country!" says Jenny. "We didn't know. Anyway, it was light out, and people were polite."

This isn't bad, Dunya thinks as she bites down on kappamaki and takes a sip of the sweet wine. *This isn't a wild party. These are beautiful girls, beautiful people, she thinks. Whatever tomorrow brings, I'm glad that this happened.*

Schedules Come Second

Never turn down an enigma, or free food.

"Uncle Clay?" Ezzie's voice trembles. Maybe it's because she's tired...she's been hiding out from Dunya, sleeping on a couch at the Olan Commons. Maybe it's because Ezzie's been eating too much chocolate, drinking too much caffeine, and having too many nachos. It's the best that the Commons has to offer. Or maybe it's this conversation she's having? Of course, Ezzie feels more comfortable around her uncle than anyone else on the planet, but...this is not a talk she's been looking forward to.

"Hi honey," comes the voice, New York distant. "How's school?"

"I'm glad I got you," she says. "I've left messages."

"I'm sorry. I've been...pretty busy lately. Lot of meetings."

"Yeah, yeah, I know about your girlfriends." She leans back against the window, relaxing, now that at least part of the conversation is falling into the furrows of a comfortable routine.

"Only two at a time," he says, "only two at a time. But honestly, this time it really has been a lot of meetings. It turns out that opossums are resistant to learning tap dancing. Dimmy has already sunk 30K into this project, and he's going to be devastated if nothing comes of it."

Uncle Clay is a talent agent.

"How are you?" he asks.

"Really, pretty not-very-good," Ezzie says.

"I'm sorry, hon. What's wrong?"

"Oh. So much. I made a mistake and ticked my roommate off, and I think one of my professors is weirded out because I...well, never mind that. Look, I have to ask you something."

"Shoot."

"Dad called me a couple weeks back."

"Uh-huh?"

"And I haven't been able to get that talk out of my head. He was...he was really drunk, Uncle Clay."

"What did he say?"

Ezzie isn't sure why, but the sudden razor edge in Uncle Clay's voice unnerves her far more than anything her father has said.

"Why? What do you think he would say?"

A sigh.

He suspects something, but he's going to make me spell it out anyway.

"Okay," she says. "He says he had to tell me that he hasn't seen Mother in years." More silence from the other end of the line. "Which doesn't surprise, me, really...I mean, okay, so it's only been two years, but their divorce wasn't a happy one. Whose is? So I don't know why he'd call me up drunk and tell me...I mean. I wouldn't expect them to –"

Clay's voice comes calm and quiet through the phone: "You lonely out there, Ezzie, in that cold, empty state?"

"Oh," she says, "you have no idea how lonely I am."

"I do," he says. "Believe it. I do. So what does this weekend look like for you? Schedule-wise?"

"It looks insane. I'm not going to have a spare minute to do anyth–"

"Is it okay if I drop in for a visit? Saturday?"

"What? That's the day after tomorrow!"

"I want to come and visit you. Take you out for brunch maybe, give you a break from all that dorm food."

Ezzie thinks. *It's going to be hard, with midterms next week and rehearsal and...I have to know what's going on here.*

"Sure," she says. "Sure. I'm...really glad to see you, Uncle Clay!"

Dunya's Crazy-Ass Party Week/End, Part 2

In inclement weather, confetti should be stored in a watertight container.

Dunya leaves Thursday in an exhausted daze and enters Friday even more exhausted. She drifts, zombie-like, through the drizzle, from class to work to rehearsal, and gets back to the Cradle just as dinner is wrapping up for the night. Samo sits on the back of the mechanical lion who guards the cafeteria. He's chatting with Giovanni Martini, who's picking his teeth with a toothpick.

"Hi. Dunya," says Gio.

"I just missed dinner," she says. It's a statement and a plea at the same time.

"Yeah."

"Fuck it all!" she yells, throwing her exhausted purse down on the pavement.

"That's gonna get wet," Samo says.

Dunya picks her purse up and stomps into Acedia House. Gio strokes his goatee. They're just starting to follow her when she storms back out, yelling, "That's it. I'm too damn stressed. I'm going for a walk."

They're startled.

"A walk?" says Samo. "A walk where?"

"I don't know," she says. "I don't care. Maybe out down West Street. Zena says people are polite out there."

"Um," says Samo. "I'm not sure you want to do that. I've been out that way before. People aren't that polite."

"Well, I'm going somewhere!"

Gio looks helplessly at Samo.

"Hey!" says Samo. "I've got an idea. Let's go for a walk with you!"

Dunya shakes her head. "I don't want any company right now."

"But I need some company," says Samo. "I'm not doing so great in my classes."

Gio takes the toothpick from his mouth. "Me too."

"Okay, okay, fine, fine, but limit your complaining. This is my pity party."

They leave the dorm sans umbrellas and spend the next half hour meandering around campus, while Dunya rages about her classes, the play, her lack of sleep. Just as she's spent and about to suggest they head back before it's completely dark out, Gio crosses his arms and says, "I want to keep walking. I haven't gotten a chance to complain about my classes yet."

"Fine," she says.

Following the margins of Winters Road east, they reach the Valley Road on the far side of I-63. Valley Road is aptly named, running along the edge of the Seller's Creek basin and, given that and the stone-thick railroad tracks and expressway, they don't even seem to be in the city anymore. But then they arrive at Peppington Road. The proud, plump smokestacks of Starr City, Arkaic's largest remaining factory, drift into view, fogging new clouds into dingy life.

"Guys," she says, "thanks for taking this walk with me, and thanks for listening." She sighs. "But I'm really tired. I am. And I don't know, I'm probably going to have to pull an all-nighter tonight. I've got to get back."

"But I haven't gotten to complain yet," says Samo.

"Why can't you complain on the walk back? It'll take us more than a half hour to get back."

She starts walking.

"Wait!" says Samo. "I want to show you my cousin's house!"

"Your cousin?" asks Gio.

"Yeah, she lives just past the factory there. Maybe they'll give us a ride back."

Samo's last point finally persuades Dunya, and they leave Peppington and wander back into the twisting side streets of the new neighborhood. It's a suburban-style neighborhood, out on the edge of town. Dunya has to admit that it is lovely. The cracked streets are paved black and look fresh and new in their wetness. Thousands of incandescent yellow and orange maple leaves arc over each street, and even at this late date, the summer scent of clipped grass spirals through the October air. It's enchanting, in fact, but the gray skies are starting to get dark.

"How much farther, Samo?" Dunya asks.

"I don't know," Samo says. "I got us lost."

They don't talk much after that, although Gio strums an air mandolin as he walks. Even in her fatigue, Dunya decides to ask him to play the real thing for her sometime. Finally, they emerge onto a new road, a broad road, and have officially left Arkaic behind. The road is lined with party stores and credit unions for the auto workers.

"Now can we go home?" asks Dunya.

"Sure!" says Samo. "I know where we are now. Follow me."

Twilight deepens into the darkness of night. One long block fades into the next, the buildings fewer and fewer, the spaces larger and larger.

"Where are we going, anyway?" asks Dunya.

"There," says Samo, pointing to a bubble of lights up ahead, sleek lines, steel sculpture, and a massive tall building of metal and glass.

"What's that?"

"Airport."

"The airport?! The airport is almost a mile from the edge of Arkaic. We're *never* going to get back!" She punches Samo in the arm.

"Ow!" says Samo. "I'm sorry. Look, I am! I just got twisted up. Maybe we can call a ride once we get inside."

"No way, Samo, no, I'm too tired, and I'm sick of this, and I think you're pulling some sort of stupid prank on me, and I don't like it, and anyway, there's a cab, and I'm getting in it and asking him to take me home. You two can come if you like."

She makes her way toward the cab. Samo stares after her for a minute and then breaks off for the airport at a run. Gio, on the other hand, flings himself in front of the cab, shouting "Thou shalt not enter!" The cabbie honks his horn, and Gio, startled, stumbles forward. Dunya jerks like she's going to make a grab at the door, but Gio holds his hands out, Christ-like, blocking the door and the face of the infuriated cabbie.

"Very nice," Dunya says. "You know what, fine. I don't care." She sits down on the wet sidewalk. The cabbie gives them the finger and peals away. Gio falls into a puddle with a loud cry. Dunya ignores him. From the other direction, from the airport, a group of feet approach at a run. Dunya is too tired and disgusted to look up and see who they are. Besides, her skirt is soaked through, and she's wet and cold and miserable and pissed off. Still, when the feet stop running, a few feet away from her, and when they stand there in silence, her curiosity gets the better of her. It's Samo (of course), Cassidy Antrim, Jenny Jenkins, Joe Newcomb, and a girl named April Silesia. There's also a man with a familiar crooked smile. Dunya stumbles to her feet.

There are sparks and whistles as Gio lights a Roman Candle and holds it aloft with one hand while handing out fizzling sparklers to each of the onlookers. Bright flames foam into the air and sear an afterimage into the low, moldering clouds. Then, when the last firework has gone out, Gio grabs a couple fistfuls of wet confetti from his pockets and flings them into the air. They mostly stick to his hands, but Dunya's eyes are on the crooked standing man.

"Dad?" she asks.

"Happy Birthday, Dunya," he answers.

Going Green

The karma of privacy affects the dharma of piracy.

Monty Valverde puts on his greenest pants. He puts on a green shirt. He puts on green socks and green sneakers. He has cut the fingers off of his green gloves and puts them on, too. He puts on a green ski mask and green sunglasses. He puts on a green backpack and straps on a headband with a portable webcam in back.

Monty has forestalled this moment for too long. He is ready to honor his commitment to the Book Ninjas.

He opens a box of the "Precious Polymer" that Argosy and Samo filched for him from Osbøe Labs. Monty lifts the box over his head and flips it upside down, covering himself from head to toe in the feather-light invisible bubbles. He turns on Samo's desktop computer and waits for it to boot up. The Wi-Fi signal is strong, and Monty's body begins to glow along with the desktop wallpaper: Frankenstein octopodes with blood dripping from their beaks. Monty turns on the camera. It records the wall behind him. Monty looks down at his body and watches as the black wall plays across his chest and arms and legs. "Let's give it a test," he says.

Monty turns out all the lights and opens the door. He steps back a half-dozen feet and stands perfectly still, facing the door.

After a seeming eternity, he hears steps in the stone vestibule. Then an animated, female voice speaks to a rough, gravelly man's voice. Dunya descends the stairs, followed by a man with shaggy hair and stubble.

"If I can get a refinance in the next month or so —" he's saying.

"Shh!" says Dunya.

She looks in through the open door, straight at Monty. The sunglasses dim his vision. Their forms are hazy and ghostly.

"What is it?" asks the man.

"Samo?" calls Dunya. "Monty?"

Monty smiles, in spite of himself. Several moments pass. She's looking straight at him from less than ten feet away. In the silence, Monty hears the clockwork tick of the chains in the metal door and the throb of distant engines. Dunya sighs.

"My friend Samo," she says. "Not very responsible. He's gonna get all his stuff stolen." She closes the door. Monty is in complete darkness. He grins and moves forward to listen at the door. Dunya's door opens and shuts. Monty quickly, quietly slides his own door open and scans the hall and stairway. Nobody. He flits up to the first floor. Rinse and repeat to the second floor. Rinse and repeat to the third floor. Rinse and repeat to the fourth floor. Rinse and repeat to the fifth floor. There are only two suites on the fifth floor: the House Masters' apartment and room 227—a.k.a. the Fifth Floor Double. Monty knows he can easily reach the roof next door by a low balcony from the Double, but he reconsiders when he hears noisy voices from inside. Krista Baroque and Velma Brass have two of the loudest voices in Acedia House. Velma laughs "Now motionless for nine hours, forty-seven minutes!" Their voices are moving toward the door. Monty slides along the purple-painted hallway until he's facing the Mavens' apartment. He listens, and not hearing anything from the other side, reaches out and turns the knob. *Locked.*

At that moment, Velma's voice rises a few decibels, and the door suddenly swings open. Monty flattens himself against the wall. Velma steps into view, followed closely by Krista. They look right at Monty but don't skip a beat, moving to the stairs and starting the long walk down. Monty tiptoes down the hall and up to the door to the Double.

"Oh, crap, I forgot to lock up," says Krista. She's returning up the stairs, but Monty has already shut himself inside and into the darkness. The key enters the door. Chlock. It locks behind him. He exhales slowly. His eyes acclimate to the darkness, or rather, the *almost* darkness. *Strange*, he thinks. They haven't left any lights on, but a soft, subtle glow, indistinct, seems to filter through the upper regions of the room, while his feet are buried in the dark. Testing it out, Monty angles his camera downward, toward the floor. His whole body turns soot black. He angles the camera upward. His body turns a dim and ruddy orange. *There is a light in here.*

But time is short. Monty checks his watch. *I've got fifteen minutes to get to the truck.* He hurries to the window and opens it. He climbs out onto a small balcony that looks out over the A. Kaufman Law Library. The library roof is about a fifteen foot drop. Monty cambers over the edge and stretches out as long as he can, so that he's holding on by the tiniest tips of his fingernails. *I'm five foot four,* he thinks. *My arms add another foot and a half. What does an eight-foot drop feel like?* He lets go and comes crashing down in the gravel. He rolls to absorb the damage but slices his glove and palm on a metal ventilation grate. The cut isn't deep, but it's long, and blood spills out and stains his glove. Monty trains his camera on the stone wall of the Cradle. Now he looks like a plane of Indiana limestone with a single, disconcerting splotch of blood floating in midair.

Got to keep moving. Monty runs along the roof until he arrives at a narrow fire escape descending into a rubble-strewn loading dock. The loading dock is gated off from the rest of the library and the outside world, and for good reason: this is where the Constellation of the Lowly Office of the Inquiscription resides. Monty discovered this academic black-op one night whilst eavesdropping on shelvers at the Olan Library. Humble custodians on paper, the Inquiscriptors actually work on behalf of the big textbook publishing houses, destroying excess copies of texts before they can be returned to distributors or turn up on the black-market. Monty nimbly descends the fire escape and clambers into the back of a black-painted rental truck. As he expects, the truck is stocked with the assigned readings for dozens of law classes. He finds a seat and hides his bloody hand. He looks like a pile of books, serious tomes, thick and packed with fine print and the minutiae of Michigan legal theory. Monty closes his eyes.

•••••

Monty opens his eyes. Muffled voices echo from the outside of the truck. They move from the back to the front. Doors open. Slam shut. The truck starts. They're moving now. Moving out from the loading dock of the law library, then rumbling along the pitted roads. Monty waits.

After about ten minutes, the truck stops. The doors open and shut again, and then two figures open up the back doors. The Inquiscriptors cut strange figures against the bleak October night. They wear black-and-white hoods and dusters and massive rosette necklaces etched to resemble stacks of books enveloped in flames. The Inquiscriptors' arms and waists are as thick as tree trunks and as hard as tombstones, and they each carry a four-foot-long flanged iron mace. Their eyes are dim and dead-looking. Monty freezes in terror. Those dead fish eyes seem to pierce right through him. Then, the Inquiscriptors turn away. Monty slowly exhales. Rinse and repeat: he waits.

For the next several minutes, low and cracking voices utter unknown threats to whatever cowering cashier drew the short stick this night, and the Inquiscriptors return again. They load huge boxes into the truck, close the gate, and are on to their next destination. As soon as the engine starts, Monty slips off his back pack and pulls out a Maglite. Then, working with an efficiency he has mentally practiced for several weeks now, he finds and frees the dozen or so books requested on Dunya's syllabi. His practice has paid off; he gets the boxes resealed and his backpack zipped up with time to spare. Now comes the delicate part. *I have to figure out where to stand so I can escape while they're not looking. I wonder what their next stop is? No margin for error now.* Monty's body turns black. *What?* Now he's covered with the familiar wallpaper of the glowing Frankenstein octopodes and numerous small, glowing icons. *My Computer. Control Panel. Recycle Bin. Oh, fuck no. Samo!* A small arrow drags itself across the dark background, floats over the Mozilla icon and opens the browser. The truck's engine stops. Monty straps on his

backpack and furtively hides behind a box of books. The arrow
selects "Start Private Viewing." The doors to the truck slam open
and shut. Unmistakable flesh-colored figures start to buck and gyrate
across Monty's body. The Inquiscriptors open the doors.

A Good Day

When reinventing yourself, it is easy to overestimate the realignment of your priorities.

Also: Mountain Dew is trouble.

Samo has survived another crazy day. He missed Crew practice for the second time (sleeping in), but he did make the Pneumatics meeting, and the coterie was so delighted by Samo's description of his potato cannons that they asked him to make a demonstration after his midterms cleared up. At lunch, the cafeteria served up a delicious course of casu marzu with flatbread. Even one of Samo's classes has started to look up. He'd been struggling for weeks with the stark Cyrillic and fluid Arabic characters, but one day, Professor Daughtry brought in a cauldron of kumis and read from the Epic of Manas. In that single moment, Samo fell into a deep and permanent love of the Kyrgyz language, and he doubled down on that class. Later, it had been difficult to keep Dunya on board yet in the dark as they had walked her all the way to the airport, but the effort paid off when her eyes went wide with shock at the appearance of her dad. Samo plans to ask her about it during tomorrow's festivities.

Right now, he figures that he deserves a few minutes of relaxation, courtesy of AU's wireless network. *Where's my Mountain Dew?* Not in his pocket. Not on his desk. *Oh well, it doesn't matter.* But after just a couple minutes, Samo's eyes happen to glimpse movement through a slit in the curtains in Monty's room, and there she is on the walkway outside: Saturnia Dyson. Walking toward Acedia House with a brisk and purposeful step. Is it the thirty-first? Samo frantically toggles the clock on his computer: "Friday, October 27, 2011." *She's still got three days! What's she doing here now? What gives?!* And in a small corner of his brain, *Why are you complaining?* But there's no time to think. Only action. Samo hears the door to the house open overhead. He stands, and the can of Mountain Dew, which has been on his lap this whole time, falls over, and the oozy, yellow-green stuff floods across the floor. *She's here!* Samo takes a running leap toward Monty's room, lands hard on his belly, and crawls under the bed. He cowers there, gasping for breath as quietly as he can, and wonders: *Why am I hiding under a bed? Don't I want this to happen?*

The Zug Island Crawl

You should always have a Plan B.

The moment the gate goes up, the roided hulks see Monty cowering behind the boxes of books. He'd figured that they'd be shocked for at least a moment at the appearance of a little Dominican boy dressed in tight clothes with glowing, graphic robot porn dancing out upon his chest. But the Inquiscriptors are immune to shock. One of them stands astride the entrance to the truck, blocking any escape, while the other clambers inside and–grab and miss, grab and miss (Monty is lithe and quick and doesn't leave much for a handhold), grab and fix–catches Monty by the collar.

"I'm sorry!" he squeaks, as the second Inquiscriptor hops into the back of the truck and unsheathes his mace. The man swings from the right, and the prongs connect with Monty's ribcage. Crack, and *pain, pain, pain*! "I'm sorry!" repeats Monty, and while the Inquiscriptor holding him breaks into a bright grin, the fellow with the mace wears an expression of stony death. The second blow catches Monty hard on the left thigh. "I'm sorry, okay?!" Monty shrieks, and the Inquiscriptor holding him starts to laugh. The stone-faced man sheathes his mace, then knees Monty in the groin. The laughing man lets go, and Monty falls to the floor. Holding his crotch, he rolls onto his back, hissing. "You can't do this to me! Who do you think you are, anyway? I'm a student here!"

The two men look at each other, and while Stoneface opens a purse holding various unpleasantly serrated handcuffs, the other Inquiscriptor laughs even louder.

"If only you knew how many of you say that!" he says, chortling. " 'You can't do this do me! I'm a student!' Who do you think steals books from us? Who exactly do you think we do 'this' to?"

"Maybe..." wheezes Monty, "Maybe I can pay you for the books?" He seizes on a possibility. "Maybe I can pay you double! Maybe you can keep whatever is left over!"

Everything Monty says seems to drive the Inquiscriptor into greater hysterics. "Oh, but we're paid pretty well," he wheezes, wiping his eyes, "I doubt you can match our salaries. Anyway, we like our jobs. We're good at them!"

The stone-faced Inquiscriptor keeps checking and discarding handcuffs; none of them are small enough for Monty's wrists.

"You can't enjoy this!" shrieks Monty. "You can't like it! Where is your humanity?!"

This sobers the laughing Inquiscriptor for a moment. "I haven't seen my humanity in a while. Sometime before I got that gig as a lobbyist for Monsanto. My colleague hasn't seen his since before he was working as Pinochet's butler. So please tell us if you have seen our humanity anywhere; we've been looking for it. Then again, if you do know where it is, you'll probably tell us under torture."

"Torture?"

"You know, the Virgin of Nuremburg, the Pear of Anguish, the Spanish Tickler, the Street Sweeper's Daughter, the Zug Island Crawl, the Piquet. Stuff like that. You'll find out soon enough."

Monty starts to tremble, then bites his lip. He decides that, if nothing else, he will keep his dignity for as long as he can. Stoneface has finally found a suitable pair of handcuffs, and both of the Inquiscriptors approach their victim. They flip Monty onto his stomach and cuff his wrists. Then they roll him onto his back and hold out a cord to bind his feet.

Suddenly, Monty's costume explodes in a searing nova of light. The flash is so intense that the Inquiscriptors are blinded. The porn flashes out and bleeds into their skin, momentary tattoos of a body-painted unicorn doing terrible things to a chrome beaver. Monty's clothes fade out. They are once again the plain green colors he'd donned at the start of the night.

Monty staggers to his feet and charges toward the truck's gate. The Inquiscriptors roar in animal rage, but Monty launches himself into the air and comes down on his toes. Tripstumble! and he falls onto his face, tearing up grass and dirt with his head. He's bleeding now. He's sore all over. But he's free! Perhaps for only a moment, though; those voices are just behind him. Those rageful, howling voices! Too close. Monty wriggles to his feet again and runs, and runs, and runs into the darkness. The voices are too loud to fade into obscurity, but at least they seem to get softer behind him. When Monty sees an open window well at the back of the Osbøe Cyclotron, he doesn't stop to mull it over. He slides past the grate and crashes eight feet down to a bed of pebbles and wilted leaves.

For the next hour, Monty hears the bellowing of the Inquiscriptors as they prowl the South Campus, feeling for him with big, hairy hands waving through the icy air. Eventually, they give up, or maybe Monty just drifts in and out of consciousness and has been captured again. *No?* No. *Oh, thank God.* It's dark out. Pitch back. Dead silent. The handcuffs dig into Monty's wrists, and his hands have started to go numb. He doesn't care. He's not learning the meaning of the phrase "Zug Island Crawl," and that's good enough for now. Monty falls asleep.

The End of October

Fortune is fickle; the good days are as transient as the bad.

One short moment after Samo has vanished under Monty's bed, he hears a fast and earnest knocking at the outer bedroom door. He finally catches his breath and holds it. The knocking repeats. And repeats. And repeats. *Will she ever go away?* he wonders. Saturnia answers with another round of knocking. *Please go away.* Silence. Finally. And then there is sudden light, and sound, and then darkness.

When the Mountain Dew fell off Samo's lap and onto the floor, it spilled under his desk and into the modem, surrounded by dust bunnies and O-KE-DOKE crumbs. The circuit broken, the modem froze, flickered, and puffed out. But it had been designed to accommodate ordinary electricity, and this is temporelectricity. A sudden wave of thought/energy/angst/ennui runs the blockade from the other side and arcs back into Samo's computer, just shy of light speed. It is a massive surge, and wires catch fire. The monitor goes black and then, instantaneously, flashes bright white before exploding. Smoke floods the room. The fire alarm starts to shriek. Samo shrieks too.

The door opens. The alarm stops. Samo hears the soft and foamy roar of a fire extinguisher. Silence again. Then footsteps.

"Nice shoes," says Saturnia from somewhere behind and above him.

Shit, he thinks.

Samo backs himself out from under Monty's bed. He gets to his feet and turns around to face Saturnia. She doesn't look happy.

"So I guess this means that you changed your mind about the end of October?" she asks.

"I don't know," Samo says.

"Classy."

"I wasn't thinking!"

"No, you weren't."

"Maybe...hm. Maybe we could talk about November?"

Saturnia thinks this over for a minute, but only to consider which of the dozens of possible retorts could be equal to Samo's insult. Finding every answer wanting for adequate scorn, she snorts and leaves, slamming the door behind her.

• • • • •

That night, lying alone in his bed, Samo realizes he would have liked to have known Saturnia better. Maybe without a deadline. Without sudden expectations. *There was just so much on the line. And of course, I was kind of a coward.* He wants to tell Monty about everything: about his frustrations, his stress, his lack of sleep and understanding, the loss of Candace and sacrifice of Saturnia. Crew. Calculus. Physics. Pneumatics. Everything. Everything in his life is so ripe with potential, and yet Samo seems to fall short every time. *Dammit, Monty, where are you?*

The Relativity of Relatives

There's no such thing as a free lunch.

When the sun rises on Saturday morning, Ezzie stretches on the curb in front of Olan Commons. Her hair is messy and her clothes are wrinkled, but she's been able to brush her teeth and wash her face in the bathroom each morning and hasn't neglected to bring toothpaste or deodorant. It's a warm afternoon–balmy, really–and the way the sun plays off the copper trees and the skyscrapers downtown suggests that Arkaic is not quite dead yet.

Ezzie's been waiting for about a half hour when a deep purple Kia Rio pulls over to the curb and the front door pops open.

"Get in!" says Uncle Clay.

Ezzie smiles and climbs inside. They make their way to South Street and start toward downtown.

"I thought I'd take you to this place called Hickory's. It's supposedly one of the nicer restaurants in Arkaic. People have been tailgating me ever since I got to the airport this morning."

"Probably what you get for driving a Kia in Arkaic, Uncle Clay!" Ezzie is smiling. Whatever her uncle is going to tell her, it's not going to be as stressful as a week of avoiding Dunya.

Hickory's is a nice restaurant, and on the surface, it's different from most of the other places Ezzie's seen in town. Massive black cherry wood panels cover the walls to a height of fifteen feet, with the exposed brick rising to the ceiling beams above. The Irish theme is proclaimed by a green backlit board counting down, "141 Days 'Til St. Paddy's Day." Ezzie orders the coney pizza. Uncle Clay orders shepherd's pie and a Harp. Ezzie tells him all about her classes, her hate-love-hate relationship with Professor Plumb, her nostalgia for New York, and her sadness over her betrayal of Dunya.

"It sounds like a mistake," says Clay. "I don't think it sounds like a betrayal."

"She seemed to think it was a betrayal," says Ezzie.

"Well, you clearly do."

Ezzie looks him in the eye, puzzled.

"Wrinkled clothes. Bags under your eyes. Your hair isn't its best. Oh, you're lovely, Ezzie, don't you worry, but is that why you haven't been sleeping in your dorm room?"

Ezzie sighs.

"You always see everything that's happening," she says. "You seem to figure everything out."

"No," he says, and there's a peculiar catch in his voice. A regret. A hesitancy. "There are things I haven't even begun to figure out."

Ezzie knows—she feels in marrowy places—that this has to do with the reason for his visit. *So let's cut to the chase.* "Uncle Clay," she says, "what was that weird call with Father all about? What did he mean when he said he hadn't seen Mom in years?"

Clay has the habit of speaking bluntly. Ezzie expects this. But nothing can prepare her for what he says next. "He hasn't. His ex-wife isn't your mother."

She takes in a breath. "I beg your pardon?"

"Ruth isn't your mother. She's your aunt. When you were born, I was married to Ruth. But she started having an affair with your father, and when your mother found out, she left. She ran away with the circus. No, I am not making this up; the circus. So it was just the three of us. Ruth didn't love me anymore, so we got a divorce, and then she married your father. They raised you as if she were your mother. I wanted to tell you when you were twelve, but they didn't agree. And I couldn't risk disrupting the life they had provided for you. I didn't think that was fair. Not to you, especially. Not then. But if he called you drunk and said this, then I think I am within my rights telling you. Anyway, his opinion on this doesn't really matter anymore. You are of age and should know the full truth. And I still think you should have known sooner. Now I suppose that my feelings don't make a difference, not in this conversation, and maybe not ever. You see, Ezzie...when children become young adults...when they become teenagers and high schoolers, and then when they go off to college...they regret the cruel things that they say and do to others...but I think that the cruel and ignorant–above all, ignorant–things that adults do are usually much, much worse. I –"

"Where is she, Uncle Clay?"

He closes his eyes. "Right," he says. "That makes sense...you'll want to know that." Clay puts his elbows on the table, his fingers onto his forehead, and they wrinkle like a pug's brow. He is usually golden retriever calm. Ezzie isn't used to seeing him worried like this. Then again, she's also not used to this uniquely physical sensation, as though a fully inflated balloon is being dragged, achingly, up her esophagus, choking her up, blocking her breath. It isn't dizziness. It's an inflated nausea. Everything is overblown, tight-strung, bleating, punctured, popped. *What sense does that make? What does it matter? Wait, what?*

"We don't know," Clay says. "We spent years trying to find her. We hired detectives, placed ads, requests...missing persons. Everything we could think of. She vanished, Ezzie. She just vanished."

"Then...when you told me...that your wife left you–"

"She did, Ezzie. She left me for your father."

"My mother was my aunt, was your wife. But my real mother –"

Clay sighs and takes a sip of his beer. "Flawed people, Ezzie. Ruth loves you. Your father loves you."

Ezzie stands and shouts: "Well I'm glad it didn't work out for the two of them, either!"

Everyone is watching now, of course. If Ezzie's mother–er, not her mother, her "Aunt" Ruth–were here, she would have started crying. Her father would have ducked his head in embarrassment or hissed at her to sit down and calm down and "just listen to me!" *Uncle Clay is better than that.* He sits there with an inscrutable face, showing no emotion, not because he feels none, but because Ezzie's moment is the important one here. *Too bad he's still fucking responsible for sabotaging me!*

"Esmeralda," he says. "I owe you an apology, and it will never be enough. I can't undo anything that has been done. Is there anything I can do for you now, to start trying to make it up to you?"

Ezzie closes her eyes. *I'm demolished*, she thinks. Or maybe not. Maybe she's beyond demolition. Beyond devastation. Maybe she has cultivated the power of feeling wrenching emotions on the inside alone. As if alone. Either way, she doesn't want to spend any more time around this man right now. Not another moment.

"What can you send me...of her?" Ezzie asks.

"I've been keeping a scrapbook for you," he says. "Nothing new. Some pictures, some letters. The most recent is fifteen years old. It's in a safe deposit box back in New York. I'll Express Mail it to you as soon as I get back to New York."

"Then please get back there quickly."

He nods, thoughtful.

"Anything else?" he asks.

"Yes. You can just let me walk back to the dorm...on my own, I mean...now. I'm not as hungry as I thought."

Ezzie takes a quick gulp of water and wipes her hand across her brow. Out of habit, she starts to lean toward Clay, to hug him, then changes her mind. She puts on her jacket and picks up her hand bag, then turns her back on him and leaves that place.

Out on the street, the fire leaves shock the crisp warm air, and the sun boils across the sky. *It's lovely here.* Lovelier than her memories, her past. She could think about this new thing, right now, and start sorting it out. A good person, a good daughter, would be sorting it out right now. But *fuck it*, she thinks. *She wasn't a good mother. She left me. She just left me. And then: I've got more important things to think about now. I've got something good here. Something more worthwhile than what I left in New York. Maybe New York isn't what I wanted after all. Maybe I wanted Arkaic. And Dunya. My friend Dunya. I am going to be Dunya's friend, and I am going to do everything I can. I deserve a second chance. What I did to her was wrong, but not like what has just happened to me. Not like that at all. I deserve a second chance. I will get it. I will try as hard as I can.*

Dunya.

Dunya's Crazy-Ass Party Week/End, Part 3

Timing is everything, in music and in self-abasement.

A few hours later, and halfway across town, another out-of-state man is taking his matriculating kin out for a meal under less-than-ideal circumstances.

"No," says Dunya.

"Dunya," says Alexander Blavatsky, "I'm not taking 'no' for an answer." He runs his hands through his hair. The band has just cleared the small stage at the The Michigan Delta Blues School Bar, and the bartender has turned off the floods. The band mingles with the crowd, enjoying a couple drinks on the house. The naked incandescents flicker overhead. The electricity is shaky and dim. Alex opens another Bud for himself and then opens one for Dunya. She takes a long drink, thinking.

"I made a couple of mistakes," Alex says. "First, I didn't make a plan to pay for your college. Hell, I didn't even think you were going to college. Didn't even think you were thinking about it. Shows you what I know. And now there's not a lot of time, but I'm ready to do what I can."

"No," says Dunya.

"Second, I shouldn't have told you about that talk I had with those anthropologists. I should have just quietly taken care of it myself. I guess when they contacted you about going to AU, I just figured they were getting you a scholarship or a loan or something. It never occurred to me that they would offer you a spot you had no way to pay for."

Dunya sighs, smiles, and shakes her head. "No," she says.

A big belly laugh from the doorman. A group of five or six are leaving, but more people are coming in, along with a strong wind that stirs up the parking lot dust.

"I'm not taking no for an answer," Alex says.

But Dunya's eyes have gone distant. She notices that there is no music, except for the music of conversation, and this has gathered near the door and the bar. The table where she sits with her dad, just twenty-four hours off the plane from California, is at the middle of an empty space. She notices the afterglow of the red and purple stage lights and the worn look of floorboards that have held dancers each week for the better part of a century. She isn't listening to her dad anymore. She gets what he's saying. It's just that she...

She gets up, walks over to the juke box, and starts flipping the CDs. She doesn't like this, she doesn't know this, she doesn't like that, she doesn't know that. This. This: Mississippi Fred McDowell. *This* is *exactly* what she's looking for. She puts in a quarter and listens as it endlessly clanks and bangs down unseen channels like a marble through a Rube Goldberg machine. The song starts playing: "Goin' Down to the River." She walks back to her seat and sits and drinks her beer and watches her dad, and they both listen to the words. Finally, the song stops, and once again, the only music is the natural laughter and talk echoing about the bar.

Dunya speaks. "It would be a Hail Mary shot, Dad, either refinancing or selling the house, and that's the only plan you've got. A humiliating plan. And even if it worked, I get one year of college. One. It isn't going to do much good if I can't pay for the next three years. And anyway, where are you going to live? So no. You will take no for an answer. Because I'm not giving you any other choice."

Alex takes a long drink.

"Well," he says, "if you say so, Dunya. I guess you're the boss. But let me ask you: has it been worth it?"

Dunya makes a fist and holds it against her chest.

Alex shakes his head.

"Well," he says. "They've got an old Buick out front that I think they're calling a 'taxi.' Let's get back to your dorm. Something about a party for you."

"Jesus!" Dunya says. "*Another* party?!"

"Don't look at me."

"I know. I know who set it up. She's my best friend. I hope you get to meet her before you leave."

Just Lyin' Around

Groans aren't exactly articulate, but they're better than nothing.

Monty has been lying in a basement window well outside the Osbøe Cyclotron. He lay there all night Friday night. Battered and bruised. He lay there Saturday morning, while Clay was taking Ezzie out for brunch at Hickory's. He lay there Saturday evening, while Alex was taking Dunya out for drinks at The Michigan Delta Blues School Bar. Now it's getting dark again, and Monty wonders how long he'll be lying here alone. The Cyclotron is a desolate place on the weekend.

But Monty has drifted in and out of consciousness, watching the clouds float overhead, far far away, distant and serene. *It's warm,* he thinks. *It must be a beautiful day up there. I'm missing a beautiful day down here.* And: *I've messed everything up. I'm behind on my homework. I'm missing all of my SO meetings. I'm failing. I'm failing.* And: *I'm winning. I'm winning! The Powers That Be fear me. And I just sent them a great big "fuck you" and lived to tell about it!* And: *I am going to learn the secrets.* Every secret. Everywhere. The sky dims. The limestone walls of the Cyclotron turn a momentary orange in the light of the fading sun, then pink, then purple, then black. The stars creep out, slowly. Monty groans, from hunger, or pain, or both.

"What was that?" someone asks.

Dunya's Crazy-Ass Party Week/End, Part 4

Drink eight cups of water each day,

and one additional cup for each drink you take.

This will keep your hangover at bay

the whole time you sleep, and while you're awake.

When Dunya and Alex get back to the Cradle, they find Velma Brass waiting for them at the entrance to Acedia House.

"Dunya!" says Velma, "And nice to meet you, Mr. Blavatsky. Hey, Dunya, we have to talk about your supplies at the Proof. I've been craving Burning Cheeze Styx for a week now, and they're always out! Here, we can talk about it in my room."

Feigning ignorance, Dunya and Alex follow Velma up to the Fifth Floor Double and gasp when forty-odd Acedians jump out of the shadows and yell, "surprise!" The men wear suits and ties, the women wear cocktail dresses, and everyone holds a photocopied mask of Dunya's face, black-and-white, mounted on a popsicle stick.

"Oh my God!" says Dunya.

"We got the picture from Ezzie," says Adina Nguyen, another first year. She smiles.

Then, the transport.

The music starts, and it opens with James Brown, then on to Coco Rosie, then Moby, then the Cocteau Twins, then Jefferson Airplane, then John Lee Hooker, then Janet Jackson, and so on. The lights here are more high-tech than those at The Michigan Delta Blues School Bar, even though the music is canned. But these are her friends, all her friends. Jenny Jenkins, with an easy smile on her face as she dances. Krista Baroque, pouring drinks and mixing them strong. Rex Nouville, ticking cards off a deck, one by one, from across the room with his whip (an even more impressive feat when one considers his lack of depth perception due to his eye patch).

Bernie Katz, expostulating on Thomas Pynchon, and how *V.* is vastly superior to *Gravity's Rainbow*. Brittany Santos, inexplicably dressed up as Johnny Depp.

The minutes become an hour. One hour becomes two. Dunya drinks beer and a screwdriver, beer and a screwdriver, sex on the beach, fuzzy navel, whiskey sour.

"But I'm just sipping!" she yells, and Alex regards her with caution and distance.

"Dunya!" bellows Samo.

"Samo!" shouts Dunya, laughing.

"Happy Birthday!"

"Thanks!"

"You know, this has all come together! This week. Haha! We got you so bad last night, with your dad."

"It's been so awesome, Samo. It's been radical, and I mean Lenin/Marx/Mao-style radical."

"Yeah! We all chipped in to bring your dad here. Instead of a new foosball table. Who needs a new foosball table? The old ones season like a skillet!"

"Haha!"

"And tonight," Samo continues, "Velma and Krista wanted to throw a semi-formal cocktail party as a big 'fuck you' to midterms. Adina and Leigh wanted to throw a Halloween Party. And Giovanni and Joe were going to take a bunch of people out to the frat parties. But then Ezzie told us all about your birthday, and we all thought, hey, let's just do that instead!"

"Hey, that makes me think, Samo, you haven't seen Ezzie anywhere, have you? Because I haven't seen her in days!"

"Huh? No, I haven't seen her, now that you mention it. Hey, have you seen Monty? I've got some stuff I need to run by him."

"No, where has he been?"

"Don't know. Last time I saw him was at lunch yesterday, but he's pretty busy I guess."

"I guess. Hey, Samo?"

"Yeah?"

"This is my last week of school. I can't afford it. I have to bail while I can still get some of my tuition refunded. I'm going to have to go back to California."

"Lucky you! My parents and I are covering my tuition with loans, but I think I'm going to flunk out. They won't love that. If you have to go back to California, at least you've got California. I'll have to go back to the West End."

"Oh no!"

"Yeah. Plus I can't get any play. You know why?"

"Why?"

"Because I'm stupid!"

And they both laugh a lot at that joke (is it a joke?), because they're tired and drunk, and most of all because they're friends.

The party continues to fade in and out, just a little out of control. Nostalgia wells up against Alex, and he gives Dunya a kiss on the forehead and says, "Have fun, be safe." He calls a cab back to his hotel. The fog machine floods the Double with haze and fumes. Bernie Katz and Alyssa Carnival dance on the table. Someone starts playing bongo drums. Someone gets sick and runs to the bathroom. The music is loud, and Dunya closes her eyes to small slits, so that tapering daggers of colored light rush from the room out into the shadows of darkened corners...darkened corners? For some reason the corners here, the ones near the ceiling, seem to have a light coming from them. It doesn't make a lot of sense.

But where is she? Dunya wonders. *Where is Ezzie?*

Ezzie is standing in the door, flicking the light switch, flashing the overhead lights, the ordinary lights, on and off, on and off. The music stops. Alyssa hops off the table.

"Ezzie?" she says. "What's wrong?"

Ezzie appears to be out of breath.

"I need Monica. And Samo. It's Monty. He's in the hospital. He's been attacked or something."

Lost and Found

Take a sick man's words with a grain of salt.

When Ezzie had finished her studies and rehearsal, she decided to take a walk. She knew that Dunya's party–the epic! cocktail/Halloween/frat/birthday party would be raging far into the night, and Ezzie needed some time to sort out her thoughts before she stepped back into that room, that house. *People make me nervous*, she thought. *People are wonderful things. I'd like to spend more time with them from now on. This is going to be a hard thing for me to struggle with. It's weird that I don't feel anything...nothing in particular...about my mother.* She wondered if she was just deferring the trauma of contemplation...contemplating someone who gave her life and then discarded her. Or, more fairly, who left her. Who left her in the care of loving allies, but who nevertheless left her. Who left her over a slight...a slight that Ezzie had not known about and could not have prevented. *All those years in New York. All that guidance. All that thought and care that went into my life. Into my education and future. Was that just their guilt? Were they just trying to make up for the wrong they had done to my mother? To make it right through me?* There was a problem with that, Ezzie knew. Of the three adult architects of her life, her Uncle Clay had been the most consistent, the most considerate, the "best." And so far, he was the only one who had felt her anger, even though she did feel that he deserved it. *Am I just too short on energy to be angry at the others? Where is my mother, right now? Why am I not more curious where she is?*

I should be more curious.

Ezzie heard a low, plaintive groan.

And that's how she found Monty, and helped lift him out of the window well, him wincing all the while, and telling her some strange stories about evil librarians on PCP with the power of life and death in their hands.

"Okay, okay Monty," she said, laughing grimly. "But what really happened?"

"Ezzie," he said, slumping against her. His face had gone green from pain and nausea. "I think they broke my ribs. Can you take me to the hospital?" Then he threw up all over his shoes.

• • • • •

Two hours later, Monty was admitted to Proctor Hospital with three cracked ribs, a dislocated arm, and a probable concussion.

"I should go get the Mavens, or at least Monica," said Ezzie.

"Yeah," said Monty. "Get Samo too."

"Samo?"

"I've got something for him. I've got a couple things for him."

• • • • •

Another hour passed. Monty drifted in and out of sleep. He was being monitored by a sitter.

"Don't sleep!" she hissed.

"Fuck you," he said, and then felt bad, and apologized.

• • • • •

And now, Samo and the RA—Monica, was it?—stand at the foot of his bed, their faces tight with worry.

"Ah!" Monty says, and attempts a smile. "You're here!"

His friends sigh in relief.

"Samo," Monty says with a wide grin, "I am going to fucking kill you. Do you hear me? I am going to destroy you. I will ruin you. I will –"

Something buzzes. Monty stops. Samo and Monica look at him with an expression that clearly says, "you've lost your mind." Monty laughs. Something buzzes again. Monica takes out her phone and looks at it.

"Aw shit!" she yells, and a couple nurses poke their heads into the room. "Code Brown?" one of them asks, but Monica begins fumbling at her waist, in and around her pockets. Monty and Samo stare at her. "Samo!" she snaps.

"Yeah?"

"There's a fire at the dorm."

"At the Cradle? Damn."

"Yeah, and I'm supposed to be there. To open the south fire escape and drop the drawbridge."

"But that's got to be a mile away."

"I know. If I run I'll be there in under ten minutes."

She starts for the door, but something silent hangs in the air. Everyone notices but Samo. Monica holds her hand at the door and swings around to face the room again, and her face is wracked with worry.

"Okay," she says. "Okay. Samo, I think I'd better stay here with Monty. This whole night is messed up. He's not right in the head. He's my responsibility. Anyway, too much is happening, too fast, right? You'll have to unlock the doors."

"What? Me?! I'm not the RA"

Monica presses her keys into Samo's hand.

"This one is for the portcullis. And this one is for the drawbridge."

"Um..." he says. He waits too long.

Monica gives him a little shove.

"What do I do?" Samo implores.

"Just be a hero, Samo!" she answers, looking at him with too much confidence.

"O-kaaaay."

"Samo...Samo!" wails Monty.

"Yeah?"

"Is...is my backpack in here?"

"Sure, Monty. Your backpack is right there at the foot of the bed."

"Take it. Give it to Dunya. Wish her a happy birthday. But don't tell her it's from me, okay?"

"Okay fine, roomie, but you'd better not kick my ass, or destroy me, or ruin me."

"We'll see," says Monty. "And by the way. Robotic unicorns and beavers?"

He watches Samo's face go slack with shock.

Dunya's Crazy-Ass Party Week/End, Part 5

When the time is right, crescendo.

The questions come at Ezzie from several angles. "Is Monty badly hurt?" "Is he going to be okay?" "What happened?" "Where did you find him?" "Where have you been, anyway?"

She answers as best she can. "Not that bad, I think, though he was pretty banged up." "I think so." "I don't know. He says he was beaten up. He had a dislocation and a concussion. A couple cracked ribs." "He was hiding in a window well on South Campus." "Oh, you know, around."

And then, suddenly, Ezzie is face-to-face with her best friend and recent nemesis, Dunya.

"Dunya."

"Ezzie!"

"Look, I need to say I'm sorry. I need to apologize to you. I didn't ask when I read your card, and I didn't ask when I –"

"Ezzie–so beautiful–this has been–my God! It has been my favorite–the best birthday I've ever had!"

"It has?"

"Yes!"

"What's happened?"

"First, Jenny, Elaine, and Zena took me out for a picnic, and then..." The whole story unfolds. It's a brilliant constellation–everyone has come through–everyone had offered to help with the parties, of course, but Ezzie hadn't expected everyone to follow through. Yet here it is. The Crazy-Ass Party Week/End to end all Crazy-Ass Party Week/Ends, and a culminating party–a party that Ezzie has just caught in the nick of time.

"Dunya!" says Ezzie. "I'm so happy. So happy. You...you are my best friend here, and I don't want to wreck that."

"Me neither!" shouts Dunya.

"And Dunya," says Ezzie, "since we're just putting it all out there, I should say–wow–I mean, jeez, but–look–my uncle was in town today. I found out that my mother was actually my aunt...that my real mother ran off when she found out my father was having an affair, and so I've never known her."

"Holy shit, Ezzie. That's enormous. That's...oh my God, are you okay?"

"I'm fine," Ezzie says. "I'm alive here now, and I'm awake. And right now, because who knows about tomorrow, but right now, right now I feel okay."

"Me too," Dunya says, "even though I'm out of money and time. Even though I'm going back to California sometime next week."

"Why are we happy?" Ezzie asks. "When everything is so fucked up with us like this right now?"

"I don't know." Dunya laughs. "Let's dance!"

They dance.

The whole house dances.

François de Rivoli and Sarah Marlowe and Argosy Jackknife and Elaine Trotter and Brent Gatsby and Joe Newcomb and Giovanni Martini and Alyssa Carnival and Bernie Katz and April Silesia and Bruce Bancroft and Dunya Blavatsky and Odin Bright and Natalie Branches and Trisha Wong and Duncan Hara and Ezzie Prentice and Adina Nguyen and Leigh Przkjtski and Rex Nouvelle and Catherine Apple and Jenny Jenkins and Cassidy Antrim and Zena Milkinovich and Krista Baroque and Xerxes Trough and Velma Brass and all, and all, and all of the others. Everyone but Sam O'Samuel and Monty Valverde and Monica Sand who are, at that very moment, at the hospital, checking out the status of broken ribs and a bruised skull. And so these others–housemates and suitemates–this primal mass–shake in the effervescence, in the foggy, liquored up '80s, '90s, aughts sonic shiver sheen of sound and fog and mist and mornings coming on soon, with and without headaches, with readiness, with spontaneous contemplation, with crashing sounds made by birds alighting on birdfeeders, of leaves winking for one last weekend before falling into mud and puddles, of stars and sun shifting southward toward the beckoning solstice, and of the music, of the four-to-the-floor, or the jello shots and the memorized lines and memorized proofs, theorems, numerals, accounts, reckonings, accents, preterites, pluperfects, perfections, precipices, priorities. Oh, you need your priorities straight when you're far from home, without help (without money) and without time, without moments, without guidance, without but with, with so much, this is an opportunity, do you know how few people in the world have an opportunity, an opportunity like this, a piece of the puzzle, a flat table to lay it on, a clear vision of where the borders belong, the interior, the exterior, the attributes, the momentarily fixed two-dimensional shapes, and many other dimensions, too?

There are many dimensions.

How will you cut and fit your pieces?

How will you find peace in the mystery, when the fog below is met by the smoke from above?

Wait. What's the deal with this smoke from above?

It doesn't have that sticky-dry smell of the fog from the fog machine.

No, this is smoke. Real smoke. Smoke from a fire. A fire? Yes, a fire!

And strange strange, but the fumes aren't coming from within the room, and they aren't coming from the hall either.

Something's happening above and between the walls.

A crack—a small fissure—in the molding at the ceiling, where someone has set something on fire—in the attic?—what's going on? Is there someone up there? Is there an eavesdropper? Is there someone lurking in the liminal space above and between rooms spying, spying? Who has been watching the party unfold through a chink in the wall? Watching, perhaps, Krista and Velma, ever since they moved in here? Who knows the Acedians and their names and their weaknesses?

What a terrifying prospect, everyone realizes at once, as the music stops and the lights go on. And "Smoke? Fire?" becomes "Smoke! Fire!"

Smoke and burning spill down and into the room through the slat in the fissure through which–*we're certain, right?–absolutely certain!–someone is there, and something is burning, and it is hard to breathe in here.*

"I can't breathe!" Alyssa yells.

Hacking. Coughing. Air trembling with heat and panic. The beginning of a stampede. Fists on doors, on closets, on windows. Not enough air to breathe. Forty-odd Acedians trying to escape, to escape all at once.

"Ezzie!" screams Dunya, and she grabs Ezzie's hands. "We're trapped! We can't breathe!"

"What can I do?!" screams Ezzie. "What can I do?!"

"You can –" Coughing. "You can –" Watery eyes, haze, panic, freak out, artificial clouds. "Ezzie, the windows!"

The windows!

So Ezzie snaps off her sunglasses and glares at the windows and–lo!–the four windows in the Fifth Floor Double crack and fissure and split and shatter and shear and rivet and crash and jags, cuts, planes, triangles, and palimpsests of glass arc up and out before raining down onto the courtyard. The sudden sharp vacuum catches whatever flame hides behind those heavy walls and snuffs it out, and the smoke pushes out the window and starts to dissipate. The smell of burning dims and vanishes. It is safe now.

But something else is happening.

As it falls, the glass changes. It morphs and shifts, its structure broken and reconfigured. When it lands, all around the old oak tree, it has become something small, and hard, and bright, and valuable.

The students don't notice this. They're happy enough to lean out of those four windows and breathe in the fresh October air. They look up, not down. They're glad to be alive, and to go on breathing fast, under all of those diamond-bright stars.

Dunya's Gift

Accept a gift with gratitude.

By the time Samo staggers up outside the Cradle, a lot of the panic has subsided. He dutifully uses Monica's key to drop the south drawbridge across the moat, and once he's crossed, he opens the portcullis and advances into the courtyard. He surveys the balconies and broken windows, all packed with shaken students, relieved students, oh boy.

"What happened?" he asks nobody in particular.

The courtyard is still empty. Nobody has come down yet. Everyone is still getting their bearings, evidently. That's when Samo spots the glittering treasures at his feet. *Fuckadoodle doo.*

Samo enters Acedia House, and the rectangular stairwell is empty. The halls are empty. Nervous voices echo up and down the space, vertically, horizontally, everywhere. *Where is Monica?* they wonder. *Where are the Mavens? What happened?*

Samo climbs to the fifth floor, which is packed with at least a dozen students. "Someone's watching us!" "Someone's in the attic." "I couldn't breathe." "Did you see what Ezzie did there?" "How did she do that?" "She saved our lives." "I know, but it's weird!" And so they talk, and don't notice Samo.

"Velma," he says, "where's Ezzie?"

Velma doesn't answer.

"Krista," he asks, "have you seen Dunya?"

Krista shakes her head, numbly.

After banging on the Mavens' door and leaving Monica's keys balanced on the doorknob, Samo goes down the five flights of stairs to the basement. Dunya's door is open and voices come from inside. The light is on. Dunya paces back and forth. Ezzie sits on Dunya's bed, looking shell-shocked.

"I don't know what happened up there –" Samo pants, "but this is yours –" and he throws Monty's heavy backpack to Dunya, "and you've got to follow me <u>right now</u>."

Ezzie stares at Samo, confused, and Dunya absently opens the backpack. She's startled. "Wait, what? But how did this happen?" Samo stomps his feet impatiently. "These are my textbooks, Samo!"

"Yeah yeah," he says, "c'mon, c'mon, follow me!"

"But...I'm out of time. I'm going back to California next week –"

"Will you shut up and follow me?!"

Stunned again, Dunya and Ezzie get to their feet and follow Samo as he sprints up the stairs and almost collides with the brick wall. He shoos them out the front door and into the courtyard before darting ahead of them again to scoop up a handful of the fragmented glass from room 227.

"Cup your hands," he tells Dunya.

She does so. Samo opens his palms into hers, dropping emeralds, sapphires, diamonds, rubies, and opals. They glitter in the half darkness, and their glint makes a kaleidoscope across Dunya's face.

"Suck on deez, California!" says Samo.

CHAPTER SEVEN
HOLLOWED HALLS

Disorderly Situations; i.e. a Redundancy

The other shoe will drop when you're comfortable in your slippers.

James Pike is a creature of routine. The salt-and-pepper headed Facilities Manager of Calliope Cradle Court sleeps just fine at night, given three things: his favorite flannel 'jamas, a VHS recording of *Murder, She Wrote*, and a night cap of brandy mixed with warm milk. Each action, no matter how mundane or eccentric, occurs in a precise order. Complex orders are subdivided into stages by protocol. At the end of the day, these orders tell one where one stands, whereas steps are useful to avoid falling. This is all very helpful. And so it is, at the end of the day, and with considerable irritation, that James eyes the ringing rotary phone at the side of his bed. He's nestled in woolly warmth with liquid heat circulating in his blood, and murder has been visited upon Cabot Cove. His red phone rattle-rings, and hasn't stopped in a good half-minute.

James answers the phone and says, "Hello."

"Mr. Pike?" It's Dr. Maureen Lawless, the Dungeon Master of the Calliope Cradle Courtyard.

"Yes?"

"We've got a situation."

James snorts. Situations are, by nature, disorderly.

Impeachable Testimonies

When your brain is out of answers, follow your nose.

It is well after midnight when Monica arrives back at Acedia House. Not wanting to wait for a bus, she walks back home from Proctor Hospital, even though this path takes her past those infernal mathematicians at XAI. It starts raining about the time she crosses the river, but her heart is a hot glow in her chest, and its heat radiates out to warm the tips of her fingers and toes. No one would know this, looking at Monica; her appearance is strictly black-and-white. Black boots, black stockings, black eyes and hair, skirt and blouse.

She is in love–something like love at first sight. Second or third sight, maybe. She had seen Monty Valverde a number of times over the weeks, but she had never looked him in the eyes before.

The first time she did so was in a hospital room, with the self-conscious anxiety all RAs possess about personally paying the price for student idiocy. She hadn't wanted the position, really; it made social demands and she only occasionally felt social. But responsibility provided free room and board, and Monica wasn't in a position to turn it down.

Monty's eyes locked onto hers, and there she saw the intensity of intricate works turning, like the gears of a Swiss watch.

Who are you? she mouthed. He nodded in response. Then Monica's phone buzzed. A text from Riley Maven: "House on fire."

"Aw shit!" snapped Monica.

"Code Brown?" asked a nurse at the door.

Monica gave her keys to Samo and sent him on his way.

Monica and Monty didn't speak. There was plenty to talk about, sure. *How many cats to own. When to move to Aughnanure. Whether to name their red-headed son Ian or Curtis.* But there would be time later for sorting out. In that moment, Monica was content to take a seat at the edge of the bed and cup Monty's hand in her own.

$$\bullet \ \bullet \ \bullet \ \bullet \ \bullet$$

An hour later, Monica has made it back to the Cradle. She is pleased to see that Samo has raised the portcullis without damaging anything, and that Acedia House looks fine from the outside. As she steps inside, Monica smells the acrid scent of dissipated smoke. Voices trail down the stairwell from the fifth floor. Monica climbs. It's Ryder Maven speaking.

"They all saw it, James. Forty-three students here at Acedia House all saw the same thing."   "They must all have had a lot to drink, to see something that wasn't there at all!"

The second voice is James Pike, the Facilities Manager.

Monica finds James and Ryder standing with Riley Maven and Dr. Lawless.

"Monica," says Dr. Lawless, "I'm glad you're here. We have an interesting situation. You should know about it." Two things are undisputed: first, that the fire alarm went off in Acedia House at a few minutes after eleven, and second, that all of the students gathered in the Fifth Floor Double saw lights moving through the cracks in the ceiling molding as the smoke poured in.

"They *claimed* to see," James corrects. "Smoke would have risen...it would have pooled in the attic if there had been a fire in there, not sunk down into a room. Plus, as I keep saying, nobody could have gotten in there."

"Wait, so there *are* cracks in the molding?" Monica asks.

"Not cracks. Slots. We just inspected the attic and the Double," says Riley. "We think they were put there to assist with ventilation. Remember, this was a mental asylum, and people lived here involuntarily. A lot of them didn't go outside much. Although we can't prove that's why it was built that way —"

"It *is* damn funny," James interjects.

"So yes," Riley goes on, "you can look into room 227, just a little, from the attic. But as James is saying, nobody has access."

"Look," James says. "There are only three points of ingress and egress to the attic. The first is obviously irrelevant. The second is the attic fan; we looked at that, and there was no sign of tampering. The dust hasn't even been touched. And the third is the door that comes in from the vestibule, the stairs we took up. Now, there are only two sets of keys to that door: my own and Dr. Lawless'. I haven't lost my keys, Dr. Lawless –"

"– and mine are right here, thank you, Mr. Pike. I keep my keys with me at all times."

"Couldn't they have come in from another house?" asks Monica. "Maybe as a prank. We don't really like each other much, most of the houses –"

"Each house has its own attic, and they are partitioned," says James. "Just like the vestibules. It's part of the reason why there are *seven* houses in the dorm."

"Or maybe," says Monica, "hm...okay, this is dramatic sounding, but maybe someone came through a wall from another house. You know, removed the bricks?"

James is getting exasperated. "We would have seen signs of that when we did our inspection just now. You don't remove enough bricks to make a hole in a wall without leaving a bit of dust and dirt behind. Especially you bookish types who can't work with your hands. Besides, there's nothing up there to hide in. We checked; there are just a few boxes and some insulation. If there had been tampering, we'd have seen it."

"James, what's the other entrance you mentioned?" asks Ryder. "The one that you said was irrelevant?"

James sighs. "There's a shaft that runs down to the chain tunnels, but as you know, there isn't any way to access the tunnels from the dorm –"

"There are entrances from each of the house basements –" begins Dr. Lawless.

"See, I knew you were going to say that, but *nobody* has the keys to those doors any more. The university commandeered them several years ago after the thing happened. Now only licensed engineers have access, and they have to enter clear across the Fairway. Hell, most of those doors are welded shut!"

A long silence.

"Well that's it, then," says Dr. Lawless. "It doesn't appear that we know anything more than when we started. Do you have any thoughts, Monica?"

Monica sniffs the acrid air.

"Where there's smoke, there's fire," she observes.

Getting Religion

Only a higher power can get you out of organizational obligations.

On Sunday morning, half of the students working with Theatre of Gold get religion in an ill-advised attempt to get out of the TOG Cleanup Day. Tedious at best, dangerous at worst, every student involved in any play or production is required to contribute at least sixteen hours on the last Sunday of October cleaning the accumulated mess from dozens of annual productions. Anyone who skips his shift, for reasons divine or otherwise, is ejected from his production. A literal ejection. A coterie of black-clad technicians reave from rehearsal to rehearsal and fling the fugitives out of whatever window or down whatever staircase happens to be convenient.

It is this event, Ezzie learns, which has earned the Theatre its notoriety with the FBI. The first few hours are pretty mundane: discarding trash and sorting old programs and lighting gels, repairing broken lighting mounts, washing windows, stripping paint left over from old stage sets. Once surface tasks are done, the chores get a bit grosser: dredging fistfuls of cigarette butts from deep puddles of stagnant rainwater; "It burns! It burns!" wails Rodney Stockpus, the ill-fated vampire of *Mad Forest*. From there it's on to discarded curtains with asbestos contamination, a cache of Sublinox®, sixty-nine gallons of expired Valspar®, a tattered missalette dedicated to "the Divine Sarah," some hard-boiled eggs that had been hidden last Easter, one of Tennessee Williams' fifths of tequila (full of hardened amber urine that briefly liquefies each February), a bildungsroman, and the half-eaten heads of Demetrius and Chiron. That's when the police are called in and Cleanup Day ends several hours early. Ezzie is so exhausted by the time she gets back to the Cradle that she drops the package from her Uncle Clay on her desk without giving it a second look.

The old Dunya liked to draw the weekends out from Thursday afternoon until midday Monday. Most weeks, her goal was to make Hump Day *the* Week Day. "The Weak Day." But this weekend has overstayed its welcome. While she doesn't regret any of her parties (or the numerous drinks), she is physically and emotionally exhausted by Sunday morning and thus too tired to sink herself into her homework. Instead, she follows Ezzie to Cleanup Day and spends most of her time chasing cockroaches down the walls and scrubbing aging floor lights with a toothbrush. She almost slips and breaks her neck when the hydraulic pump that raises the stage suddenly extends while she's kneeling on the edge. Then she gets the word that Syd Barrett is at the Secretary of State's office downtown, signing autographs. She gets excused early by taking over Rodney's cigarette butt duty, but by the time she makes it two miles through driving rain to East Street, the Octopus has moved on. So Dunya walks back home (more rain), and the purpling twilight is brightened by gurgling sirens and many orange motes on the horizon. It's Devil's Night in Arkaic, Michigan.

Back at the dorm, Dunya meets Samo and Ezzie at dinner. "Where's Monty?" she asks. He's still at the hospital. They won't discharge him on account of gnostical turpitude. Rumor is that he has hooked up with Monica. If they become an item, maybe he'll get an RA position next year, and free room and board to boot. "Lucky guy," Dunya says. She palms one of the polished emeralds in her pocket before heading off to take her shift at Proofs. *Am I going to have any time at all for homework tonight?* At midnight, she closes up shop and mentally steadies herself for sleep, but Argosy shows up and asks if she's going to go to the study break.

"Study break?"

"One to three a.m. at the Commons. Hot fudge sundaes and banana splits. And coffee. Dozens of midterms tomorrow. Maybe hundreds." *Midterms I should be studying for, but...* "Sure!"

By three a.m., Dunya's finally back in bed and drifting off into a hazy BEEEEEEEEEEEEP! goes the alarm. "What?!" she screams, leaping out of bed. BEEEEEEEEEEEEP! "What?!" BEEEEEEEEEEEEEEEEEEEEEEEEEEEEEEEEEEEEEEEEEEEEP!

All of the students of the Cradle stumble out into the courtyard, worried and shaking in the northerly wind. But they can't escape. Nobody's there to let them out. Fifteen minutes later, Monica arrives–"I'm sorry! I'm sorry!"–and raises the portcullis. "Where were you?!" asks Riley Maven. Monica blushes, probably down to the tips of her black boot-covered toes. She murmurs something.

"Proctor Hospital?!" Riley cries.

"It's a good thing that wasn't a real fire," mumbles Ezzie, shivering in her flannel 'jamas next to Dunya. "We'd be toast."

• • • • •

After the Arkaic Fire Department arrives, late and annoyed to find a false alarm on the busiest night of their year, the "all clear" is announced, and the three hundred exhausted students return to their rooms and beds. The sky is already turning from black to purple over the Happy Hunting Grounds and the power plant as Velma and Krista climb the last flight of stairs. They love the view from fifty feet up, but they detest all those stairs. They love their RHs and RA, too, but they hate the fact that the Mavens are reaming out Monica in their apartment. Hate that they're doing it so loud, and doing it *right now*.

Krista sticks her tongue out in the direction of the ruckus.

They also hate where they're going. Room 227 is the most coveted suite in all of Acedia House. As they reach the end of the hall, Velma even sighs as the sound of the angry Mavens has faded to a whisper. There's no way the two upperclassmen will hear it *inside*. Adult histrionics are an acceptable alternative to isolation when isolation is scary. Even when fear is irrational. Even when fear is called irrational by "very responsible people" like James Pike.

Krista fits her key in the lock, and the deadbolt slides open. She reaches out and turns the handle. The door opens into the cavernous suite. Krista and Velma stand, statue-still, in the doorway, willing, it seems, to let only their shadows enter. To probe the dimensions of the hidden rooms. To see if they're really empty.

The Fifth Floor Double is something of a legend in Acedia House. It has always been occupied by charismatic upperclassmen, stalwart in the dormitories, willing to go to great lengths to throw the best parties and make the best noise. Each room is almost twice the size of those on the lower floors. The inner room looks north onto the Arkadian skyline with the Pyramid Building perfectly framed at its center. The outer room commands sweeping views of the Hunting Grounds and the Quints to the east and south. Not even the privacy of the large Acedian singles lives up to comfort of the Fifth Floor Double, to say nothing of its storied reputation for Dionysian debauchery.

"It's a state of mind," Velma says, theatrically. She laughs loudly for a moment, but the silence sweeps back in. It is a state of mind, that comfort, that reputation. But now the suite is empty. Black and bleak and barren. Unilluminated. Something white billows across the space and breaks the spell. It's the gentle movement of a bed sheet. They've hung them from the ceiling, around the entire perimeter of the rooms, and while at first they were unnerved by the constant movement–drafts from the attic–it reassures them to know that they cannot be seen from outside the room. The girls enter the suite and close the door.

Wordlessly, they undress and climb into their beds, deliberately keeping the door open between the two rooms. The sun is readying to rise outside, but with the windows blocked by both curtains and bedsheets, they'll be able to enjoy the darkness for a while longer. On her back, in the outer room, Velma thinks she can relax herself again. She's already comfortable with the darkness. In fact, the darkness is comforting. No unknown glows from the molding. The silence still seems strange. "Maybe he's right," she says out loud. "Maybe James Pike was right...that we imagined it." She pauses. "I mean, we were drinking a lot. There was fog. There was loud music. There *was* a fire somewhere, because we could smell it.

Maybe we just got a little ahead of ourselves. Maybe the lights from the attic weren't a real thing."

"I saw it, Vel." Krista's voice is defiant from across the vast empty. Almost angry. Not with her, but with dismissive administrators.

"Well," says Velma, letting the word draw out, "maybe we did see it then. Maybe we saw it, but it was just something more innocent. Like a light that someone left on up there. In fact, if there was a light and it burned out suddenly, like it burst, couldn't that have started the fire?"

"Whatever." There's a definite edge in Krista's voice. The two have been friends–best friends–since they were first-years, and claiming the Fifth Floor Double had been the crowning achievement of that friendship. Now, for the first time ever, Krista sounds annoyed with Velma. Velma's considering what to say when Krista's voice rings out across the room again:

"What? Speak up!"

"I didn't say anything," says Velma.

"Yes you did. You keep whispering. It's annoying."

"But I'm not."

The silence draws long.

Opportunities Under the Horizon

Keep your ears to the ground.

Text message from Travis to Samo:

> hu bak 4m bos wknd + crs bak 4m chi + mrk. Sta @ AU w u fri nt

Samo writes back:

> sry, 2 mch hwk. Crew fri / sat am. Mdtrm ths wk a nxt. Thksgvg?

Travis:

> Lissa 2???

Samo:

> c u fri

• • • • •

from: Dunya Blavatsky <dblavat@arkaicu.edu>
to: Esmeralda Prentice <eprenti@arkaicu.edu>
date: Mon, Oct 31, 2011 at 9:24 AM
subject: Fwd: Hope to meet you soon

Shit. What am I supposed to do with this?

----------------Original Message----------------

from: Andreas Rochet, PhD <arochet@arkaicu.edu>
subject: Hope to meet you soon

Dear Ms. Blavatsky,

The Department of Anthropology is delighted by your attendance at Arkaic University, and we hope to see you soon. Perhaps we could arrange an informal wine and cheese reception with a few of our senior faculty. I'm sure that if you were to demonstrate "ghosting" for us, and be ready/willing to discuss some of the anthropological implications of your work, you would find us to be a very enthusiastic audience!

Please write back and let me know if 6 PM this Friday (November 4th) is a convenient date/time for you.

Sincerely,

Dr. Rochet

Andreas Rochet, PhD

Arkaic University of Department of Anthropology, Department Head

----------------End Forwarded Message----------------

· · · · ·

No reply after five minutes. Ezzie must be in class; she never checks her phone there. Dunya's head drops into her folded arms. It's been a frustrating morning. No, the bursar doesn't accept emeralds, or diamonds, rubies, opals, or sapphires. She'll have to try a pawn shop. She fell asleep in her hum class and is way behind on her studying, and now she's hallucinating that someone is knocking on her door.

"Stop hallucinating," she tells herself.

"Um, Dunya?" comes a female voice from the other side of the door.

"Oh, hi," mumbles Dunya. "Who is it?" she calls out.

"Um, it's Riley Maven. Could I see you for a moment?"

Dunya answers the door to find both of the Mavens and a tall black man with stern eyes and a perpetual frown.

"Dunya, have you met Mr. Pike, our facilities manager?"

"No. Nice to meet you."

Dunya rubs her eyes before mumbling an apology and shaking Mr. Pike's hand. He nods.

"Dunya," Riley goes on. "You work at Proofs, right? Do you have a key to the basement?"

"Oh, yeah. I mean, I don't use it often, but I guess it does go into the basement. I mean the outer storage area."

"That'll do. I don't have my set handy and Monica is out and away somewhere. Do you think you could let us in?"

Dunya leads the three staff members down the stairs beneath the dining hall, past Proofs, with its gum-crusted couches and lopsided chairs, past the laundry room and an exercise room stripped of equipment, and toward the hulking bulk of the double basement corridors. She fits her key in the lock and leads them into a dusty, narrow, humming, dim catacombs-for-bricks-instead-of-skulls-type passageway. James and the Mavens pass her. "Thank you, Dunya," says Riley. *What the heck*, Dunya thinks. Adventures, it turns out, have a stimulant effect. She closes the door behind her and follows.

From above, Calliope Cradle is shaped, more or less, like the letter D, with the straight part of the D representing the dining hall and the seven sinful houses arrayed along the curve (Acedia House being the second from the bottom). Beneath the dorm, the subterraneous tunnels radiate out from the center of the dining hall to each house, while another passageway links all the houses to each other.

The passages are punctuated by a chamber beneath each house, and each chamber has three doors. First, there's a gate to a summer storage closet. Second, there's a stair that parallels the house stairs with entrances to the main vestibule and then, much higher, a door to the attic. Finally, there's a steel-reinforced door to the chain mazes.

The chamber beneath Acedia House is bricked off from the room accessing the basement dorm rooms, including Dunya's. The lack of connection confuses her, but then, much of the Cradle's architecture does. So she's all ears when James turns to face the little group and speaks.

"So there is *something* going on here. It isn't what your students think, but we've had fire alarms two nights in a row, without any *compelling* evidence of an actual fire, and it makes most sense that there's a short in the wiring. Have you heard of Occam's razor?"

They nod.

"Well I'm going to tell you a bit about Pike's razor. It goes like this: other things being equal, a duller explanation is better than a more exciting one."

"I see what you're doing," said Ryder, "but you're actually deriving your theory from an incorrect understanding of Occam's razor. Simplicity isn't sufficiency, you see –"

"I fully understand what I mean and what I'm saying, Mr. Maven. Now." He unlocks the second door, leading to the stairway. "What is this?" He thumbs a dull, gray band stapled to the mortar.

"Wire," they others say, dully.

"And how does this wire look?"

"Is this a trick question?" asks Ryder.

"It looks pretty worn," says Dunya.

"Bingo," says James, clicking on a schmitty. "A short waiting to happen. Now this is just a line running up to the hallway lights, so I doubt there's anything wrong here. But we're going to go up to the attic and see what other electricals run around room 227, and maybe we can find something that sparked up and caused a fuss."

As Dunya follows the tiny group up the stairs, she salivates, just a little, imagining all these passages that twist through the dorms, just a few feet from where the students walk every day. After a dozen or so stairs, they pass a door with light spilling in through the crack at the bottom. *That would be the door to the main vestibule*, Dunya thinks. After another several more minutes, they reach another small door, which James unlocks with his key. It swings open, and just like that, Dunya is the first ordinary student in many years to set foot in the house attic.

Her eyes adjust from darkness to deeper darkness, and then she realizes it isn't really dark. A weak, pale, white sunlight sheen seems to just touch the floorboards up ahead. Dunya watches James as he locates a nest of wires and cables on the far wall, forty or fifty feet ahead, and begins to do an inspection.

"Not surprised the students are seeing things," Riley's saying to Ryder behind her. "Three years ago, a girl *hung* herself in that room."

"I'm not sure they're wrong," Ryder answers. "They told me someone was *whispering* at them last night."

Up ahead, James coughs loudly. Dunya and the Mavens (a great band name, no?) cross the attic, and now Dunya is able to see the source of the light. It is sunlight coming in through the windows of room 227, dim already through the multiple blinds and curtains hung by Krista and Velma, and then further dimmed through the slats at Dunya's feet. It gives her a strange feeling, a sense of existential vertigo (Nietzschean vertigo?) to be on the other side. To be in the place where from whence the other night's glow originated, and moved from darkness into light.

James' feet, however, are firmly planted. "As you can see, these cords are in terrible shape. They're shorts waiting to happen. My guess is that mice have been gnawing on them the last several winters. It's hard to keep mice out of here, and if they get hungry enough, they'll eat plastic." His flashlight follows the cables down toward the floor, to the most distant corner, where they vanish behind a pine and plywood crate overflowing with foam peanuts.

"If we move that crate, we'll find the sub wall where the cables run, and if we're lucky, we can see where the short is. Then I just have to find the service panel, take it out, replace the wire, and we'll have no more problems with ghosts or false fire alarms."

With a grunt, James drags the crate away. As promised, the wires vanish down a chute that plunges back toward the earth below. But the chute is much larger than they had expected, easily three feet in diameter. More, it is covered by an iron grate locked to a similar frame which has been fitted to the floor.

"Hmm," James says, "that seems excessive. Why would they make this so big? And why would they bother *locking* it?" He takes an enormous key chain off his belt, with big keys, small keys, rusty keys and shiny keys. He tries at least a dozen in the Gothic-looking lock, but nothing fits. James puts the key ring back on his belt and stands again, his hands on his hips. "My guess is they put this grate up here back when this was still an asylum, and somehow, they didn't update it when they renovated the dorm. Tell your students to brace themselves for more fire alarms, because it could take me a week to locate that key."

"Where does it go?" Dunya asks.

"The room we came from?" James asks.

Dunya shakes her head.

"What about the dorm side of the basement?"

Dunya shakes her head again.

"Then it must be the chain mazes. There's nowhere else for it to go."

CHAPTER EIGHT
THEOSOPHICAL CONSTANCY

Indiscretion and Action: a Correlation or a Causation?

As you watch, you are being watched.

Monty looks up into the starry shadow that is Monica's face. At the moment, she is surrounded by a hellish halo from the fluorescents in his hospital room. Monty hates the lights; they are cold suns that bleach the room antiseptic. And yet, with Monica half-lying on him, her face floating above his, the pale light casts her as a marble statue at noon. She is, after all, perfect.

"I've got to go," she whispers. "They'll need me back at the Cradle when the alarms go off tonight."

Monty sighs, and his heart breaks. He speaks above his shattered heart: "So it's not even an 'if' anymore, but a 'when.' "

Monica stands up and straightens her blouse. "It's a problem with the wiring, they say, but they can't get at the wires to inspect or fix them."

"That's stupid," Monty says.

"Same time tomorrow?"

"Sure."

"Bring your homework?"

"Please."

She leans close to him and whispers in his ear. "It'll be nice when you get out of here. You don't have to go back to the basement. I've got plenty of space in my room. It's definitely more comfortable than the rooms you first-years get."

A stupid grin spreads across Monty's face. He tries to pull it back because he doesn't want to look like an idiot. Monica gives him a light kiss on the corner of his mouth and turns to leave.

"Wait a minute," Monty says. "Why am I still here?"

"Observation," she answers, "for Scrofungulus."

"Shit," he says.

Monica turns the light off on the way out.

• • • • •

That night, the fire alarms go off.

The next morning, Professor Periwinkle turns the light on as he walks into his classroom. The physics students stir. They are all dazed and half-asleep. They are not impressed by the tray or its projection. The magnet, black as an Aztec sword, hovers over a tiny ocean of gray mist.

Samo thinks about 'Lissa and gets an erection.

"What is that?" mutters a student sitting behind him.

"It was on the list for Artemis' Hunt a couple years back."

They're talking about the ocean and the magnet.

• • • • •

That night, the fire alarms go off.

The next afternoon, Ezzie is in her bedroom, putting on her earrings, her scarf and shawl, and her favorite peacock feather hat. She checks herself in the mirror, and her eyes fall on the box from her Uncle Clay. Her heart pulses, hard, and her hand twitches in direction of the package. She sighs and grows angry.

"I'm sorry, Mother," she says. "I don't have time for you right now. I have a Humanities midterm to finish. Not that you'll ever know about it."

She turns the light off on her way out.

• • • • •

That night, the fire alarms go off.

A master's candidate will use this phenomenon for his thesis paper, charting the midterm performance of students from Calliope Cradle against those from other dormitories. The Cradle has a collective IQ that lowers by the day. Her residents look ever more green and bedraggled. By Friday, they'll be drooling zombies.

Except for Monty. Monty spends his days under the diabolical white light of the hospital fluorescents, but his nights are still and only occasionally interrupted by the nurses checking his vital signs. He studies for his midterms, which he expects to ace as soon as his Project Blue is cured and he's officially discharged.

• • • • •

That night, the fire alarms go off.

The next day—Friday—Samo's classes seem to drag on forever. Lunch drags on forever. So does dinner ("Refried Isoptera Paste," a.k.a. R.I.P.). When he gets back to his room, Samo throws his sooty computer into the closet and lights incense to spice the air with something delicious. He opens back the shades in Monty's room to let in the xenon flicker from the courtyard. He has even installed a dimmer overhead to drop the perfect hues of muted beige over his white walls and cheap furniture.

Someone knocks on the door.

His heart jumps.

He answers.

It's just Ezzie.

• • • • •

Bundled against the cold, Dunya knocks on the door.

The door opens.

"Dunya Blavatsky! Please come inside. It's a cold night, tonight, and we have some Stinking Bishop in here that is sure to warm you up." His smile is all kinds of Bela Lugosi charming.

"Thank you," she says.

· · · · ·

"Where's Dunya?"

"At some meeting of the Department of Anthropology?" says Ezzie. "Don't ask me about it...I didn't think she was even into anthro."

Ezzie steps inside.

"So," she says, "where's Monty?"

"Still at the hospital. Help yourself to a beer from the fridge. I stocked up good."

· · · · ·

Monty twiddles his thumbs.

Monty watches *Jeopardy*. Post-Watson. Anything goes, now.

· · · · ·

"So you seem nervous," says Ezzie.

"Yeah," says Samo, taking a seat on his bed. "I'm seeing some people tonight I haven't seen since high school. Mostly good friends of mine. And this one girl."

"An October girl?"

Samo looks at his feet. "No, not her."

"That Indian girl?"

"Um, no..."

"Someone you knew from high school."

"Yeah. Her name is 'Lissa. And um, I..."

The pause draws out.

"Come on, Samo," Ezzie says. "We're both *Basement People*."

"I don't know," says Samo. "I had a big crush on her for years, but I'd already written that whole thing off. What happens in high school stays in high school for a reason."

"I don't understand. What happened in high school?"

Samo sighs. "Absolutely nothing."

· · · · ·

Monty looks out the window. The parking lot is yellow and black. Recently paved black pavement and yellow streetlights that shine down upon it. They shine down upon the yellow parking lot lines, too.

· · · · ·

Dunya steps into the room. She hears the silver scrape of steel forks against crystal plates. The clink of crystal glasses quietly colliding. Modest, muted toasts. Loafered feet shifting weight on thick, soft carpet. A sleek and pearlescent light suffusing over this most exclusive apartment of the Department of Anthropology.

"You must" she says, "be Dr. Rochet."

"Andreas, please," he says, offering his hand.

His hand is clammy. His handshake, weak.

"Please come inside."

"So she doesn't even know that you –"

"Oh, she knows."

"Did something else happen?"

"Yeah. On the day before I came away to college here, I thought I'd give her a call, to wish her luck at SMU. But before I called, I thought, 'hey, maybe I should just tell her how I feel.' And then and there I decided, if she'd broken up with Twist, I'd let her know how I felt. So during our talk, I said, 'so hey, how's Twist?' And 'Lissa said, 'Oh. I don't know. Okay, probably.' And I said, 'What do you mean?' And she said, 'We broke up.' And I said –"

Knock knock knock!

Biting down on his teeth, Samo steps to his door. He looks back at Ezzie, who gives a nervous, reassuring smile, and opens the door.

On the other side stand Velma and Krista. They're holding their pillows and a few blankets. "Samo," Velma says, "I don't suppose we could crash in Monty's room. Monica says he's still at the hospital. We could sleep in the lounge, but this would be a lot more comfortable. If you don't mind."

"Sure, but...why?"

• • • • •

The television has gone frothy like the one at the beginning of *Poltergeist*. It is the foam of truth that smashes illusions with its static cacophony. Lives manipulated and warped. But out the window, the parking lot, still and glowing, radiates peace, stability, and full recovery. Take a deep breath.

Monty sees the irony. That the view out his window–three-dimensional–is an illusion, as if its many depths and colors are nothing but a scant millimeter of paint spread upon a beige canvas to cover up a safe or a secret passage. Whereas the TV screen–demonstrably 2-D where it hangs upon the wall–actually hides unseen depths. Studios in other countries. Radioactivity. And something else. Something that hides behind all that static. Signals. If one could only learn how to read them.

He thinks it's a shame that others do not see this. That nobody else is present in this room to witness this perfect analogy for fact and dishonesty in the world and its systems.

Then again, he feels a prickling sensation, like eyes playing across his shoulders from behind, much as fingers might.

This is what Monty thinks as he drifts off into slumber.

• • • • •

"– and then we heard laughing!" says Velma. "Laughing! From the walls!"

"And then there was a huge wind that came from all around us," says Krista. "Like from the four corners of the room –"

"– from the walls –"

"– and just like that all the curtains we hung up fell down."

"I screamed!"

"We both screamed."

"It was pretty dark in there, but you know, with all the streetlights on South, it never gets all that dark on my side."

"It was pitch dark on my side.

And that's not all –"

"No it's not!"

"What did you see?" asks Ezzie.

"A shadow right off to my side...like a human head. And it was breathing in my face. And it had the worst–I mean, the very worst–breath I've ever smelled. It actually smelled like –"

Knocks on the door. Samo leaps off his bed and swings the door open in a single, sweeping movement. Noise crashes in from the hallway beyond. Two boys and one girl.

They invite themselves right in. One of the boys, wearing a track outfit and sunglasses in the dark, is blowing big pink bubbles and popping them against his wrist. There's also a white girl with her nose buried in her phone, and another boy who seems happily at ease, except for his slightly too-large smile.

"You're finally here!" Samo says with a grunt. "My college friends: Ezzie. Krista. Velma. Meet my high school friends: Travis. Chris. Mark." And then, "hey, where's 'Lissa?"

"What, she's not here yet?" says Travis as he enters the room.

• • • • •

Dunya breathes deep and sweats, but thanks herself for at least having had the sense to wear her single dressy outfit. It's a black skirt, black tights, black high heels, and a black blouse with tiny little white sequins and pearls worked in. Her black hair is up in a bun. She wears red makeup. She doesn't look goth, but it will have to suffice. The Anthropology Department exhales an aged odor of academic predation that she has only just begun to notice.

"So Ms. Blavatsky," says Andreas Rochet, "tell us about your time at Arkaic University so far. How do you find the college? How is the city?"

"I'm glad you wrote me," she says with loaded gratitude—gratitude loaded with qualifications, that is, though they are welcome to misconstrue it if they wish. "I wasn't even planning on going to college until I got your letter."

"It's only fair that I'm frank with you at last," says Andreas, and Dunya can hear the other lips in the room quietly blow off their conversations. She can hear the minds turning, willing ears to eavesdrop. "We didn't bring you here simply for your own benefit. We're very tidy about our Google Alerts. We read about your successes with ghosting."

Dunya nods, smiling. She has expected this much. She decides to show her own hand–her confusion–in the obvious response: "But what does that have to do with anthropology?"

"All in due time," says Andreas. "Tell me first. Why have you joined the Anthromancers?"

"The Anthromancers?"

· · · · ·

After a week of uncertainty, Velma and Krista finally feel safe among noisy basement company. Travis, Chris, and Mark are happy to be drunk on Arkaen terra firma. Even Ezzie is happy for something to distract her from the endless march of midterms and Uncle Clay's revelations. Everyone is joyous but Samo. Samo laughs too much, drinks too much, and is distracted. He's giving stupid answers. Laughing at stupid jokes. Staring at the door.

A knock on the door.

With impudent speed, Samo leaps to his feet with a grunt and pulls the door open wide. There she is, her straight black hair (*as always*), her tip-tilted nose (*as always*), and her cunning little eyes (*just like I remember*). His own eyes open wide.

"You're beautiful," he says.

· · · · ·

"The *Lovers of Man*! A deadly, evil, occult coterie, and that's just where it starts. They take the crucified effigy of Eric Wolf, and shove their door stoppers up his decomposing –"

"But Andreas," interrupts Dunya. "I didn't join the Anthromancers. This is the first I've heard of them! I joined the Anthrostrologists."

"Oh. Well, that's completely different."

And too late, Dunya realizes she would have liked to have heard more about the Anthromancers.

· · · · ·

Travis and 'Lissa are both talking at the same time.

"– not just the good stuff –" says Travis.

"– so she called you again –" says 'Lissa.

"– but the gooooood stuff."

"– but you didn't pick up."

"We're not talking Cinderella 99. We're not talking Sleeping Beauty 1001. We're talking Wolfman One Fucking Billion."

"I'm missed all of you. I really have. Southern Michigan is a good school. It's underrated. Not just like I got stuck there and so I have to find a way to be happy about it."

"One pinch of this bit and you won't feel a 'no' but heaven'll be ticklin' your toes."

"They don't have the rep, so they have to make something amazing out of nothing amazing."

"'High as a kite,' they say, but I'll teach you to fly faster than the speed of light."

"Urban gardening. Water reclamation. Blue and green and purple innovation. Downsizing cities; that is, right-sizing them."

"Past the pulsars–"

"Radical reinfranchisement–"

"Past the quasars–"

"Demographic contraposition –"

"To the edge of the universe –"

"Y'all have quite a setup here. I can see why people are excited about AU. I guess we're more humble at SMU. Just us working class kids. Poor kids. Just trying to pay our tuition. Taking out a billion loans. Because this is our future."

Samo squirms. Ezzie, Velma, and Krista are stony-faced. He can't tell if they're embarrassed, offended, or whatever the fuckall.

"It's going to blow your fucking minds!"

"But I don't know you...I'm sorry. I shouldn't assume. I've had a long day."

And 'Lissa buries her face in her hands and heaves an exhausted sigh.

"We aren't all from such privileged backgrounds, 'Lissa –" says Ezzie. Thinking of Dunya. Of Samo, too.

"I'm sure you aren't!" says 'Lissa, seriously.

"Oh, no, I am. My family is loaded. But many of us aren't. Samo isn't."

"So," says Samo. "Um..." He hesitates between fruitless(?) and fruitful(?) awkwardness and plunges ahead. "How about 'I Never?' "

Travis blazes.

· · · · ·

"Dunya Blavatsky," says Dr. Rochet. "A first-year student in the College."

Polite applause. Quiet, but not hesitant. Hands that know the appropriate soft volume and tempo for an academic event.

Dunya strides soundlessly across the plush carpet and up to the podium.

She carries two trays and Monty's laptop. She plugs it in and primes her presentation. The screen opens up. She unveils the first tray. Dirt. She puts on a pair of latex gloves, then plunges her hand into the soil. Her dirty fist emerges. She unclenches. A white seed with a black spot.

"Ghosting," she says.

"I don't know exactly *why* it's worked out, but I am pretty sure it *does* work out, because every time, I'm able to predict the actual event with complete accuracy. Obviously, you need a good specimen," holding up the pea, "and good soil, moisture, et cetera. Basically, you need everything you would need to grow a black-eyed pea in the first place. We'll call these the initial conditions.

"And now," she says, "applied ghosting."

"You plant the black-eyed pea about one index finger deep in rich soil. For the other to be formed *ex nihilo,* you'll amend the soil with what I call divine dews, a nitrogen dioxide supplement to your regular water supply. This is the still the initial phase of ghosting. It must be applied just before germination, so that the peas aren't involved in nitrogen extraction on their own. This is actually one of the hardest parts of the whole thing. Now, the ratio of nitrogen dioxide to ordinary water comes from a Teleological Ratio I've devised, modified by a Theosophical Constant. I've only fixed the Constant very approximately, in accordance with the number of vowels divided by the number of consonants in your typical Italian terza rima. The more samples we get, the more accurate we become. Then, through an argument taken from the writings of Augustine, Laozi, and Gira—I call this the law of Concyguinity—we modify the Constant down by a fixed value. Divide the absolute value of 661-673 by 13. Don't have your calculators?"

Dunya laughs nervously.

"The answer is 0.9231 repeating...approximately."

While she speaks, the PowerPoint presentation paints her story upon a screen for her silent audience. A black-eyed pea gives way to a screen full of dizzying equations. Dozens upon dozens of Σs and $\sqrt{}$s and $\int$s and ξs and $\hat{H}\Psi=\bar{E}\Psi$s and ☺s. At the bottom, the equations boil down to something almost comprehensible, if not elegant.

"I've been told that this is a Rössler attractor, but I don't really know what that means. It's what we need, however." Dunya removes her gloves..."Here's what happens when you apply the Constant with nitrogen dioxide in mixing." She presses a button to advance to the next slide.

Click!

The screen shows two atoms, side by side.

"Stannic acid," says Dunya, and she wrinkles her nose in disgust. "But we can bypass undesired reagents by aerating with a tiny bellows after germination has occurred." Dunya demonstrates, pumping with her thumb and index finger.

Click.

"Two atoms, good and evil."

Now onscreen: two men, side by side. Mannequins.

"Because aren't women always the metaphor? Well, I decided to mix it up a bit. These will stand in for the peas we're growing."

One mannequin stands with a swagger. The other has been castrated, and his eyes are gouged out. It doesn't hurt. He's just a fucking mannequin. But it plunges him ever deeper into the gloomy bowels of the uncanny valley. Dunya is judgmental over him.

"I should have foreseen the problem I will shortly demonstrate. You see, these formulae, and even the methodology here, are inescapably an articulated Manichean manifold. The natural cosmic equivalent is matter and antimatter, and we know how those two feel about each other."

Click. Now: a somber eyeball bedewed with a milky crust. Now: umbrellas with tentacles instead of handles. Now: wretched, wretched worms. Now: a belly button swearing like a sailor through its yellowed, crumbling teeth.

"It's an ugly business."

Click. Now: pinwheels spinning. No, wait, those aren't pinwheels. It's the perichoresis of ifs, ands, and buts, each oozing a brown organic pus from its beautiful wounds.

"Every man is either a saint or a gigolo."

• • • • •

    The pipe passes around the room. Everyone descends into their various moods. Samo wishes he had brought along his blacklight posters and blacklight. Someone has put an empty beer bottle into the middle of the room. Someone spins that bottle.

    "Oh boy, here we go," says Samo.

• • • • •

Someone watching.

    Monty opens his eyes. A cloaked and hooded figure stands over him. Its face is empty.

    "What, is this, the Renaissance Fair?" he asks.

    But there's something familiar about the figure. It's wearing a shinobi shōzoku.

    "You!" says Monty.

    The figure holds out a slip of paper. Monty takes it and reads.

You have done well.

    "Um, thanks."

    It holds out another piece of paper.

We particularly admired your clever escape from the Inquiscriptors. It seemed like they had won, but with your friend's mishap, you seized the moment and made a most dramatic impression.

"Thank you. Although I would rather have avoided getting beaten up altogether. Now I'm stuck in the hospital with a bunch of infectious diseases I've never heard of before."

Ah yes. About that. Does that seem quite credible to you?

"It does seem kind of strange. I've never heard of someone being kept in a hospital for so long over such minor injuries."

Do you think that is what has happened to you?

"I'm getting suspicious." Monty sighs. "Do you think that someone is keeping me in the hospital so that I don't figure out some of the strange things happening at the university?"

BINGO!

• • • • •

Krista Baroque is doing her famous impression of Richard Nixon. Travis laughs, too much, at this. It's funny. It's not *that* funny. 'Lissa seems distracted, however, and looks out of Monty's window, into the courtyard.

"You okay?" asks Ezzie.

"Huh?!" says Samo, too loud. "Yeah, I'm fine. Why wouldn't I be?"

"Shouldn't we close those curtains?" asks 'Lissa.

• • • • •

"It's almost erotic, when you watch it finally happen," says Dunya.

She has turned off the PowerPoint and uncovered the second tray. The stalk of the black-eyed pea has doubled and divided, inexplicably, except explicably, because Dunya had just proved the entire process by which the whole thing happened, though she had been unable to distill the elemental elements of the process. Such things are hidden from the mind of man.

But also as predicted, the Manichean tragedy of the whole experiment plays out. The white-eyed black pea has fixed his hungry eye upon his sister and has curled his stalky leaves around her, throttling the juices out of her capillaries. Her leaves are brown and wilting. She dies. They both die.

"A saint," says Dunya. The black-eyed pea. "A gigolo," says Dunya. The white-eyed pea.

"Anthromancy," whispers someone out in the crowd.

• • • • •

Not just you. Your friends. You have come too close to uncovering secrets that powerful people wish to keep hidden.

"Who?"

Powerful ones. We dare not write their names,
lest they obtain power over us.

"Really?" Monty puts on his most skeptical face. "I thought that was the other way around."

Names are complex and unpredictable.
Haven't you ever heard of a Rössler attractor?

Monty shakes his head, but the Book Ninja gives him another piece of paper. He opens it eagerly:

Ordinarily, in the course of things, we would initiate you now, but there are more pressing matters in this instant. One of your friends is about to embark on a very dangerous adventure. We will help you escape from the hospital, but you must intervene. Then we will turn to more routine matters. You cannot go on indefinitely in our service or benefit from our aid without having been initiated into the higher degrees.

"I understand," says Monty. "How am I going to escape?"

There is a drawer of sanitary napkins near the commode. They have adhesive properties when wet. If you fashion a rope from these, you can escape through the window. We will ensure that you are unmolested as you exit the hospital.

• • • • •

Several hours into the party, and the room has changed considerably. The air is heavy with the pungent stink of pot and patchouli and the wetter stench of spilled beer and malt liquor. The students sit slowly in a dazed and naked circle. Platonic ease whatever, Samo is happy to be surrounded by four sets of happy breasts. Ezzie's timid little radio dials. Velma's broad, pink pillows, with their razor-sharp laser sights. Chris' prim twins, placidly staring off in different directions. And 'Lissa's bare breasts. Samo cannot bring himself to look at them. They're there, he knows, in the periphery, but he remembers wondering about them in ninth grade, and not knowing. He feels fifteen again and looks away.

For the most part, the girls seem ambivalent to the three naked men, although a surprised shout went up when they all discovered that Travis wore a friendly uncircumcised sleeve. And while Samo carefully avoids looking here, too, he cannot fail to notice that he's longer and thicker and balder and bolder than either Travis or Mark. Poor Mark who, if anything, might have come to the party after swimming in the snow. It's a good news morning, meaning that if it's good news for anyone, it's good news for Samo.

The bottle and the joint had ruled the night, and determined that Krista, alone, would keep her clothes, and Chris her panties. Meanwhile, Samo was made to do jumping jacks, and while everyone laughed at first, his heart bloomed like rose blossoms when the room fell silent save for the sound of his dick slapping his belly twice for each jump, jump, jump. And then someone dared Velma to bring out a straight razor and scrape off her lazy landing strip, but the whole thing just seemed too awkward, so they called that one off. The game wound down after that, with the half-guilty but sleepily elated lethargy of people who have seen each other naked. Except for poor, sulking Krista.

Samo doesn't know what this *means*. Certainly, this is the kind of occasion he has hoped and prayed for every night since he graduated high school, and even before. It's a world beyond the electrical currents that ran through his skin when Candace Bhatt sat on his lap on the bus just over a month ago. *Only a month ago!* But there are strange things happening, too. His high school life has collided with his college life. And nakedness–a feast for the eyes–is great, but...it isn't nearly the apotheosis of the flesh he has hoped to script for the last several months. Not that his audacity knows no bounds, but a bit of boldness, a bit of hope, may be called for to carry him further into the realm of grown-up opportunities.

"Dare me to do something!" he says.

It is a loud sound against the drowsy silence.

Ezzie blinks her eyes, sleepily, registering the words that have come through the fog.

"What's that?" 'Lissa asks.

"Dare me to do something," he repeats, carefully avoiding those dark chocolate nipples on that milk chocolate chest. "I–I mean—I want to do something. Something to make tonight even more memorable than it already is. Tell me what to do."

And he waits, but not patiently, for them to answer.

· · · · ·

The polite applause is equal in volume and duration to that which brought her to the podium, but she's sensitive enough to recognize that a subtle change has come over her audience. The warmth has been bleached from their faces. Repressed repugnance has replaced restrained adulation. The anthropologists don't want to touch her. Don't want to look at her. They see something vile and decadent and thoroughly unclean in Dunya Blavatsky. Their steely eyes tell her this. They don't seem interested in hanging around to discuss her research any longer.

It's their reaction to the evil pea. It is an abomination. I had the same reaction the first time I saw it.

But as she excuses herself from the room, putting on her coat for the walk across campus and the Fairway, she can't help but wonder if it's her they're repulsed by. As if, in demonstrating a literal Manichean inversion, the evil twin, the evil mirror image, she had become inverted herself.

I sure hope not! she thinks. *They asked me to come here when they liked me. Maybe now they'll ask me to leave.*

She steps out into the angry, billowing night.

· · · · ·

Touchdown. Monty looks up at the string of pads swaying gently in the breeze. Suddenly, it whips out of his grip with ferocious speed. Monty can't see the clouds in the dark, but the lack of stars and the roar of wind warms him that a storm is coming on. Worried that someone will have seen his escape, he hurries off down the block.

Proctor Hill is one of Arkaic's many notorious neighborhoods, although it has been less so since most of the houses burnt down and emptied out. Now, with just one or two houses standing on each block, the city has turned off the streetlights, and Monty can't even see the naked oak branches rattling in the howling wind. He is seen, of course. Young, slight, fragile-looking. He'd make an easy target for any urban predator. But the few predators watching know that there's no room for a wallet or keys under that hospital gown. And if this kid is crazy enough to run around at night in a storm wearing nothing but that, who knows what else he'll do? In fact, there are few predators. Instead, everyone curls up in their dark unheated piles, just trying to stay warm, listening to the roar overhead.

• • • • •

At night, the Fairway is one of the darkest, widest, wildest places on campus. It stretches, like a vast river of grass, between North Campus and the Quints, and turns as dark as pitch once the xenon lamps have powered down for the night. Some of the students walk out of their way to follow South Street, with its ugly yellow lights, but Dunya isn't squeamish about a night walk. She strides right down the middle of the Fairway, or on the other side, even, where the thick boughs of the Hunting Grounds frown out at her.

As she walks, she thinks about the fundamental problem with ghosting. It is as seemingly intractable as the impossibility of spontaneous generation in the first place. *But spontaneous generation is possible!* she thinks. *I figured it out. And if I figured that out, then maybe I'll figure out the answer to Manichean manifolds.* In her mind's eye, she sees horrible things: children starving to death. But given ghosting, they might live. At what cost? She imagines a combine rolling out over a field of the peas, and they bleed with the harvest. Their bright white blood drips down like nucleic sludge and crusts the soil. It becomes a parasite of the earth. An abomination. A hateful thing.

"Dunya Blavatsky?" says a familiar voice behind her.

She whips around, but can't see a thing for all the darkness. Above. Below. It's everywhere. She's been swallowed by the night.

Room 227

Anxiety makes for poor studying.
So does Mickey's Fine Malt Liquor.

Samo stands fully dressed beneath the flickering fluorescent of the fifth floor hallway. In one hand, he holds his calculus textbook. In the other, a forty of Mickeys. Beneath him, Acedia House is silent. Behind him, nobody stirs in the Mavens' apartment. He is completely alone. Samo reaches out and places his palm upon the cool wood. It's as if a current passes down his arms and body and legs and vanishes into the floor. He shakes his head, smiling at himself. "Spend the night in the Fifth Floor Double, and figure out whatever the *fuck* is going on in there!" Krista had said, but it was 'Lissa who watched him with a strange intensity playing across her face. As if her teeth were unconsciously clenched. As if she were consciously avoiding blinking. It wasn't the dare he had expected– what *had* he expected?–but it was exactly what he had wanted. A chance to break through. Not to prove that he's better than the others here, but that he can stand tall and proud. That he can accomplish something all on his own. That the compromises of his past are not going to determine his future.

Samo turns the knob and opens the door. The room beyond is dark, but Samo steps inside without hesitation and closes the door behind him. He waits a long, long time with his eyes shut, waiting for them to adjust. It's part of his plan, and the results comfort him. When he opens his eyes, he doesn't see a glow of any sort coming from the molding near the ceiling. There's no light at all, in fact, except for a feeble trickle that creeps in under the door to the hall.

Breathing a sigh of relief, Samo crosses to the inner room and turns on the overhead light, then, finding it too garish, trades it for a lamp beside Krista's bed. A soft, orange glow spills out over the room while leaving the deeper shadows undisturbed.

For a long moment, Samo peers into the shadows of the room, then makes a show of yawning, then lies down on Krista's bed, the covers tumbled just as when she had taken flight with Velma. But it isn't comfortable–too hard (most of the Cradle's beds are too soft)–and anyway, Samo is distracted by the stillness and the piles of curtains lying on the floors. Velma said that they had fallen down, all at once, and all on their own. Samo sits. He taps his feet. He grunts and walks around the suite, gathering the sheets in his arms and dumping them in a pile. Then, annoyed by the obnoxious stillness of the air–aren't those cracks in the molding supposed to *ventilate* this room?–Samo crosses to the south-facing window and pushes it open.

It doesn't last long. A spitting wind darts in, rips a stack of papers from Velma's desk, and throws them across the floor. Samo slams the window shut. Through the stillness, now, he can hear the faint sound of thunder.

He returns to Krista's inner room, closing the door behind him, and takes out his pocket flashlight. For many minutes he stands on each piece of furniture–headboard, desk, chairs, radiators–and peers into the black slats of the molding. He can almost smell the mothballs in the attic beyond, but there's nothing to see. No light. Only dark.

Climbing down, he spends a few minutes playing with the knick-knacks and oddities on Krista's desk and dresser: Pez dispensers, Detroit Tigers bobbleheads, scratched-off lottery tickets, and tiny animal skulls. *Maybe they are imagining things*, he thinks. He cracks his knuckles. He stretches his arms out behind him. He pulls the desk chair out and sets it near the table lamp. He sits down, props his feet up on the bed, and opens his calculus book. By Sylvanus P. Thompson. Another name worthy of nicking.

"Considering how many fools can calculate, it is surprising that it should be thought either a difficult or a tedious task for any other fool to learn how to master the same tricks."

Flipping ahead:

"In the first place, any function of x, such, for example as x^2, or $\sqrt{x}$, or $ax+b$, can be plotted as a curve; and nowadays every schoolboy is familiar with the process of curve-plotting."

As Samo becomes absorbed in hard, cold numbers and emotionless reason, Krista and Velma's fears seem more and more absurd. Of *course* they imagined it. Even now, when he is attentive, Samo can hear the distant sound of doors slamming in the house, footsteps between rooms and bathrooms, and even the occasional bit of talking. He even hears the silence broken outside the dorm by the groan of the wind and the tip-top-tap of rain against the glass. The storm has begun. It comforts him. It almost relieves the heat of stillness steeping inside the room.

Anyway, Samo hadn't been in the room during the fire a week ago–he trusted his friends that there *had* been a fire–but he has an overactive imagination himself sometimes. Besides, Housing's explanation of a short in the walls explains the light, the fire, and the nightly alarms. It's not only plausible, but likely, given the many changes made to the old building in the last few years. Samo pauses a moment.

It's several hours past midnight, and there hasn't been a fire alarm.

"Huh," he says.

Maybe they're going to spare us tonight, he thinks, and then: *Who is "they?"*

Samo doesn't have a problem set due on Monday. He just needs to read the next section on transcendental functions and review the proofs. He cracks open his forty, takes a swig, swallows the bittersweet liquid, and fixes his mind upon the formulae.

$$f_1(x) = x^x = {}^2x$$

It strikes him as elegant and beautiful. Simple and complex. Easy to see and difficult to understand. Difficult, but possible. In fact, all of his calculus has seemed possible ever since Monty helped him with the delta-epsilon proof. *Maybe I'll pull this off after all. Sam O'Samuel, the rocket scientist. Sam O'Samuel, astrophysicist and astronaut.* He sighs. Takes another swig. *When is Monty getting back, anyway? That's whack for them to keep him so long, just for observation. What is it he's got that they're keeping him there, anyway?* He takes another swig. Many more swigs.

$$f_1(x) = x^y{}_0(ma)_2$$

His head starts to swim a little; he's already lost track of how much he had to drink at the party, and a forty of Mickey's can pack a kick. He takes a look at the pee-colored liquid, filtered green through the moss-colored glass. The bottle is half empty. "Damn," he says aloud, "I drank that fast!" He ratchets his attention back to the page. He opens his eyes wider, as if that's going to improve his mental acuity, but those lovely, elegant symbols are going all fuzzy and drifting together.

$$f_1(x) = x^{wtf}$$

I'm not getting much accomplished here, am I? he wonders. *Oh well, I'm studying on a Friday night. That's an A for effort, right?* The symbols answer by drifting even closer together and fading out into darkness as Samo's eyes drift shut.

$$f_1(x) = z^{zzzzzzz}$$

Outside room 227, Acedia House falls ever deeper into slumber.

Outside Acedia House, the storm rages on.

· · · · ·

Samo has a strange dream. It's strikingly simple, but nevertheless different from any dream he has ever had before. He sees the room he is in, from an angle above his own body. He's looking down on himself and watching himself sleep. Samo sees the wind-lashed rain streaking the windows. The buzzing glow of the table lamp. The rise and fall of his own chest. But someone else is there, and then his point of view returns to his own. He is looking out, it seems, through his own closed eyes. A shadowy form is at the foot of Krista's bed. Peeking out furtively, but not carefully enough to avoid being seen. It notices this, flinches, and draws back. It hides until Samo has almost forgotten that anything was there at all. And then the thing peeks again.

Samo and the shadow dance this dance a dozen or more times—he really doesn't know how many—until his heart starts to flutter with uncertainty. He lurches awake with a gasp. He blinks his eyes in shock. It must be near dawn by now. He feels as if he's been in here for hours. Days, even. And yes, it must be late, or early, rather, because all sounds of footsteps and doors and voices have vanished from the dorm. But the dark is still unending outside, and the storm has shown no signs of stopping.

With a clarity and concentration he was unable to muster for his calculus homework, Samo fixes his eyes onto the spot at the base of Krista's bed, looking for a shape or shadow. Minutes crawl by, but he doesn't see a thing. Then, still a little uncertain, he leans even further forward and looks into the shadowy corners of the room, and especially into the black attic slats. Again, nothing. He heaves a weary sigh and leans back in the chair. That's when Samo feels the subtle shiver of presence at his right shoulder.

He turns his head to the right, toward the bed, and six inches away floats a decomposing, tottering-rottering skull with stony, ochered flakes clinging to its face. The eyes and nostrils are packed with dirt, a thick loam, clay even, wet and dense, and the teeth are too huge, too yellow, loose in the jaws, bending out, even splitting, in an expression of the most anguished apathy. That's when the stench hits. That wide mouth and its snagglysplit teeth are curled around a glistening tube of human shit, and the fetters drop off the thing and hit the floor and stain the bed sheet. The sight is so shocking, the smell so ghastly, such a mixture of blood and phlegm and sewage and waste, that Samo falls back out of the chair and hits his head on the floor.

CHAPTER NINE
ABSENCE MAKES THE HEART GO PONDER

Anthroway Icksday

In college you will learn to critically examine even "noble" inclinations.

As one late hour becomes the next, the storm rolls itself like a flopping lump of dumpling dough. Chill ice on the inside, now the outside, arrows down toward the earth. In the morning, it will take the students off guard. They have been engrossed in studies and stridulae and have no time for weather reports. They don't expect Friday's high of sixty to be followed by a Saturday high in the upper twenties.

But not Monty Valverde. He feels the change raw against his skin. It's only a couple hours from dawn when a little old lady in a '65 Dodge Coronet (D-500) drops him off on the Quints. His hospital gown lies sloppy and wet against his skin, and his toes feel as though they're attached to his numb feet with toothpicks.

"Maybe next time you want to carry a map?" she says. "But I'll give you a ride any day." And away she goes, at many thousands of rpm.

Gutter floods light sharp sleet. Monty lifts his heavy head. Still. Is what it ought to be. But now Monty sees, oh so dimly, a stir of activity along the eastern fringe of the Hunting Grounds. A faint ribbon of glowing light. He sets off toward it, but angles to the north so that he's also moving toward the entrance to Calliope Cradle. As he gets closer, he realizes that the ribbon of light is actually made up of many individual flares. Dozens of them. Monty gets closer still— just a couple hundred feet away—and sees that the lights are torches carried by many men and women, all fifty years old and older. And they're not just carrying torches; many of them have pitchforks and scythes. They start to veer away from the Hunting Grounds, toward Monty, and he realizes that they're marching on the Cradle. *What the–doesn't matter–don't get cut off.*

Monty clenches his teeth against the pain in his side and half-jogs to the stone dormitory. He makes it the last several hundred slippery feet to the dorm and doesn't stop until he's standing behind the raised iron portcullis. Monty peers back out into the gloom. The torches come into focus. Then the mob is silhouetted by a flash of lightning. Hundreds of furious, seething old men and women. It starts to snow. Thunder crashes. Monty turns and enters the vestibule.

He goes through the gate, up the stairs, and down the halls of Vainglory House to an imposing cherry wood door with "DR. ENDOLYNN LAWLESS" etched in gold lettering on the nameplate. Monty bangs on the door, and after a moment, it opens. Dr. Lawless stands there, placidly, as if she has been expecting a soaking first-year in a hospital gown to fall on her doorstep at four in the morning.

"Oh, you're dripping all over!" she snaps. "What is it?"

"Angry...pitchforks...torches..." gasps Monty. "What do they want?"

"Christ," she mutters angrily to herself (though not in answer to Monty's question), steps out into the hall, and closes the door behind her.

$\bullet \bullet \bullet \bullet \bullet$

The mob has closed to within a few dozen feet of Calliope Cradle when Dr. Lawless emerges from the vestibule with Monty shivering at her side. Her expression is firm, unyielding, and unsurprised. Her lips are mathematical in their zero-slope horizontality. It's the first time Monty has really ever noticed her appearance; she certainly hasn't been gifted with imposing genes. She's tall and pale, with straight gray hair and large, thick bifocals. Everything about her suggests long nights reading and daylight hours spent poring through windowless library stacks. When the crowd sees her, they begin banging their axes and scythes and pitchforks together in feral rage.

"Really?" asks Dr. Lawless, in a deadly voice. "This is exceptionally unprofessional."

There's murmuring from the horde. Someone, their spokesperson, takes several steps forward.

"Dr. Lawless?" he says.

"Dr. Rochet." Her icy voice chills the storm. Andreas Rochet flinches. He rallies his nerves and soldiers on.

"We demand the surrender of first-year student Dunya Blavatsky to the esteemed tribunal of the Anthrostrologers and the Arkaic University Department of Anthropology. This is not a trifling matter of tampering with seminal cultural relics or fraternizing with the cargo cultists. She has been charged with First-Degree Anthromancy."

The crowd behind Andreas thunders in affirming rage.

"I see. With regard to her pole-bean experiment?"

Andreas is flummoxed by Dr. Lawless' evident inside information. "That...is the business of the tribunal!"

"Well I hope it is not, because I do not understand the she has actually performed any acts for the clear benefit of humankind, or has expressed the intention to do so. You had better be able to prove that she has or it will obviously be *cogitationis poenam nemo patitur* from her defense, and you will have wasted all those torches and pitchforks."

"We know our business on that front, Dr. Lawless, as you are well aware."

"So you *do* intend to dispense with her defense?"

"It is our departmental practice, as you well know."

"And did not your department specifically request Dunya's attendance on the strength of her discovery of ghosting?"

Andreas leans to his right and whispers something to a woman at his side, presumably about identifying and murdering the leak among the anthropologists. He returns his attention to Dr. Lawless, saying:

"It's *ad quod damnum vis a vis* damage potentialities for homo sapiens."

"It's *non est factum vis a vis* her admission to this institution, contingent on the university's approval of her high school record specifically."

"*Res ipsa loquitur. Salus populi suprema lex esto.*"

The crowd gives an approving roar.

"*Vigilantibus non dormientibus aequitas subvenit,*" says Dr. Lawless.

The crowd is cowed.

"*Somnium, somnium,*" Andreas stammers.

"Ouyay areway anway assway," Dr. Lawless says.

The strength of her conviction manifests as a chilly wind against Andreas' chest, lifting him from the earth and tossing him like a pigskin into front line of the mob. They, of course, don't want to catch him, and so he crashes into the sleety grass.

He staggers to his feet. "Nevertheless," he says, "you will surrender Dunya Blavatsky at once."

"I won't," Dr. Lawless says.

"I have the writ here." He holds up a scrap of muddy paper.

"Is it stamped by the provost, as protocol demands?"

Andreas bites his lip. "That's just a formality!"

"It's a necessary formality. I shouldn't wonder that its procurement earns you a reprimand for jeopardizing our accreditation with a clown show such as this."

The crowd gnashes its teeth, swearing and stamping their feet.

"Good night to you all," says Dr. Lawless, as she turns her back on the horde and returns to the Cradle. The mob bristles, and then, to Monty's surprise, their shoulders slump in defeat. They turn their backs and let their pitchforks drag along the damp grass as they slowly make their way back toward the Hunting Grounds.

Monty catches Dr. Lawless right at the door to her apartment.

"What was that all about?" he asks.

Her answer is weary. "The one thing that the lumpers and splitters hate more than each other is an altruist."

She closes the door behind her.

M.I.A.

Knock before entering.

Monty runs down to the basement of Acedia House and flings open the door to his suite –

"Samo, we've got to find Dunya, because the, ahhh!"

No Samo. Instead, he sees a naked boy he does not know sprawled asleep across the floor, plus various other boys and girls sleeping, wearing a motley collection of towels, bathrobes, pajamas, and T-shirts.

"Velma? Krista? Ezzie? What?"

They dazedly wake and sit up.

"Um..." says Krista, running her hands through her hair.

"Where's Samo?"

"Don't worry," Krista says, "he's in the Fifth Floor Double."

"Wait, why aren't you in the Fifth Floor Double?"

"That's a funny thi–"

"Wait, Ezzie, where's Dunya? I have to talk to her now!"

"Oh, I don't know. She went out to some reception with the Anthropology Department, but she should be back by now. What time is it, anyway?"

Monty has already left. As he crosses the hall, he overhears Velma's voice. "Isn't he supposed to be at the hospital? And where are his clothes?"

"You're one to talk, Velma..."

Monty bangs noisily on Dunya's door.

No answer. Silence, in fact. He sighs and turns the knob. The door is unlocked. The room beyond is blank and empty. He turns on the light. Dunya's bedroom is the same cluttered mess as always, but the air seems still and undisturbed. He doesn't *feel* the presence of anyone in the room. Just to be safe, he checks under the bed and in the closet, and then beyond, in Ezzie's room. *Who knows?* he thinks. *Maybe she heard them coming. Maybe she's hiding.* Still, he feels awkward calling out for her like a parent after a wayward toddler. "Dunya? You here, Dunya?"

"Monty, what's going on?" It's Ezzie. She's standing alone in the doorway. Monty looks out into the hall, past her, but everyone else is still in Samo's room.

"Close the door," he says.

She does.

Monty hurriedly tells her about his escape from the hospital, omitting the Book Ninjas (of course). It troubles him, not mentioning it...but you can't un-tell someone something. He doesn't want to get drawn into a discussion of his bizarre relationship with the SO or give away more about his run in with the Inquiscriptors. *Caution, caution,* he thinks.

"So you broke out of the hospital, Monty?" Ezzie says, her brow furrowed. "I don't think they can keep you there if you want to leave."

"I wasn't a patient, Ezzie. I was their prisoner." Again, he's on the edge of uncharted territory. "Never mind –"

And then he tells her what he saw—what anyone who had lingered on the Fairway that dark and stormy night would have seen—the march of the anthropologists, and their demand of Dunya Blavatsky.

"Shit," Ezzie says. "That does sound serious."

"There were a few hundred of them. I don't know what they would've done if Dr. Lawless hadn't stood up to them. They looked like they were ready to tear the Cradle apart, stone by stone, if it would help them catch Dunya."

"So what now?"

"We need to find Dunya. And I think...I think..." He *wants* to know what Ezzie has discovered about Professor Plumb and the shattering glass–*God, that feels like months ago now!*–and what Dunya knows about the anthropologists. But to find out, he knows he'll probably have to divulge his own secrets. *I need to buy time, but I need to move forward.* "Let's go get Samo."

• • • • •

Standing outside the knuckle-scarred door to room 227, Monty and Ezzie are startled by the perfect silence. But they have taken courage from the gently graying light of dawn trickling in through the windows in the stairway. Inside, it will no longer be completely dark.

Monty knocks softly, waits a moment, then knocks loudly.

"Samo's a pretty heavy sleeper," he tells Ezzie.

But there's no answer.

"A *really* heavy sleeper," he says under his breath, as he reaches out and opens the door.

The stale air floats out of the dim room beyond, and while the gray of dawn has begun to drift in through the un-curtained windows, it is still very dreary outside. The storm has (finally) collapsed into icy stillness, but the hungry clouds still hang like webs over the campus. In the room itself, Velma's furniture and bed are indistinct, almost humanlike in shape, and nothing whispers or breathes.

"I can see why Velma and Krista wanted to come downstairs," Ezzie says, to break the silence, but even this low muttering seems to intrude, and she finishes the statement under her breath.

"Right," says Monty. "Well, he probably slept in Krista's room. It's got the better view, hasn't it?"

Ezzie shrugs.

With a sudden movement, not willing to trust their resolve for too long, they hurry across the space and open the door to the inner room.

The stillness and darkness within Krista's room is even more oppressive than in Velma's, and they stop again, cowed, at the edge. Curtains or none, there's next to no light coming in through the north-facing windows here. Monty feels bile rising in his mouth.

"Oh, Samo," gags Ezzie. "What have you been eating?!"

Monty wonders the same thing. The stench is some horrid mixture of excrement and death. Everyone knows about the gastrointestinal chaos that the dining commons inflict upon the helpless students, but this is worse than anything he's ever smelled in his life.

Assuming that Samo's lying on the bed, Monty starts across the room, only to stumble over something on the floor. He falls with a scream and a crash. The spell of silence broken, Ezzie reaches out and turns on the overhead light. Monty rolls onto his back and sees that he has tripped over Krista's bedside chair, which has been toppled, along with the bedside lamp. Monty's hands just miss the broken light bulb.

Monty gets to his feet and looks all around him, still squinting from the ugly smell. Then he sees something else, glassy and shiny, but unbroken, at his feet. He reaches down and picks up the overturned forty. Most of the remaining liquor has spilled onto the concrete flooring, and it says something that he can't even detect its powerful odor above the foul stench of shit and decay.

"Where is he?" croaks Monty.

Ezzie shakes her head, frowning.

"Let's get out of here," Monty says.

• • • • •

Back in the fifth floor hallway, with the door to the Double shut behind him, Ezzie and Monty each take a deep, clean breath.

"Um," Monty says. "I'm going to need a bit of time to think about everything that —"

"Me too," says Ezzie.

They stare awkwardly at their feet.

"Um," Monty begins again, "do you think you could get all those nakedish people out of my bedroom?"

"Sure," says Ezzie. "You might want to put on some real clothes yourself."

The Sensible Conspiracy Theorist

Signal trust through speech...

Tired as he is, Monty decides to take a shower before returning to his room. To warm his fingers and toes. To wash the stink away. While the hot water soothes him, the dull bruises and sharp pains along his sides remind him that he broke his ribs, climbed down a five-story rope of sanitary napkins, ranged through an icy Arkaen night, and outran a mob of angry anthropologists. Still, it feels good to get out of all the dirt and grime and to slip into his smooth, silk pyjamies.

On his back, in his own bed for the first time in a week, Monty feels clarity return to his brain again. Clarity about the comfort of being home. Not clarity about the deep secrets that surround him. Goodness, no. *Christ, I already know about a conspiracy to extort ridiculous money from students for textbooks, and a covered-up faculty disappearance that resulted in exploding windows. Which has also involved one of my best friends here. And that someone wanted to keep me in the hospital, for whatever reason. And that the Book Ninjas wanted me out. That those anthropologists wanted to abduct Dunya...and Dr. Lawless very much didn't want them to. Dunya's missing. Samo's missing. It's too much.* Monty's wish to witness secrets had been fulfilled. But he never expected it to be fulfilled so quickly or thoroughly. His thoughts are more tangled and confused than ever.

And yet, such confusions turn him toward another clarity. A clarity of perspective. His SOs, his own scholarship, and his good luck have not been enough to solve any problems. His own mental resources are insufficient. *There's something I need to do to make progress. Something I haven't done. What haven't I done? I've done everything. I've looked everywhere.* There's got to be something else. Something more.

As a conspiracy theorist, Monty knows that he's noticed things that others have not: a disordered section of a bookshelf, a missing page from a ledger book, or a sullen Russian with wretchedly mutilated genitalia. He has a high opinion of his own ability to notice.

But as an unusually self-aware conspiracy theorist, Monty knows that he, too, is a victim of human nature. He is not immune to bland self-interest or the casual addiction to habit that blinds the public at large. So when the sun rises in earnest and filters through his curtain in a wholesome brown glow, and Monty sees and feels with clarity, this thought comes: *As a conspiracist, what are my liabilities? What is my bias? What tools am I ignoring?*

Having asked these questions with courage, the answer is now obvious: *Trust. Implicit trust. Complete trust. Complete vulnerability. I don't like it. But that's the only way that I'm going to get answers.*

Monty knows exactly what he needs to do. He needs to trust. But he doesn't trust his resolve to do so, so he pulls his laptop onto his bed and taps out a quick email to Ezzie:

"We're in trouble. Samo and Dunya are missing, and a lot of strange things are happening. Meet me at the oak tree later, when I'm up?"

Monty sets the laptop down and is about to close his eyes, but a chime tells him that Ezzie has already replied. He reads her message:

"Okay. :)"

Not Quite the Bodhi Tree

...and listen to learn.

Monty expected to sleep through most of the day on Saturday but is nevertheless surprised to find that it is fully night again when he wakes. He climbs out of bed and puts on a pair of jeans and a polo shirt. *First quarter of college, take two. Might as well get a fresh start.*

Outside, he finds Ezzie sitting on the ground with her back to the oak tree. She waves. Monty pulls his coat tight against the cold, crosses to the tree, and sits down. Ezzie holds a heavy Thermos between gloved hands.

"Sorry I've been asleep so long," Monty says. "Have you been waiting a long time?"

"I wanted to get outside," Ezzie says.

"What are you drinking? Is it alcohol?"

Ezzie winces. "I felt more like tea. Especially after last night."

"That's right. You aren't Samo." He smiles, worried. "Any sight of him?"

"Nope. Or Dunya. Nobody knows where they are."

"Mind if I have a sip?"

She hands over the Thermos. Monty takes a drink.

"Ezzie, I think —"

"Let me say something first, Monty. Okay? I knew this was a strange place as soon as I got here...in fact, before I ever got here. But I didn't expect it to be as strange as this. I mean, I've seen a *lot* of strange things since I got here. My headmaster really pulled some strings for me to get in. Then I started breaking glasses when I looked at them. Prof. Plumb put an end to that by suggesting I wear sunglasses." She taps them. "It works. But then you also found out that weird thing about someone shattering windows all over campus during an initiation. And there's more than that, even. Weird suicide woods on campus. Strange things turning up at TOG. Even my own personal life is weird and fucked up. So before you say what you're going to say, I just wanted to tell you that I think we should come clean with each other and try to figure out this stuff together. I'm ready to tell you everything."

Monty nods his head, slightly.

"Wow," he says. "That's pretty much exactly what I was going to suggest, myself–"

Then the oak tree explodes.

CHAPTER TEN
ELISION

A Fate Worse Than Death

If you can reserve your confessions for people instead of machines,
so much the better.

This soul. This human. This man is not a weak-willed or dull creature. But for all such essence, he is near the source. And the source speaks. It speaks like a metronome. Loudly. Like a loud metronome. Some metronomes say *click click click click click click click*. Some say *tick tick tick tick tick tick tick*. And some say *dock dock dock dock dock dock dock*. But ships dock at harbors. Harbors require sufficiently deep water. They also require a shore. Here there is deep water, but no shore. Only endless depth. And so when the man opens his eyes, all he sees is the complete absence of light. All he hears is the utter presence of sounds. Of *clicks*, and *ticks*, and *docks*.

Let us see what he sees.

An unknown city flows out beneath him. Beneath his fingers and toes lie the lights. But this is not a wealthy city, nor a happy city. This is a confused city, sad at its lack of sentient vastness, and there are many empty spaces where houses have been condemned, burned down, or demolished. The man stands on a major street downtown, and here there are cars and lights. An extraordinary building, topped with a pyramid, lighting out, lighting down. He walks with friends. He has friends. New friends. People he hasn't known long but with whom he has already trusted many secrets. It isn't that they have done anything to earn his trust yet. It is his discovery that trust is not something to be begrudged. That he should be free and easy with his secrets. With himself. So he shares them on a long walk through sharp September puddles, and the wind steals his words and hurls them out into the world. Very well. The world will have them. He doesn't mind. He's willing to share himself. There is plenty of him to go around.

And then, focus is lost.

The lights blur bright, then dim.

The *click*, the *tick*, the *dock*.

Where is he?

He is here. A light *phlashes.* A photo strobe. A foto phlash. Splash! His shoes are soaked. His mother is chiding him. He's forgotten something. She's annoyed that he forgot. But there's a line of cat gut running from the back of her throat to her front teeth. That's what he thinks of in the little vibrations of her words...like a thin line trembling...like a fishing line. She loves him and worries for him. It makes her voice tremble like a line. A fish hook. Her anxiety for him causes her pain. She loves him! Ah, wonder. As he walks the street with his friends, his face is clouded, unknown, unrecognizeable, so he must make do with his own silhouette, a somber thing, smooth on earth but shaggy in the soul. It is cold, so he sits with his knees clasped to his chest, a little boy, and rests his eyes, and worries. And his mother worries for him, again, again, and his mother worries for him. Anyone can see him now, on the main street of this sad, dying town, sitting like a bum on a bench with his head on his knees. They will think he is drunk, but he is only tired, and his heart is full, full of the love from his friends, and full of the worry of his mother.

He blows on his hands in the outside air.

Tries to warm.

The lights blur. Why won't they stay in focus? What is that scent? Sharp? Ozone? Why can't he focus? He's in a neighborhood. A lonely place where he went to get something cheap, something he would have had to spend money on earlier. The world, his life, is full of promise and potential, but he measures it out in apprehensive fistfuls of grain and chaff. All worries, weighted by his own anxiety, balanced by giddy-tinged anticipation–has he fallen asleep?–the ballast of his mother's worry, those beads, those beams, those heavy things relieved by her love for him. The glow of her heart makes heavy things buoyant, like bubbles, and so their fears float, and the *clicking, ticking, docking* machines hear this, and it fills them with hunger.

Again, they splash a flash across the space, and in it, his beautiful boy's face comes into focus–into itself–for a moment. He almost remembers his name and sees a perfectly perfect metallic smooth wall with perfect machines and their perfect baby chains, all in spirals, snaking around him, tracing lightning from their locks to their lips.

I love you, he thinks about fleshly creatures. *I like people*, and his smile is so bright, so full of the world–young children and adolescents are not so full of the world as this–they don't know what they see–and adults and old men and women are jaded by all they have seen–all they have learned–because at a certain point the learning–the realizing–the losing–teaches you reluctance–bitterness– sighs and remove–you cannot ever connect–you have to let go–it is unavoidable–always–and for all–this–this–this–*click–tick–dock– Click–Tick–Dock–No!–They have already taken my name, and they want to take more than that from me, but I won't let them have it!*

He walks alone down a street near his house. It is cold, midwinter, and he has been warned by his parents not to walk alone around here. *But I've got to!* Probably to get a ball back from a friend, or maybe he was just hungry for one of the glazed donuts they sell at the corner store. He walks quickly and tries to avoid the shadows.

Now he's walking across campus, and *aren't there gargoyles out there?* Up there? It's cold. It's so cold. He blows on his hands. To keep warm.

He blows on his hands as he stands on the porch outside his house. Right there. On the wooden front porch. The blue paint has started to peel away from the planking. To chip away, rather, lifting in jagged, wave edges, up just a nail's width, rising like tiny tsunamis that break from the oceans and tear toward heaven on hurricane winds. These...beautiful...children...

And turning from his porch, this beautiful boy, his eyes take in the world, but why won't it stay in focus? Why does it haze and flutter and blur? The green traffic lights, the yellow street lights, the white street lights, the white of the moon, white of flood lamps, gold of porch lights, glisten on grass, on glass, on dew? They all go haloes, and he is alone.

His feet feel cold, and his belly, his chest. He's cold, and he knows he won't be beautiful forever. He'll get old. It aches him. Those *clicking, ticking, docking* machines hear this feeling, this moment memory, and this hungers them too, so they flash and strobe out like a camera. Just like a camera–a big camera–an older camera–well–not digital–is what I mean–and a soft electric noise–a wheeee that starts low and then goes high–a hyperbola curve–up and up–and for a moment, he sees the actual machines as they steal his memories–bright and feral and made of *clicking, ticking, docking* whirring bright–dim eyes–comforting–comforting–be comfortable, they say–*we are just stealing your memories*–to keep the world *ticking*–to–to–*to keep the world clicking, ticking, docking*. And they strobe against him and steal his name, his self, his memories, but he, he, he has read a bit about these things–he's game–he's game!–and when they strobe, he catches a quick glimpse all around–corridors and passages–slight and stainless steel–wet subterraneous places–and also, he's sitting beneath a brick chimney–there are handholds–and while he doesn't know who he is–doesn't know *why* he is–disorienting here–he has some memory of space–has always had a knack for space–and the only escape that he can see is straight up. Is he being restrained? Nope. Only the flash of the –

Flash! Strobe!

What? Who? No...his mother twists her hands like there's a rag between them that needs to be wrung out. His father smiling. His sister smiling. Why such tragic smiles? "_____, mow the lawn!" his father says. "Sure, Pops!" *Pops?* Not a name, exactly, but it must be enough, because he hungrily lifts himself from the hungry chair and places his hands on the hungry bricks above his head, and lifts, although his feet lift heavily, as if they are mortared to hungry and mournful bricks.

He looks up into an unreasonable light. It's an interior space, but God, there are so many stars there. *So many fucking stars!* He wanted to see them, always. Wants to see the atmosphere peel thin around him like the layers of an onion, removed. His hands move up and grasp a brick, and he pulls, pulls, heavy, heavy, and up he goes. One arm up. Another. Slowly. It's cold out in the city. He blows on his hands to keep them warm, twists them in worry like there's a rag between them. Wringing, wringing. Sincere smile. So much promise. Much hope for this beautiful boy. He hears the *clicking, ticking, docking* machines beneath him readying their camera charge. No more playing around; they mean to rip him apart this time. Rather than lose those delicious memories. But he hears a girl's soft voice whisper, "here......I'll help you..." and as she cradles his feet in her invisible palms, lifting upward, he bends his will to his hands, and pulls, and pulls, and holds on tight, tight to the sound, the rhythm, the lights that won't stay in focus, where he might worry, where he might collapse on a park bench and keep his eyes shut nightlong with worry, or even sleep for hours on the rising tides of his own front porch.

He lifts.

But those fucking machines flash out at him again. They've almost got him now. They mean to–they mean to–God, he finds his mind stretching and dimming–they're doing it–they're almost there–they–are forgetting him–as he–has forgotten himself–forgotten it all–hands afire–arms numb–right?–and the air gone thin and dusty and cool–and the brick walls turning into pure air–dead air?–and all his lovely promise stretching away–and his mind, stretching down their camera whine–their awful strobe–their murderous *click, tick, dock*–stretching his feet downward like rubber–erasing his brain–it will finish him–he can't keep going–he is too weak–stretched and expanded out to sleep–and his body has ceased to be–and he feels himself fading away–being erased–elided–from the universe. He cranes his neck to look up at the brick tunnel above him, and it flies high with vertiginous speed. It reminds him of one last thing–"the Space Shuttle," says the girl's voice–and of outer space soaring above him–the rockets that soar in vain pursuit. How sometimes, by scattering their contents to the atmospheres–their passengers?–they rise. "Get out of here," says the girl. *It rises like the sun!* She lifts her prayerful palms, one last boost, and he sees Mallery's Storage on the horizon, where the sun set on the first day of Orientation, and he stood next to Monty Valverde and introduced himself to that night of promise and apprehension:

"Sam O'Samuel."

That's my name! I know my name!

The killing charge pulses out beneath him, but it meets with an unexpected resistance. The force field showers him with sparks and pushes him up the tunnel, higher and higher, to the top, the apex, where he crashes through the crumbling bricks and the rotted pulp and the rotten bark beyond. The oak tree explodes in a rainbow of Technicolor light. Samo sails into the air, clinging for dear life to a shattered branch that twirls like a helicopter blade, flying far out over the Fairway, some magical drag slowing his descent, before spinning and whirling him down to the earth. His feet hit the frosty grass, all cold, and he stumbles to his knees. He's alive.

Touchdown.

CHAPTER ELEVEN
STUNNING FREEDOM

Pyrotherapy

Protection is best. Penicillin is next.

This soul. This human. This man has been consigned to various hells ever since he tried to sprout his angel's wings. A few weeks–or maybe months–after he lay down with one of the prostitutes living in hovels outside the West End X factories, his back erupted with hundreds of glossy crimson papules. They rose up along his upper spine, then spiraled out about his shoulder blades before curving gently, a graceful sweep, down toward the small of his back. Angel's wings, clearly. He felt the bones and feathers, wings and tendons stirring and struggling beneath his gritty skin. It pained him, the efforts of emergence, and for the next several weeks, he lay prone on his floor, swearing at the pointy-hatted gnomes who banged on his head with their miniature croquet mallets. He sweated like a dog. He wailed on the chamber pot. Heat flooded his eyes with an angry red light. Through the dimness, he made out a photo of his mother, gazing at him from his bedside. "Why," she might have asked, "did you ever lie down with a prostitute?" "But mother," he said in his delirium, "I am becoming an angel. Maybe I'm on my way to heaven. Maybe I will fly. Maybe I will even get a little rest."

In the seven years since he'd left the farm, he'd seldom gotten much sleep.

Eventually, his body gave up on wings and flight. The fevers and pains receded, and the lumps on his back diminished and faded, leaving nothing behind but a few faint scars where ruptures had occurred.

"I guess I failed the test after all," he said ruefully to the mirror as he got ready for work in the morning.

It was only the first taste of his earthly purgatory.

His life never turned out as he had hoped. He went to dances, went to church, lived quietly and meekly. He faithfully submitted his draft card despite his own Hunnish heritage and said a quiet prayer under his breath when they didn't call him up. He lost two fingers to a grinder on the line and afterward was an even less-desired dance partner than before. He visited the prostitutes from time to time but never made a habit of it. He was too forlorn. He'd learned a few lessons in pain, but the harder tracks were field courses in despair. After all: he was a dull man. A listless man. He had little hope not to dissolve to nothing. Nobody loved him. Nobody at all.

If the ever-optimistic angels had made a play for the man in his youth, then the devils claimed his old age. Before his hair had gone completely gray, he started forgetting things. He'd walk to work through the snow without his shoes. He'd wet his pants in the middle of a church service. And then one day, staggering about his job, he fell forward and put his whole hand in the grinder. They staunched the blood, drove him up to the asylum, and diagnosed him with "general paresis of the insane." From there, it got worse. He saw the horrors of war, the horrors of the line, riding by, those grinders devouring jagged rods, tossing out sparks that burned like bitter fireflies, incinerating the final summers he'd never enjoyed. A sundered June smells like brackish bitumen. Cindered July is bleary brimstone. And in the depth-vents of his waking dreams, he saw men and women with loose shirts and thick blue pants moving about his bed. Some of them brought in even more dangerous engines, silver, bright, and hard to look at. These were seemingly intelligent. They glared. They swung sledge hammers. With them, they broke down the last of his beliefs: heaven and hell, heaven and Earth, metal and flesh, prostitutes and prophets. It all fed into a slate gray haze.

Whenever that happened, some devils would flutter down and cut him up with tiny swords and bleed him up with fires and ovens. Then the engines got hotter still, brighter still, and he closed his eyes and sighed.

Multivariable Vertigo

Your mother's right to worry about the "nice looking" ones.

She sighs and opens her eyes. A will'o-the-wisp in the moat below. No, a reflection, actually, fireflies flashing their warm green lights in the air above. The white and violet-colored airs, cold and perfect from the xenon lamps. *Xenon lamps!* she thinks. *This place is strange.* The woman looks up at the vast stone walls of Somnium Hall rising above her. Twilight has lingered for hours, but now, at last, at ten p.m., the shadows stretch across the Fairway as hard and as sharp as obsidian swords. She looks out. She sees them. The tenured humanities faculty, striding in slow steps across the field and trampling its lustrous spears of grass. They look bizarrely imposing, menacing even, dressed in the voluminous coils of their Chandrian-black robes. And she sees the Other she's been expecting.

It's strange, really, that the woman did not notice him first of all. After all, he's brighter than the humanities faculty, brighter than the xenon lamps, brighter than the fireflies, brighter than the setting sun. A beautiful boy dressed in wrinkled robes of white muslin, tied with a bright white cord. Shaggy brown hair the color of rice chaff. Wheat-brown eyes. And freckles. Sunspots across his skin. He isn't smiling–his mouth is a flat line–but he seems to radiate smiles and light, as if he has somehow captured the mirrored luminescence of an equatorial island, straight down from the sky and up from the water. He seems to scatter light from his fingers and toes. She sees his toes. He is barefoot.

One of the black-robed figures speaks.

"Huh?" she asks, her attention pulled back to herself.

"I said, 'Greetings,' and 'We are ready.' "

She knows the voice. The belligerent, impatient voice of Dean Plumb.

"I am ready, too," she says, determined to match his arrogance with her own strength and severity.

"Then let us continue!" says the beautiful boy, and it is as if there's an angelic chorus.

As his voice sings out, the woman feels an awful vertigo. Not the sharp sensation of falling up she got once looking up at Manhattan skyscrapers. Nor the somersaulting forward through darkness she felt when she drank too much and put her head on her knees. Rather, her mind and eyes rotate out from her stationary body to look down on the small crowd from above. She sees radiation pour down around her, bright through the twilight. The sluggish, hungry infrared that drips horizontally across the vertical, standing bodies of the crowd. The fuzzy, jagged ultraviolet darts that quiver from surface to surface. A gravelly sound of rings circling crescents out of the xenon lamps. They flare. But even this strange vision does not conform to her personal, interior logic. The black-robed faculty members look to her standing body, waiting for her to reply, but the beautiful boy looks up at her disembodied eye, and she knows that he knows what he's seeing her see.

"– !" says Dean Plumb.

"Pardon?" she gasps, looking out through her own two eyes again.

"Pay attention! This is important!"

"I'm sorry, Percy," she says. "I will pay more attention. You know you need me, so you should respect me."

Plumb is annoyed at her lack of deference, but he stifles his retort. "We've got to get moving," he says.

He fumbles in the robes until he produces a large key.

Once the portcullis has been unlocked, two professors take positions at either end and haul the squealing mass up. Plumb speaks. "This is going to be a dormitory. Right now, the space beyond the Fairway consists only of the power plant, but soon students will be staying here as well."

"What are they going to call it?" the woman asks.

"I don't know," Plumb says. "The trustees haven't decided yet, but I'm sure they'll name it after some Olan or another."

They enter the hall through one of its many vestibules and take the stairs down to the basement. There are three doors. Two of them are plain wooden doors that lead to the former residents' cells. A third door is thick and made of reinforced metal.

"They brought these out from Chernobyl," says Plumb. "The Ukraine was selling them at auction, and A. Olan couldn't pass up the chance."

"Chance for what?" asks one of black-robed faculty.

"Oh, who knows," Plumb answers. "Some sort of symbolic gesture or warning."

He thumps on the door with his fist. The black-robed figures flinch and recoil.

"What lies beyond these doors," Plumb says, "is more deadly than what burns in the core of Unit Four." The boy, however, smiles without smiling and steps forward to place his palm on the door. It isn't like the rough, angry crash of Plumb's fist. No, this touch is fond and familiar, as if calming someone, or trying to gently rouse a sleeping creature.

And then the woman's perspective shifts again. Sharply, as if she's been hit by a violent earthquake. She puts her foot out to keep her balance. She extends her arms, pinwheeling them wildly. Her eyes go wide, and she looks to the motionless, black-robed faculty. But she can't see their faces, can't see their eyes.

In the middle of the door, a sigil has started to shine like molten metal.

It looks like

and fills her proud heart with a bottomless regret. Things she's done that she cannot forgive, and she's done them every day. Calls never made. Letters never written. All the beauty of this exotic and mysterious world, kept to herself, to herself. And she rises, through concrete and brick and stone, above the slate shingles of that monstrosity of a building, and on up above the fledgling North Campus of Arkaic University, and over the whole city-thing of Arkaic. She wriggles her toes, and the tiny lights twinkle in response, the Pyramid Bank brighter than the others. She smells honeysuckle on the thermocline. The clouds are little eggs. She makes a grating sound deep in her throat that recedes back down into her belly–all the letters and calls she can't make now–and swallows. He is watching her from the past. And she is watching her from the future. And he is watching them all, and is warned by them. They want to intervene. It is their greatest desire, because soon they will be beyond call or contact. Somewhere else. Somewhere in between. She lets her breath out in a sudden rush.

The boy turns the handle. Opens the door.

Getting One's Just Desserts

Fatten yourself for winter whenever someone else is grabbing the check.

"Samo?" she says.

He opens his eyes. Ezzie stands over him with a worried expression. Just behind her is Monty, wincing as he clutches his side. Samo takes in the clouded sky and bitter cold.

"Are you okay?" Ezzie asks.

Samo gets to his feet, shakily. "I," he says, "uh, gotta go do something."

He walks away, toward the dorm. Monty and Ezzie follow him down to the bathroom, where he gestures for them to stay outside. Several minutes later, he comes out.

"I haven't gotten to go at all for hours," he says. "What was it, a whole day?"

Samo walks back to his room with Ezzie and Monty in tow, checks his email, then takes out his phone and makes a call.

" 'Lissa, hi, it's Samo. Yeah, it was weird, but I'm fine. I'll tell you about it later." He pauses as she speaks on the other end. "Yeah. Look, you want to meet up for dinner this week? No, not really. Well, yeah, I am asking you out like that. No, I am. Okay, what day? Where? You pick a place, drop me an email. Yeah, I can dress up. I don't mind. It was good to see you...all of you. Ha ha, thanks!"

He hangs up. He looks at his friends.

"Damn," he says.

He looks at the walls.

"We shouldn't talk about this here."

Ezzie and Monty nod silently.

"Where's Dunya?" asks Samo.

• • • • •

An hour later, Ezzie, Samo, and Monty huddle around a dark wood table in the pleasant dimness of Hickory's downtown. As Monty tells the story of his encounters with the Book Ninjas, the Inquiscription, and his escape from Proctor Hospital, Samo stabs and stabs again at his baked potato, loaded with chopped chives, the sourest cream, and little flakes of shredded cheddar cheese. While Ezzie explains her sudden, last-minute admittance to AU, the mystery of her mother's whereabouts, and the sunglasses and strange goings-on with the Humanities Department, Samo dips the biggest spoon into the creamy swamp of his peppered Guinness beef stew and slurps up every last bite and drop. He quietly sips at his Harp (since nobody cards nobody in Arkaic) as they tell him, in hushed tones, about Dunya's disappearance, the march of the anthropologists upon Calliope Cradle, and Dr. Lawless' sudden intervention.

"And that," says Monty, "is all we've got. What about you?"

Samo begins.

It wasn't all magic. The skull, he figures, was a real skull. The shit, real shit. But the arms that flipped him onto his stomach and the knee that pinned him to the floor had the stench of sweat and the feel of muscle. Hard muscle, real muscle, but mortal, and for a moment he was almost able to break free and escape. They slid a hood over his head, tied his hands behind his back, and picked him up off the floor. Samo couldn't see where they were taking him—they, surely, for he heard several voices whispering roughly all around him—but he's always been good with space and distance. The quiet creak had to come from the direction of the bed...from within the bed, specifically. The smell that drifted out, almost overpowered by the smell of poop, was one of dust and mothballs. *The attic!* Samo had thought. *So that's how they got in. That's why that bed felt so hard.*

After they pushed him inside, he lost his orientation. He recalls a long, painful descent down a long, long ladder, so old that flakes of rust crumbled off in his hands. It was terrifying, because the whole way down, the ticking sound from below grew louder and louder. He knew where they were taking him. To the underground. To the chain mazes. How long he'd been left alone there, he wasn't sure. At some point, his hands had been untied, his face unmasked, but he was too lethargic from radiation to remember who he saw, or even how *many* he saw.

The last part–the moments of his imminent destruction and inexplicable survival–are almost impossible to explain. He remembers, in meticulous detail, every feature of the active turbines: their fan belts and strobes and slick plastic interlocking parts. But he doesn't remember who helped him escape. It was as if she were invisible. Her voice sounded young. About his age. But he couldn't connect the voice to anyone he knew. And yet he knew, as surely as he had once gone to the corner store for donuts, or worried his mother on their porch, or laughed with Monty, Samo, and Dunya on their long Orientation walk, that this girl had saved his life.

"So," Samo says. He belches. "What now?"

"We've got a plan," says Monty.

"Shoot."

"The first thing," says Ezzie, "is Dunya. Firstly, is she okay? Secondly, where is she? The anthropologists and anthrostol– anthrostrologists really wanted to hurt her. But I've asked around, and the last time anyone saw her was at her big talk yesterday. So I think –"

"I think –" cuts in Monty.

"I think she might be hiding," says Ezzie.

Samo nods. "Sounds good."

"First, we need to cover for her. Go to her classes. Her meetings. Her rehearsals above all. We can't have her come back and then fail all her classes or something because she was missing."

"Should we report her missing?" asks Samo.

"We talked about that," says Monty. "We're going to wait until Friday..."

"Is that a good idea? The trail might go cold. Police need tips, most of the time."

Monty shakes his head.

"Wait for it," Ezzie says. "We have an answer on that too."

"Second," Ezzie continues, "we can't flunk out just because things have gotten a bit weird here. My midterms are all done. Are yours?"

Monty nods. "I actually had plenty of time to study when I was in the hospital."

Samo thinks. "I've got one more. In Kyrgyz."

"Don't fall behind on that," says Ezzie. "If we flunk out, then everything is for nothing."

"If I flunk out, I won't get to be an astronaut," says Samo, his lips grim. "I'm not flunking out."

"Third," says Ezzie, "we have to keep chipping away at this. Maybe these are all a bunch of unrelated things, but I don't think so. My school's headmaster wanted me to come here, *specifically*."

"And," says Monty, with a sidelong glance at Ezzie, "the Book Ninjas insinuated that things were connected. That there are people out there who don't *want* us to solve these mysteries. Or, at least, to solve only the parts that don't implicate *them*."

"Fourth," says Ezzie, "we stay in touch, but electronically or in a place like this. You notice how the weird things all seem to happen in an old-fashioned way? I mean, Dunya pisses off the anthropologists while delivering a lecture, or Monty is beaten up by thugs in a truck, or you're taken through a secret doorway. Even me, my sunglasses keep me from breaking glass when I look at it."

Samo hesitates. "That isn't exactly old-fashioned..."

"They don't seem to be able to accomplish anything electronically," Ezzie says. "Computers are apparently useless to whoever–to all the whoevers–we're dealing with."

"Whomevers," corrects Monty.

Samo nods, slowly.

"We need," says Ezzie, "to meet up off-campus once or twice a week to talk this all over, the three of us. But if we need to talk about it sooner, we do it by text or email or something. We can't talk in our rooms, because we know that they can listen through the walls. And we can't talk about it on campus, because someone who overhears might have a stake in it."

"That all sounds fine," says Samo. "But what about reporting Dunya missing?"

"That," says Ezzie, "is fifth. Okay. Look, we don't want to be like some dumb kids in a young adult novel who don't go to authority with all the junk that's happening to them. Those kids always get in over their heads, and are saved by luck, but we don't know that we'll be lucky. Or clever. The problem is, we have to be careful who we go to–"

"To whom we go," corrects Monty.

"I mean, Prof. Plumb knows things, for sure, but he was somehow involved in the shattering glass incident. We can't go to him. Dr. Rochet knows things, but he wanted to hurt Dunya, so that isn't good either. But we know that they are both high up in the university–they both are, or were, deans–and the university is tight with the Olans. If I'm right –"

"You are," interjects Samo.

"– being tight with the Olans is the same as being tight with the police. And the whole rest of the city government, for that matter. If Dunya is hiding, and we report her missing, and then the police find her, that's pretty much telling the university–telling Rochet or whoever else is looking for her–where she is. But we do need to tell someone in a position of authority. And Monty has a good idea who."

"I do," says Monty. "Dr. Endolynn Lawless. She's already had our back at least once. And she *definitely* knows some of the things that are going on."

Samo thinks for a long moment.

"I like it," he says. "It's a good plan. We'll be busy but...hey, that's cool."

"Should I get the check?" asks Monty.

"I kind of want some pie."

Fate Train

First impressions deceive.

But as Dr. Lawless is gone for the rest of the week at GenCon 2011 (Collonge-Bellerive), awesome plans notwithstanding, the three students are stuck in a holding pattern.

Monty has been assigned to Dunya's classes, as well as his own. When Monday, November 7th splits the skies with a yawning, gray, phantom light, he hopes that he can rise to the occasion with the articulation of Ikea instructions. You know:

The happyman! has a Flat-head Screwdriver. And a Hammer. And a Pencil.

He is not a sadman! ill-equipped and without help.

He is a happyman! with the necessary tools and assistance.

He is not a distraughtman! who bangs away on a hard floor and breaks things.

He is a happyman! who does his work on a carpet.

Wind the crank. You get it.

Monty's classes are awesome, since he's been studying his entire time at the hospital. His SOs are suffering. He finds unanswered emails from the Eggplant, the Psychedelics, the Skeleton Keynes, and the Dominicans. The Aaron Burr Society has in the meantime imploded, pending a federal suit brought after some kid from Madrid got snitchy, so that's one less thing to worry about. But catching up on Dunya's classes is a challenge. It means going through her room to identify precisely what classes she is taking. So there's...the Classic Vampire? And her hum sequence: Nietzsche Say, Nietzsche Do. And an Intro to Anthro class (complete with glowering anthropologists). And one more...probably a math class. Most first years try to kill their math requirement up front.

Monty recalls that Dunya said she wasn't much of a student in high school, so he figures he should drop a line on the non-calculus courses around campus. There are only a few that offer credit, but after attending three of them, Dunya's name hasn't come up. Monty spends a couple hours scouring listings and section websites for various bio sequences before he comes across the crumpled remnants of problems sets. Calculus. He's underestimated her. In fact, she placed into the mid-level, non-tutorial sequence. *Samo would be jealous.*

Three out of four professors buy his excuse that she's been called out of state unexpectedly. She is a Californian, after all. Such things are to be expected.

A train whistles across the midnight horizon, like a harsh horn.

Romantically, he misses Monica. She'll be upstairs, doing some studying of her own. He should join her. Maybe they can work together. They'll work like a freight train, chugging away through the night.

There's a Sprocket in my Pocket!

It is both simple and difficult; relax into yourself.
That's when good things can start to happen.

And as Samo stands against the urinal, resting his forehead on the cool metal pipe, he falls suddenly asleep and sees...

One little part, just one little part of the temporelectrical turbine contains more nauseating effluence than if all the toilets in Arkaic had flushed at once, causing compression in the pipes, pressure from beneath, and the bellowing eruption of geysers of gristly filth. Witness the stator. As with any old armature, it features coils of metal. The oldest of these were forged from a concentrate of argyrial silver (Item #492, 2008 Artemis' Hunt), but the later models were made by wires of Olympian ruthenium (Item 17, 2009) cooled by a Sisyphrigerator (Item #189, 2008). The memories and dreams that splash this high—shattered and smashed and dragged up the walls by centripetal force—are vicious and viscous, corrosive and corrupted, and redolent of death. When they react with the armature, they throw out a smell of ozone with a whiff of cadaverine. The stench is still thick in Samo's nostrils when he wakes and opens his eyes.

"Huh," he says.

He zips up, leaves the bathroom, and returns down the long hall, to the main dining room of Hickory's. 'Lissa smiles up at him as he sits down.

"Were you always so tall?" she asks.

"Huh?"

'Lissa blushes at her own question and looks down at the table.

"Um, no," says Samo. "I used to be very small, actually. You won't believe it, but I used to be as small as a baby."

"When was that?"

"Oh, about nineteen years ago."

"Nineteen. Wow, you're old."

"Not you?"

"Eighteen," she says.

Samo nods, finds himself yawning, worries that it looks rude, and puts his mouth into his armpit to hide it. 'Lissa laughs.

"You look really tired," she says.

"You have no idea."

"School got you down?"

"That's some of it. I have my last midterm tomorrow."

"They're serious about their midterms over there, aren't they?"

"I have three classes. This is going to be my seventh midterm!"

"Wow."

"But that's not all of it...I've...we've...got a friend whose gone missing. We're covering for her, picking up her homework and...well, I'm in touch with the different clubs she belongs to. And I just found out she wasn't able to pay her tuition, um, normally, so she pawned these huge gemstones–um, and now she's getting these threatening calls. She's in over her head." Samo muses. "I think I am too."

'Lissa rubs his hand comfortingly. "We're all in over our heads, Sam," she says.

She's about to pull her hand back to her menu, but Samo puts his other hand on hers. 'Lissa's brows knit in an expression of...irritation? Animation? What?

Samo speaks. "Something strange happened to me after I saw you at the party last weekend," he says. He licks his lips, which are suddenly dry. "It won't make sense to you right now, so I won't get into it. But it was...a...hm. It was a moment of reckoning, okay?"

He releases her hand, and she pulls it back, clearly annoyed. Samo feels nonplussed. No, wait, nonchalant. His emotions don't make sense to him, to himself. It might just be because he's tired. God! He is so exhausted this week. But the exhaustion is welcome, because he isn't worried. He just isn't worried what 'Lissa says or does right now. If that spark, that old shine that cut along her hair on the cloudiest days, when they were both ninth graders, and punctured his heart meant anything, she'll get it. She'll get it. And if she doesn't, well, then it's time to move on.

"What are you saying?" she asks.

He realizes that his lips have been moving. Echoing his thoughts.

"I was saying you should get the cherry pie. It's really good."

The waitress comes. They order. She leaves.

"What were you really saying earlier?" 'Lissa asks.

"You know, in high school, you were always on my mind. And I'll say it, I mean, it would be shitty to lie, it's partly just that you're so fine. But...hey 'Lissa , you always talked to me. And most of them didn't. You were always easy to talk to. Which was funny, because it made me nervous. Made me scared to talk back to you. So I didn't. I wish I had."

"Do you think I was leading you on?"

"No. I mean, how could you –"

"Then I don't think you have anything to complain about," she says, but her smiling tone tells him that she's teasing now.

Samo hedges for a moment.

"What do you say," he asks, "to us being a thing? You and me?"

"A *thing*?" She laughs so loud that she snorts, then covers her face, embarrassed. "Sam, man, you are a trip. No not the idea of it, just the way you *say* it. 'A thing,' well, wow, that's romantic, isn't it? I get to be a *thing*."

That stings a bit. Maybe Samo isn't as impregnable as he thought. He can't meet her steady gaze. She doesn't blink or look down. She's on the offense now!

"Sam," she says. "I dated Twist all through eleventh and twelfth grade before he dumped me out of the blue. I went to our prom stag. Now I'm just starting to get around. I'm dating whoever I like, whenever I like, and I *like* it. I'm not willing to give that up...yet. That freedom. It is freedom! It really is. Who knows what the future has in store? I'm not ready to close that book yet. Not even a little. Not even temporarily. I mean, I'm at the bookstore. I'm just browsing."

Samo sighs. "I understand," he says. Then, self-pitying: "It's something I'm getting used to hearing these days and —"

"Stop whining," she interrupts. "You might change my mind."

"What do you mean, change your mind?"

"Well, I was going to say, if you wanted something a little less serious, you know, something for fun, maybe..."

She taps her finger on her napkin in something that could be Morse code, or at least, the signal seems plenty clear to Samo.

"I'm not," Samo said, "um..." He hesitates. "Experienced?"

'Lissa laughed. "I don't care!" she says.

They pass the rest of their dinner in laughter and mischief. After they eat, they dance to the Irish ska band that has set up in the front window and then go outside to wait at the curb, in light snow, for the city bus that takes them back to Calliope Cradle. Once there, they hurry with turbulence through the halls, and their merry voices sound like chimes in the night. For the briefest moment, they can be glimpsed by other students, but it's just an instant, and then they are gone. Down into the basement. Behind the door to Samo's empty suite.

It is 10:30, maybe 10:45 p.m., that Tuesday night when Samo and 'Lissa baptize that basement bedroom with a sweetness it has never known as either dorm room or institutional cell. But don't worry. We're not going to go there. Lucky college students, on their very first go, are blessed with a grinning gargoyle that shushes would-be voyeurs and even writers of prose fiction. It waves its clawed fingers in front of its fanged mouth, and to answer an earlier question, its intentions are as protective as its instincts are deadly.

Behind those doors, the celebration of life and love is even more varied and vigorous than the most ambitious romantics can imagine.

Goodnight Hume

Whatever you think you know about your parents in their young adulthood,

the truth is seventeen times more lurid than you think.

And as Ezzie, the most exhausted of all, closes out the week—the longest week she's ever had, of reading, and writing, and going through the penultimate week of rehearsals for *Hamletmachine* as well as disguising herself as Dunya for rehearsals of *The Moldy Fountain*—her head comes down hard on her copy of *An Enquiry Concerning Human Understanding*. She was to have finished it on Wednesday, and she sat, beleaguered, as the hands flew up around her, barking answers, whispering arguments, and generally withering under the excessive skepticism of Professor Plumb.

The paper is due on Monday. There are fewer than eighty pages left, but they are eighty dense pages. Can she understand *Human Understanding* on less than four hours of sleep a night for a whole week? Has she even slept that much? She certainly can't add for shit right now! Through her gray shades, her eyes catch the buff color of an envelope corner peeking out from under steely gaze of a rotund Hume. It's the envelope her Uncle Clay gave her.

That'll kill a few minutes, she thinks. Then: *I haven't got a few minutes to kill.* Then: *I don't care.*

She tugs the envelope out from under the mass of papers. She untwists the tie and opens it. *This is going to be awful*, she thinks, fastening her hands upon the mass of notes and photographs and newspaper clippings. *But at least it won't tax my brain.*

"Time to meet you, mother," she says.

But it does tax her brain, in an exquisitely wrenching way. Because there is her mother, with full and bright blonde hair and sparkling green eyes, as different from Ezzie as day is from night, except for a certain tension about her waist, a tilt of her head, a narrowing of her eyes. It suggests a spontaneous hope, energy, creativity, tamped down by overwhelming anxiety but reawakened by overcompensating pride. That...Ezzie knows that posture well. It is her own.

She flips through the clippings. Her mother was accomplished, socially and academically, and also bizarrely. Here are some borderline scandalous photos of her working as a burlesque impresario on an improvised Coney Island stage. Ezzie's mother must be what–twenty? Twenty-two?–in these pictures. Then come the articles and rejected notes for a half-pondered memoir from San Francisco in the late '80s. At that time, Ezzie's mother was earning her doctorate in musicology at SFSU, but she was also learning to walk the tightrope, to swing the trapeze, and to compose for the calliope. This is incredible! Do you know how many full-time post-modern baroque steam-calliope composers live in the US today? Not including Ezzie's mother, the answer is a prime number of digits on the single hand of a Yooper who blew off one his fingers with a bottle rocket. It's that freaking special.

Ezzie's mother's early career culminated when her composition "I'll Still be Tendin' my Still, Bill" was played at the Clinton inauguration in '92. Then she married Ezzie's father, an ex-Green Beret (*too many family secrets*, thinks Ezzie). A few more years passed with more photos but fewer clippings. Ezzie's mother seemed listless at home, frustrated with her more sedentary life. And then Ezzie was born. The affair was discovered. Ezzie's mother ran away with the circus.

Dazed–no, stunned–no, shocked–Ezzie's arms fall mechanically into her lap. She's only taken a glance, but her mind is crowded with this incredible, insubordinate, immaculate, impetuous woman she cannot remember. Her genetic mother. The mother of her blood. This Dr. Lorraine Prentice née Glass.

Ezzie blinks.

She realizes and opens her eyes. The lenses–the *plastic* lenses–of her sunglasses fracture.

Lawless

Areca is cool, but have water handy.

When Sunday tumbles along, Ezzie spots Dr. Lawless' Chevy Volt stashed in one of the back parking lots.

"Tonight," she says, and Samo and Monty nod solemnly.

As the three students make their way down the cobblestone path, the xenon lamps winking beside them, Monty smiles at Samo.

"You look a lot better today," he says. "Get caught up on sleep last night?"

"I didn't sleep at *all* last night," laughs Samo. "Where were you?"

"I've been staying with Monica," says Monty.

Ezzie glares at them.

When they knock on the forbidding Vainglory door, it opens at once, as if the good doctor has been expecting visitors.

"Monty Valverde. Sam O'Samuel. Esmeralda Prentice. Why am I receiving a visit from 6.8 percent of Acedia House tonight?"

"Dr. Lawless, we..." Ezzie trails off, staring at her hair. "Um, you have a bunch of leaves stuck in your hair."

Dr. Lawless plucks a small twig with oak leaves off her head. "Come in," she says.

All three have been in Dr. Lawless' apartment before, for her reception during Orientation Week, but in the darkness and chill of late autumn, it seems quite different. It has all the necessary accoutrements of an academic party, including alright wine and cheese. *Was she expecting us?* Monty wonders. There's also an array of tasteful but not-too-expensive clay vases and locally painted pictures. And the houseplants. The houseplants! It's a little overwhelming. Potted bougainvilleas with limpid purple blossoms. The luminescent princess flowers. The thick-lipped heliconias and the dozens of orchids. The thirty foot coconut palm, balmy and drenched in a moody purple light. Ezzie feels on edge. As if she's in the remotest jungle and Shere Khan is hiding behind the curio cabinet (nice Fiestaware though).

"Sit," says Dr. Lawless. "I will get you refreshments."

She leaves for the kitchen.

"I'll have some of that wine," says Samo. "Can I have a glass?"

"You're all severely sleep-deprived," comes Dr. Lawless' voice from the dark. "Wine won't help."

She emerges, holding a tray of what look like tiny avocados and a cup filled with fine white powder.

"Guacamole and cocaine!" says Samo. "Awesome!"

Dr. Lawless laughs at this. "It's betel nut," she says. "Better than coffee."

Fifteen minutes of dizziness, nausea, and pumpkin-y phlegm later, the students are wide awake. Only then does Dr. Lawless finally pour them some wine.

"Um," says Samo. "Maybe we should go somewhere else to talk? Not in the dorm?"

"Being overheard," she says. "A very rational fear of yours, I know. Don't worry, I had this apartment extensively soundproofed when I moved in. Now let me tell you what I already know about your situation, and you can tell me what I do not." She studies them for a moment. "Your friend Dunya Blavatsky has gone missing, and you're covering for her. You, Monty Valverde, are involved in many SOs, but most significantly, some unknown actors have managed to get you to challenge the Inquiscriptors who roughed you up a few weeks ago. You, Sam O'Samuel, were recently abducted and wound up in the chain mazes yourself, but you escaped when the oak tree in our courtyard exploded the other day. I'm going to have to replace that, by the way. I'd like to go with a sycamore tree, as in William Shakespeare, as in the Sycamore Grove. *Romeo and Juliet*. A fine place. Which brings me to you, Esmeralda Prentice, who must have recently discovered that you are the daughter of Dr. Lorraine Glass, who vanished in the chain mazes four years ago and inspired the name of this dormitory."

Jaws drop.

"How...do...you...know?" stammers Ezzie. And other obvious questions.

Dr. Lawless shrugs. "I observe. That is all. Now tell me what I don't know."

They do that thing.

"And now," Dr. Lawless sez, "let me tell you what I know, and what you do not..."

She starts speaking, and speaks for a long time.

Going All the Way

The exercise of power hangs on the question of leverage.

This has all happened in Arkaic. But this is bigger than Arkaic.

So far as I can tell, when A. Olan decided to open a university, his intentions were naïve. What I mean is that he didn't intend anything more than to open a university. Prestigious, sure. Revolutionary even, fine. But not otherworldly. Not supernatural.

Be that as it may, it remains that from the moment the ink was dry on the deeds to acquire the Arken County Lunatick Asylum, there were already two groups here vying for supremacy. Where they came from, I don't know. How long they've been around, I don't know that either. They had both been around for a while. They already hated each other. I was one of the first faculty at this school, and I had been recruited into a tenured position to help establish our credibility early on. I was in a unique position to observe what was happening behind the scenes, as I held two doctorates, one in English and the other in sociology.

The first group to approach me was Via Positiva. They were covert establishment players. Somehow, they'd already gotten the ear of the administration before any students arrived. They must have had contacts on the board of trustees and down through most academic departments because, by-and-large, tenure and appointments proceeded from Via Positiva. Funds for fellowships and residencies flew out of hidden coffers. Long-neglected dissertations received attention and acclaim. For many academics, this was all too good to be true. And naturally, scholars in the humanities were the most destitute, so they found Arkaic University to be the most seductive. Via Positiva may have been manipulating the administration, but they were quite overt in their takeover of the Department of Humanities. Anything significant that happened in that department had surely been rubber stamped by Via Positiva. As time passed, they also entrenched their power on campus through other institutions. They enabled the Inquiscriptors to control the textbook market here in exchange for their own access to forbidden texts. Via Positiva also infiltrated the Utilities Department and convinced the Olan Foundation to explore alternate methods of powering the campus. Not wind power, oh no, not solar...something much more exotic.

Their agents in the Humanities Department contacted me that first year and asked me to coordinate with them. To help them build "a real, first-class educational institution." But their methods seemed both duplicitous and autocratic. And I was already tenured. So I declined. Politely, of course.

A few months later, I heard from the other group. Via Negativa. They had been much more discreet in their operations. In fact, their agents had been speaking with me for months before I even learned their names or identities. Even in those early days, Via Negativa was seemingly on the defensive. Their meetings weren't held on campus, but in the Happy Hunting Grounds, where they allegedly practiced bizarre and demoniac rites. At least, those were the rumors circulated by Via Positiva. But the agents of Via Negativa were cunning and audacious, and somehow they established a foothold in the Department of Anthropology, which has finally become their principal power base. They even went so far as to establish an official organ on campus; the Department of Anthropology includes, of course, everyone who teaches anthropology, but all of the faculty that run the Anthrostrologists are Via Negativa. They asked me to join them as a spy. But this sounded risky, and I did not trust them, and they had no leverage on me. So again, I declined.

"Wait," says Samo. "Via Positiva? I knew that sounded familiar. Isn't that the SO that puts on Artemis' Hunt each year?"

"Oh," says Dr. Lawless, "this is only the beginning."

· · · · ·

For the first couple years it seemed like these two groups, warring behind the scenes for control of AU, were evenly matched. They both had plenty of talent and wealth at their disposal. They used their tools differently. Via Positiva would orchestrate an elaborate coup in a distant banana republic in order to seize some rare mineral or endangered orchid. A professor hostile to Via Negativa would supposedly commit suicide in the Happy Hunting Grounds. But the truth is, they were never evenly matched. One of them held the advantage from the beginning, and when students began to formally enroll, that advantage became more clear.

While Via Negativa exercised their influence through the Department of Anthropology and the Anthrostrologers, the greater influence of Via Positiva enabled them to establish themselves directly through the student body as well. This took the form of Artemis' Hunt, the second largest scavenger hunt in the Solar System. As you may have heard, it's no ordinary scavenger hunt. It's a brilliant scheme, in both elegance and effectiveness. Artemis' Hunt allowed Via Positiva to discreetly assemble the necessary ingredients for their most ambitious project. Under the guise of the Hunt, Via Positiva obtained the materials and expertise to build temporelectrical turbines. To link them. To increase their efficiency by bonding them to a common field. In short, chain power.

Much has been written about the technology—about the sheer genius of it all. That something as ephemeral as *time*, as abundant as *memory*, as renewable as *thought* could provide us with energy. Engines that amplify and convert neural activity into usable power. And of course, research is nascent, but much has also been written about the hazards of such power. The toxic waste they leave behind is capable of burning through diamonds. The known unknowns and the unknown unknowns. We've only scratched the surface of what temporelectricity *is*. What it *does*.

Via Negativa's relationship to the turbines is shrouded in secrecy, but I have a slightly better understanding of Via Positiva.

You see, their influence is such that they could have established themselves anywhere. Why not Stanford or MIT? Why here? What is it about this school? I have a theory. The decline of Arkaic over the years has left a wreckage in which emotional distortions and risks can be easily masked and neglected. And the temporal detritus left by Arkaic's violent and destitute history has left plenty of raw material for the turbines, nowhere moreso than at the former mental hospital. It is, essentially, a place in which the side effects would escape scrutiny. And that's why Via Positiva came here. And that is significant. They aren't *from* here. They *came* here. They are *outsiders*.

Regardless of whatever preparations or allowances they may have made, it was a dangerous game to play. I still remember June 30th, 2009. The night the full field first went live.

"Was that the night when my mother vanished?" asks Ezzie, her face pale.

Dr. Lawless nods, gravely.

"Even the students noticed strange things happening. But they didn't know the half of it."

· · · · ·

From the beginning, Via Positiva had been in the habit of "initiating" humanities professors into tenure as a way of ensuring their loyalty. But Dr. Lorraine Glass was a strange case. Erratic as a bat, even after she'd been teaching here for a year, Dr. Glass had discovered a lot of the conflict through her own ingenuity. But no one knew where her loyalties lay. I had been able to maintain neutrality, largely by staying above the fray, but Lorraine wanted to play the pieces like a game of chess. I wasn't a witness to what happened in the chain tunnels under the Fairway that night, but I was on campus, working late in the library. I was walking back to the bus stop when all hell broke loose.

"What happened?" asks Monty.

"I just told you," says Dr. Lawless. "All hell broke loose."

The first signs were subtle.

"Do you understand what the word 'psychedelic' actually *means*?" asks Dr. Lawless.

"I do," says Monty. "It was the first thing they taught me at the Psychedelic Association."

"Ah yes," says Dr. Lawless. "I funded the PA–anonymously, of course–so that there would always be a few students who could recognize the effects of concentrated temporelectrical radiation, who could differentiate it from, say, ordinary recreational drug use. Very well then, Monty. Be a good student and tell us what 'psychedelic' means."

"It's Greek. *Psyche* is the soul and mind, as one thing. As our combined mental identity. *Delic* is representing something to the world. So 'psychedelic' is a manifestation of our mind."

"That's right," says Dr. Lawless.

"The effects were psychedelic. No drugs, you understand. Temporelectrical radiation. Psychedelic. Otherwise, the facts just don't add up. Impossible things happened. Everything became bright in the dark. Green grass went Jungle Green (#29AB87). The trees' leaves turned Emerald (#50C878). Moss became Persian Green (#00A693). An Egyptian Blue sky (#1034A6). A Jet colored road (#343434). An earth of Brown (#964B00) and Vermilion (Cinnabar) (#E34234). My blue-green blouse went Teal (#008080), and I felt a breeze on the side of my cheek, but it wasn't a coolness. It was a tingling, like an electric kiss.

"It so chilled my icy heart, that solid tears fell from my eyes like sad little ice cubes, but baubled bums belching drunk bubbles caught them in sterilized stemware and guzzled right-wing martinis wearing cheap fuchsia suits. And I meant for that comma to drop, dammit! We all sat down on the bright-eyed smiling bench for the wheels on the bus go round and round, like I know a girl got a lot to lose, so come, gather 'round people. Round about then, the late night dews soaked through my panties and excited me. My nipples stiffened, and little goose bumps popped up along my thighs and calves and stockings. I wrapped my arms against my chest, even though it was warm and moist out, because I wanted to keep the bums from leering at me. I put my hair into pigtails to convince them of my innocence and painted my glasses gray, but muggy, runny sweat damped my cheeks.

"The whole while, that electrical breeze kept running tingling currents down my spine, tugging at my clothes, urging me to greater life. *This is life,* it said. *Enjoy it!* Life propagates life. Let there be propagation! 'Endolynn isn't young anymore!' I said. Then the bus came all over the pavement and opened wide, and we all stepped inside.

"I observed that the driver was wearing browned briefs in need of a good washing, and he leaned heavily on the chortling wheel as he drove. He drove quickly, played a nasty beat, and grinned and crumbled into unhappy dust. But the bus drove on, whining about our weight. My sore feet, poor bunions, trotted me down to a vacant place, and I settled in for the ride. Passengers of all ages, races, accessories, and dispositions took off all of their clothes before the grime-streaked windows and Peeping Tom pedestrians. Summer was there. The time was right for dancing on the seats. But all was not well, for where I had expected to admire or ignore a pleasant cross section of healthy genitals, I saw winking bear traps, watercress, dandelions, quarantines, tambourines, tangerines, concertinas. Wire disconsolate that it had only been designed to wound other things. Still, I felt many wrinkles across my own body being smoothed out by the blast of air conditioning, and looking around, the plump roseate butts on the bus, bare and buttressed, were magnificent, and bounced in time to a beautiful salsa beat. Time travelers brought down the Fresno and the Foxtrot. The Mad Bomber danced a tap. The Killer Clown cackled and pirouetted. They bit out each other's throats and eyeballs and swallowed them down in big gulps like bread buttered with piquant piggy pâté. Things got all troubled up in there. People started climbing all over each other, mating and killing everything. They tried to pull the pins from their hand grenades with their teeth, but their dentures popped instead. Now, the passengers ripped off their own arms and used them to beat and molest one another. They had kept all their funk bottled up their whole lives. Now it cracked and erupted their porcelain sides, all that violence with which they would bridge their divides. I had to escape from the lecherous ogling and murder, so I distracted those commuters with hypnotic spasms and wily ways. Look deep into my eyes! I am mesmerizing you! Hands flashing like headlights, and illumined by the death rays of the flying saucers making their final descent outside. Every human head became a big boar with pineapple eyes and cherry pupils. Every human heart became a chocolate coconut nectarine. A Satanic goat ate a junkyard. When everyone's gaze went momentarily vacant, I hopped out the window and made a run for it.

"I was free. But still, that electricity. It was a stunning freedom, if you know what I mean.

"Back at home, where we fucked for our lives with the flowers and stars, all the plaid and the paisley ignited the sun, for the varying love of the gods, and it supernovaed and gave us a light for the party where we, wearing down, wearing costumes, combined connoisseurs, or the old Martian ladies pretending to be sexy cops, and they say 'trick of treat' on Halloween, even though it ain't classy to go at that age and expect you will get invitations. To make booty calls that will work, you must be oh so honest, you know. There is recreation in the syndication of procreation so long as one has sufficient medication, or so I have heard it reported before. It would be fairly acknowledged. But there's no way they were going to get me back on that bus, or back to that campus, that night, no way. So I put my boot on this student's heel, and took his wrist in my arm, and put my back against her side, and I pulled so hard that they tore right in two, with geysers of blood inkjetting black spray across the glistening marbley spine."

Ezzie's phone shivers. She takes it out of her pocket and looks at the glowing screen.

"Hey," she says. "I just got a text from Dunya."

CHAPTER TWELVE
A LAZY ALLIANCE

Chill of the Deep Sea

*Even college students should keep a stock of practical tools, like
sweaters, flashlights, and first aid kits.*

It's been a strange week for Dunya. When an odd man caught
up with her on the Fairway after her ghosting presentation, he
mentioned that he had been hired by a despicable cult. That didn't
comfort her, and she was about to run, when he added that "those
who want to destroy the turbines would also like to destroy you!" So
Dunya stopped and listened while the man breathlessly explained
that he had infiltrated a secret society on campus and learned that it
meant to annihilate her that very night. "But I remembered you," he
said in an evocative voice, and Dunya felt a shock as she remembered
all that coffee, that ceiling fan, those names, those hours, and oh, the
man in the moon.

"Chris?" she asked.

Yes, it's been a strange week, hiding out at the Atlantis,
biding her time, knowing that her friends are worried, and worrying
that she is losing her job, failing her classes, and getting kicked out of
the play. But Chris and his brother, Brendan, had leveled a strict
injunction of silence when she arrived, and when Dunya had balked,
they had explained just what was at stake–how she and her friends
might lose not only their lives, but also their minds, memories,
identities, and souls.

Each night, between midnight and one, the Atlantis closes,
and Dunya is left on her own. She fries potatoes. She scrambles eggs.
She slaps butter on Texas toast. Mostly, she drinks coffee and studies.
The world is silent except for the hum of the furnace in the back, the
occasional swish of traffic through slush on Ash Highway, and the
howl of the sequestered wind. Sequestered? she asks. *I probably
mean uninhibited.* Inside, the place is hers. On happy nights, she'll
see the moon. On other nights, at least she sees the stars. At least she

sees the bilious clouds. *Bilious?* she wonders. *Billowing, perhaps.* There's a sort of still, nightlong divinity.

Each morning, when the sun rises, Dunya reluctantly slides from the booth and prepares herself for an icy nap, hiding in the walk-in meat freezer. For a bare minute, before the big door swings shut, she sees the outline of many cardboard boxes. Boxes full of frozen Viennas. Boxes full of hamburger patties. Then the dark and the cold. It hints at the chill of the deep sea. Dunya wraps her arms around her shoulders. At least she's got a sweater. And so: sitting in the dark. Asking it questions, like, "Would you go away with me? But you wouldn't go away without me, would you?" She wraps herself in a blanket, gazing out through the abyssal shine–a sleek blackness borne of bleak density–and thinks herself to sleep. It's a peculiar kind of cold in there. A peculiar kind of lonely. A peculiar comfort in hiding. But who would understand? The Robotic Cetacean Deep-Space Gospel Collective. That's who. We know that the transcendent loneliness of non-corporeal angels who rise, awkwardly always, and skyward, though up, is relative.

It takes a full week for Dunya to crack. It's almost midnight, and the last customers have just left for the parking lot. Dunya stands in the sickly green fluorescents of the kitchen.

"I'm telling my friends I'm okay," she says.

"Wait, don't!" yells Brendan, lurching across the diner like a stumbling Olympian. But Dunya has already pushed the buttons.

Hiding. OK.

It only takes a moment for Ezzie–four miles away–to write back, but when she does, Dunya almost drops her phone.

Hiding frm /-\?

Brendan stops up short. Chris has locked the front door and looks in curiously.

"But how do they know?" wonders Brendan.

Dunya types:

How u know?

This time, it takes several minutes for Ezzie to write back:

Hang tight. Stay safe. Quiet. Got a plan.

Fictional Inscriptions

Read critically, always.

Ezzie exhales heavily. "I told her," she says. "Slash dash backslash?"

"It stands for Via Negativa," explains Dr. Lawless.

"Huh," says Monty. "I get that."

"That's subtle," says Ezzie. "Not!"

Dr. Lawless laughs. "Well, no. And Via Positiva is slash plus backslash."

"Wait a minute —" says Samo, his brow furrowing.

"Are they trying to make it easy or something?" asks Ezzie, but Monty shakes his head.

"If nobody knows who you are, it doesn't matter if your logo is obvious," he says.

"Precisely," says Dr. Lawless.

"But then again," says Monty, "that still doesn't sound like due caution from two groups who prefer to work in strict secrecy."

"It is a mystery of their behavior," she admits.

"Not to change the subject," says Ezzie, "but what is this plan we have?"

"For starters, we're not going to play by their rules," says Dr. Lawless.

"We have rules?"

"They try to teach you rules that make it easy for them to win. Deceptions. And we are going to mindful of the big three."

Samo starts to speak, but Monty silences him with a hand. He fixes Dr. Lawless with a newly skeptical look.

"You're describing this in a very peculiar way, Dr. Lawless," he says. "Tell us what you're going to tell us. Don't drag us along like we're Dr. Watson, asking expositional questions convenient for a slower-than-average reader. *Pretend*, at least, that we are as smart as you are."

Dr. Lawless laughs. "This is very good," she says. "You're already starting to break them. The rules. But I'll be straightforward. You all know—you, most painfully, Monty—about Via Positiva's dealings with the Inquiscriptors. How is it that they operate so blatantly, but with such impunity? Don't worry, I'm going to tell you right now. They brainwash you into carelessness. After all, the Inquiscriptors control the publishing industry. That industry chooses what books to publish. And so they publish books for young adults, featuring young adults going on adventures. These characters make decisions that work out well in a fantasy but end badly in real life. This has been going on for hundreds of years. Think about every adventure about preteens and adolescents that you've ever read."

As she speaks, Dr. Lawless strides to her shelves and begins amassing a stack of books in her arms. She slams them down on the coffee table as she talks: "*Nancy Drew. The Hardy Boys. Romeo and Juliet. The Princess Diaries. Treasure Island. The Chronicles of Narnia. A Wrinkle in Time. Oliver Twist. The Catcher in the Rye. Alice in Wonderland. Harry Potter and Twilight. Negative Dialectics.* I could go on. There are exceptions, of course, but film echoes these conventions. Imagine every children's movie you've ever seen, by Disney *or* DreamWorks." Down crashes a stack of Blu-ray discs featuring various princesses and their sequels.

"Mind you," Dr. Lawless says, "you aren't supposed to know that anything strange is going on at all. But if you do discover something, the Inquiscriptors, and Via Positiva by extension, want to make sure you're inclined to do the stupidest thing possible. We are going to pursue a different path. We are going to break these rules they've taught you by osmosis. And then, maybe we can find out why Via Positiva abducted you, Samo, why Via Negativa hunts Dunya, who the Book Ninjas are and why they are recruiting Monty, and Ezzie...why you're shattering glass all over campus."

Dr. Lawless stands before them, hands on her hips, cool but defiant.

The First Rule

"Never confide in authority. Keep your secrets to yourself."

Don't do this.

"Never confide in authority," says Dr. Lawless. "Keep your secrets to yourself. What idiocy. Think about this for a moment. You four are students, just trying to figure out how to survive your first year of college. Your adversaries are illegal conspiracies meddling with dangerous technology. Who do you think is more at risk of exposure? So, confide in authority. Tell everyone what has happened."

Which is why, the next day, Monty will get on the phone and call the Arkaic Police, and he will drop tips to the AU administration, the board of trustees, the FBI, CIA, NSA, and IRS, and the boudoir of one Paula Broadwell. He will incriminate the Inquiscriptors (tips re: black-market trading and antitrust violations), Via Positiva (tips re: breaking and entering, suspected abduction, and even necromancy), and Via Negativa (tips re: attempted abduction, academic misconduct, blackmail, and fraud).

Samo will take the bus to a wretched hovel in the Os, where he will rouse two filthy, drug-addled PhDs with Monty's information on the Inquiscriptors' book caches. Their eyes will gleam with a feverish light as they imagine millions of dollars to be made while exacting their revenge on the publishing industry that spurned them.

Ezzie will simply stand up in her humanities class, look Professor Plumb in the eye, remove her sunglasses, and say, "I want my mother back, you son of a bitch." At this point, all the windows will shatter.

The Second Rule

"A lie will always come back to haunt you."
Don't believe this.

"A lie will always come back to haunt you," says Dr. Lawless. "Bullshit. Have some understanding of your own strengths and weaknesses so you can avoid conduct that will make you nauseated in the morning, but keep in mind that nobody has a fixed identity in the first place. We are all changing, all the time, and we must wear many hats during our lives. As for lies, keep them clean and simple, don't contradict yourself, and you can stay ahead in the game."

Which is why, the next day, Ezzie will compose an email to Dr. Rochet, saying, "I believe that the Anthrostrologers have murdered my roommate Dunya Blavatsky, and I'm just waiting to finish my decryption anthology. If there's anything you'd like to get off your chest, you know where to reach me."

Monty will unearth the email listhosts for both the judges and the team captains of Artemis' Hunt, writing, "Members of Via Positiva started a fire in room 227 of Acedia House on Saturday, October 27, and I have photographic evidence. We'll see if that ends up being an item on this year's Hunt. I think it's doubtful; photos won't help build a temporelectrical turbine."

And as for the turbines...

Samo will make a silkscreen T-shirt featuring his own precise rendering, from memory, of a temporelectrical turbine, labeled according to his own careful deductions. The sketch shows a third of a turbine, which is all he can remember. The back of the shirt features an enormous, throbbing brain, and the words, "The Rest of the Plan is in my Massive Hanging Hemispheres."

The Third Rule

"Virtuous protagonists will not die."
It isn't always true.

"Virtuous protagonists will not die," says Dr. Lawless. "Straight-up nonsense. Via Positiva kills. Via Negativa kills. None of us are invincible or even close to it. Any or all of us could end up dead before this quarter is over."

Stunned quiet.

"Um," says Samo, "what do you want us to do about that rule?"

"I want you to be fucking careful," says Dr. Lawless.

Blindsided

Play the pity card.

Waves are made.

Alyssa Carnival loudly denounces Monty in the cafeteria ("Now Acedia House is going to be on the judges' hit list!"). Ezzie is suspended from her classes "pending appeal to the Administrative Division." Samo is actually summoned by campus security and the Dean of Housing, where his shirt is confiscated (although they do leave him with a wife-beater). The three feel, maybe, a little less isolated in their *Sturm und Drang*, but these exploits don't ameliorate their work load. Extracurriculars. Classwork. But Monty, Ezzie, and Dunya are sleeping less than ever. Not four hours a night, but three. Sometimes not three, but two. They get by with a heady mixture of caffeine and cocaine and ginseng and betel nuts. Maybe not cocaine. Maybe, but maybe not. One hour.

Monty sleeps fitfully, his head resting on the velvet bolster of Monica's harem bed. It is early evening–five or five-thirty–but the sky is already the dim, bloody color of a crushed thrush. Behind him, the door knob twists with a squeal. *Maybe Monica will give me a massage*, Monty thinks. *I need a massage.* The door opens. *But Monica would have needed a key to open her door. It's probably the Book Ninjas.*

Monty rolls over onto his side, sits up on the burgundy mattress, and faces the black-clad figure in the blackening room.

"Who are you?" he asks.

"We are the Book Ninjas," says the figure. Its voice literally sounds like Vincent Price with a frog in his throat. As in, every time Vincent's larynx contracts to breathe or speak, it chokes the frog, who lets out a feeble bleat that dimly resembles an English word.

"Who are you, really?" asks Monty.

"I think I will ask the questions!" The figure lifts its fingers into the air, somehow throwing a secondary shadow over the dark room.

"No, you won't. Because if you do, I'll turn on the light and try to pin you down, and if I do, then you can answer the same questions for the university and the Olan Foundation."

"Ha ha ha," croaks the figure. But it doesn't seem too certain.

"Are you with Via Positiva?"

"No."

"Are you with Via Negativa?"

"We are with ourselves."

"What do you want?"

"We are the good guys. We want to keep you all from getting hurt."

"Why?"

"Ha ha ha!" croaks the figure.

"You said that one of my friends was going to 'embark on a dangerous adventure.' Did you mean Samo or Dunya?"

"Ha ha ha!"

A squeal, and the door opens again. The bright light catches Monty off guard.

"Monty?" says Monica.

"Stop!" yells Monty, but the ninja has already darted across the room and launched itself into the air. It crashes through the window and vanishes into darkness below.

"My God!" Monica shrieks. "That's a six-story drop!"

They rush down the stairs, open the portcullis, and race out onto the Fairway. They quickly find the twisted and crumpled robes and shinobi shōzoku, all wrapped in a mass. There are some socks and slippers, silver daggers, a copy of Ovid's *Metamorphosis*, and a pair of Spongebob boxers. But no body.

Monty looks at Monica matter-of-factly.

"I'm going to need some sex tonight," he says.

Updrafts and Air Conditioners

When you do find yourself in "the zone," don't relent.
You never know how long it's going to last.

from: Percival Plumb, PhD <pplumb@arkaicu.edu>
to: Esmeralda Prentice <eprenti@arkaicu.edu>
date: Wed., Nov 16, 2011 at 7:22 AM
subject: Academic Reinstatement

Ms. Prentice,

I have spoken to the Dean of Humanities and explained that the incident in class this Monday past was a simple accident. I trust you will take all due precaution to ensure that it does not happen again. If there is any matter of comment or complaint you wish to register regarding myself or my class, I kindly ask you to speak with me during office hours. If you do not feel comfortable making such comments in person, please schedule an appointment with either your Academic Adviser or the Secretary of Humanities. They will respect your privacy.

Sincerely,

Prof. Plumb

• • • • •

"It's working!" Ezzie says. She stands in the doorway to Samo's room, waving a piece of paper over her head. An orange-lipped Samo looks up from a pile of Cheeto and Dorito crumbs. The sun is just now up, and the world is a haze all around him.

"Don't talk about it here," he slurs. "They might hear you."

"I won't," says Ezzie. "Here, read." Samo takes the page and strains to read the email while Ezzie talks. "Up all night? I was too."

"Yeah..."

"You look tired."

"You don't look tired." He pauses. "I am. I had to finish my potato cannons for the Pneumatics and drill down on this problem set. And I just got back from Crew a half hour ago. But I'm not half as busy as Monty. He seems as wide awake as you do. Did he tell you about his run in with the BNs last night?"

"He texted me about it."

"Crazy, huh?"

"We've got them on the run, Samo!"

"Well, I don't know that we're quite that far..."

"I feel like an angel!"

"That's just the caffeine talking –"

But she does, and as a matter of fact, she did dream of angels, but–when could she have dreamt of angels?–she hasn't slept at all! *A waking dream.* "I'm awake." The thermals blew them upward.

"The longer I'm awake, the more power I feel." Or was it something stronger than thermals? "It's like I'm rising above everything." A fierce updraft that tossed the feathered souls up toward the heaven they mourned. "Above the static." They weren't fallen angels, but striving souls. "Above the noise." *Like Clarence or something.* "And I can just imagine those machines, ticking down there, even when I'm far from them, but I understand the noise they're making." Perhaps they're blown by the world's biggest, boldest air conditioner. "We're breaking the rules in the books, Samo, and something is shattering, other than glass." A spirit, prime pump through fully charged condenser coils. "We're holding up the light of truth, and they are afraid." A wind that can be felt but cannot be seen, that flows from the skull, follows the white arrows on green backgrounds, angles downward first but ultimately up, as if Newton's law has been applied in reverse. They build speed, these feathered things, bigger than neutrinos, and faster than space inflation. "And we are young and curious, and we have the whole world ahead of us, and Samo, I'm writing plays, and they will be *seen*, and the angels will stretch their wings, and we'll take lovers and love them, have friends and hug them, make enemies and yell over big wooden tables, and, and, and...and we have the whole world ahead of us —"

Samo's glass cracks. He quickly picks it up and drinks the last of the milk inside before it starts to drip.

"Sorry," says Ezzie.

"I remember when you were shy," muses Samo.

"What do you mean? I am shy!" Ezzie cackles like a banshee.

Her phone buzzes. It's a text from Dr. Lawless:

Friday night, you have to go to the Atlantis Coney Island. It is on Ash Highway. You have to devise a way to get there without attracting notice or suspicion. And you also have to be able to accommodate a very important guest.

"She spells everything out when she texts," says Ezzie. "Who does that?"

"Dr. Lawless," says Samo. "I need some sleep. What were you saying just now?"

"That there was this incredible ladder. A ladder of electricity. The angels went up it all night long, and their wings were like smoke."

An Acedian Thing

Even perceptive students won't notice
how many strings are attached
until they're hopelessly entangled.

"It's a Basement People thing," murmurs Monty.

Monica rolls her eyes. It's a clichè, true, but that's what she does. She stands before him, hands in the pockets of her track pants, and makes a slight swivel of her head, taking in the vaulted ceiling of the Olan Library. *Dammit!* Monty thinks. *That's distractingly adorable.*

"I just had my window smashed by some lunatic in mummer's robes who launched himself from the sixth story and vanished before he hit the ground. A week ago, you were sitting under the oak tree in our courtyard when it *exploded*. Samo went missing and I still don't know how he got back. Dunya went missing, and I still don't know where she is. Then there was all that weirdness with room 227. And you still haven't told me what landed you in the hospital."

Monty pushes aside the Ovid and opens a massive catalogue of Salvator Rosa. The page opens to a landscape painting featuring a young woman holding a pile of dirt, and an almost-naked man who appears to be blessing her. The river water behind them seems to be pulled in by the gravity of these two figures. The verdant cedar branches ache with the desire to touch them. The very sun attempts to reorient its orbit around them.

"It's very lovely," says Monica with a petulance.

"I am so close," whispers Monty. "So damn close!" he hisses.

"So close to what?"

"It's a Basement People thing."

"Okay," says Monica.

She slams the catalogue shut with a violent thud. Graduate students glare across the space, but Monica doesn't notice. She's glowering down at Monty.

"Listen, *boyfriend*," she snaps. "I am the RA of Acedia House, and you so-called 'Basement People' are part of my house. You don't get to pick your own little tribe. And I'm your *girlfriend*, so if you have a clique, I'd better be in it. This isn't a basement thing anymore. It's an Acedian thing. Now you can tell me what's going on and how I can help *right now*, or I'll take this straight to the Mavens."

Monty blinks, coming out of a trance. "Of course," he says, too loudly. More glares, but: "Rule One. Duh! Yes, Monica, you can help us."

"First, you have to tell me what's going on," she answers.

"First, we have to come up with a list of people we can trust in Acedia. Not a long list. Just three or four people."

"First, you have to tell me what's going on."

"First, you have to get that psychopath Alyssa Carnival off my back!"

"Monty?"

"Yes?"

"What's going on?"

No Apologies

Often the Room with a View comes at a price.

"Why are you wearing a dress?" snarls the professor.

"It's called a utilikilt, Dr. Plumb," answers Cassidy Antrim. His voice is smooth and even, as always.

"Hmph!" Plumb answers. "Have a seat."

Cassidy sits. "You have a nice view up here."

Plumb shakes his head. "The lighting is atrocious."

They're both correct. The peaked Gothic windows are on the second-highest floor of Olan Commons, offering a commanding view of the Arken River valley, from XAI to the downtown skyline. On the other hand, the white walls and white fluorescent lights dangling from the overly high ceiling give the office a cell-like feeling. As afternoon draws toward evening, the ceiling seems to grow higher, and the walls more severe.

"What may I do for you, Mr. Antrim?"

"I'm actually here on behalf of Esmeralda Prentice –"

"I have no business discussing other students, Mr. Antrim, but you would do well to reexamine the *so-called* arguments you made concerning alleged trysts between William Kent and –"

"Picture it, Dr. Plumb." Cassidy produces a stainless steel flask. "Care for a tipple, Doctor?"

"You're underage!"

Cassidy takes a big swig.

"I am unaccustomed to being treated with disrespect –"

"Then you must be very concerned about what I know about Lorraine Prentice, to tolerate such disrespect."

Plumb breathes for a moment, then another. "You must all think you are so very clever," he says in a low voice, "and that you can blackmail me. You must think yourself so very superior to *me*. You did well in school. Got away from your parents. Got a tidy bit of money. But you make stupid mistakes. Blackmail requires a crime. Blackmail requires vice. I can tell that you don't have proof of anything. I know that you don't have proof, because there isn't anything to prove. I've no reason for guilt. Case closed."

Cassidy shrugs. "Three years ago, you were dean. Now you are not."

Plumb purses his lips. "See? It appears the situation has already been remedied."

Cassidy stands. He stretches. Stretches like a cat. He's a broad, tall guy, so it's a tiger of a stretch.

"I don't think Ezzie thinks it's been remedied," he says.

"Then she can come and see me!" snaps Plumb.

"I'll leave this for you." Cassidy sets the flask down on Plumb's desk. "You look pretty stressed out."

"Leave, now."

Cassidy walks slowly to the door, opens it, and ducks out, closing it softly behind him. Then he steps to the side and waits. Several minutes pass. Beneath the door, the office light clicks off. Just as he expected, Plumb is sitting in the dimness and considering his darkening view. Cassidy hears a soft tap, of metal on wood. Just as he expected, Plumb has set the flask of whiskey down after taking a long, deep drink. Cassidy takes a deep breath and opens the door again. Plumb wheels back to face him, his cheeks wet in the angry yellow hallway glare.

"That looks like guilt to me," Cassidy says.

"I told you to leave!"

Obsolete Technology

There is a time to keep silent, and a time to speak.

"I can't hear you!" Samo's voice rattles through the plastic walkie-talkie.

"That's because I'm whispering, idiot!" 'Lissa hisses.

"What?"

Why did you insist on walkie-talkies? 'Lissa has quickly learned that her friend-with-benefits will go with the technological anachronism each and every time. *Cell phones? Oh, no, way too convenient.*

"He's entering the Fairway," says 'Lissa.

"Follow him!" Samo's voice booms through with a cackle of static. It's so loud that Dr. Rochet hears and looks behind him, but 'Lissa has ducked behind a stone staircase. Rochet sways for a moment, uncertainly, then turns and continues along his path.

'Lissa risks an answer: "I am following him, fool!"

"What?!" yells Samo on the other end.

That's it, she thinks, and turns off the walkie-talkie. *You stick to your strengths: drawing.* "I'll handle the espionage."

It's a warm, comfortable night, and for several minutes, Rochet affects a casual stroll. As he gets farther from campus, however, and deeper into the Fairway, he becomes more and more agitated. Not in a comic book way, furtively glancing side to side, but walking with short, sharp steps. Trembling, maybe. Shaking, even. 'Lissa slinks along the edge of the looming trees—*They call it the Hunting Grounds?*—and even if Rochet looks her way once or twice, there's no way he can pick out her slight figure among the towering trunks. 'Lissa's self-satisfaction vanishes when she realizes that Rochet himself is walking closer and closer to the trees. Fortunately, by the time he's standing on the eaves of the forest, he's so visibly shaken that he doesn't seem to notice anything around him at all.

They move along, Rochet hugging the shore of the forest as it slopes away to the east and into the rising moon, and 'Lissa creeping along behind him. At length, the campus vanishes behind them, and even South Street is nothing but a distant line of pinprick street lamps. But another building has emerged into view: a vast, concrete sarcophagus-obelisk-type thing that seems to thrum with chained power. "Chain power," 'Lissa says, softly, and clicks her tongue. She notices that Rochet has vanished.

She freezes. Checks her sides. Looks behind her. Nothing. *If he's seen me, he hasn't let me know it –*

A branch snaps somewhere ahead. *Two o'clock.* After an anxious moment, 'Lissa slinks farther along and discovers a small path leading into the forest. She peeks around the frost-licked brambles, and her eyes go wide. Rochet is standing in the middle of a small clearing, and stringy shapes dangle from the tree branches. They sway with a lively motion, even in the slight breeze. Nooses of many sizes and varieties. In the center, with his jacket cast to the ground, his shirt untucked and ripped open–bright buttons everywhere–stands Rochet. He's pulled off his necktie–burgundy gone rust red in the steady silver moonlight–and appears to be tying it around and around in his hand.

"I'm sorry," he groans. "Tell my wife!" he wails at the trees. The branches click against each other in answer. "I'm sorry!" Rochet yells. "Tell my wife!" he screams. The winds rise, dispelling the warmth, filling the air with menace and ice. 'Lissa sees that Rochet has fashioned his tie into a crude noose and is fastening the opposite end around a low-hanging branch.

Horror-stricken, she backs away from the scene. She fumbles with her jacket–her pants pockets–her jacket. Her cold hands–icy fingers–finally find her cell. *Get away from him*, she thinks. *Got to call. Can't be heard. God knows what he'll do if he hears me.* An instant later, she's back on the margins of the Fairway, and out of view, out of earshot, but she can't find a signal. *Can't find a signal?! Where's my signal?! I'm in the middle of the city. There's a signal everywhere here.* She spins in frustration, and then she knows. She understands. The pulsing glow of that sepulchral power station. She can just feel something unholy shimmering through her, disrupting all kinds of fields and connections.

"Oh, my God," she says in sudden wonder. "He was right. God, thank you, Sam, you were right!" And she takes out the walkie-talkie. "Sam, Sam, Sam!" she says into the speaker.

"Oh, hey, you're there!" he cheerfully answers.

"Get on the phone. Get emergency. That professor, he's going to hang himself in the forest! He's trying to do it right now!"

No Time to Be Scared

Don't get so wrapped up in life-altering moments
that you miss out on the day-to-day mundane things,
because it is the day-to-day mundane things which will most often
alter your life.

Thursday night. Forces deployed. Despite Dr. Lawless' encouragement, Ezzie feels a little nervous about the broad circulation of secrets. Still, the confessional has lightened the oppression and even enabled her to delegate a bit. So yesterday, Cassidy went to pry information from the steel jaws of Professor Plumb, and tonight, 'Lissa will follow Rochet in the hopes of learning more about the Anthrostrologers. Monty told Monica everything, and while Ezzie was angry at first, she has to admit that he couldn't have chosen a wiser confidante. Argosy Jackknife, Giovanni Martini, Krista Baroque, and Velma Brass have all been told—to varying degrees—about these Autumn Quarter struggles. They've contributed their trust and talent, from compiling a list of every faculty member and student who has joined the Anthrostrologers since the SO was formed, to packing a furious Alyssa Carnival away to Seattle for the week.

Last night—*mercifully!*—Ezzie slept.

Tonight, Ezzie has lonely work, but it's ordinary work, and it's wonderful. It has nothing to do with glasses shattering, or secret societies, or even reaching across the comfort barrier to make new friends. She's doing something old and comfortable in a new and exciting setting: she's promoting her play. Tomorrow, *Hamletmachine* will open at TOG, and afterward, the Acedians will enact a piece of Rube Goldberg performance art to safely land the Basement People at the Atlantis. Tonight, her mind is on a more ordinary audience. She has helped to build this production. Its metallic, serrated, mechanical magnetism. Its political edge, special and sharp in 2011 AD. In the diminishing wake of Occupy. The continuing surge of election year primaries.

"Are you coming to *Hamletmachine* tomorrow?" she asks Bruce Bancroft in the Acedia House vestibule.

"Um, how much does it cost?"

"Five dollars."

"Sure. You did something with that?"

"I am its shimmering dramaturg, but if you look closely, you'll also notice that I painted half of the set pieces."

In her arms, she carries a stack of high-gloss 11 x 17-inch posters. The cast has already papered half of the campus, and it's a good thing, too. *Hamletmachine* had almost slipped between the cracks, between last week's pungent magnificence of *The Night of the Iguana* and next week's hyped-up *The Moldy Fountain*. Ezzie is determined to go above and beyond. She isn't content to advertise on campus. She has—she said it herself—the whole world ahead of her. Time to take a few practical steps into it.

Ezzie catches the South Street bus and rides it downtown. She starts on East Street near I-63. She papers all of the telephone poles in front of City Hall and the county jail. She imagines the lonely prisoners looking out through their narrow windows, seeing the posters, and wishing that they could attend. Then, further north, there's a block of churches: Presbyterian, Methodist, Lutheran, Episcopalian, Roman Catholic, and Christian Scientist. They'll all wake up in sere sunlight to face Müller's puckered frown. She's surprised to find an open party store on a side street...she had thought that downtown Arkaic would be closed up by this time of night. It sets her back three dollars but nets her a processed donut and some dishwater coffee. That's okay; she's happy to have the sweet and warmth. The only thing she can't stand are these stale Michigan bagels. New Yorkers have no patience for such things.

The next block presents businesses: restaurants, bars, coffee shops, and more eccentric offerings. There's a hat shop, a board game store, and a wig outlet. And finally, there's the Arkaic campus of Southern Michigan U., where 'Lissa goes to school. *I wonder how*

'Lissa's doing out there, anyway. Will the SMU students rip down my posters? How do SMU students feel about us over at AU? I guess they probably think we're all spoiled brats...like me? Ha!

As Ezzie crosses the brick street, back and forth, papering every bulletin board and light pole, the hope that has chased her all week wells up in her throat again. It clouds her eyes. It's a wonderful feeling. She suspects it won't last. Good things never last forever.

"But neither do bad things," she says.

It isn't that I'm less shy. I...I...people are hard to talk to. People are weird and alien things. She shrugs. But when people are doing such amazing things–when I'm doing amazing things–there just isn't any time for it. "No time to be scared," she says. *Fuck it.*

Ezzie turns back down East Street. She's papered downtown Arkaic from tip to toe, but she saved this place for last. The happy, warm glow of Hickory's, open and crowded at this late hour. She leans against the window and waves until the host sees her. He smiles. She points to her poster and then to the broad glass window. He nods, grinning. She gives him a thumbs up. Then she hears a rustle or, no, more like a gentle roar coming from the east.

Ezzie looks up and watches a gust of wind–visible in its blasted dirt, the swirling papers, the spinning leaves, kicked up and made instantly more brittle. This wind, advancing fast upon her, is nothing more or less than the arrival of winter. It is something she might have seen in New York, or many other places, for that matter, but it is magnificent, even though it has nothing to do with weird technology or bizarre cults or her mother.

My mother...

The wind arrives.

It suddenly wrenches the few remaining posters from Ezzie's hands and dances them up into the midnight blue sky. The temperature drops ten degrees. Ezzie tastes the promise of snow on her tongue, and she laughs with it. The posters vanish into the distance.

Ezzie gets out her phone and calls her Uncle Clay.

"Ezzie?" he says.

"I love you, Uncle Clay," she says.

"I love you too. Thank you for calling. How are things?"

"Things are...insane and all over. But I'm not going to tell you about that tonight. I'm just going to tell you one thing. My play is opening tomorrow, and I'm excited. I'm putting up posters for it right now. Tonight is a wonderful, clear, cold, cruel night, and it makes me glad to be alive."

"I'm glad you're alive too, Ezzie," Clay says, and his voice is warm. "The world is lucky to have you."

"The world is a wonderful place!" she says.

Then she leaps in the dark.

CHAPTER THIRTEEN
THE COUNCIL OF ATLANTIS

Quantum Cortázar, Part 1:
Don't Garrote My Parrot

"It is extremely easy to assume things have gone off the rails."
—The Editor

If the plot of Shattering Glass *blows you like a strong wind, and you wish to "get on with it," kindly hop forward to the part of this chapter titled "Stockholm Syndrome for Everyone."*

If you wish to take a leisurely walk down a windswept and haunted lane, and to contemplate contradictory things such as the longevity-by-proxy of The Many Loves of Dobie Gillis, *by all means continue reading right here.*

Theme Song: "Milkshake" by Kelis

Evil sparrows fall providentially from a high library window. A fog congeals. It forms the words:

"DON'T GARROTE MY PARROT"

Cut to Alphonse, a masculine, cigar-smoking parrot. Cut to darkness on the face of the deep. Monty, Dunya, Ezzie, and Samo walk across the screen with Alphonse perched on Samo's shoulder. They are being watched from behind by Professor Plumb. Cut to Dunya being chased by the Anthrostrologists. Cut to Monty being nabbed by the Inquiscriptors. Cut to Alphonse molting. Cut to a skeleton with a shit-eating grin. Cut to the fivesome running away. Cut to a temporelectrical turbine erasing some poor student's memories. Cut to Samo comforting Alphonse. Cut to the fivesome eating at

Hickory's. Cut to Samo riding a giant potato through outer space, to somewhere offscreen. CRASH! Cut to Samo sitting in a urinal. Cut to Alphonse cackling at Samo. Cut to Ezzie gasping in horror. Cut to Monty twisting about. Cut to various sere-faced professors glaring in their disapproval. Cut to Alphonse holding a terrified Samo. Cut to October Girl shrieking in demoniac fury. Cut to Alphonse flying away in a tiki mask disguise. Alphonse collides with a squid-headed demon from space. The tiki mask falls off. Alphonse looks up. The creature stares at him. Cut to Samo tweaking. Cut to everyone dancing in room 227. Cut to Alphonse advising Samo on his income taxes. Cut to a gargoyle disapproving of lewd dancing. Cut to Alphonse smoking the Sybil's ashes from her ampulla. Cut to the fivesome huddled over a copy of Ovid's Metamorphosis. *Cut back to the words floating in front of the library:*

"DON'T GARROTE MY PARROT"

Cut to Alphonse pecking out the robotic eyeballs of a predatory and fake Jimmy Buffett singing "Cheeseburger in Paradise" off-key.

"Featuring Special Guest, THOMAS PYNCHON!"

• • • • •

"Stars are awful," says Ezzie. "They look down on everyone. They know too many of our secrets." Yesterday's exaltation has faded with the nervousness of today.

"Stars are the only reason we're alive," says Samo.

"You two ready?" asks Monty.

'Lissa perpetually waits in the psych wing of Proctor Hospital, waiting waiting, in case Prof. Rochet tries anything weird.

Monica has camped out in the vestibule of Acedia House, ready to field any unexpected questions.

Everyone else is in position and ready to roll.

"Nothing to fear but death and elision," says Ezzie.

"Let's go!" says Monty.

• • • • •

The Acedia House lounge. It's eleven p.m. of the opening night of *Hamletmachine*.

"Nine days. You're toast!" yells Thomas Pynchon.

"Dammit," says Samo, throwing the controller with a fury.

They're huddled on the floor in front of the Wii. Ezzie reclines on the couch, dazed by the success of her show.

"I thought you were doing pretty good," she says.

"No," says Samo, resetting the game. "I wasn't."

"If he doesn't beat it in eight game days, he doesn't get the best ending," says Thomas.

"What happens with the worse ending?" asks Ezzie.

"You die from the infection of Dracula's curse."

"Are you sure this is worth the trouble?"

"Are you saying that difficult entertainment isn't worth your time?" (Dead people laugh offscreen.)

"No...I'm not."

"Well, I am!" says Samo. (Dead people laugh offscreen.)

"Awk! I hate *Vice*!" says Alphonse. (More laughter.)

"An ethical parrot," says Thomas. (More laughter.)

"An awetarded magazine," says Samo. (Loud laughter.)

Monty enters the room.

"Hey guys," he says, "I was just up in Monica's room, and there's something strange going on downtown."

· · · · ·

Monica's suite. They look out the window. The downtown skyline sprawls before them, but Arkaic is a city in decay. Other than the symbolic illumination of the Pyramid Bank Building, and its cousin, the Mesopotamian, most of the buildings there are shuttered. They say (with annoying regularity (Dead people laugh.)), "last one out, turn out the lights." But tonight, lights are on in the gutted nightclubs, abandoned banks, and skeletal, cathedralesque things raised by the riches of the auto industry. Seemingly every light bulb in a square mile has clicked on for the evening.

"Woah," say the Basement People (sans Dunya).

"By Byron!" exclaims Thomas.

"Awk, that's weird, woo hoo!" says Alphonse, flicking ash from his cigar.

He's right. It doesn't look like the thriving city of the 1940s or '50s. Most of these buildings have been abandoned for decades. The water has wormed its way in and leeched the mortar from between the bricks. Downtown shines with the pallor of a poorly reanimated corpse.

"Hey everyone," says Monty. "It looks like we've got a mystery to solve!"

"I'm ready," says Ezzie.

"I'm hungry," says Samo.

"Why should things be easy to understand?" asks Thomas. (Dead people laugh.)

· · · · ·

The city bus leaves our heroes on the corner of East and South Streets. It leaves. The world is empty but bright.

"Guignol!" says Ezzie. " What's going on here?!"

Nobody can question the light that blazes on the wrought iron arches straddling the brick streetscape, or the sound of milkshakes churning in resurrected drugstores, or the rush of music floating out from the derelict Burgundy movie palace.

"I've got the munchies, Alphonse!" says Samo. "What say we go grab a bag of Fritos from that party store over there?"

"Awk! Free to eat Fritos!" says Alphonse. (More laughter.)

• • • • •

Samo and Alphonse go to the party store. They jokingly ask the empty counter for Fritos and Vernors. They laugh at their imaginations. As if by magic, the food appears in front of them.

The others enter the Burgundy, where *The Ten Commandments* is screening for an audience of none.

"Shall I project a world?" asks Thomas. (Laughter.)

They sit down to watch Charlton Heston part the Red Sea. Monty receives popcorn from Ezzie, Ezzie receives popcorn from Thomas, and Thomas receives popcorn from...who is it?!

Nobody is there.

• • • • •

Samo and Alphonse leave the party store. The autumn air smells of crisp cinders, apple cider, and fog. A shadowy alien thing with a bright glowing head marches by, and a theremin trills. A flexatone pleaws. The figure is gone in the blink of an eye.

"That looks like something extraterrestrial," says Samo.

"It looks like a freak of nature, is what it looks like!" says Alphonse, flicking ashes from his cigar.

They follow it into the unlocked lobby of the Pyramid Bank Building, but it has vanished. An ATM spews hundred-dollar bills from its robotic mouth. Samo stuffs his pockets.

"Now I can get a new stereo! And a new car! A microkini for 'Lissa and some kicks to pump up," he says. "But..."

"But?" asks Alphonse.

"Starving."

"We just ate a bunch of Fritos."

"No," says Samo. "Not me. I am fed. But I grew up on a block of cookie-cutter houses. Every house has the same dimensions. The same floor plans. They don't look the same any more. A third are fine. A third are trashed. The last third are empty or burned out. Now my parents take out a second mortgage and half a dozen loans so that I can go to this school here, and eat in that cafeteria every day, and study for my future, and smoke up, and get laid by 'Lissa, and there's kids on my block don't even get enough to eat."

"So you're going to use that money to feed them?"

"Don't go all supply-side on me, Alphonse. I can't even do that. I'm not ready for the responsibility."

"Nobody wants responsibility."

"I want to plant a money tree with this shit, and then it isn't even my problem."

"Look up."

They do. The twisted head of the alien demon has an illithid squid mouth, and its tentacles part to issue a petrifying cry: "Woowoowoowoowoowoowoo!   Yayayayayayaya!! Yeyeyeyeyeyeye!!!"

Samo and Alphonse flee from the bank.

They hide in a dumpster.

They wait until the terrible sound has died.

· · · · ·

Monty, Ezzie, and Thomas are halfway down East Street when all the lights–buildings, traffic lights, street lights, and marquees–flicker and die.

Suddenly, downtown is pitch black.

"Clearly," says Thomas, "we are not among those chosen for enlightenment."

"Guignol, I don't like it here anymore!" says Ezzie.

"It has gotten rather spooky," says Monty.

A hollow wind curls a few dead leaves along the bricks inlaid in the street.

"Hey, it's Alphonse and Samo."

Their friends, shadows now, cross East.

"We saw..." And Samo tells them about the squid-skulled ghost.

"I know one person who might know what's going on," says Ezzie.

"Who is that?" asks Monty.

"He lives over there!" She points across the river at a stoic stone hotel, nine stories high, dating to the 1920s. The recently restored Ashburn Hotel.

"Do you mean –"

"Yes! A. Olan himself."

· · · · ·

A dapper gentleman, wearing newly pressed pants and a double-breasted charcoal suit, black rubber boots, and a red silk tie, meets them in his penthouse suite on the top floor.

"That is quite impossible," says A.

"It is not," says Monty, firmly. "All of the lights were on, in all of the abandoned buildings, just a few minutes ago."

"It was creepy!" says Samo.

A. sniffs a cup filled with brandy dating to the Roosevelt (Teddy) administration.

"All of those properties have different owners," he says, and takes a quick drink. "And many of them are out-of-state. New York. California. Colorado. Florida. Speculators. I can't imagine how any one person would coordinate what you just described."

"That isn't the half of it, Mr. Olan!" says Samo. "We saw a squid-headed alien–

"An alien?!"

"Like, the extraterrestrial kind!"

"Oh."

"And he ran into the lobby of the Pyramid Bank, and the ATM was just spitting money all over the place!"

Samo draws wads of hundred-dollar bills out of his pockets to illustrate.

A. cups his hands around Samo's comfortingly.

"I understand most of you attend my school, AU. You're not from around here. Your ways are not our ways. So listen when I tell you that in the darkness of many abandoned buildings, it is not unlikely that you saw some northern lights, or some haze of clouds moving about the moon. It can confuse unfamiliar souls. Yes, I am sure that this is what happened to you." He draws the money from Samo's hands and folds it on a neat stack on a nearby desk. "As you can see," he says, gesturing out his window at the close view of the cityscape, "all is dark. All is empty."

"But I am from Arkaic!" protests Samo.

"Give it a rest, Samo," says Monty. "Thank you for listening, Mr. Olan. We'll be on our way now."

Alphonse poops on the carpet.

"Awk!" he says, "Uno deuce."

• • • • •

Outside the Ashburn.

"That man doesn't care about the facts," says Ezzie.

"Facts are fiddlesticks for businessmen," muses Thomas.

"So what now?" says Samo. "Defeat makes me hungry. I have an idea. King Carol's in the Os is open twenty-four seven. Let's go there now. We can get coneys. I'm getting a Grand Rapids coney and a Flint coney and a Detroit coney, and gravy fries and –"

"Sunflower seeds! Yeah! Yeah!" chirps Alphonse.

"You two!" says Ezzie.

"I'm hungry, yo," says Samo.

"Shhhh!"

They turn to gaze across the river into the shadowed depths of the East Street cavern.

The lights of the Mesopotamian flicker on. Then the party store where Samo and Alphonse got their Fritos. Then the Masonic Temple and the Presbyterian Church. Then the Burgundy and the Pyramid. But this time around, the enlivened streetscape is less functional than before. All of the potted plants in the Mesopotamian have been smashed. Rammstein replaces the bland Muzak in the lobby of the Burgundy. The streetlights and arches flash on and off like a thousand concert strobes.

"This," says Thomas, stroking his beard(?), "is truly an anonymous, mysterious enigma."

Wacky hijinks follow. They have to. The plan must keep them occupied downtown until at least two a.m. And so they chase the high, glowing, squid-headed space demon, who runs through the alleys, distributing cans of beer in every alcove and chanting: "Woowoowoowoowoowoowoo!   Yayayayayayaya!! Yeyeyeyeyeyeye!!!"

Fireworks tear upwards between the skyscrapers and shower sparks down upon the low-rises which, catching flame, send clouds of smoke across the sky. The fire hydrants blow their tops and extinguish the fire. The space demon is escorted through the side streets by pealing teams of swans. Theremins and flexatones pleaw and wuh-aaaaaaaahhhhhhhh among the fogs and embers. That's when the tables turn. The space demon realizes, evidently, that it is larger than the humans and endowed with psychotic psychic powers, no doubt. It ought to be the hunter, the students its prey. It begins to chase them as it screams: "Woowoowoowoowoowoowoo! Yayayayayayaya!! Yeyeyeyeyeyeye!!!"

"I'm not paranoid," says Thomas. "I'm scared shitless!"

It starts to rain, then stops. Then Monty pours a cauldron of lava onto the sidewalk, and the space demon, running in pursuit, is caught fast. The soles of his rubber boots melt upon contact with the molten earth, which binds him to the pavement. Twist and turn as he will, he's stuck for good!

"Those boots look familiar," says Monty. "Let's see if our extraterrestrial friend can breathe Earthling air." As he pulls off the demon's helmet, its tentacled, chitinous face falls to the ground, revealing a human face underneath.

"A. Olan?!" the group exclaims.

A. looks out at them with a scowl.

"Guignol! I get it!" says Ezzie, slapping her hand to her forehead. "Everyone knows that Mr. Olan is trying to buy up property downtown for redevelopment. He already has the municipal government and the local nonprofits in the palm of his hand, but he couldn't do anything about squatters or the out-of-state speculators. By making everyone think that downtown Arkaic was haunted, he would lower the property values and make it easier to acquire deeds for his own nefarious purposes!"

"It was probably a great way to lower his tax contribution, too," adds Monty.

"And get free Fritos, too!" says Samo.

"Awk, free Fritos, woo hoo!" chirps Alphonse.

"But what about all those lights?" asks Samo.

"Easy," explains Monty. "As majority deed holder, A. was able to access each building through adjacent properties that he owned. He had only to run from building to building and turn on the lights!"

"And the ATM?" asks Samo.

"A. also holds a controlling stock in Pyramid Bank. Manipulating an ATM would be child's play."

"It was a good plan. Almost too good, Mr. Olan," chides Monty.

"Yes," he says, "and I would've gotten away with it, if it hadn't been for you busybody students!"

The group laughs.

"I think it's time to get Mr. Olan to the county jail," Monty says. "The board of directors will have some strong words for him after these antics."

"Just a minute, just a minute!" caws Alphonse. "This right here is a momentous moment. I want to get a picture." He pulls out his smartphone.

Thomas breaks out in a cold sweat. "Um, please don't," he says.

"What's the matter, Tommy boy? Am I rainbowing on your parade?"

"No," Thomas stammers, "it's just that...well...to be honest, I'd rather not be photographed."

"Aww, lighten up and say 'Mozzarella!' "

Alphonse takes a picture.

"You fucking bitch of a bird!" shrieks Thomas and leaps at the parrot. Alphonse tries to flap away, but Thomas catches him around the neck and begins to shake him roughly, back-and-forth, banging his head against the sidewalk. "Bitch of a bird! Bitch of a bird!"

"Hey!" yells Samo. "Don't garrote my parrot!"

END CREDITS.

· · · · ·

Mad applause from the peanut gallery. The twenty-odd people in the audience have enjoyed this show, eclectic as it was, held in an abandoned storefront of Owen Road in the Os. It has taken a couple last minute phone calls by A. Olan to have the heat and electricity turned back on, and the place is still a mess. There's a shattered pile of chalk and asbestos (probably?) wherever the ceiling tiles have fallen in. Water always finds a way, so mold grows in in the corners. But any doubts in the audience were assuaged by a cooler full of free chilled Mickey'ses and a tray of very special brownies waiting at the door.

The house has been a tight grid of folding chairs.

The stage has been nothing but a white curtain strung from one wall to the other.

And now that the show is over, on cue, the electricity cuts out again.

Still, people hang out in the "lobby," chatting about the experience. What it means for them in terms of reification, and gestalt, and pastiche, and hubris. The shadow of Ezzie's head floats out to the middle of the stage, and she speaks to the audience directly.

"Thank you for coming out to see our impromptu performance."

Wild cheering.

"I want you to know—I want you to know—that the mold and the mess here...we didn't have the time to clean it up. The words we said and the emotions we expressed were real. We're all scraping through a forest full of dense, dead trees. And we're looking for a path. Who knows where it goes, but we think we'll know it when we find it. Who knows where our path will take us? And maybe we'll find the right path, the wrong path, by luck. It's time to look and look hard. Who knows if we'll get another chance. So that's all I want to say, at the end of this show. Pull your jackets and scarves tight against the wind, and don't be afraid of the werewolves or the monsters hiding behind each tree–they're just men and women wearing masks, anyway–and hurry, hurry, hurry toward your goal before it slips between your fingers."

She holds up her hand and makes a quick and gentle fist. It's too dark to see much of anything, exactly, but everyone feels, in their held breath, something invisible, like a quick, streaming sand of time, slipping inevitably through those delicate, closing fingers.

And so the show is officially over. The audience, including Cassidy, Argosy, Krista, Velma, and many unknown others, files toward the exit, debating which bar or restaurant to hit up.

"Thank you for this opportunity, Ezzie," says Thomas. "I need to get going, however. Melanie will be expecting me home in time for dinner tomorrow."

"Thank you Mr. Pynchon, and don't be so hard on *The Crying of Lot 49*. It really is a bright and challenging piece, and it's a good little start for those of us too impatient to dive into your other stuff."

"Yes, well I don't want to hear that," he says with a sniff, and leaves through the back door.

"Excuse me," says A. "May I leave too? It's already quite late for my evening cordial."

"Unless," she says, "you want me to tell your wife about your second affair, you'll say and do and stay and go exactly what and where I tell you."

A. is quiet.

"Ready to go?" asks Dr. Lawless, stepping out of the wings.

"Yes," says Ezzie. "This will work. Nobody's going to think it's strange for us to go celebrate after our successful performance. Let's go get our Dunya!"

Stockholm Syndrome for Everyone

Sometimes, True Loves aren't even people at all.

A gray haze–blurry lines–beleaguered confusion.

Is Dunya going crazy?

Sleepy, yes, but that's not the worst of it. The worst is the weary exhaustion. Two weeks now without enjoying the sun. Two weeks now of sleeping in a freezing meat locker.

Everything is headache gray. The door. The lights overhead. The food. The coffee. The windows, unstreaked. The gas station across Ash Highway, and behind that, the trains that chug away nightly. The door. The door.

Everything is gray and blurry.

• • • • •

Nevertheless, Dunya has come to love this place. It has been her own island. Her oasis. Her home, and in some ways, it's a more permanent home than any she's known so far. During her time here, she has inhabited the place fully. Chris and Brendan entertain her with anecdotes and fairy tales each day, to pass the hours by. The sharp bite of new coffee, gurgling into life with water. The moon's nightly seductions, seductions. And even the untouched outside–Ash Highway–well, she said it up front: this is where Richmond, CA and Arkaic, MI could theoretically join hands and dance.

So it's a home, and a strange music to her, these weeks, this time, it is sharper now than anything she has experienced in her short life.

Is this even a little bit of Stockholm syndrome? she wonders. *I mean, I'm staying here for my own protection. And really, I could leave any time I wanted.*

She taps her foot. She is emotionally overextended. Fragile. Confused. Oh, yeah, gray and blurry.

I want to leave. But if I ever were to find out I was going to die, this, this is where I would come.

Somewhere outside, the moon looks down. Chris has put on another pot of coffee. The water sputters for the one-thousandth time. And then the door opens, and Ezzie steps inside, with Samo and Monty behind her, and behind them, A. Olan and Dr. Lawless. Dunya leaps off her seat and hurls herself toward Ezzie, knotting her arms around her, and she's, she's, she's suddenly crying. But Ezzie is crying too, and so is Monty. Samo is not, but his face looks stricken.

"What," asks Dunya, surprised at the rough sound of her own voice, "what has all of this—time—done to us?"

Ezzie pulls back, wet shimmer all over her smiling face. "I'm figuring things out now, I think, Dunya. It is making us into something more than we ever were before."

A muffled voice comes from the back of the group. "I, I, I," it says, "love you too."

It's A. Olan speaking, of course.

"Okay, this is fine," says Dr. Lawless, briskly. "I would like to call us to order. What is this, the Atlantis Coney Island? Okay. So let us begin the Council of the Atlantis. I'll have two up with extras and a cup of coffee. And Mr. Olan, you might want to take off that ridiculous jacket. You aren't going anywhere anytime soon."

Absolute Values

You'll think better on a full stomach.

Several minutes later, sufficient food and insufficient explanations have been served.

The sufficient food: for Dr. Lawless, two Flint-style coneys (Koegel on a bun with mustard, onions, and sauce (ground beef, beef heart, beef liver, paprika, and the secret spice (better than Detroit))), french fries swimming in brown gravy and black pepper, bright cold cole slaw, coffee, and more of the similar all around.

The insufficient explanations: A. Olan is simply the chair and heir of the Olan Foundation and the founder of Arkaic University. Chris and Brendan are saints or something who, finding Ralph Nader and Ron Paul insufficient to the exigencies of Arkaen desperation, stumbled upon Via Negativa and then, finding it to be eeeeevil, defected. Samo, Monty, Ezzie, and Dunya are college students, duh. And Dr. Lawless is basically the Aughra, the Miyagi, and the Lidenbrock. Apprehensions all around.

"What's going on?" asks Dunya.

"Tell them," says Dr. Lawless, gesturing to A. before taking an enormous bite of her coney.

"None of you are here because of your applications," he mumbles. "Some of our, um, benefactors contacted us through the Humanities Department. They...they wanted Dunya and Ezzie at the college. And, um, given their generous support of AU's endowment, I was compelled to give their recommendation of your talents the best consideration."

A car rushes by outside.

"Via Positiva," says Dr. Lawless between bites. "Go on."

"And as for the other two of you...there were high ranking members of the Department of Anthropology who actually invited you to the university without prior approval."

"Via Negativa," says Dr. Lawless.

"Does he understand this stuff?" asks Ezzie, gesturing to A. A. squirms.

"Oh, he understands," says Dr. Lawless. She takes a drink of her coffee. "Can I get a Coke, too?" she asks Brendan. "He doesn't want to talk about it."

"But why?" asks Samo. "And how is it that we all ended up together? I mean, in the basement of the same house...of the same dorm."

"That...isn't just a chance," says A. "They...the Humanities Department and...the Anthropology Department both thought– separately–that you belonged together. That you would benefit each other as students, being in proximity to each other. And being in the basement of Acedia House."

"I can see my meal will have to wait!" says Dr. Lawless, crossly. "And all because Mr. Olan knows much more than he is willing to say up front. You ought to know, Mr. Olan, what I know and how your reputation depends very much on what happens over the next few weeks. But that's okay; I can explain." She takes another bite and chews. "Okay then. What we know: you haven't spent much time in the other dorms or houses, have you? Because if you had, you might have noticed that dorm rooms are generally not placed below ground. Too close to the turbines and chain mazes. Too much risk of contamination. And none of it makes sense, anyway, because Calliope Cradle is far closer to the chains than any other dorm. So obviously they wanted these students contaminated. The alternatives defy the odds. But what about the selection?"

Brendan sets a Coke down in front of Dr. Lawless. They watch as she takes a long pull. "Bittersweet," she says, cupping her black coffee in one hand, her sparkling pop in the other. "There are a few possibilities. They each chose two of you without knowing the others' plans. Or Via Neg went first and Via Pos responded. Or Via Pos went first and Via Neg responded. I don't know that we'll ever figure out that part of it. Maybe they wanted the other team's choices kept out, or maybe they wanted you together after all...as spies. There is a bit of evidence of that, Monty Valverde. But we may not know the details of this either. Here is what I suspect...

"Monty Valverde. You came here as a prospie, honestly enough. But you noticed something on that early trip. The secrets that lay beneath the surface. Most of your friends and family back home thought you were full of shit, but one hunch out of ten was true, and that's enough to make a scandal. Your noticing was noticed by Via Negativa. They knew you could, and would, discover them. So instead, they decided to co-opt you, recruiting you to AU and then setting you on the trail of the Inquiscriptors and, by extension, Via Positiva."

"So the Book Ninjas are Via Negativa?" asks Monty.

Dr. Lawless looks at Chris and Brendan.

"Um," says Brendan. "Not really. The Book Ninjas are independent contractors hired out by Via Negativa. They, um, they spread disinformation, sow discord, and cause confusion and chaos. You know."

"And they're vampires," adds Chris.

"You mean, parasites? As in, they prey upon the world?"

Dr. Lawless looks at him seriously.

"Oh," says Monty, "you mean that they are literal vampires. That drink blood and can't stand the sunlight and all. Well, that does explain a lot."

"Dunya Blavatsky," Dr. Lawless says. "You believe that you came here at the behest of the Department of Anthropology. That couldn't be further from the truth. When Via Positiva's agents in California learned of your work with ghosting, they knew at once that this could counteract the necromantic powers of Via Negativa. 'Anthromancy,' they call it. It was Via Positiva that ensured your admission to this university and tried to secure you a full-ride scholarship. Unfortunately for them, Via Negativa saw their move and preempted it. They invited you themselves, hoping that you'd flunk out or go broke, and at the very least, they could keep an eye on you. But their anxiety overcame their prudence, causing them to show their hand when they tried to lynch you two weeks ago. You are very lucky that Brendan and Chris defected as they did."

"Damn," says Dunya.

"Sam O'Samuel," says Dr. Lawless. "Via Negativa wanted you. We know this because Via Positiva showed their hand when they tried to elide you in the chain mazes. During high school, you were here in town, and I have reason to believe that the Negatives have been in Arkaic longer than the Positives...the Negs have haunted the Hunting Grounds for a long time. You must have some kind of aptitude for engineering, because they caught that proficiency and pegged you as a person who could quickly learn how the temporelectrical turbines work. Who could engineer and even reverse engineer a turbine. You can, can't you?"

"No," says Samo, sheepishly. "I mean, I just memorize what I see."

"Right," says Dr. Lawless dismissively.

"And you, Ezzie," says Dr. Lawless. "You. A bit of a mystery to me. More than the others. The connection is the most obvious here. Sometimes, you break glass by looking at it –"

"And plastic even..." murmurs Ezzie.

"Plastic? Well. And then you are the daughter of Lorraine. I just don't know. You fit the profile of the 'typical' student here more than the others, but I can only imagine they–Via Positiva–think that you can complete what went uncompleted by your mother. It might have to do with your ability to shatter glass on campus. Or it might have to do with whatever happened that causes you to shatter glass. But what is the significance of the shattering glass? I don't know."

"I've almost got that figured out," says Monty, meekly. "I'm about 90 percent of the way there..."

But Ezzie has gotten to her feet. "I've got to take a moment," she says. "Take a breath. Fresh air. You know." And she steps out through the door.

Monty follows her.

• • • • •

"You shouldn't smoke," says Monty, sternly. His eyes are wide with worry, but it isn't worry about the risk of annihilation or murder or elision. It's worry about cancer or addiction.

"Jesus, Monty," Ezzie says. "I don't smoke. I mean, I got this from Brendan. Don't you see what we're up against?"

Monty sighs deeply. In the cold air, his breath makes some smoke of its own, which makes him feel guilty. He tries to regulate his breathing. Ezzie coughs and chuckles.

"You don't seem so shy right now," Monty says.

"Who has time?"

A car swishes past.

In the distance, that train.

"Who has time?" Monty chuckles. "Two months ago, you couldn't even look up when we talked to you. Now, you look us right in the eye."

"I'm getting a feeling–a sense–in dreams–angels climbing up and down–of what's going to happen at the end. It isn't exactly a happy ending. It doesn't exactly leave a lot of room for me to be timid. The timidness is expendable. So I tossed it."

Monty smiles, nervous.

Ezzie takes a long, last pull on the cigarette. The smoke fills her lungs like dry spice and speaks a word to her: east. She turns her head to the east and blows the smoke from between her lips. The wind blows it westward into her face. She coughs and sputters at this surprise and laughs, tears in her eyes. Monty laughs too.

"Oh, Monty!" she says. "Let's go back inside."

• • • • •

"You're changed," Dr. Lawless says as Monty and Ezzie return to the booth.

"Who, me?" asks Ezzie.

"No, all four of you. I think I've figured this out. Yes, they had to put you in Calliope Cradle to do it, it was the only dorm close enough to the chains. But I am the Dungeon Master of the Cradle. They clearly underestimated me. Ha! They'll think again before they make that mistake."

"What do you –" asks A.

"Look," says Dr. Lawless. "What is elision, exactly? We don't have a complete theory, but we do have what one could call plausible speculations. For example, a turbine can't interact with naked time. You need the perception of time passing in order to create power. You need memory, and so you need some form of sentience...of intelligence. This is proven. The turbines turn from the motion of our memories through time. We emit these, radiate them, in the same manner that stars radiate light and heat. But within the temporelectical field, the power of the turbines stretches actual minds. They 'lens' them, so to speak, especially those not sufficiently athletic to resist. This stretching is a *physical* effect, such that self-consciousness and, with self-consciousness, the actual, physical self is elided."

Dr. Lawless pulls a pen from her hair and scribbles a formula on a napkin:

$$\frac{pd}{t\phi}$$

She continues: "p is called presence, which we cannot yet accurately quantify, but it's a mental or spiritual quality, and d is distance. t is time, and ϕ is the temporelectical constant."

"What is the temporelectical constant?" asks Samo.

"It's the inverse of the theosophical constant," says Dunya with a shudder, and Dr. Lawless regards her with surprise.

"Anyway," says Dr. Lawless, "the point is, if something sentient—something intelligent or even merely *alive* is too close to a turbine for too long, it is erased. It is difficult to prove, because the erasure is complete. It acts upon the memories and minds of the living as well, but there would be scraps of evidence. Artifacts. Inconsistencies. Have entire human beings been elided? Who knows. Probably, I think. But most likely, we wouldn't know, because our memories of the people would be erased along with the victims themselves."

A long silence.

"But I was put down, and..." Samo says. The blood drains from his face. He blinks several times. "Um," he says, "excuse me while I go vomit."

He stands and stumbles toward the hallway, while A. follows him, muttering, "I'm sure she's wrong on this point, boy. We wouldn't let something so dangerous –"

Samo's voice echoes from the back: "Fuck you man, you're The Man. Bleahealehehaehaeha!!!"

When Samo returns from the bathroom, Dr. Lawless continues. "We also know that the turbines, and especially their chain power, create radiation with psychedelic effect, and that these effects would be stronger, the closer one is to the temporelectrical field. I think we've got it!"

"Got what?" asks Ezzie.

"You were each recruited to AU because of your special talents: Monty's sleuthing. Samo's engineering. Dunya's ghosting. Ezzie's...shattering? But these were natural powers. They wanted to get you as close to the field as they could without killing you. And to thereby make your natural powers *supernatural*. It's very poetic, when you think about it. Almost Shakespearean. They sculpted you as weapons to be used against each other, but here, you have become friends. Friends engineered for mutual destruction. Oh, we are close to the heart of it now!"

The students are aghast. Chris and Brendan too, and even A., the intemperate tycoon. Dr. Lawless breaks her own concentration for a moment to grin at her brilliance.

"I've untangled the motherfuckers' webs," she says. "And now I want another coney."

· · · · ·

They sit and watch while Dr. Lawless devours her third Koegel. Everyone else has somewhat lost their appetite, although Samo (never one to turn down free food) surreptitiously munches on some gravy fries.

"Well," says Dr. Lawless with a contented sigh. "I am very pleased with myself."

"But what are we going to do?" asks Ezzie.

"Huh? Do?" asks Dr. Lawless. It's a sharp, despairing laugh. "What are we going to do? These are millennia-old societies with all kinds of money and technology at their disposal."

"We're going to George W. Bush them," says Monty.

"What?!" asks Dunya.

"Yeah yeah," says Monty. "Fuck Bush, right? But listen. They're setting us up for a fall...one that will work for them. Via Positiva. Via Negativa. They're playing their little chess game with us. That's the way a conspiracy works. There are players and there are pawns. We are pawns. So what if we decide not to be mere chess pieces?"

He pauses and chuckles, then adds: "I was the champion of my high school chess team, you know."

After a moment, nobody speaks, so Monty goes on: "Look, we obviously got some of those powers, right? I mean, I've picked apart a lot of the history here, just like Samo's figured out the turbines, and there's Dunya's ghosting and Ezzie's shattering. But there's more to it than that. I mean, this thing, this power...it's basically made us into the X-Men. If we wait for the Vias to act, they'll do what they want with us. Personally, I don't want to end up with the Inquiscriptors again. But if we take things into our own hands –"

"Spell it out for us!" says Ezzie. She smiles. "Pretend we're Dr. Watson."

"Right," he says. "They both want to use us to leverage the turbines for their goals. That's clear, isn't it? So remove the turbines, and we remove the threat. And maybe expose them and escape them. We take control. We don't wait. We take the initiative."

Monty stands and starts pacing.

"Ezzie, you're a powerful writer, right? We saw that tonight. And Dunya, you maybe didn't know it, but you're a powerful actor. If only there were a play coming up...a script...an opportunity to turn expectations upside down. Oh wait, that's right, *The Moldy Fountain,* based on *The Holy Mountain,* Jodorowsky's psychedelic masterpiece. What if A. were to get us a turbine in exchange for us ending our blackmail and probably saving his pet university? What if Ezzie were to rewrite the script a bit, and then Dunya were to draw the audience in, get them involved, and prompt a protest, or something like that? Raise the students against the Pos and the Neg. While they're on the defensive, we can get to the chain maze. Samo, you get us close to the turbines safely, and Ezzie, you shatter the critical part."

"And what happens, Monty," challenges Dunya. "What happens if you 'shatter the critical part' of a temporelectical turbine? Do you think we just walk out of there, unharmed?"

Static across Monty's eyes.

He thinks.

"Hell if I know," he says.

BACK MATTER

Note

We are concerned that, after the excitement of the grand finale, you may be less likely to read the back matter of *A Manual on How to Survive Your First Year of College, This First Reckoning to Address Matters Pertinent to the Autumn Quarter Most Concisely Summarized by Issues Embodied in the Observation of Shattering Glass*, because your mind may be sufficiently blown as to inhibit productive neural functioning.

With this in mind, we are situating the back matter here, between Chapter Thirteen and Chapter Fourteen, for your use and enjoyment.

Epilogue

The Cradle is almost silent, now that the last shuttle has left for the airport. It is noon. The last few students have until twelve thirty to pack their shit up and get the hell out of Dodge.

Samo only has to get the hell out for a few miles. His Moms has noticed, he's sure, that despite the mere fifteen thousand-odd feet between them, he's only been home once since the quarter started, for Thanksgiving. Samo's been to the Atlantis, to the Os, and to the airport, but he hasn't had much hunger to go back to his own little neighborhood across the river. He knows what he'll see from his front porch, standing in an egg beater breeze, facing down those shake-sided ranch houses. In three months, they've only aged a little. Their paint has grayed a bit from sleet and exposure. Shoes have scuffed a few stones loose from their concrete porches. Their windows fogged up when the heat kicked in for the first time. Their change has been slow.

But Samo has changed entirely. Cataclysms. Ruptures. Sunderings. Oh, how much has happened in three months. Three months is not three months, because while those houses stand strong or gradually weather in the darkening air, he has seen whole realities turned inside out. The realities of his future as a student and as a man.

He hears a very neat and organized clatter from the inner suite room. Monty is packing up his things.

"You almost ready?" Samo calls out. "We get fined if we're here a minute after twelve thirty."

"I've been ready since ten, Samo," comes Monty's voice.

"Then what are you doing in there?"

"Ordering my books for next quarter."

"Already?! You know they'll have them at the bookstore in a couple weeks. Or in the Os, for that matter."

"I get a good deal if I order in advance. I found a dealer who can get me most of them used."

The door swings open and Monty is ready, suitcase in one arm, laptop in the other.

"That's a big suitcase," says Samo. "You know it's just three weeks."

"I like to be ready for anything," says Monty. There's a knock on the outer door. Before he can move, the knob turns and the door flies open. Argosy stands in the hall.

"Come on!" he says, loudly. "I don't want to get a fine."

"What did you do to your hair?" asks Monty.

Argosy's hair is pink.

"I don't know," he says. "I woke up in the projects with a tattoo on my leg and my hair all pink. I'm still trying to figure it out. And a —"

"Okay, well, you're all packed, right?"

"Packed?" asks Argosy. He scratches his hair. Snow falls.

"Hey, that's fine," says Samo. "I'm sure Monty's got something you can wear."

"Wear?"

"Where is your mom picking us up?" asks Monty.

"The bus stop on South Street," says Samo. "I'll call her when we get outside."

"I called her this morning!" volunteers Argosy.

Samo punches his shoulder.

"Ow!" says Argosy.

Then, in one motion, they take up their belongings and step into the hallway.

Samo turns back at the doorway to hit the light switch. With just a pale cloud-light wafting in from outside, the windows are dim, and the room looks as empty as the moon. Unspoken stories float there. The fantasies of students moving and speaking. Etching a new mythology from scratch, upon the floors and walls and their own lives. But for all that, the room still looks cold and empty.

"Okay," says Samo. "Let's go."

Afterward

I should properly say that *Shattering Glass* was written as a synthesis of my experiences as an undergraduate at the University of Chicago and my many years living in Flint, Michigan. Two odd places that seemed fit for each other and able to cohabit in the imagined city of Arkaic. Acedia House and Calliope Cradle are based on the former Mathews House in Burton-Judson Courts, just as Artemis' Hunt is based on the University of Chicago Scavenger Hunt (the largest in the world), and Theatre of Gold corresponds to the student-driven University Theater as it existed in the late 1990s. This is what was nominally in my brain when I received a summons from the Robotic Cetacean Deep-Space Gospel Collective.

Acknowledgments

First thanks go to my wife and daughter, Jessica and Mary, for their love and support.

This novel was executed with support from the Gothic Funk Press, and especially with the many long hours and hard work put in by editor Reinhardt Suarez and illustrator Sam Perkins-Harbin.

Additional thanks go to my parents, Shannie and Gregory, and my whole family, Elisabeth Blair, Skylar Moran, Paul Lathrop, Gemma Cooper-Novack, and Lyn Slayton. I'd also like to thank many friends in Flint, Chicago, and beyond who have been enthusiastic supporters: Jeffery Renard Allen, Jan Worth-Nelson and Ted Nelson, Gordon Young, Bryan Alaspa, Chris Ringler, Michael Kennedy, Shane Gramling, Ken VanWagoner and the Good Beans Cafe, the Jamesons, the Kennedys, Arlow Xan, the Atlas Coney Island, Destiny Dunn, Donald Harbin and Elizabeth Perkins-Harbin, Amber Staab, Jonathan Williams, Meridith Halsey, Irène Hodes, Mehrunisa Qayyum, Scott Larner, Sean Conley, Helen Colby, Colin McFaul, Melissa Arminio, Melodee Mabbitt, Michael Davidson, Eleanor Tutt, and Leila Sales.

The publication of this novel was supported by a Kickstarter campaign, and the following backers gave generously to bring the project to completion: Cathy Amboy, Dean W. Armstrong, Sheila Reinhard Augustine, Frank Bednarz and Meridith Halsey, Judd Belstock, Seth Berlin, Mark Bibbins, Elisabeth Blair, Peter Borah, Christine Borne, Alex Brandt, Jodi Bufford, Robert Burack, Katie Call, Katie Cawood, Helen Colby, Gemma Cooper-Novack, Shannon Copp, Catherine and Cody Coyne, Doug Diamond, Aunt

Sue Diveley, Thad Domick, Judge Jim "Boots" Duehr, Heather M. Dumdei, Sebastian Ellefson, Marty Embry, Lisa Feiertag, Kristin Fitzsimmons, Nora Friedman and Colin McFaul, Samuel Friedman, Jenny Gavacs, Mercedes Gilliom, Angelika Sophi Glogowski, Helen von Gohren, Ben Golden, Laura and Sawyer Gosnell, Here's the Story, Rebecca Holm, Amber Hurt, Joseph Irvin, Jessica, John, Christian Kammerer, Jeffrey Kitson, Jen Knickerbocker, Melissa Arminio Kops, Bernard J Kravitz, Amy Lamboley, Nicholas Lapeyrouse, Paul Lathrop, Ann Marie Lonsdale, Gardner Linn, Bob Mabbitt, Melodee Mabbitt, Liesbet Manders, Shaun Manning, Marco and Camellia, Evan Mencke, Ashley Meyer, Milligan, Minnie (the World's Greatest Chihuahua Ever), Skylar Moran, Edward Moser, Nathaniel Mosher & Emily Perkins-Harbin, Josh Nachowitz, Natasha and Bill, Nicolle Neulist, Nick and Kat, Julia Nielsen, Chris Noto, Lisa M. Ogle, Rich Pak, Hosanna Patience, Sara Patrin, John Pendell and Vickie Larsen, Elizabeth Perkins-Harbin, Sam Perkins-Harbin, Projective Industries, Jon Quinn, The Reading Family, Erin Robinson, Jasmine Robinson, Austin Robison, Rock 'n' Roll Dino Productions, Sara Ross Witt, Jim Ryan, Armand Ryden, Vivian Chang and Eloise Ryden, Leila Sales, Shannie and Greg, Lyn Slayton, Sam Smith, Thomas B. Spademan, Amber Staab, Nicole Steinberg, Steph Lane, Reinhardt Suarez, Sumara, Kimmy Szeto, Emily Taylor, James Turnbull, Eleanor Tutt, Benjamin Umans, Jonathan Williams, Xana Wolf, Kim Wolfgang, Joan Wolkerstorfer, Jan Worth-Nelson, Jody Wright, and Gordon Young.

A very special "thank you," also goes to a backer, friend, and mentor, Michael Patrick Dugan. He passed away before I could present him with a copy of the novel he supported, but I am very grateful for years of his support, humor, and kindness, and so this book is also dedicated to his memory.

And the marvelous Vehicle City of Flint, Michigan, and the divine University of Chicago 1997-2001, shot with shades xenon-sharp.

And all thanks go to God Almighty.

Postscript

Want to follow the further adventures of the Basement People as they strive to survive their first year of college? The epic struggle of Winter Quarter will play out in:

SPLITTING CELLS

Ah, but there's a catch. See, I'm still paying down $50K in student loans for my creative writing master's and taking care of my kid while my wife brings home the bacon. I want to bring home some bacon too. I just got a water bill from the City of Flint for about $115. So when I earn enough off Shattering Glass to pay my water bills for four months, I'll drop everything and start putting out *SPLITTING CELLS*. Considering that this novel took about three hundred hours to write and edit, this is a pretty sweet deal for my readers. So if you want to hear more about Samo, Monty, Ezzie, and Dunya, get your friends, your family, your coworkers, and your enemies to buy *SHATTERING GLASS!*

Appendix: Things That Really Happened

(An incomplete list.)

My best friend at college had multiple parties thrown for his 21st birthday which was, incidentally, on Halloween. These included most of the adventures imposed upon Dunya, as well as a midnight train-and-SUV trip halfway toward the dark heart of Wisconsin.

It seemed like practically every audition form for University Theater asked whether actors were willing to perform in the nude, regardless of whether or not the production involved any nudity. I think that directors sometimes did this to make their projects seem edgier.

When some friends and I took the bus too far on an Orientation "night out on the town" we had to walk the length of Chicago's Loop to get on a train back home. We were half-lost and delirious with expectation.

There are steam tunnels running under the Midway at the University of Chicago that can be accessed from the basement of Burton-Judson. By rumor, they were exotic, dangerous places, and breaking in could get one expelled.

Each Autumn Quarter, Mathews House would host a semi-formal cocktail party, during which we'd wear our finest to the dining hall before returning to the Fourth Floor Double to get drunk. One year, a new student got so trashed that the RA and I had to carry him to the hospital, where he threatened to beat me up (for no particular reason). About the time this happened, we were called back to the dorm because the fire alarm had been set off.

I did spend a University Theater Cleanup Day picking up hundreds of wet cigarette butts, which both stained and burned my fingers.

There were, in fact, bidding wars between directors of UT plays. Since most students auditioned for multiple (or all of) the shows, these contentious negotiations involved chalkboard charts, begging, and dickering.

October Girl is real.

We all hungered to get off campus. Instead of Arkaic's East Street, we fled to Chicago's magical intersection of Clark and Belmont. It was a much longer trek, though.

As a first-year at the Registered Student Organization (RSO) fair at the beginning of the Autumn Quarter, I signed up for way too many clubs (from the Gymnastics Club to the Young Democratic Socialists), which subsequently pushed my sanity to the limit.

A few undergrad directors achieved a sort of legendary status at UT, both for the ballsiness of their work as well as the professionalism of their product. Amanda Delheimer was one such director, and we talked about her greatest success, Charles Mee's *Orestes*, for months. It was, in fact, one of the few plays that did involve actual nudity, which led to one friend calling it *Oresticles*.

Court Theater's production of *The Iphigenia Cycle* was also powerfully memorable, as was JoAnne Akalaitis' and Philip Glass' production of Kafka's *In the Penal Colony*.

There was once a crazy party in a dorm room—mine—and while everyone's clothes stayed on for the duration, nobody much wanted to talk about the event after it happened. It was weeks before my floor didn't smell like malt liquor.

The Atlantis is based on a specific coney island in Flint, which was called the Grapevine in the late 1990s. It has had a few dozen names, it seems; today it is Tom's Coney Cafe. Other great Flint Coney Islands are the Atlas, the Starlite, the City Diner, Tom Z's, Angelo's, Star Bros., the Olympic, the Golden Gate, the Capitol, and, until recently, the Colonial (may she rest in peace). Chicago diners include the Golden Apple, the Golden Nugget, the Green Light, the New Archview, Huck Finn's, the Hollywood, Mitchell's, and

Standees (may he rest in peace). Everyone had to have, I think, some 24-hour greasy spoon refuge far from campus.

The Fourth Floor Double of Mathews House is a contentious subject to this day...it is true that the residents were alarmed to hear noises and see lights shining from the attic through slats in the molding, and that at the same time, the fire alarm was going off nightly (in the midst of midterms) due to some sort of "electrical malfunction."

A girl flirted with me on a crowded bus during O-Week. I got her phone number and everything. But she wouldn't date me because I wasn't Korean. (Or maybe I'm thinking of another girl who also gave me her number, but wouldn't date me because I wasn't Jewish.)

We did dance to loud techno with fake fog and strobes under the frowning portrait of former University President Maynard Hutchins.

Papering the town with fliers for a play at one a.m., two a.m., three a.m., and four a.m. was a real and affecting thing. The cold wind looms, the play (Tennessee Williams' *The Long Goodbye*) is going to be great, and when Borders opens at ten a.m., I get to buy the first new R.E.M. album since 1996.

Burton-Judson had a basement snack shop called the Pit. Thank God there was never a health inspection.

Midterms span from third week to eighth week in an eleven-week quarter.

I took a class called The Slavic Vampire, and it was the most fucking awesome course I ever attended. The reading list–several thousand pages in under three months–was also the most intense I ever encountered.

The oak tree in Burton Court became diseased and was cut down, and we all mourned. Several Mathews House residents (Mathewsniks), including yours truly, wooed our spouses beneath the besquirreled boughs of that grandfatherly tree.

It was hard to write multiple scenes about sitting in class, but anyone familiar with the University of Chicago knows what a memorable experience this can be. Especially in the Common Core humanities sequences, students engage in debates of an elemental intensity and rigor. Nothing in high school had prepared me for such a wonderfully violent collision of ideas, facts, and strong opinions.

Samo and Ezzie and Dunya and Monty are each based on real people I've known, but they're also based on me, and probably on you, too. Those of us who, at college or not, felt a real sense of possibility, risk, and vertigo on the edge of our adulthood.

Appendix: Moments Elided

Consult future releases of *Shattering Glass* outtakes.

A girl from Ezzie's playwriting class has exactly the same taste in music, and the chemistry is pungent, but it is sadly a one-way street.

Thudding off-campus house party, c/o the Psychedelics Ass. Five DJs in three apartments and the basement. Wait a minute, how did they get access to the basement? And why does it look like a catacomb, with niches and skulls and sulfur and vapour and shit?

The Classic Vampire involves crosstown field trips to the theater. It doesn't unfold exactly like in Anne Rice, but the resident goths have brought along chemical amenities, and the professor has words to make students fall in love with her even as she flays their brains with her serrated intellect.

Acedia House, the North Campus Champions of Intramural Ultimate Buzkashi!

Appendix: Additional Advice

Organize your computer from day one. If you make a mess, it's going to stay there.

Listen. Fucking listen. At seventeen/eighteen/nineteen/twenty/ twenty-one/twenty-two, you are likely to either clam up or to say some stupid shit without thinking. Listen first and then answer. You'll still embarrass yourself occasionally, but not irrevocably.

Take the initiative. Get to know your employers, housemates, RAs and RHs, coworkers, and profs. Make sure they know your name.

Foosball is 90 percent psychological.

Work hard, but don't stay in your room and study. Your most important education will happen outside of the classroom.

Mechanical pencils and ballpoint pens are cheap, so get many and don't run out.

Differentiate between "risks" and "the deep end." "Risks" = good, but nobody ever enjoys "the deep end."

Explore the neighborhood. Explore the town. Explore it with a friend. Better, make a friend while you're exploring your neighborhood and town.

Drink orange juice. It's awesome.

Once you join a mailing list, you will never escape it. Never.

Discover new music.

Have fun. Don't get killed. Make sure someone's got your back. Tragical shit can happen.

You cannot read enough. Read more. Read more!

Don't try to avoid falling in love, but realize that falling in love will not make your life any easier. It will make it harder for you to work and study, and it will unscrew you emotionally, because love is a screwy thing.

Caffeine may help you, but it will not be enough to save you.

This is probably both the most hopeful and the most obnoxious you'll ever be.

Take walks.

Bibliography

Not comprehensive, but here are some things you should check out.

Special Music: Elisabeth Blair, Arlow Xan, DJ Psycho, Mama Sol, Millimeters Mercury, Planck Length

Older Music: Ladytron, *604;* Moby, *Everything Is Wrong;* Björk, *Debut* and *Post;* R.E.M., *Up;* Laurie Anderson, *Bright Red;* Kraftwerk; Pearl Jam, *Vitalogy;* Sufjan Stevens, *Michigan;* Nine Inch Nails, *The Fragile*

Newer Music: Underworld, *Barking;* MGMT, *Oracular Spectacular* and *Congratulations;* Zola Jesus; Gazelle Twin; Moby, *Destroyed*

TV: *Scooby Doo, Taxi*

Film: Baz Luhrman's *Red Curtain Trilogy,* Alejandro Jodorowsky's *The Holy Mountain,* Katsuhiro Otomo's *Akira,* Darren Aronofsky's *Pi,* anything by Jane Campion, *Nosferatu*

Playwrights: Tennesse Williams, Charles Mee

Authors: Plato, Nietzsche, Doestoevsky, David Bradley, Italo Calvino, Ann Radcliffe, Zora Neale Hurston, Thomas Pynchon, those bloody Romantics, Anne Rice, Laurence Sterne, Djuna Barnes, Toni Morrison, Joyce Carol Oates, Jean-Jacques Rousseau, China Miéville.

Colophon

A look into your future.

You will be put to the test, after all. But before the final battle, you'll lie on your back in bed, and it will be dark above you, because it will be night time or the early hours of the morning. If you look carefully into that darkness, you will see glowing dragonflies whizzing to and fro, just a few feet above your head. You will feel the grass pressed with rich scent beneath your bare and dirt-streaked feet. And so what, maybe your knees will ache with many hours' standing, but they are your knees. Your very own. Imagine them relaxing.

By means ordinary or extraordinary, the choice is ours,

And we can pick the time, perhaps, and we can decide

When to go all inert like the fans, the phones, the boats, the cars,

The whatever that happens when the universe elides.

Hold your breath.

Count from one to ten.

Peer closely into the dark right above you.

Don't you see it?

About the Author

Blah blah blah, blah blah. Blah blah blah blah blah, blah blah. Blah blah blah blah blah. Blahblahblah. Blah, blahily, blah blah, blah, blahing, *Blah Blah, Blah blah blahblah, Blah, Blah, Blah Blah Blah, Blach blah blah blah,* blah *Blah.* Blah blah blah, blah blah. Blah blah blah blah blah blah blah. Blah, blah blah blahblah blah blah. Blah blah, blah. Blah blah blahblah, blah blah blah? Blah?! Blah. Bla-blah blah blah blah blah blah blah blech!

connorcoyne.com · facebook.com/connorcoyne · twitter.com/connorcoyne

CHAPTER FOURTEEN
THE PAST IS RUPTURED

Before the Storm

Go easy on Thanksgiving turkey; tryptophan and finals do not go well together.

For the next two weeks, life is as close to normal as it has been since the beginning of the quarter. The four students strive to soothe any Positivan or Negativan suspicion with their own plausible boredom. After all, they sleep so close to the chain mazes that one might believe, perhaps, that the engines have lulled the memories of recent weird occurrences into an unsettling dream. Appearances are important. Problem sets are answered. Papers written. Rehearsals attended. Studying, studying, studying for the imminent finals. Passing grades are also important. Dunya makes sure to pay the interest to her pawnbroker on time. Samo drills down on calculus and physics. Monty stays up late talking to Monica and learns that she, like most South Philadelphians, believes that trees are "kind of gross."

Communicating their plans by email and text and handwritten note, and touching base daily with Dr. Lawless, their webs begins to tighten around their invisible adversaries. 'Lissa reports back that Dr. Rochet has been permanently institutionalized out of the county, having fallen into a sort of catatonic fugue state. Professor Plumb conducts his last few classes with an air of dejected fatality. The early antagonistic energy is gone, and he speaks slowly, dragging each word up from sea bottoms. He sits in his chair now, and his sunglasses are cloud-gray dark.

Each morning, Samo and Ezzie take a short walk and discuss his experiences growing up in a crumbling Arkaic. Each afternoon, she talks with Monty about his daily discoveries; now that he's cracked the outer shell of conspiracy, the yolky mess of history dribbles down to crust his world with a salmonella-rich resin. It isn't a question of how to prove the real and conscious presence of interference; it's knowing where to even begin.

That is Ezzie's job, and so after dinner, she camps out in her room or the library, or coffee shop, or a Coney Island off campus, and writes and writes and writes. On her left is Dunya's script of *The Moldy Fountain*. To her right are her notes from Monty and Samo. "Liz won't mind or get involved if I go off script," says Dunya, "as long as she thinks I'm improvising. That it's a moment's inspiration that changes the course."

"That's your job, as an actor," explains Ezzie. "I can't write that. You're going to have to pull it off."

And so Dunya practices her lines, new and old, late into the night.

The nights fly by with surprising speed.

Samo invites Ezzie and 'Lissa to spend Thanksgiving with him and his family.

Dunya and Monty spend theirs in the libraries and cafeteria, finishing up the last of their work.

The last regular week of the quarter passes, and the night of the performance arrives. Monica brings their closest friends in Acedia House up to speed. They'll be a Secret Service of sorts, so everyone dresses up on the opening night of the play: Ezzie and Samo and Monty, 'Lissa and Monica, Argosy and Cassidy, Krista and Velma. Only Dr. Lawless is missing, having to attend a meeting of the Housing Department. Dunya prepares with her cast. The students breathe clouds of fog in the cold air as they follow South Street and then Franklin to the Turner Center for the Arts.

Shhhhhhh!

At a live performance, your neighbors' manners will reflect upon yourself as well.

The Turner Center, a new, sleek, glossy building welded onto an older brick-and-stone thing, is the seat of the Arts Programs and Theatre of Gold. But the glossy part hasn't been completed yet. *The Moldy Fountain* will be performed in an intimate cubbyhole of a proscenium theater, all painted black and drab, the arch less than fifteen feet high, with narrow wings and gloomy windows masked with dark cloth. The space has a capacity of maybe two hundred. Maybe. Every seat has been sold for this, the debut performance of the infamous Elizabeth Kraus' thesis production. In one of those seats, in the very front row and far house right, Ezzie spies Professor Plumb, who leans forward sullenly and scrutinizes the carpet. The Acedians seat themselves house left, halfway back. Ezzie sits one seat in from the aisle and fidgets with her skirt and her scarf. Music commences in some strain of Ossetian techno. Ezzie takes off her scarf and places it upon her knees.

What if it all goes wrong? she thinks. *What will happen to Dunya and us? What catastrophe?*

"Excuse me," says a tall Asian man with a narrow goatee. He wears a black suit with an ascot designed to look like the Mongolian flag. He munches popcorn out of a red and white striped bag. "Is this seat taken?"

It isn't. "But," says Ezzie, "you aren't allowed to have popcorn in here."

"Oh," he says, "sorry."

He leaves.

The lights dim.

The house manager begins her schpiel about donations and turning off cell phones and blah blah blah. The Asian man noisily returns and seats himself next to Ezzie.

"Is that Samuel O'Samuel?" he mutters in her ear, gesturing down the row.

"Yes," she whispers.

"Oh," he says, "he doesn't have a seat open next to him, does he?"

"What?" she asks. "No!"

"Oh, that's a shame. See, I'm Agent Francis Costello."

"Esmeralda Prentice," she says, and shakes his hand.

"Pleased to meet you. I'm with NASA2–kind of like the CIA in space–and I am here responding to a tip submitted to our Washington office by Samuel regarding a Professor Percival Plumb, whom I believe to be that individual wearing sunglasses indoors over there."

Ezzie feels the blood drain out of her face, but she manages to give a noncommittal nod.

"Say, why are you wearing sunglasses in here?" he asks.

She gives a noncommittal shake of the head.

"Huh. Well anyway, tell Samuel not to worry." Agent Costello chuckles. "I have secret agents planted throughout this audience in case he tries to escape!"

"Shhhhhh!" hisses someone a few rows behind them.

"Don't do anything yet," whispers Ezzie. "We're going to give you a smoking gun tonight."

The house manager has finished. She leaves the stage and the lights go out completely.

The Moldy Fountain begins.

The Star

Show your audience your deepest, darkest self, but never show them your hand.

The lights rise on Dunya, wreathed in fog and backed by a Venn wash of bold blue over primary green light. She wears a black Delphos gown with a silver ribbon tied in a bow at the front. She is the star. Burning fills the air.

The star looks out into the dark house. She sees the audience. It sees her. She shakes her head autumnally. A cloud of leaves falls down about her. Taps on the floor. The audience watches in breathless silence. The star takes steps toward the house. She stops to think.

"When I was a kid, before my mom died, I got signed up for swimming lessons. I was eight, maybe. One winter day–I don't know if you know, but in Richmond, California, half the leaves stay green through the winter, and the rest turn brown and dead. One winter day, we were driving to my swimming lessons, and my mom saw a big bird–a raven–with a broken wing crossing the highway. It was a busy, six-lane road, and the raven was maybe a third of the way across. The speed limit was forty-five, and it was rush hour, and my mom said, 'he's never gonna make it.' So she pulled over to the side of the road, and everything seemed...wet and cold and dangerous. Stinky with risk. But she was going to try and save him, no matter what. I was anxious about the bird and terrified for my mom. Big pickups and big SUVs shot by close–way too close–to where she was, and she was just...just trying to make it to the middle, safe but fast. And those cars around her made her seem even more alive, because death was just a foot or two away. Rolling on its way to 7-Eleven or Speedway. Anyway, she didn't get hit, but then the semi hit the bird and its beak and feathers and its whole life dissolved into a myth –" and the star pulls on the silver ribbon and breaks the secret string, and every stitch, every thread of her dress disintegrates into foam and imagination.

But she is a virginal star. The audience and the other actors and crew don't see shit, because at that moment, a vast bank of Fresnel floods flashdial up to eleven, and their dry and screaming heat becomes a blindness of spectral lines—jagged purple and electric blue, celestial seas and magma scarlet—all fuzzy circles, round afterimages that hang on for minutes, even though the small stage is now empty and dark.

• • • • •

Monty blinks his eyes. *Well*, he thinks, *that was unexpected.* He'd always figured that Dunya was the only person he knew at AU more prudish than himself—straight-edge, almost, in a non-dogmatic sort of way. Then again, what *had* he seen? Only part of a silhouette, and that for only a slight second, and why does it matter? *It matters because it matters to Dunya, and because she projects that it matters. Her privacy and secrecy, more decisive than mine.* He understands, suddenly, the justified hype behind Elizabeth Kraus, a director who pokes about the stifling campfires of confused collegiate souls and fans their tiny sparks into flames that burn bright with vulnerable heat. The power of a director. The power of an actor like Dunya, trusting enough to let that flame be fanned, and yet guarded enough to raise walls of timber, battlements against siege engines, provisions for a long winter. The tension in simultaneously taking from and giving to an audience. The power of a playwright, like Ezzie, speaking in code, recasting glyphs as words, spells as stage directions, runes writ for flesh and pulp and motion. He gets it now. For the first time, Monty really gets art.

Somewhere at the back of the stage, Elizabeth Kraus stands up in the sound booth and calls out, "she's gone off script! She's gone off script!" A half-naked boy with a beard stands in the wings of the stage and looks out at Elizabeth, though she must be invisible to him. Has Dunya gone rogue so soon? Or were her line readings, as well as Elizabeth's response, a channeling of Andy Kaufman? Monty doesn't know, and Elizabeth doesn't answer the question. Instead, she slowly sits again, wearing her favorite poker face.

The play continues.

Quantum Cortázar, Part 2:
Not a Fool, but a Damn Fool

"Why does the reader have to go through all of this in such detail?"
– The Editor

If the plot of Shattering Glass sucks you like a swift current, and you wish to "keep it moving, keep it moving," kindly zip on to the part of this chapter titled "The Turbine."

If you wish to trace the Chekhovian tale of Michigan's ecstatic agony of decay after its too-brief moments of prosperity, follow this way, follow this way.

The half-naked boy steps onto the stage. His beard isn't simple and scraggly, like Jesus', but ornate and Teutonic. He twirls his mustache. He is twenty years old, or maybe twenty-one.

"I'm a Damn Fool," he says, likably.

The Fool sits at the dinner table with his parents in the Arkaen suburb of Arkadia. They eat Thanksgiving leftovers and dream the sweet dream of cedar mulch that scents like Lebanon.

"You know?" the Fool says between mouthfuls, "Sweet potatoes and marshmallies go back to the Civil War. It was originally yammies from the South, and maple syrup from the North. We got them ate as a sign of nat'l unity."

His father grunts.

The Fool takes a big bite.

"Have you chosen a major?" his mother asks in a slightly overplayed, condescending voice.

The Fool flexes his muscles for them, and the light flickers.

"I haven't decided if to put more salt on my soup."

"Add the chipotle bouillon, sweetie."

He does. The table begins to shimmy like a disco dance floor, but it has started to rain outside, and the walls are made of paper. They dissolve. The Fool stands.

"Wait!" says his mother. "Don't you deserve a sidekick?"

"Maybe," the Fool says. "I don't gots one."

The Fool walks through the torn-open wall and into the water. The rain increases. The spots flicker.

"What about your job?" his mother calls after him. "What about your loans and your sister and brother? What about your library fines?"

The Fool is already gone.

• • • • •

In the next scene, the Fool stands and observes as a couple stagehands drag a wading pool onstage and begin to fill it with a thick, smelly, greasy, yellow goo. An actor dressed up as Michigan Governor Rick Snyder–it isn't the real Rick–this isn't libel here!– steps out onto the stage guiding a rapidly blinking, indecisive waif wearing clogs and a sash reading "Miss Michigan." Rick delivers a long and beautiful monologue crafted by cunning philologists about the nature of nerd-dom, and how, while his credentials are unestablished by popularized internet tests and memes that really just reinforce tired tropes of the past, he is of a special pedigree, as the master of a computer company. "That is why you college kids should stay in Michigan and take advantage of the opportunities I've given you!" he says. "To learn real skills, from me, in your poverty. We'll let you pay more, earn less, and discard superfluous dignity." He puts his hands on his hips. "'Michissippi,' they call us!" he snorts with contempt. "We are the very frontier of American asceticism." It is his glory, his vision of the future. "We're all anchorites now."

Rick strips down to his Presbyterian Speedo and proclaims that it is his intention to bathe the state in butter. "No no, don't complain. Virg couldn't have afforded anything better than water, and Mike Cox would have used prison moonshine, as only an adulterer of unparalleled experience can. Let's not even get started on Hoekstra!"

Someone in the audience stands and says that this representation is not fair; Snyder is, after all, a moderate, and a pragmatist, and his policies are less onerous than those of his main rivals. Someone else proclaims that the complaints about Snyder are completely legitimate, but that putting an actor onstage in a Speedo distracts from his record by making him into a caricature of reality.

At any rate, the shaggy-headed governor lifts the waif in his arms and hurls her headfirst into the butter-filled pool. Her spine snaps, but that's okay, because, as Snyder points out, he has taken the money he saved buying this cheapass pool and given it to her boss, who has (presumably) supplied her with insurance options, or at least COBRA. So her treatment ought to be covered in part. She is carried offstage by the stagehands.

The Fool laughs, eats a coney and a KFC Famous Bowl, and dances to "Amnesia," Chumbawamba's would-be second hit. Their guitars are so svelte, for an anarchist collective. That girl rocks the short-hair-and-no-bangs way better than Dolores O'Riordan, with wittier lyrics, too. *Do you suffer from long-term memory loss?* The Fool nods his head happily. He sprays his hands with an antibacterial solution and finds himself sitting in an empty parking garage with a professorial centenarian suffering from advanced Alzheimer's. The prof wears the stereotypical tweeds, and a pipe dangles flaccidly from his lips. Cobwebs stretch from his elbow pads to the floor. The Fool is happy to have a captive audience, and he tells the old man a long and rambling story about the cats that his father brought into the house. They were brought in because his father has a soft spot for animals, but their stated *raison d'être* was to catch mice. There were no mice, so the cats learned to hunt each other, at first playfully, and then with serious rivalry, finally appropriating paring knives and meat cleavers from the kitchen to murder each other in cold blood. This was, naturally, futile, as cats lack opposable thumbs, elastic elbow joints, and sufficient strength. Then the 1980s drift down from the sky, and tattoos spontaneously erupt all over the young Fool's body, to his evident horror. He hurriedly pumps more antibacterial spray into his hands, but to no avail: he is inexorably covered with coded references to a variety of products (the red-and-gray smiling-and-saluting Stalin, for example, being a subtle paean to Coca-Cola).

Meanwhile, bright white lines streak the gloomy black stone, and here on the giant picturesque lawn, a group of shambling, brain-eating cadavers makes its final advance upon our heroes. "Brains...brains!" they seem to be saying, but every few feet, one collapses and (re?)expires. By the time the beasties have reached our fool, only one is left, smoking an Ojibwa pipe. "Claims...claims!" he says, and then his eyes open wide, and he fixes the Fool seriously and says, "Gigii-wiidigemaag gidaanis(im)inaanig. You are our ever friend." The zombie chief hands the Fool an elegant piece of paper wrapped in red ribbon and collapses into ash.

"I'm cold," says the Fool to the professor. "I'll give you this deed in exchange for your coat."

The moribund man does not answer.

The Fool takes the prof's coat, puts it on, and then places the paper into his hand and leaves that place, never to return again.

• • • • •

The next scene takes place in a house in Arkaic, because, as with most broken cities, the heart of civic life does not play out along the paved central canyons as intended. For squatters, renters, homeowners, and home-dwellers, the "house," the "shell," is the nexus of industry, commerce, prayer, and recreation.

"How do I get these tattoos off?" asks the Fool.

This house is par for the course. "Poverty in the wake of prosperity," comes the offstage voice of the world, "is neither absence nor abundance. It is worthless abundance piled high to try to fill the gaping hole." And so this Gothic room of an arts and crafts style home on a tiny Victorian plot is filled to the gills with flotsam and jetsam. Bold, conical pyramids and elongated obelisks of TVs lean, their vacuum tubes sadly smashed like crystal chalices. There are proud trophy deer and ducks bedewed with scummy cobwebs, their mouths wide with defilement, a carburetor, a generator, and calculators, and typewriters, and comic book stacks sticky with mildew, but still the empty hole looms wide with hunger.

Inside sit three friends, one in his thirties, one in her forties, and one in his fifties, drinking beer from bottles and tapping their feet to the beat of their cheap and unsavory consumption.

One of the broken televisions turns on to show a stereotyped sequence of daytime talk shows, reality TV, and occasional news, undercut by ads for political campaigns and Disney princesses. Its volume gradually increases through the scene. As the TV gets louder and louder, the Fool starts asking for directions to Arkaic University, but the figures cannot hear him over the sound and fury. Instead, they smash their beer bottles, spraying foam over the carpet and junk, and begin dancing in rough circles. They step on cut glass in bare feet, and cherry red Aunt Jemima spreads down the floor of the room. The friends don't notice but slice up each other's faces with ragged punches, and the TV gets so hot white that it might as well be a solar flare. The metal starts to rust. Sparks shower down from naked and overfed extension cords. The Fool cannot make himself heard, so he leaves. As he closes the door behind him, the whole Arkaen house falls into a kitchen sinkhole and dies.

• • • • •

Now, the Fool walks through Arkaic...not the South Side, but the West, North, and East. He passes a mile-deep brownfield with spring-fresh poplars erupting from the flagstones to take a peep at the surrounding neighborhoods. They, too, are being overtaken by weed trees. The field had been gated off by a chain-link fence, but the linkage has been cut away by scrappers. Only the aluminum posts remain, and a thick, black X Valentine with chrome hubcaps and Frank Sinatra on the radio. A cup holder, wide for champagne bottles. A tinted window rolls down. Inside sits a clean-shaven businessman, an automobile guy, not a car guy–this guy can't change his own oil–forty-seven years old, wearing a flickering Technicolor dress shirt and a paisley tie, but no jacket.

"Where are you going?" asks the businessman.

"College," answers the Fool.

"So you *are* a college student."

The Fool nods.

"I drive my own damn self," the businessman says. "Get into the car."

The Fool does.

"How do you like my shirt?" the businessman asks.

"It isn't as beautiful as a beautiful girl," the Fool says honestly.

"Have some Champagne. The real shit. Cuvée de Prestige. Unless you'd prefer Blue Nun."

"Champagne is fine."

They drink.

"You look out at this, and you see a waste," says the businessman, "and that's what it is. But I have a pretty potion here." He reaches into his pants pocket–he's wearing plain, black slacks–and brings out a two-colored capsule: a rich, umbral moss and a crisp rust red.

"You can't save this town," he says. "It's too late for that. We intended to give it a blood transfusion, but we accidentally drank it up instead. However, we do still have a chance to make a bit of money off of it. Waste not, want not, right? It would be unenvironmental to let it go completely to waste. So listen, you can do this, but you have to go to that school of yours and major in engineering."

"But I don't want to do engineering. I want to be a clown!"

"Aw, shut up," says the businessman. "You learn how to be an engineer and then–and only then–you plant this little pill in the brownfield. You'll see. It'll grow you a brand new machine that will make you lots of money. Then you can drive your own Valentine and drink your own Blue Nun."

• • • • •

At this point, the show leaves the gentle fool for a few minutes to find itself strolling along the storied promenade of Venice Beach, L.A. But no, it is actually the Coney Island Boardwalk in New York. In fact, it's neither. It is the outer stretches of Whitmer Road in Arkaic, MI. There's no ocean to speak of, nor any large lake. Even the river is a mile to the west. So what then? What gives?

Whitmer Road is one of the streets that the city descends upon on a hot summer day to walk through dust, kick barefoot through flashing red sun, and lick thick ice creams. To drink cold beers, order up coneys to go, and shout at motorists shoving by. To plod on by on mopeds. To hold empty straws and Pixy Stix up in the chilling north wind.

It is a dark and sunny day, full of heavy heat.

Take a deep breath in this new and exuberant environment, because we are about to meet her. His *other*. The *Cybergoth*.

She stands in a church of many stained glass windows, which is presently a used paperback store that is only open for two hours on two days of the week. There is no sign to mark it, but you can see the books stacked high from out on the street, behind the plywood sign. The books have all been painted with highlighters. She has been painted herself. Eyes drawn into crimson flames, but these are her flighting contacts. A thick mane of purple wires and tubes, but these are dreadfalls and extensions that sprout like sharp ambitious weeds from jagged red bangs. Chrome and glass goggles, each lens etched with a deadly glyph: Ω. The fact that $\Omega = 2$ is bad news indeed. Her shoulders are netted with black fishnet beneath a fitted, black rubber

356

bodice. Her equally black skirt has been modded from cut-up car tires, accented with the crimson of her eyes and the violet of her hair. Dr. Seuss socks. Platform boots. Ready to kick you and stoically judge you. The Cybergoth browses the collection of books here–Hegel, Engels, and Mao–and finds them wanting. She looks in the mirror and is pleased with the result. She looks as she wishes to look. As it is necessary to be.

The proprietor, heavy set and hand-wringing, steps to the front of the store.

"Are you going to buy a thing?" he asks.

She stares at him.

"Then we are ready to ritual," he says.

This scene plays out onstage in glorious black and white, with a background orchestra sweeping through suicide-inducing chords of grace. The proprietor puts a wriggling worm in the Cybergoth's ear. She takes it with a straight face. There is a lot of static and interference. The proprietor puts on his hazmat suit. The Cybergoth regards him coldly. The proprietor hands out snacks and goodies to all of the animals waddling about and browsing his collection, then calmly turns on a Bunsen burner. He plays the music that they love, which is electrified 90s blues. Grubs begin to pupate in a beaker. Machines click and whir and begin turning sheets of steel into a fine, silvery thread. Hundreds of books fall from their shelves, tumble open to a certain page, and spew locusts around the room. The proprietor, surprised by this (though who knows why? This is, after all, the *plan!*) swats at them angrily, but the Cybergoth does not flinch as thousands alight upon her skin and nom on her like she's broken crackers. Some of the locusts plunge through the Bunsen burner, fall onto a book or two, and set the whole store on fire. The Cybergoth pulls on her gas mask. The proprietor draws out a fire extinguisher and fights the flames as they spread. There is little hope. The flames spread oh-so-quickly.

In the end, they both survive, but the proprietor's business has been forever ruined. More importantly, the monochrome gloss is burned from their eyes, and Technicolor reality bleeds through in all its insouciant joy. With nothing holding the roof up over their heads but a few charred timbers–and the road and its turning transpiring in open air a few feet behind them–they look side-to-side at the rubble.

"I am covered with soot," the Cybergoth says.

"You will not live long," answers the proprietor. "But you will not be long remembered."

The Cybergoth turns toward the sidewalk and sees the Fool walk by.

"Where are you going?" she asks.

"I am looking for college," the Fool answers.

"I'll go with you."

• • • • •

Their honeymoon is transfigurationally radiant and poignantly brief. They sun has just set as they enter the ambered glow of the Prahova Family Restaurant at the city limits and order up the *ciorbă de burtă* and *tochitură moldovenească* with crepes and coffee and dry *pálinka*. From there, they cross the street in deep purple twilight and down several pints of PBR with a Somalian émigré and a Michigan Supreme Court justice who won't stop chattering about font hue and size. Then the Fool and the Cybergoth go next door to the Frosted kiosk and buy several popsicles, which they lick up-and-down suggestively while walking the last mile of bleak darkness to Arkaic University. They hold hands as they walk.

Their time together has been ruptant and kaleidoscopic, but it has already come to an end.

They are ready to meet the star.

The Turbine

Danger has its own intelligence, sentient or not.

And so, after many adventures, the Damn Fool and his lover, the Cybergoth, have arrived on campus. Their next encounter takes place on the Fairway, so the black screens covering the windows have been lifted to show its distant, gray expanse, stretching beyond the sullen towers of Calliope Cradle and the shimmering power plant. As the lights rise, the star is sitting at center stage, dressed in a white Delphos gown with a gold ribbon tied in a bow in front.

The Fool and the Cybergoth enter from stage right and left. They stop, several feet away from the star. Just outside of striking distance.

"I want to be a star, like you," says the Fool.

"You are a Fool," says the star.

She stands, and as she does, the sound of sharp humming radiates from beneath her feet. The grass changes. Glows. Flexes and flicks out at a beat, and the star starts to tap her feet. The lights pulse in time. The sky becomes magma, with clouds transformed into charcoal mote that scuds along with gray streaks behind it. The two adversaries circle each other.

"I have a knife," says the Fool.

"I have a word," says the star.

The Fool lunges at her, but the star opens her palms, and they emit a flood of spectral energy. It strobes the entire audience, and the Fool falls to the ground, clutching at his eyes.

"Go to him," says the star, and she steps to one side. The Cybergoth crosses the stage and kneels beside her lover.

"What have you done to me?" asks the Fool.

"I haven't hurt you," the star answers. "I have opened your eyes."

And now, for a flicker of a moment, Dunya looks from the stage and makes contact with Ezzie. *Do it!* she thinks, and tries to say with her shark-wide eyes. Dunya looks at Samo. *This is the moment,* he knows she is thinking. Samo nods his head slowly. He has spent a whole week on this part of the illusion. Dunya smuggled him the pill after rehearsal one day, and he spent the whole week reverse engineering its origami in the cyclotron and the labs of XAI. He's pretty sure this will work. *Pretty sure.*

Dunya's attention snaps back to the Fool. "Plant your seed," the star says.

"I am not a gardener," he answers, dumbly.

"No," she says. "It is the pill that the businessman gave you."

The Fool digs a hole with his hands. The Cybergoth cups the dirt in her palms. The Fool drops the pill in the hole. The Cybergoth fills it. They stand and step back.

A beat shudders out and through the house.

And now another. And another. The stage thrums with authentic energy. Waves of trembling radiate out, and Samo can feel the carpet shaking beneath his feet. Onstage, a metal spoke projects through the dirt and grass. Stretching like a blade of grass toward the sun, it reaches four feet into the air. Its top splits, and two rods slide supple from their metallic sheath, rotating out until they hang perpendicular to the earth, a wiry letter 'T.' Then, more wire-thin rods slide forth from these points and extend until the skeleton of a cube has been assembled. The dividing and extending continues, and now there are two cubes, and now cantellated cubes, and pentragrammic crossed-antiprisms, and glomes, and so on. Faintly glowing fluorescent sheets drop down between the skeletal shapes, linking them together and hiding the space in between. The boxes unfold and multiply, unfold and multiply, until at last the strange, expansive, glossy, and faintly abominable package takes up the entire stage. Elizabeth's script had called for a symmetrical yoni, into which the Fool would journey alone and learn from the star how to pursue the quest of the Moldy Fountain, but Samo's design has gone far off script. His creation sprawls horribly across every empty and imagined space, a bizarre, multi-dimensional, Escher nightmare.

The star turns out to look at Elizabeth. "Trust me!" the star cries, "this plot is the real plot, and its conclusion, the real conclusion." Then, to the Fool, "shall we unwrap this delicious present?"

· · · · ·

It is, actually, the first time Samo has ever seen one of the turbines in full light. When a turbine had fallen out of the rafters of the Commons at the SOs Fair, it had been broken and half-disassembled. And when Samo was imprisoned in the chain mazes, in almost complete darkness, he caught only a few solitary glimpses when the lenses flashed. This turbine, brought forth from the chain maze and hidden by A. Olan on Dr. Lawless' orders...this is the real deal. Samo knows exactly what he is looking at, and even if it is something to be feared, he is captivated by the pure genius of the thing. It takes his breath away, literally. He goes a long time without breathing and doesn't even notice. *Does anyone understand how much danger we are in, right now?* he wonders. Samo leans forward to get a closer look.

The thing is too complex to take in all at once.

Samo sees the safety toggles, secure in place. The field settings, which he manually turned to the lowest rate of intrusion. The precision lensing, with lasers to access fiber-optic leads. The clean layers of blue and white plastic parts, crisply labeled in sharp, black lettering. The balanced angles between paraconductors reducing flux and stress, to avoid temporelectrical warpage. The carefully vented exhaust ramp. The turning unit, preprogrammed to orient receptors toward the optimal oneiric induction in five unconnected dimensions. The inkjetted label admitting everything: "Manufactured by Via Positiva Under One or More of the Following Patents," with countries listed from Algeria to Zambia. The bright blue turning wheels–the cause of the beat–the *click tick dock*–the singing rotor.

A deep hush has fallen over the crowd, as if they know that things have gotten realer than real. Elizabeth leans forward, eyes wide, chin resting on her folded palms. Beside Ezzie, Agent Costello is slack-jawed in awe. Up front, Plumb stares at the floor like a sick man. The Fool, the Cybergoth and, yes, the star, all hold their breath.

Flick the fifth switch, Samo prays to himself. The star has donned gloves, and she positions herself behind the thing and presses down on a flat, blue switch, the last of five.

Now step back, Samo thinks. *It knows what to do from here.* As if she can hear him, Dunya takes a step back. The Fool and the Cybergoth follow suit.

"It," says the Cybergoth, "it's just a fake, right? It's just a model?"

The turbine makes the tiniest *click*, and its fans start to quietly spin. External valves turn themselves, fine-tuning their own settings to account for the atmosphere, the electromagnetic field, and solar effects. The turbine's computer is slightly confused. It detects an abundance of proximate sentience, but its settings have been manually downgraded. Moreover, the machine it is not accustomed to separation from the chain, and it cannot detect any connection to an optical network. In this context, it must function as a lone driver. It takes a few seconds to make the necessary adjustments and then uses its battery to prime the engine. Shafts begin to rotate. As the whirring grows into a soothing whine, a blue light flicks on at the shell of the beast. It is online.

"That's not a model!" yells someone. "That's the real thing!"

But nobody stands or leaves. They're all transfixed.

The rotor begins to turn. It starts slowly, rotating clockwise, then counterclockwise, then clockwise again, while the input drives, twitching tentatively at the air like tiny antennae, turn subtly toward the audience. As the rotor spins ever faster, it becomes a vast fan that drags Dunya's hair from its braids and whips it wildly around her face. She faces the house. *Click! Tick! Dock!* The turbine sings its sonic lullaby behind her.

"Now we'll confront the Moldy Fountain," she says. "For the Fool has gone on many journeys. He has confronted double-dealing politicians and the walking dead, his doomed fellow citizens and their corporate pimps, the death, the drive, the depth, the rising tides of a pure and true love erupting within him. And now he has arrived at Arkaic University, where he finds not a fountain of flesh, but a fountain of time. The fountain has erupted. The past is ruptured. The machine will try to eat up our present and our past, but we can resist. And through this rupture we can look into this past. Let's take a look. Let's see what has happened."

This is a well-trained cast.

They are prepared to follow the story, whatever labyrinth it pursues.

And so, with Fool and Cybergoth at her side, Dunya steps into the new role that Ezzie has written for her.

The Cumaean Sybil

Most fairy tales were not originally written for children.

One of the most popular SOs on campus is Artemis' Hunt, a grand scavenger hunt, ambitious beyond mortal peer. But for all that they are steeped in the trappings of a game, their constitution suggests something more serious:

Artemis' Hunt exists, and thus, the apotheosis of human kind is achieved through the mutuality of power and freedom. Power, to be obtained through the imposition of order. Freedom, implying the presence of chaos. Hence, an immortal paradox that plagues our pretensions to immortality.

We hold these truths to be self-evident, and so, in our desire to forcibly elevate the University to empyreal status by imposing a condition of powerful freedom at the Olan Commons, where teams shall accumulate items enumerated per list and with discrete point values, under the direction of the judges, a.k.a. Via Positiva. Each team, and each team member, imposed upon by a condition of powerful freedom, shall bring us closer to the new Age of Enlightenment, in which we shall all aspire to become true gods.

As the star explains, they do not lie. And so, in ages beyond mortal memory, there existed powers—for convenience, we'll call them "gods." The gods struggled against each other, and the struggle of two siblings—for convenience, we'll call them "Apollo" and "Dionysus"—went bitter and bloody. Amoral and non-deistic, these gods were never impartial, and they meddled ceaselessly in the workings of the universe. Apollo ever sought to build the particles of existence into their most intricate and delicate—life!—forms, while Dionysus sought to scramble and disperse them in frenzies of rage.

In four dimensions, Dionysus must win, but in sufi and zen and gnostic truth, Apollo held the upper hand. Their duels—our actions, in light of them—have slaughtered billions. Hence the story of the Cumaean Sybil, which Monty has discovered:

• • • • •

The Fool has now become Apollo, and the Cybergoth is the Sybil.

Apollo sits, harp in casual hand, upon a weathered lumber stump. The Sybil stands beautiful, young, god!, eternally young, without wrinkle or crease, doubt or apprehension. With clear gaze. A state of youth that seems equally removed from both birth and death. From any form of non-existence. The clouds swell large and heavy. The river water seems to drag itself toward the two of them. The branches of the pine and cedars pull toward them in an invisible wind, and even the sun feels the effect of the gravity of this singular moment.

"I love you," says Apollo, "I want to teach you with my body. I need you. I have to have you. I have to merge. I want to blend with you, and to become one body between us."

"I am only myself," says the prophetess. "I am not anyone else."

"I want you so badly. I would give you anything. Anything! If you would just blend with me and become one thing."

"Ha!" she says, laughing.

She doesn't need him.

"I'm young," she says. "I'm wise. I guess even the gods want me! I don't need anything you can give me! What could you possibly give me that I would want?"

"What do you want?"

"The only thing I want is to be like this forever."

"Like this?"

"Alive!"

"I can give that."

"You can?"

"Yes, I can."

She thinks, then says:

"Do it."

She laughs merrily and scoops up a pile of sand in her hands. "How many grains of sand are here? Ten thousand? One hundred thousand? That's how many years I want to live. As many years as there are grains of sand in my hand right now. Because it sucks to die, to stop being, and I don't want this, and the beautiful world doesn't want it either. So make me live this long and yeah, I'll fuck you, Apollo."

"Then you will live that long."

She thinks some more.

"Then I don't need to fuck you. Do I?"

She scatters the sand in the wind.

Apollo frowns. The sun frowns brightly. The clouds billow darkly. The river ripples, but the Sybil knows and doesn't know. She knows the heart of the god, but she doesn't understand what he has done to her.

• • • • •

It was many years before she understood what happened that day. What the god, and the sun and clouds and trees and river had witnessed and recognized, but she did not. *She* figured that she had not followed her word, and so neither had Apollo. But he had, in fact, honored the covenant. He did vouchsafe her request to "live as many years as there are grains of sand in my hand," even without freeing her from the tragedy of painful transience. And so, she turned sixty and felt arthritis; seventy, and felt a closeness in her chest; eighty, and felt her memory start to slip. Then she turned ninety, and one hundred, and one hundred and ten. Only *then* did she understand, although the memory had dimmed for her, a strange and hazy, half-dreamed hallucination from ninety years before. Ninety years later, it had receded into a nightmare inscribed in dew on fog, because as she aged, the years slipped by ever more quickly, as a testament to her changing orientation toward time. For each year she lived, the next represented a smaller portion of her overall life. And so she withered and diminished at an ever-accelerating rate. Generations died. Civilizations died. No one spoke. No one knew. Her limbs became so stiff and unyielding, her eyes so sullen and cataracted, her mind so subdued, that existence fell into the humorless haze of a Rorschach zoetrope, spinning spinning. Three hundred years. Five hundred years. Seven hundred years. Aeneas slipped by like a shadow in the night, and she found the slippage so quick—so fast and yet peculiarly unending—that she was reacting to her conversation with him centuries after he had become dust himself. Dionysus watched her from afar. Apollo watched. They wondered what the Sybil portended.

That is where this all began.

The other stories proceed from this one. How the Sybil sold her stories to King Tarquin of Rome for half the price of the kingdom. How Flavius Stilicho destroyed them a thousand years later. How the Sybil diminished further and further until nothing was left but a voice. A haunted voice that drifted among the cedars and under the blazing sun. A haunted voice that finally found refuge inside a glass ampulla.

During the years that her stories resided in Rome, scholars studied them and came to different conclusions.

One group of Egyptian scholars called themselves Via Positiva, The Positive Way. They considered themselves servants of Apollo, but they really wanted to create a million new universes, in which they would each be a god who could create their own creatures that would worship only them. They knew that they could accomplish this if they captured the Sybil and bound her to their machines, because Apollo had gifted immortality upon her.

Another group of Mesopotamian scholars named themselves Via Negativa, The Negative Way, as worshipers of Dionysus, but they, too, wanted to be masters, and to cut short their own suffering and pain by prematurely eclipsing the universe. They knew that they could accomplish this if they destroyed the Sybil, because the chained human chaos within her had already thwarted Apollo's plans.

And so they have fought through the centuries and millennia–Via Positiva and Via Negativa–through wars and plague and poverty. One advocates absolute ascension, the other complete negation, though for those of us just trying to live our lives, the result is the same. They bring suffering.

• • • • •

This is the moment. Onstage. With tragedy before and behind. With this thing whirring two feet in front of me. The rotor blades turn with a blue flicker, so silent that they make less noise than the exhale of a sleeping child. So fast that it doesn't seem to be a cutting at all, but a cool wash of comfort and healing. So deep that she forgets the audience sitting and watching on the other side. She could lean right in to it. She could kiss it. It would calm her. It would comfort her. *Don't consider what it wants!* Dunya stands bolt upright. The Fool and the Cybergoth stand at her side, worried. The silent audience is out there, watching. *Time to bring it home,* Dunya thinks.

Throughout her performance, so far, she has been speaking in a near monotone and holding back the emotional reservoir that first germinated during her auditions in the forest so long ago. "Now," she says, leaning onto the rounded syllables derived from inked shapes that Ezzie gave her on paper, "let's see how this *machine* works."

The turbine phlashes, a bright light, a *click, tick, dock,* upon the audience. It is being pried about, and it doesn't like this. The pod at the center of the rotor is utterly inhuman...three black dots twirling on blue casing, but they nevertheless suggest to Dunya a curious and suspicious face.

She finds the panel that Samo has described, loosens the screws with a simple hex key, and opens the center frame. Air hisses with decompression as Dunya lifts the plate, revealing a core of spinning gears and crankshafts, spattered with emotive and cognitive detritus. And there, in the middle, is a small glass filled with glowing, amber fog.

"They are here," Dunya says, "Via Positiva and Via Negativa, and everything they do is for this." She touches the glass chamber, and it chimes in response as if fearful at the contact of young flesh. "Which is why, several years ago, Professor Lorraine Glass was lured into the tunnels underneath the Fairway to be a literal sacrifice–a human offering–as someone still corporeal and full of flesh and impetuous passion–just like the Sybil herself–to bind the turbines together into a matrix, a field of energy. It absorbed her–Dr. Glass. And now that they are online and functioning, Via Positiva and Negativa need someone–someone special–to shatter this reality into an annihilation of creation or an impregnation of destruction."

"You see," she continues, running her hand affectionately along the glass chamber, "the turbines are what they both want and need. To fuse the Sybil and create new universes. To destroy the Sybil and destroy all universes. It can be accomplished through the alteration of the turbines' glass. By splicing all things together or shattering them into a million shards."

And then, Dunya's voice drops like a guillotine:

"Perhaps you should ask Professor Plumb, over there, about this." Professor Plumb looks up at the stage for the first time in a long while, and his face is gray. A grim corpse face. He has taken off his sunglasses. She continues. "When you bound Lorraine to the Sybil in her glass, you became averse to glass yourself. What is so special about Esmeralda Prentice? What does Via Positiva need her to *do*?"

Maybe Plumb is trying to speak. Maybe he's trying to shake his head. Dunya laughs down at him.

"Any sympathy for someone who inflicts this kind of torture on someone, bound by chains, by mazes, by temporelectrical turbines?"

She flicks the glass with her hand, and for an instant the fiery fog disperses, showing the ghost of a woman, a bald-headed, wide-eyed, sad and pathetic thing, three or four or five thousand years old.

Dunya sweeps her arm forward in a broad arc, taking in the two hundred souls in the audience.

"They mean to do this to all of you," she says. "In fact, they've been doing it for years. Erasing your memories. Erasing your minds. Erasing...you."

CHAPTER FIFTEEN
THE MAZES PRESENT

Violence/Death

At Arkaic University, you can get a beer and a plate of hot chicken wings for three dollars each Friday.

Your campus probably has a similarly good deal somewhere.

Seek it out.

"That clinches it," says Agent Costello, standing in his seat. His voice shakes with emotion—what anxiety, what agitation—but it is loud, and anyway, it is the only voice, other than Dunya's, to break through the tocking and whirring of the turbine. He holds up a badge that is invisible in the darkness of the theater. "I know everything I need to know. My name is Agent Costello, and I'm here with NASA2, ancillary to the CIA, the FBI, and the NSA, and everyone in this theater is to stay exactly where he is. Or she. Or...dammit, can someone turn the lights on in here?"

Sounds of shuffling, mumbling, grumbling. The house lights come on. Ezzie squints in the bright light, but she isn't comforted by what she sees. Clearly, Dunya's performance has had an effect on Agent Costello. He is flushed and sweaty, weighed down with the burden of Atlas and Sisyphus, because he, more than anyone else, has grappled with both emotion and evidence. He feels the implications of the millennia of struggle Dunya has described, and he also knows about the cults and the global implications of their power play.

But if Costello knows the gravity of the situation, the audience knows its intensity. Their senses are primed by anxieties growing day by day, week by week. Prohibitive debt. An uncertain future. Tenuous health care. The fate of parents, the elusiveness of children, and the fantasy of stability. Sickness. Competition. National delusion. Confusion. Oh! Their ephemeral ambitions, stirred into a froth by Ezzie's supernatural script, Elizabeth's supernatural direction, and Dunya's supernatural acting. In a dark theater on a Friday night, sleep-deprived from studying for finals, many of them two or three drinks deep (the Turner Center's Pub sells dollar Shiners and hot wings for two), the students now hear a true story. That the game is rigged. That there is no assurance, no comfort, no consolation, for them, or for anyone. Every so often, a large percentage of humanity is wiped by fate from the cutting board of history. Bad timing? Bad luck? It may be them. Probably will be them. And you too, perhaps.

The chords of their own anxieties sound in the god's wretched answer to the Sybil's sass, and aluminum adrenaline floods their mouths. The color red floods their brains and eyes when they hear about the wealth and manipulation of Positiva and Negativa. And they feel fire, an authentic heat–their bodies become *enfevered*– when Dunya tells them of Professor Plumb's sacrifice of Dr. Glass to the turbines.

These emotions are drawn in by the turbine onstage. Processed down into trash and waste. Projected outward in its temporelectrical field. Reabsorbed and reimagined as violence and death and darkness upon the horrified crowd. And so death and violence circulates through their veins.

Oh fuck, thinks Ezzie. *What have we done?*

Agent Costello doesn't seem to notice. His attention is completely fixed upon the stage and on Plumb in the front row.

"Agent Chaplin? Agent Keaton? Please apprehend the professor."

A man and a woman in the house have just stood and started to move toward Plumb when the audience rises as a mass, shouting, pointing, swearing, demanding. Plumb shouts in a ragged voice and makes a lunge toward the stage, but several students near him have leapt to their feet and grasped him about his jacket. He kicks violently, gets one leg free, and manages to get purchase upon the stage with his foot. He wraps his arms around a curtain to lift himself up, but the students catch at his pants and jacket, and now twenty, thirty, forty people press in upon him.

"You don't understand!" Plumb yells in a cracked voice. "I...am...innocent!" His trousers come flying off of his pasty legs, even as more students crowd forward. "I...I..." and a loud scream goes up from his throat as four, five, six arms pull on his legs. Agent

Keaton draws a pistol and fires it into the air to quell the crowd, but the only effect is that he shoots a spotlight operator in the thigh; she falls to the floor and squeals as arterial blood jets out of her leg and stains the carpet.

Costello and Chaplin make an honest attempt to reach Plumb, but they are thrown back into their seats by hungry hippies and angry neocon econ majors. And just as the agents start getting a beatdown for its own sake, even more students leap onto the stage, rip up pieces of the set, and rush backstage to grab hammers and awls and sanders and files from the scene shop. The kids rush back onstage and begin beating and banging upon the hated turbine. *Click tick dock! Click tick dock! Click tick dock!* It whirs, its rotor spinning faster and faster. Plastic and metal though it is, it somehow expresses thought through all the thought it has leeched and drained, transferred and retained, and knows that its end has surely arrived. It spins sporadically, beeps and whirs, and in a final act of desperation, vomits a jet of tarry nightmare upon some drunk fratboys. No dice. Several frenzied hands reach through the rotor blades and, though they get all chopped up, manage to pluck essential wires from their moorings. The students rip metal fixtures apart. They smash plastic plates. The turbine heaves an exhausted, despairing sigh, and gives up the ghost. Fists beat and bang against the glass cylinder and shatter it, and a splinter of Sybilline ghost escapes into the rafters.

At that moment, the curtain collapses upon Professor Plumb's shrieking and frenzied agony, and both fall in a tangle to the floor. "I'm sorry!" he screams. "They were going to kill me!" he begs. "They were going to kill my family!" he yells. "I'm not a part of Via Positiv –" The words are cut short as a scrawny geometer kid has wrenched a huge metal sphere from the turbine and hurled it full force onto Plumb's head, which explodes like an overripe honeydew, the most delicious melon of all (although you often get inferior servings when you eat them at hotel continental breakfasts).

By now, a horrified Dunya, along with the Fool and the Cybergoth, have fled the stage and made it to the Acedians in the house, screaming, crying, trying to escape, trying to figure out how to help, *but we have to survive,* we can't die, *I can't die in this thing!* Only Cassidy, filled with bloodlust (he will later claim on account of his Scottish heritage), has hurtled toward the stage, foaming at the mouth, venting his fear and rage, and Ezzie can see that Elizabeth Kraus has also gone feral and succumbed. Some of the students are ripping off their clothes, and some of them are dragging lights out of the grid to set the seats and stage on fire. The mob hurls the dead and headless Plumb onto the stage, rips more pieces off of the turbine, and proceeds to beat the corpse until it is nothing more than rattedy-scratchedy strips of clumpy, bloody bones and flesh, hideous, unformed, abhorrent.

That's when the same enraged geometer who ended Plumb's life plunges a fork (where'd he get a fork?) into an outlet (why?) and causes a short in his electrification. The lights go out, except for the flickering body of the geometer.

"We gotta destroy those turbines!" someone yells in a fevered voice. "We gotta wreck the maze!"

"It's under Calliope Cradle!" yells another in the dark. "We gotta burn it down!"

They're both boys. *It's always boys*, thinks Ezzie.

"Listen! Listen!" she hisses to the Acedians and Agent Costello. "We've got to get out of here. This is insane! *Insane!* They don't know what they doing! They're not thinking! When they get to the Cradle, they'll just kill *everyone!*"

The dark and the calm of Ezzie's voice, intense but composed, holds the Acedians' attention.

"Right," says Monica. "If we can jump the moat, I can get us in quick with the portcullis."

"There's a trapdoor in the scene shop," mutters Dunya. "We can take it out of here and beat them to the dorm."

So even as the raging, feverish crowd of students tramples their way out of the theater by the main exit, asphyxiating three of their own en route, the Acedians cross the stage in the darkness, enter the scene shop, lift a secret door in the floor, descend the stairs that pass the student union's indie rock radio station and the unending battle rapping of The Beat Hip Hop Club, and leave the Turner Center for the Arts.

• • • • •

Time is short.

As the Acedians (minus Cassidy) and Agent Costello hurry down the hill and across Sellers Creek on the way back to the Cradle, they can hear, rather than see, the raging mob, just moments behind them. Monica pulls her key ring from her belt while running and, as she tries to pick the right key for the portcullis, drops the whole thing.

"Ahhhh!" she yells. "No, it's a nightmare, a nightmare, a nightmare," she mutters in a still, low voice, and she claws through the grass feeling for the cold metal, looking for the glint of reflection.

"I've got to—they'll kill them—I've got to—they'll kill them," she says, slowly.

Monty catches her hands.

"Monica," he says. "There's no time."

She stands. She nods. On they run.

The Acedians enter the Cradle by the main entrance, and the languid attendant looks up at them with a bemused frown.

"You've got let us in!" implores Monica.

"Had a bit to drink?" asks the attendant. "Have your ID? Or your keys?"

The first of the mob slams against the door outside. Monty jumps against the door and manages to slam it closed. "I'm small," he says, and so Samo, Argosy, 'Lissa, Dunya, and the Fool lend their shoulders.

"We're under attack," shrieks Monica. "And...and...I'm an RA!"

"If you're an RA, then you know better than to speak to me like that."

"We're under attack!"

The attendant puts on her headphones and loads a new playlist onto her iPod. Monica is incredulous.

"You don't even have a smartphone?!"

A glare of fire out the window, then a big boom, and another crash. The feral mob is pushing again, and harder. How many bodies are shoving against the door from the other side? Six? Eight? Twelve? The Acedians brace themselves. Agent Costello lends his weight to the door.

"Wait a minute, wait a minute," says Samo. "I'm from Arkaic, Michigan. I got this shit."

He reaches into his pocket, all MacGyver-like, unfolds a paper clip, and–one, two, three–picks the lock to the dorm. The students shift their attention from the outer door to the inner, slipping into the courtyard and leaving the attendant to haggle over access policies with the mob.

The Acedians hurry down the cracked cobblestones, past the xenon lamps, and into the vestibule of Acedia House.

"What was that explosion?" asks Monty.

"It came from the Dungeon Master's apartment, I think?" says Samo.

"It must have been Dr. Lawless. She'll keep them out for a few minutes!" says Monty.

Samo bumps into Alyssa Carnival in the vestibule.

"Samo!" she says.

"You bitch," he says, fast. "Your fault. Your damn scavenger hunt. Crazy motherfuckers. Where is everyone?"

"I don't know," she says. "The Mavens thought they saw a mob coming at us from the Turner Center, so they evacuated Acedia House through the back."

"Thank God," says Monica. "Who is left?"

"Me? A bunch of first years? The other houses? I don't know."

A crash. A yellow. A yellow glint of fire.

"Fuck-fuck," says Dunya.

"They're in here!" yells Monica. "We have to get out of here!"

"Where can we go?!" yells 'Lissa.

"If I had my keys, I could open the portcullis."

"The basement!" says Ezzie, in steely calm. "We can go into the basement. I think I know how to get us out of here. Follow me."

• • • • •

Mob logic is dumber than a toddler. If Turbines X have some connection to Dormitory Y, well, just burn down Y, right? And so they throw rocks, books, backpacks, whatever, themselves against the windows of Calliope Cradle until they get inside and grab matches or lighters or laptops or televisions or whatever and try to start fires. It works amazingly well. You wouldn't think that a Slavic thing made mostly of stone would catch fire so easily, but the truth is that old buildings like this make use of a lot of wood. Cherry wood, walnut and oak, cedar and pine, lots of white pine, pine for the cheap shit, two-by-fours2x4s and somesuch–students don't need nothing fancy, right?–and when that wood stuff (not to mention all the books and carpets and papers and other bullshit) gets hot enough and fast enough, even the stones get hot and look like burning. They burn bright enough to turn black with soot and cinders. And so columns collapse, flames blast windows out into open air where the fire can freely breathe, and plenty of the rioters get lost in the evaporating oxygen, or worse, in the pure heat and glare of the cannibal flames. Fortunately, the mob has concentrated on the building, not its inhabitants, and so while a few confused or angry students get burnt to a crisp (especially since the fire alarms have been turned off in the wake of incessant malfunctioning), most of them escape through the main entrance, crawling, gasping, onto the Fairway.

The only other refuge inside the Cradle is the basement of Acedia House, and that's where Ezzie leads her friends.

"What now?" asks Argosy.

"I don't—ahhhhh!" yells Ezzie.

She yells because there's a stranger there, leaning against the door to her own suite.

She has never noticed him, never seen him before. The first thing she sees are freckles scattered like sunspots. *That's a lot of freckles*, she thinks. But he is beautiful. Solar. Illuminatory. Kind and patient. He wears a white robe of muslin tied with a white belt, and he smiles at her.

Everyone freezes behind her, waiting to see what she says. What she does.

"Who are you?" she asks.

"I don't think you have time to chat about that," says the boy. "Don't you want to get out of here?"

A lateral explosion. The boiler has gone. The Cradle is burning faster and faster.

"We'll suffocate down here," Ezzie says, "even if we don't burn alive. We've got to get into the chain maze."

"That door?" he asks, gesturing to the forbidding thing that stands, almost rusted shut, between the two bedroom suites.

"Yeah," she says, then, dripping with sarcasm, "what? You got another?"

He laughs. "You have changed a lot over the last ten weeks, Esmeralda Prentice. You should be proud. How few know themselves so well at the moment of their death! Anyway, yes, you can open that door. You could have opened it any time you've wanted."

"What do you mean? Who are you? Why are you here?"

"I'm just the custodian. And I'm here now because, now, you are ready to believe me. You've seen it all, haven't you?" The boy laughs again. "It is so easy, Esmeralda. Put your hand on the door, and it will open for you."

"And that's all?"

"That's all."

A roar from the conflagration upstairs.

The Acedians huddle closer together.

Ezzie looks at her hand as if she has never seen it before in her life. Creased. But young. Not scarred by many years. Injuries. Confusions. She turns her palm out tentatively and leans, reaches, puts her palm against the hard, metal door. It is cool. It is a comfort.

There's a moment of nothing, but then a sigil starts to shine like molten metal:

"Son of a fuck," says Samo.

Ezzie reaches out, turns the handle, and opens the door to the chain maze.

The Chain Maze

If you are attending an official function in an unfamiliar part of your campus,

you should take a map, so that you do not get lost,

and make sure that you have plenty of time to spare.

Let's take account of who is present in the doorway to the chain maze beneath the Fairway and Calliope Cradle. You have the Basement People–Ezzie, Monty, Dunya, and Samo–and some Acedians–Monica, Argosy, Velma, Krista, and now Alyssa–and five other people–'Lissa, Agent Costello, the Fool, the Cybergoth, and the unnamed beautiful boy–right there, in that moment.

The door swings open.

A subglow from the aboveground xenon lamps trickles down into this cavernous place, a silvery white light that glares off of the plain bricks and mortar. Narrow passageways, obsidian black, spoke out into the shadows, but this inner vestibule is drab and ordinary. Brick and stone. The weirdness is in the *click tick docking* of hundreds of turbines whirring in the maze ahead. The gradual convergence and divergence of their various rhythms; they all keep the same regular tempo, as the machines are perfectly calibrated. It is *time* that is unhinged here, and its uncoupled meters surge and fold, surge and fold, until the ticking rolls like a solemn blue tide over the students and into the walls. It is soothing. A binaural whirring. Behind them, the air burns hot. The smoke stinks. The students step into this calming new space.

And the shit hits the fan.

"Glass shatterer!" croak two Book Ninjas, and their claw-like hands bend and flex toward Ezzie.

"Leave off!" bellows a grim-looking, goggle-wearing Inquiscriptor, swinging a mace above his head before throwing it with deadly force at the Book Ninja, who dissolves into smoke at the last moment. Another Inquiscriptor steps out of one of the passageways and draws a big, serrated blade from his belt. He leers into Ezzie. She screams and hurls herself straight into the nearest of the branching corridors. She's vanished, but Dunya is right behind her, chasing the white and pink heels of her friend's sneakers. Agent Costello surprise!punches the nearest Inquiscriptor on the chin and barrels after Ezzie and Dunya, with Samo, Monty, and the beautiful boy right behind him. And then they are gone, leaving the noise and confusion and many of their friends behind them.

"Stop! Wait! We want to help you!" hisses the Book Ninja, lifting into the air and batwinging, hellbent upon pursuit. But Argosy dives forward and throws his arms around the thing's ankles. From within its mask, the Book Ninja lisps. Argosy wails with frostbite but stumbles to his feet and plunges into the passage after his friends. At the same time, a recently tenured humanities prof, sophisticatedly sexy (she had taught the popular Neitzsche Say, Neitzsche Do class), steps out of an alcove triumphantly, ready to stop the Book Ninja. The Book Ninja floats right through her, and she clutches her heart and falls dead to the stone floor. More figures rush out of the alcoves–Inquiscriptors and hum profs and Anthrostrologers and Book Ninjas–and suddenly everyone is divided and confused in darkness and on their own.

• • • • •

The vibrating pulse of the turbines, above, below, left, and right, the contractions of the chain maze–*it's like running through abstract air*–bedizzies Ezzie. Jet black walls. Glowing xenon ceiling. A black and gray checkerboard floor of granite tiles, receding into infinity. Every dozen or so feet, an alcove with a turbine. Every other dozen feet, a new passage, splitting off at right angles. *Cutting away.* The turbines watch with their rotary eyes. They chirp like crickets, and Ezzie's thoughts spiral. She hears a human scream. An explosion. She turns a corner. The new passage is identical to the last. She hears the sound of metal scraping along a wall. She turns another corner. *Click, tick, dock, click, tick, dock.* She turns again. *If these passages are all right angles, then this should be a grid. It isn't a maze at all. But it is a maze.* Every path feels exotic, and so, as she twists and turns and worms her way closer to the core of a tempogravity well, she knows in her heart that she has not yet recrossed her own path.

Click clack! her feet go. *Click clack!* They sound as if they are tapping along a sheet of thick plastic, but this is grim granite beneath her. It looks like the floor of a mausoleum.

"Does this floor sound like plastic to you?" she asks the light-haired girl who is right behind her. *Who is she?* she wonders. *Must be another student.*

"What's granite?" asks the light-haired girl in a loud, amused voice.

"Wait a minute...what's your name?"

"What's *my* name?"

"Yeah."

"D...Dunya?" the girl says, as if it's a question. "What is yours?"

"Esmeralda, I think," says Ezzie.

Somehow, a boy has caught up with them. He has a lot of freckles.

"Who the hell are you?" asks Ezzie.

The boy shrugs.

"Hey look, the corridors are circular now," says Ezzie.

● ● ● ● ●

The corridors are circular now. Monty has tried to keep up with his friends as they move deeper into the chain maze, but Ezzie makes a turn too quickly, and Dunya is right behind her, and Monty misses them. *That's okay,* he thinks. *There aren't any dead ends, and all of the angles are right angles. This "maze" is a grid, and I can just turn and turn and find them.* He doesn't find them. "Which way did they go?" he asks the men behind him, except the men behind him are gone. The Book Ninja is not. The Book Ninja is there and advancing, his feet silent on the glowing, blue floor. *The floor is glowing?* Monty looks at the Ninja. It has gray claws, so Monty turns and runs some more.

Sure enough, ribbons of blue light–teals and aquamarine and deep dark sea–run toward him and flash all around, just beneath the surface, beneath the skin of the tunnel. In their racing, he sees zeroes and ones, *a*s and *z*s, alphas and omegas, and other glyphs he doesn't recognize. The circular passage has changed again. Now, the new passages shoot out at odd angles, some slanting up and some down, and his path starts to turn some angles of its own, with no particular rhythm or regularity. Snaps to the side-the side-or up-up-down. It puts him in mind of the code to Contra. A-B-A-B tracers glide by, down the wall or along his brain. He laughs. There are just as many openings as there were before, but fewer of them are branches in the passage. More of the openings hold turbines. Turbines with their rotors. This earthquake-heaving passage. *There has to be some pattern*, he thinks, and he starts to puzzle it out. *Why am I running?* he wonders. There's an angry shriek behind him. *Oh, right, that thing.* He slides his finger along the blue, flashing ceiling as he runs. It gives him an electric thrill. *At least there aren't any dead ends.*

The passage ends.

Abrupt stop. A turbine there. Nowhere to turn. Nowhere to escape. He turns to face the Book Ninja.

The Ninja stops when it sees that its prey has been cornered. It sizes up the situation for several long moments. The turbines thrum. The corridor flushes blue and dark, then light, then shadowy again. The Book Ninja jabs a shrouded hand out at the boy, and he flinches in pain. The thing emits a terrible, croaking laugh.

"Ahhhh!" the boy says. "Dementors, Nazgul, whatever, why do you things always wear black robes and have awful voices? It isn't discreet!"

This baffles the Ninja for a moment, and the boy moves back as far as he can, so that he's standing right in front of the turbine. He can feel its waves in time with the blue pulses, in pulse with his own heart, vast waves, strong waves, cresting in his soul, a bedazzling blue breaker. He communes with the turbine and through it, through the chain, and with all of the other turbines as well. They are singing to him. He wants to laugh. He stops himself. He fastens his attention upon the advancing Ninja.

"You. Are. A. Vampire!"

The Ninja stops again.

"How did you know?" the creature croaks. Then it laughs. "And who are you?"

The boy thinks. He doesn't know his name, but he can remember a thing or two. "Someone who figures shit out."

"Lawless told you!" hisses the Ninja.

No, I know, the boy thinks. *I know, I know, I know!* And almost without knowing what he's doing–but wait, no! He knows exactly what he's doing–he holds out his arms at his sides, Jesus-like, his fists clenched. And then, with the creature just a dozen feet away, he opens his left fist.

He isn't looking, but he knows what is written in ink upon his palm:

She did tell me.

He fixes the Ninja with an unblinking stare and opens his other fist. The ink reads:

But I would have figured it out on my own.

The creature stops for a moment, baffled.

"But we did not teach you this gift," it says. "How did you learn it?"

The boy clenches his fists again, then opens the right:

I taught myself.

And his left:

Don't you know? I am the Master of Secrets.

Again, this brings the Ninja up short. It waits a long moment in uncertainty while the boy clenches his right fist so tightly that his nails draw blood and stars flood his vision. He stumbles back against the turbine, his left hand on the rotor casing, his fingers just an inch from the slicing blades. The Ninja laughs.

"You have divined our secrets, but you have mortal discomfort. Worry not. I am not mortal. I can destroy you, secrets or no, though it is tragic to lose such a talent as yours to such a meaningless death."

The boy opens his right fist for the third time, and a long string of words dances up along his forearm:

When I first came here, I felt a strange wind, and I looked at the trees, and they opened their secrets to me. They told me which stories were true and which were false. They told me that I was to come here and discover the darkest mysteries that history had hidden. I am meant to be here. And so I ask you, little vampire, who is meant to survive this battle, and who is going to be destroyed?

As the Ninja reads the long scrawl, Monty feels the vibrations straight from the source. The chain is rooting around in his memories, in his thoughts, and he can hear it whispering to him. He has officially acquired the gift of premonition. In the future, he sees his victory. He sees his past. His past: a long ago dusk, when he visited Arkaic University for the very first time. There was an imagined thunder in the wind, and the trees danced and whispered. The sky went red with a rust blood tint. The dorms and campus were set aflame by the setting sun. Behind him, the cold and burning magnet feeds on this memory, but he borrows it for a moment before giving it away.

The Book Ninja looks up.

The boy opens his mouth and eyes, and from them–from his nostrils and fingernails and navel–floods the solar glow of the distant evening. It is palpable and present and washes through the room with its soft and ruddy hue.

"That's not fair!" wails the Ninja and crumbles into dust.

The blue racing streams have sped up. The boy feels a crushing, sharp pain in his head, and he stumbles into the pile of ash and soot in front of him. The turbines. Their consonant waves are trembling across his brain. He feels them pulling his mind apart. It is too much knowledge. Too many dreams. Too many ideas. Too far, too fast. He vomits food, and vomits bile, and falls, hands and knees, into his own vomit. It's too much. It's going to kill him. It is killing him right now. Above him, the pulsing walls have started to change colors.

• • • • •

Running through the mazes because, hey, why the hell not, everyone else is, Samo loses Ezzie and Dunya in the distance first, and then Monty takes a wrong turn (a right turn) and, well, at least Samo's still got Argosy and Costello with him. *But where did Monty go?* Samo wonders, and then he immediately understands. *The temporal manifold changes with time. We can't even go back the way we came.* Be that as it may, the Inquiscriptors are hot on their trail. And so the two students and the agent run onward. The passages, once so neat and crisp in their angular twist, have become sinuous and serpentine. The passage curves upward and to the left before narrowing into a small tube that slides sharply downward. It then opens to the width of a football field, rolls, pitches, yaws, straightens out, and then seems to rotate down the middle so that the three men are running along the ceiling like scurrying insects.

The tall student can't even pick apart the sounds of the individual turbines anymore. Their tocking has folded together. Taken on a cubical sound that blocks out on his ears in endless succession. T-t-t-t-t-t-t-t-TOCK! The shifting colors have solidified, turning in pale bars–xenon bars?–mellow yellow and aquamarine, clementine orange and ultraviolet. They radiate on by in jagged bands. The air is thick with the stench of ozone. The turbines are fused into alcoves on the ceilings and floors, growing like fleshy things, but that's okay, because gravity appears to pull toward the nearest surface. The fugitives may run where they wish.

Except they cannot run anywhere anymore. They've been cut off at last, in a narrow stretch of passage lined with three of the whirring turbines. Up ahead, an Inquiscriptor resolves in the dark like a BDSM nightmare.

He stops.

"What is it?" asks the other student, who has more dandruff falling from his head than the tall student has ever seen..

"Um..." he says. "I heard about this guy."

"What do you mean?" asks the other boy.

"Some guy I knew blinded him with some sort of light show...sometime, oh, I don't know when."

"How do you know?"

The Inquiscriptor is wearing goggles. "Those goggles. They aren't just safety glasses. They're optical-neural receptors that magnify high-spectrum light waves."

"Speak English."

"Means that blind people can see."

"There's another," says a nervous-looking Asian man wearing an ascot.

"Do I know you?" asks the tall student.

"I don't know," says the man, "but I'd rather know you than him."

Sure enough, the other Inquiscriptor has caught up, goggles on his face and a morning star clenched tight in his fists. It doesn't matter what colors cut past him, his face is deathly pale.

"We," says the Inquiscriptor, "are going to slice and dice and mince and mice you!"

"'Mice' us?" yells dandruff boy. "What the fuck does that mean?!"

"Shut up!" yells the Inquiscriptor.

On their other side, the other Inquiscriptor advances.

The tall student thinks.

"Hey, Dandruff and, um, Ascot...can you buy me thirty seconds?"

Argosy and Costello look at each other.

"I think I can buy you twenty," says Ascot.

"I can buy you at least...two," sez Dandruff.

"Do that," says the tall student, and he takes a bent paper clip out of his pocket and sets to work on the nearest turbine.

Dandruff and Ascot face off against the advancing piles of ripped man-meat. It turns out that their estimations of their own powers were amazingly accurate.

The tall student has managed to fashion an Allen key out of the clip and wrench open the maintenance panel on the turbine. Ascot takes off his shoe and fiddles with it in an attempt to activate a built-in laser ray or a projectile razor blade–or to at least remove the laces so he can attempt to garrote the Inquiscriptor. Having only managed to unlace one shoe before the silent Inquiscriptor arrives, Ascot leaps at the man, right as a kick is aimed precisely at his neck. The Inquiscriptor's foot catches Ascot in the stomach instead and knocks the wind out of his body. Ascot's hands manage to reach the big man's groin and curl themselves around the bulge in his pants, but there's nothing to squeeze. If only Ascot had read his file on the Inquiscriptors more closely, he would have known that they were castrated upon swearing fealty to the order, their unmanning accompanied by copious injections of testosterone directly to the pituitary gland.

On the other side, the tall student has just managed to pry open a flange panel, exposing the naked circuitry beneath, when Dandruff closes in with the other Inquiscriptor, who keeps telling awful puns:

"This is going to be the last study break of your life. Because you'll be *broken!*"

And:

"You know that song 'Do the Twist?' Because I'm going to twist your neck!"

And:

"You're going to be tired. Completely pooped. Because I'm going to beat you until there isn't any shit left in you!"

Dandruff lifts his hands to claw, catlike, at the Inquiscriptor, but the thug lunges out, gets a good grip on the boy's neck, and starts to squeeze.

Meanwhile, the tall student sees a poorly placed screw between two wires, plants his clip in the crack, and gives the turbine a rough kick in its belly. A new whine cuts through the surrounding sound, a high-pitched squeal that disrupts the perfect thrumming of the chain, and the Inquiscriptors freeze where they stand. *I got it!* The tall student thinks. "I'm sorry," he sincerely apologizes. "I am. Because this is a real fucked-up way to die." He twists the paper clip, compressing the wires. The pitch goes up. The field contracts, gets funky, radiates, and turns sporadic. The colors intensify and strobe by with blinding speed. In those nightmare pulses and Hiddekel dreams, ultraviolet rays become X-rays. X-rays become gamma rays. Gamma rays enter the Inquiscriptors' goggles and flash fry their brains.

"I demand a penance!" shrieks Argosy's Inquiscriptor as he drops his victim. "No, I mean it, I mean it, a penance, a recompense, my mommy, my Sally, my priest, my –" and that's all he says before collapsing into a smoking pile of death.

The other Inquiscriptor sighs, turns around, twice coughs blood onto his hand, wipes a tear from his face, sits down, and solemnly gives up the ghost.

"We're saved!" squeals Dandruff, flinging his arms around the tall student.

"You're incredible," wheezes Ascot, his voice hoarse. "You just saved us."

"No," whispers the tall student sadly. "I just gave us all cancer."

The stream of lights coloring down the Klein bottled tunnel has become a raging torrent. It rages and foams and loses form and stability.

• • • • •

Screams all around, trembling up through the dark tunnel that goes bright in turn, shivering in a foam of static color and harsh gray noise.

"What is that?" asks the dark-haired girl.

"I...don't know?" says the light-haired girl. "I...think that those are our friends. Do you know?"

The tunnel contracts and winks, eerily.

A group of spiders come around the corner.

"I hate spiders!" says Dark Hair, flinching, twitching.

"Wait!" says Light Hair. "I know these guys...these aren't spiders. They are people!"

And they are.

Is this an optical illusion? wonders Dark Hair. *Is this a hallucination?* Now she sees a dozen old academics dressed in gray robes.

"I can't rememb..." mumbles Dark Hair. "It's bad," she croaks. "We've got to..."

The other girl–What's her name?–is unmoved. She stares down the academics with hate and clarity.

"Hey, you," says Dark Hair to Light Hair. "We've got to..." her lips flap as if they're loaded with Novocaine. "Deactivate...deac...the...chains."

But it isn't working.

Dark Hair closes her eyes and concentrates. Concentrates on making such speed stop. And, though her eyes are closed, she sees him. A beautiful, freckled boy, who has really been at their side this whole time, raises his hand and helps her to slow everything down. They turbines obey, in a resentful, temporary sort of way. The chain goes momentarily slack. The maze loosens a bit. When Dark Hair opens her eyes, she sees that the crazy boil of color and gray sound has settled down into a comfortingly random cascade of white. There is no strobing, no splashing, no raging. Now, the gently shifting lights–really, the only substance that defines the boundaries and limitations of space–have arrayed themselves into quietly gliding luminescent strands...like silk. Like silk scarves that a certain someone puts on each day, to feel that an ordinary day might be special somehow.

Damask.

And there is a door there.

In that damask foam.

A door like a black hole.

An opening.

The beautiful boy stands at the threshold and beckons for Dark Hair to follow.

Light Hair turns to Dark Hair and says, "My name is Dunya. You go do what you've got to do."

Ezzie blinks, because she's awake now.

"Dunya?"

"I've got something to say to these people here...these *Anthrostrologers*."

"Dunya, I've needed friends..."

"We all need friends."

"But I haven't had any. You're my first friend. And my best."

Dunya smiles.

And she sings.

About her disbelief in predictable rumors. About the *controversy*.

The Anthrostrologers rush upon her, but Dunya gives Ezzie a rough shove, and the boy puts his arm around her shoulder and guides her into the black hole. It quickly resolves into a plain, ordinary brick tunnel. Ezzie hears Dunya yelling behind her.

Is she white or black? Is she straight or is she gay?

And shouting: Do they believe in God?

And screaming: Do they believe in Dunya?

Those rough and torn notes, off-key and sloppy, are still dense and dripping with emotion, with anger, with confusion, with determination and pride. The heat of Dunya's resolve seems to melt the passageways far behind and above Ezzie.

Then it is cold and silent.

She moves on with the boy.

Then again, not quite silent.

Not quite still.

There's still the click and tumble of the numberless turbines.

The Grand Elision

Always beware of beautiful boys.

And yet, going deeper, father, darker, even the turbines grow softer. Fainter. Silent. It is all silent. In their feet. In the stones. All around. Everywhere. Time slows. Time stops, it seems.

Finally, Ezzie and the beautiful boy emerge into an unadorned stone room. It is round with a domed ceiling, and white and coldly bright, although there's no sign of any light source.

"Where are we?" Ezzie asks.

"This is the heart of the chain maze," says the boy.

"But there aren't any turbines."

"It doesn't matter. When the turbines were chained together, the field became all. This is its center. All of its energies converge on this point."

"But there's nothing here."

The boy shakes his head.

"What is here?" asks Ezzie.

He gestures to the floor.

Ezzie looks down and sees a faint, dim, mostly-scrubbed-away red stain.

"Is that from —" she starts to asks, but the boy doesn't answer, and anyway, Ezzie already knows the answer. She crouches down to the ground and presses her palm against the rough concrete floor, hoping for some moment of communion, of connection, to this, the last trace of her mother. But it's all gone. It's only a stain. Only a color, left on a sterile, gray nothing.

She crouches in the cold light and cries.

"It is..." comes a voice. "It is okay for you to cry, you know. I cried a lot." It isn't the voice of the beautiful boy.

Ezzie feels a comforting touch, a strong but nervous touch, upon her back. She squints and looks up.

A gray, plain-looking man with a kindly face, a confused and scarred face, stands over her. "There, there," he says. "It's pretty bad, right, but it isn't awful, right? There you go. It got better for me. It'll get better for you, too."

Ezzie notices that one of his hands has been amputated. His face is horribly pitted and deformed, but his smile is sincere.

"And we are very grateful for you," comes another voice, also kindly, although where the man's voice was dull, this low, calming, feminine voice is just tired. Ezzie looks up at a girl her own age, with sleepy, heavy-lidded eyes and dishwater blonde hair. "We have been waiting for you here," she says. "And for a very long time. There isn't really any time here, which you'd think would make it a short wait, but anything feels like a very long time."

"But who are you?" asks Ezzie.

"My name is Ada!" says the girl, and her eyes light up for a moment. "It is so refreshing–so light and wonderful–to be able to remember my name! I was in your house–Acedia House–but only that first day of Orientation. Do you remember me?"

Ezzie thinks carefully, and she then realizes that–yes–she does remember this girl, though faintly. She seemed shy and withdrawn, confused and bewildered. *She seemed even more at sea that first day than I did.* Ezzie nods dumbly. Then, "I do remember you."

She turns to the old man.

"And you are?"

"You've never met me, but I still feel like you've known me, because you've put me in every play you've ever written. I'm Alphonse!" And he grins a happy, sad, innocent smile.

"Alphonse," says Ezzie in wonder. "You...you broke the fourth wall."

"Yes," he says, "yes, that is exactly what I am doing."

Ezzie looks back and forth between the girl and the man.

"But what happened to you?" she asks.

"We were elided," they answer.

"Forgotten by everyone," says Ada.

"Wiped off the whole thing," says Alphonse.

"We were erased from the universe," says Ada.

"We're all gone from it," says Alphonse.

Ezzie thinks. "But then how am I talking to you?"

"Ezzie?" comes a voice.

A rich voice with a steely core. Tentative now. Like Ezzie. Not like Ezzie. Like a complete confusion.

"Mom?" Ezzie says.

And she looks upon Lorraine Glass. Haggard, worn, hopeless, drawn, but completely relieved and ecstatic.

"I just –" says Lorraine.

But nothing.

They hold each other for a long time.

Or maybe, for no time at all.

"And who are you?" Ezzie asks the beautiful boy.

"You know who I am."

Ezzie nods. Sentimentality isn't going to help her cause now, so she plows on ahead.

"Why did you play her like that?"

"The Sybil?" asks Apollo. He shrugs. "You're humans. You're usually beneath my consideration. It was immature of me, because it compromised me, but that's the extent of my guilt."

"That isn't even guilt," Ezzie observes.

"Perhaps not," he finishes.

She can see that it's a pointless argument, so she smiles.

"So what's going on? Why did you bring me here?"

"Via Positiva has won. They've had the upper hand all along, and before winter break, everyone in Via Negativa will be driven away or dead. But Via Positiva has betrayed me. They have done this for their own glory, not mine. And they don't realize that if they annihilate this universe to create others, they will also annihilate themselves. And me. I wish to stop them.

"You see, when Positiva channeled the Sybil's immortality as a focus and sacrificed your mother to the chain maze, they thought that their act would rupture the membranes between universes and create new Big Bangs, new universes, that they could each construct and manage on their own. They were mistaken. The bond they created is too small, too fragile, and the incision is wild and ragged. But elision is seldom complete. A thread connected Dr. Glass to her only living blood–to you–and so they were hoping to complete in their second attempt what failed in their first. Congratulations, by the way...you had been accepted at Yale until Positiva intervened."

"I don't want to go to Yale," says Ezzie. "I want to go to AU."

"Be that as it may, you aren't going anywhere now."

"You don't understand!" Ezzie shouts, and everyone but Apollo takes a step back. "This year, this term, is the most important moment of my life! I am young! And now I am confident! After all these years, I am ready to be someone. *I am ready to be something!*"

"I don't care," says Apollo.

Ezzie stomps her feet and growls in sheer frustration.

"So what, am I elided right now?" she asks.

Apollo laughs. "Not yet, Esmeralda. You can go back the way you came. You can find your way back to your dormitory."

"And if I do?"

"Monty is being destroyed by a turbine. Samo and his companions are dying of radiation poisoning. Dunya is already half-elided."

"So you're saying that my sacrifice can save them?"

"For a while, maybe."

Ezzie chews on her lip.

"What else?" she asks.

Apollo smiles.

"I mean if I go back," Ezzie explains.

"Well," Apollo says, "it could take a few hours, or days, or weeks, but the bond between yourself and your mother would cause greater and greater tremors. You've already been threaded through the eye of the Sybil. It's only a matter of time. At some point, some random moment, the maze will shatter, the membrane will rip, and the universes will meet one another and vanish. That's the end."

"The end of me?"

"The end of you, me, them. Of everyone touched."

"I see."

She scuffs her foot on the concrete.

"So what do *you* want me to do?"

"I'm glad you asked!" beams Apollo. "It's called the Grand Elision. You stay here, feel the machines eat away at your identity, and then, at your last moment on this earth, you break all the glass in all the turbines, freeing and killing the Sybil and breaking the chain maze."

"And that'll save everyone?"

"No," says Apollo. "We can't stop what our enemies have put into motion. The incision remains. But we can buy your friends some more time to figure it out and shut the process down. I'll be here. I'll help them."

"So I get to choose between certain death for me and probable death for everyone."

"Not death for you," Apollo corrects. "Elision for you. The erasure of identity. The destruction of memory."

Ezzie shakes her head. "That's not much of a choice," she says.

She stops.

She looks over at her mother. Lorraine bites her lip and looks back. She holds Ezzie's gaze in her own.

"Well what about *you*, Mom-who-was-gone-my-whole-life? What do you think I should do?"

"I think you need to decide for yourself –"

"I'm tired of figuring everything out for myself! I'm tired of not determining anything –"

"This way," says Apollo, "you get to determine *everything*."

"You are telling me," screams Ezzie, "that everything I've ever done will be forgotten and undone! That it will be like I was never alive!"

Apollo's eyes brighten. "Is that your worry?" he asks. "No, nothing will be undone. Your memory, your identity, all recollection of your presence, will, and intellect will be gone, yes, but time is just a coordinate of position, and your actions are permanently imprinted upon it, even if your vector is erased."

"But I won't get a grave, or a funeral. Monty and Samo and Dunya...and Uncle Clay...and Mom and Dad...they won't even remember me and think about how much they loved me. I won't even get that."

"You don't get *anything*," says Apollo.

Ezzie scuffs her feet against the concrete.

"Ada?" she says.

"Yes," says the girl.

"Hold my hand, please."

Ada does.

"Alphonse?"

"Yes, Esmeralda."

"Is there a new universe beyond the fourth wall?"

"I don't know. I haven't been there yet."

"If there is...will you...will you be with me?"

"I will try my best."

Ezzie nods.

"And Mom?"

"Yes, Ezzie?"

"So, this is a long shot, but if there is a new universe, and if we are born into new lives there, and it is a life like this life, and you are my mom, and I'm your daughter, and they have colleges there, will you send me to college, and give me a chance to do the things I wanted to do here but never got to do?"

"That's a lot of ifs, Ezzie," she says. "But I will do what I can."

"Okay, then," says Ezzie.

She takes a deep breath.

Two.

Three.

"Apollo?" she says.

"Yes," answers the god.

"Fuck you."

For the second time, every glass on campus shatters.

CHAPTER SIXTEEN
FUTURITY

Benediction

At some point you may wake up and not know
whether you are hungover or still drunk.
You may desire fried eggs on such a morning,
and this can make a helpful test:
Try and fry some eggs. If you are able to keep them down,
then you are probably hungover.
If the egg misses the skillet and splatters all over the counter,
then you are still drunk.

The next morning dawns like an obnoxious hangover: too much clarity, too much noise, too much all at once. The events of Friday night stack like a translucent deck of cards, superimposing sense-reality (that *totally* happened), nightmare (that *couldn't* have happened), and strange collisions of the two. What is remembered cannot be forgotten, and what time on campus has caused to be forgotten cannot be remembered. Still, there is evidence scattered about, most visibly in the puddles of sticky blood and mangled flesh upon the floor of the theater at the Turner Center, and again in the charred and scorched remnants of Calliope Cradle Dormitory.

The night's death count is thirteen. Five students from fire or smoke inhalation at Calliope Cradle, three stampeded at the Turner Center, two dead of unknown causes, one cardiac-arrested hum prof, and one fried geometer. The thirteenth corpse is damaged beyond identification until dental records prove it to be Professor Plumb. There are few who miss the man outside of his family, but there are also few who don't recoil at the savagery of his demise. And yet, nobody remembers precisely who did it or how it happened. Cognitive dissonance? Nobody, even those who were at the show and who woke up with strange bits of brain, blood, and bone crusted to their clothing have a clear recollection of who gave the beating. It must have been someone else, right? *Surely, I am not capable of such a thing.*

Another sixty or seventy students wind up at Proctor Hospital, which finds this a major crisis; it's the worst flood of patients since the Arkaen Spring, fifteen years before. They are treated mostly for first-, second-, and third-degree burns, smoke inhalation, broken bones and concussions, and, most perplexingly, for severed hands and fingers.

The strangest thing about the whole situation, however, is the lack of emotion, of passion. Deep shock? Maybe, but shouldn't shock be followed by a total freak out? It doesn't happen. The dead students are buried and stoically mourned, the injured students are treated and stoically consoled, and the city and university get back to their business of preparing for the holidays and finishing up the quarter. It's as if they made a collective agreement to put this tragedy behind them–to not speak of it–*we don't want another Arkaen Spring, really*–and so it really *is* more like a hangover than actual shock. *Bad things happened last night, and we slept it off. We've been sleeping for a long time, but now we're awake. Let's move on.*

Then the students get back to their dorm rooms and find them burnt down, or back to their apartments and find the windows blown out. The entire campus is without electricity. *Oh well,* they think, and resume studying.

Extrication

If you don't have anything useful to say, don't say anything at all.

Samo wakes up right as the xenon light starts to fade and die, but now that the chain has been shattered, an appalled silence replaces the constant, comforting whir of the turbines. He wakes in a plain brick hallway underground. Agent Costello and Argosy are lying between the corpses of the Inquiscriptors, which are sticky with boiled blood. Samo rouses his friends, and they follow their footprints in the dust (thank goodness for the dust!) back to the main corridor. More footprints lead to the sleeping forms of Monty and Dunya. As she sits up, rubbing her head, they notice the frantic, running footprints of the Anthrostrologers that Dunya drove into mad terror with her song. Two other sets of footprints vanish into another passageway, circular, brick, and just a few feet across.

"Maybe someone got hurt down there," says Dunya. "Maybe they need help!"

"There's nobody down there," says Monty. His voice is firm.

"How do you know?" Dunya asks.

He shrugs. "I just know. Somehow."

For a long, hesitating moment, they look into the dark. Then Dunya takes out her phone and turns on its flashlight.

"I'm not taking your word for it," she says. "I'm going."

They wait in watchful apathy–confused apathy–*why do we feel apathetic?*–for a long time, while Dunya is gone.

Then again, who knows how long it takes? They aren't keeping track, and anyway, there aren't any turbine ticks to mark the passage of time.

Dunya comes back.

"Did you find anything?" asks Costello.

She shakes her head.

"It ended in a little room, a dead end. But there's nobody there. The footprints just disappear."

• • • • •

The students do, eventually, make their way back to the basement of Acedia House and climb up to the first floor. They notice that it is gray morning outside, but all of the lights are out. Shattered glass covers the grass and flowerbeds, as if blown out from within. But the glass is only the beginning of the damage. Acedia and Wrath and Lust Houses still tower proudly above the courtyard and the Fairway, though they are scarred by soot and smoke. The other four houses look like they've been through a blast furnace, with little left except for cave-like skeletons of blackened stone and twisted metal. Nobody is there.

"Holy shit," says Argosy, but his heart isn't in it.

They look out onto what was recently the courtyard. They hear the wind. A plastic bag that has been ripped through one of the open windows floats down, blows up and down, and eventually vanishes through the open portcullis.

"I guess Monica must have gotten the gate open and evacuated the rest of the dorm," says Monty.

"It feels like snow," says Dunya.

They watch some more.

Then Agent Costello separates himself from the group, looks at them all, gives a succinct nod of respect, and says, "well, I'd better go and write up my report."

He leaves through the open portcullis.

The remaining students watch some more.

"Let's go to the hospital," says Monty. "People got hurt. I bet that's where Monica and the others are."

They turn and leave the broken dormitory.

It starts snowing.

Reassurance

The end of the term is a good time to do something small and useful.

Something that will help someone.

The rest of the day passes in a cloud of mystery, of history and futurity and liminal intersections of the two. They all understand, they think, the essentials of what *happened*. Dunya's acting, informed by Samo's research and Monty's secrets, incited a riot against the secret societies and didn't give their enemies much time to react. But the students' efforts overshot the mark, and so an angry mob killed Plumb and burned down Calliope Cradle. The Acedians and their friends escaped to the basement, somehow – how?– gained access to the chain maze, and bested their adversaries with their new superpowers and good luck. And then–what?–the turbines stopped working. The chain ceased to be.

"Maybe the turbines knew that we were coming and they just suicided," muses Samo.

"Were they intelligent?" asks Dunya.

"I don't know."

It takes almost an hour to walk to the overstuffed hospital, and once they arrive, they don't know what to do with themselves. Extra supplies and cots have already been brought in from around the county and set up in the ER and the atrium. An exhausted-looking Monica sits slumped in a purple plush chair with her booted heels dropping dirt onto an ottoman. Monty calls to her, but she doesn't notice. Then he sits down on the ottoman and gently pushes on the tip of Monica's nose with his thumb. Her eyes fly open.

"Monty!" she yells, and her eyes and mouth open in a big, bright smile. They hug.

Everyone's apathy starts to thaw a little.

It thaws further when their feet and hands and eyes are finally put to work. Dunya and Monty sort through students' items retrieved from the Cradle and organize them on folding tables to be claimed later, while Samo makes a few supply runs with the Mavens to a Meijer in the suburbs. Argosy vanishes into the crowd and eventually turns up playing games of solitaire with a group of disgruntled third-years. He manages to win about forty dollars off of them. The brief hours of daylight pass, and Monica is finally given permission to leave. Proctor's parking lot is choked with cars and confusion, so they walk a flat mile to the high-rise Armitage Hotel downtown, where they've been placed while the Cradle is cleared of debris.

"I saw that everyone attacking us in the basement was mostly after you guys," Monica explains, "and I couldn't keep up. I couldn't figure out who was going where. I just had to figure that Monty and the rest of you would be able to take care of yourselves. That was when I started hearing the screams from above, in the dorm. I had to figure out a way to get the portcullis to open. I had to!"

"How did you?" asked Samo.

"We were down with the turbines, Samo. You know how caustic that temporelectrical waste is, right? Well, it corrodes metal, but it doesn't corrode PVC, so I scooped some goop up in a pipe, carried it back to your room, and loaded it into one of your potato cannons. I was able to blow the lock clean off!"

"Monica, you are a hero," says Monty. "You *are* the hero."

Monica sighs. "Now that Calliope Cradle is gone, maybe a silver lining is that I can stop being RA. I knew it was going to be stressful. I knew it wouldn't pay well enough. I didn't know it was going to be mind-bendingly insane."

They've arrived at the East Street bridge, and all the ruin and chaos of the day has melted away in the new, glorious darkness. Now that Thanksgiving has come and gone, the poor city has managed to scrape together shiny things to celebrate the darkest month of the year. A. Olan is behind most of it, of course, and many will complain that this money should have gone–should not have gone anywhere else but–to the hungry and the cold. The iced wind is

407

bitter against the students' backs, but they smile unrepentantly in the yellow, green, gold, and blue C9 lights that wink across each of the street-spanning arches and curl up around the miniature maples. The warm amber of the street lights and the bronzed cast they light off of the snow-covered street and sidewalk. The thick fur of evergreens huddled on the median of the bridge. The Armitage Hotel and its warmth are waiting for them. They go inside.

Up on the tallest hill in town, Arkaic University is dark and empty.

Relief

Sometimes you will be tempted to cut back on sleep in order to study,

but never cut back on sleep so much that your studying becomes ineffective.

All of the AU students put up at the Armitage have to sign in on a special sheet, and the four friends are relieved to see that almost everyone they know is accounted for. Velma and Krista have been put together in one room on the seventh floor, and Cassidy is safely ensconced on the eighth. There's no word on the Fool and the Cybergoth yet, but they didn't match the names of the students who wound up dead or hurt on Friday night. For that matter, nobody's seen hide nor hair of Agent Keaton or Agent Chaplin.

"No news is good news." says Monica.

Samo calls 'Lissa for about the nineteenth time, and her mom finally answers the phone. "She's what?! What the fuck! Oh no, sorry Ma'am. No, I'm sorry, I mean–She hung up."

Everyone looks at him questioningly.

"She's out on a date," he mumbles.

• • • • •

Samo and Monty are assigned a room with a southwest view on the fourteenth floor, while Dunya and Monica are grouped together on the sixth floor. After a short discussion, Dunya and Samo agree to trade so that Monty and Monica can be together. There is much to talk about, of course, but little talking, as they ride the elevator skyward. Seventy feet up, Monty and Monica say goodnight, and Samo and Dunya ride to the top floor and walk down the narrow hallway to a small, hotel-sterile room with two twin beds.

Samo claims the bed nearer the window, opens the curtains, and takes a seat.

"Are you upset?" Dunya asks.

"Huh?" says Samo.

"About 'Lissa? On a date? I mean, weren't the two of you kind of dating?"

"Not really," says Samo. He lies down on his back, on top of the blankets, clothes on, eyes closed. "You can turn out the lights whenever you'd like to."

Dunya does so. She takes a shower and puts on her pajamas, and a good half hour has passed by the time she's back. Samo lies in exactly the same position. He hasn't closed the curtains, and it has started snowing outside. The light from the streets below, magnified by so many snowflakes, seems to intensify the brightness of the night. Diffused light. As she looks out the window in the dark, over the river, into Arkaic, she realizes that she is facing the hospital, and beyond it, the neighborhood of South Branch. Where Samo's family lives. He grew up out there, although there doesn't seem to be much light outside of downtown itself.

"I'll probably be upset about it tomorrow," he says softly from his bed, "but right now I'm just too tired."

Dunya slides under the covers of her bed and enjoys the coolness and closeness of the sheets and the freshness of a pillow that was laundered that morning. She's drowsy but says, "If you want to talk about it, Samo, we can talk any time."

"Thanks," he says, and then, "I've got Crew practice in the morning. I'm looking forward to it. We're going out on the river. It'll be cold, but foggy, I think. Nobody is awake on a morning like that. Almost like nobody's alive out there. Just the sleeping trees. Because it's winter –"

And just like that, Samo's asleep.

Dunya turns onto her back.

"Because it's winter," she says.

She's troubled.

She's worried that she's forgetting something, but she can't say what.

She's forgotten.

She stares up at the ceiling for many hours, waiting for sleep to relieve her exhausted body.

Finals Week

It is easy to underestimate research papers.

With a test, you only need to invest the time necessary to answer the questions correctly.

Research papers take time, no matter how well you understand the subject.

Arkaic University shows its commitment to the path of stoicism throughout the week. Despite the student casualties, not a single exam is postponed or canceled. Despite his almost universal unpopularity, the Elysium Chapel is standing room only at the candle-lit funeral of Professor Plumb. The casket is closed, of course, and the icy air and cold December gray shining through the crushed panes of stained glass give the event a ghoulishly gothic feel, but the muted feelings among students and staff prevent anyone from commenting on this. Likewise, the national press, which hung out on campus a few days, trying to sensationalize the events of that fatal Friday, gave up when nobody was willing to weep or scream or implore justice in their interviews.

"You went to the funeral, didn't you, Samo?" Dunya asks that evening.

"Yeah, you?"

"I did."

"Why?"

"I don't know. I didn't know anyone who knew Professor Plumb. I guess I was curious because he had that connection to Via Positiva."

"Yeah, how did we get started on that, anyway?"

"I don't know," she answers. "But it bugs me."

The more they dive into their studies and extracurriculars, the more things seem to return to normal. Elizabeth Kraus calls a meeting of *The Moldy Fountain*'s cast and crew. She has stitches across her cheek where another student bit her, and several of her teeth are missing. She explains that the other two performances of the play had to be canceled, but that nobody could sanely deny that the production testified powerfully to relevance of live theater.

Samo, on the other hand, has been told that he is too tall, too awkward, and too rhythmically impaired to make an adequate coxswain. He's invited to come to Crew meets for free, however. He sighs.

"Just let me ride on the river with you one last time," he says. His request is granted. The black river mirrors back the sparkling stars that shine in cities where most of the lights have gone dead. The icy water is as still as a plane of glass.

• • • • •

The strangeness of life at the hotel also quickly melts away. The continental breakfasts and dinners are, by and large, not that different from the cafeteria food, and the rooms aren't much larger or smaller. Arkaic University has managed to restore electricity to about a third of the campus by midweek, and rooms are rented out at Southern Michigan University downtown for the rest of the classes. Samo calls 'Lissa each day, hoping to meet up for coffee or dinner, but "she's out with her man," 'Lissa's mom tells him, with sauce.

"Man, fuck that bitch. And her mama too!" he says, and Dunya watches him sympathetically.

As for exams, even the quarterly panic has been muted by the recent catastrophes. Students file in and out of their classrooms, sit calmly, fill out their Scantrons and notebooks, and march the results up to the professors. Often, the whole room fills and empties in three hours without a dozen words being spoken by anyone.

Monty aces all of his exams.

Samo squeaks by on his—not extremely well, but within the margin of safety. He's not going to have to reconsider his concentration yet. He still looks at the contrails arcing through the air above him and wonders what they must look like from far overhead.

Dunya only has two exams, and they are easy enough; she had two weeks of nothing but study at the Atlantis, after all. Her paper is much more difficult. She signed up to write a piece for the Classic Vampire about links between Longinus, Carmilla, and the Blue Öyster Cult's *Imaginos*. It isn't an easy task, as there was no easy way to conduct research from the Atlantis, and now she's almost a month behind. This week, she sleeps even less than she did during her midterm work-study-rehearsal binge, reading/writing/revising, rinsing and repeating, and beating a dead horse.

And then, on Friday, the paper is done, and Dunya receives an email from the university:

from: Michael Davis <mdavis@arkaicu.edu>

to: Dunya Blavatsky <dblavat@arkaicu.edu>

date: Fri, Dec 9, 2011 at 8:45 AM

subject: Acedia House, Calliope Cradle

Dear Student,

We are pleased to inform you that your residential house (Acedia) at your dormitory (Calliope Cradle) has been properly secured following the fire of last Friday. We encourage you to return to your suites there for the night tonight, and check out according to the end-of-quarter policy by noon (12:00 PM) tomorrow, the 10th of December, Saturday.

Regards,

Michael Davis
Dean of Housing

·····

Dunya returns to Calliope Cradle that very day, as soon as she's handed in her paper at Valentine Hall. It's only ten in the morning, and the dorm is still and almost empty. The windows to Dr. Lawless' apartment are dark and quiet, although Dunya does notice a small hill made entirely of charred and blackened tropical plants below one of her windows.

Although the dorm has been "properly secured," it still looks hideous, with large swaths broken and uninhabitable, as if they had been struck by meteorites. But of all the houses, Acedia seems to have weathered things the best. Dunya notes a few glossy panes of newly fitted windows, contrasting with dozens of sheets of plywood securing the rest of the dorm. When she steps inside the house, she welcomes the chortling and banging of the radiators; evidently, there's an old coal plant half-buried in the Hunting Grounds that was reactivated for the short term. In the long term, the is going to reactivate the tunnels beneath the Fairway, this time using the power of steam. There were early discussions about replacing the turbines and erecting a new, even larger maze, but such talk suddenly went silent. Dunya wonders if Agent Costello's report had anything to do with this.

It starts to feel like any old day at Arkaic University as she walks down the stairs to the basement and sees the familiar doors to her left and to her right, and the industrial door straight ahead, closed and flush to the wall as if it had never been opened at all.

How did we get in there? she wonders. *I don't think I had a key.*

No...no, things aren't quite back to normal here after all.

For one thing, the humming and whirring of the turbines through the walls–that was a constant thing–soft as it was, she could always hear it. Now, all is still.

And then Dunya notices the paper taped up onto her door.

DUNYA BLAVATSKY
RICHMOND, CA
and
ESMERALDA PRENTICE
NEW YORK, NY

That's strange, she thinks. I don't have a roommate. She must have dropped out or transferred before she ever got here. Strange that I didn't take this down before.

Dunya rips down the sign, crumples it up, and puts it into her pocket.

She goes inside and lies down on her bed.

I must be hallucinating, she thinks –

– and falls asleep before the thought is complete.

I Am...

*Movies will seem trippy if you watch them on too little sleep,
and movies that are already trippy will push you over the edge.*

Bang bang bang bang bang!

Dunya snaps up in her bed. She had been having a nightmare, but indistinct, how, what? A hundred cloaked figures–vampires?–chasing her through a brick tunnel, then on and on again, as fish and anemones, through an inky ocean. She was just waking up, being offered a choice between immortality and dea– *bang bang bang!*

"Just a minute," Dunya calls out.

She walks to the door and opens it to find Monty and Monica on the other side.

"We're going to watch a movie," Monty says, "want to join us?"

"I, um, think you just woke her up," says Monica, with an apologetic smile.

"I'll watch a movie," says Dunya.

They're joined in the house lounge by Velma, and the movie is *Akira*.

Dunya saw it once before, but it was a long, long time ago, before she ever fled from assassins, incited a riot, survived a fire, took two finals, and spent sixty-two consecutive hours awake, writing a paper about vampires.

She sits on one of the understuffed couches and watches Tokyo get all ruined by a boy who becomes an octopus-tumor and makes people explode.

"I am Tetsuo," the movie says as it fades into darkness.

The words are reflective of something. Dunya doesn't know what. She feels as if she's just a hallucination.

"I'm hungry. I feel like I just crawled out of an Egyptian pyramid. Who wants to go to Hickory's?"

They stare at her.

It Isn't...

You've watched your friends in the intensity
of study and work all term long,
so don't pass up the opportunity to see them in the intensity
of partying during the break.

An hour later at Hickory's. It's Samo, Monty, Monica, Argosy, and Dunya.

They all look like they've been run over by a bus.

Monty and Monica didn't sweat their finals, but they've been catching up on time together and missing out on sleep for that reason. Dunya's evidently pulled some herculean all-nighters completing some paper; her eyes are red, and she has a red nose and stares fixedly out the window onto the brick street. Argosy looks well-rested and relaxed, but he never folds his clothes or combs his hair; his natural state is hobo-ish. As for Samo, yeah, he stayed up plenty studying for those exams, and he's still recovering from last week's antics, but more than anything, it's 'Lissa on his mind, turning his guts inside out.

"We all look awful." He says it.

Monty looks at him quizzically, and Dunya gives a cynical, worn laugh that comes from a place too tired to match words to thoughts.

"I'll have two coffees and a coney pizza," says Argosy. "What?" he asks the rest. "I'm not tired."

"I'm forgetting something," Samo says. "I know I'm forgetting something. I think it has something to do with the turbines. I think that now that they've all been destroyed, I can't remember how they fit together any more. A week ago, I could have built one from scratch if I just had the equipment. Now, I don't think I could even assemble the battery kit."

"I think that the quarter is over, Samo," says Argosy. "I think you need to relax."

Samo stretches and thinks. Then he sees. There's a girl at the bar, slim with swagger, leaning happily forward, waiting for her drink. It could be 'Lissa, "but it isn't."

He realizes he's said this out loud, because his friends look confused. He looks right back at them.

"Well, it isn't!" he says.

They stare some more.

"Okay, look, I've got one life, and I'm not going to burn it out waiting for one girl to come to her senses. There isn't any time to waste, and I mean, not one more day."

"Are you looking at a girl?" Monty asks.

"No, Monty, I'm looking at you." Samo jabs at his suitemate with his finger. "How about you and Argosy come and stay with me for winter break? We'll tear this town down. I'll show you that there are real parties here–real getting crunked and breaking into abandoned building parties–for Christmas, New Years, Kwanzaa, Boxer Day, and –"

"I'm down," says Argosy.

"Cool!"

"My parents will want to see me –" starts Monty.

"That's too bad. You tell them you can't. You have to stay here in Arkaic. With me."

Monty smiles.

"We'll see."

What Happened?

Do not wake those who have earned sleep through hard work.

After days of studying and tests, after nightly shenanigans with Monica, after *Akira* and Hickory's, Monty knows that his body has given all that it can. He's the one who suggests hiring a cab, and he's the one who pays their fare back to the Cradle. When he and Monica slink down the stairs to his suite with Samo (because the basement rooms are the only ones that don't smell like burnt popcorn), out of their clothes, and into bed, he doesn't expect to be awake for long.

But he is.

What happened?

Some things just don't add up. He thinks about his first encounter with the Inquiscriptors, when he fell down a grate and waited all day to be rescued. And then he wound up at the hospital that night. Had someone helped him? Not that he can recall, so he must have climbed out himself and walked. But that's not possible!

At around the same time, Monty remembers sneaking into Professor Plumb's class with his unearthed copy of *The Arkadian Archive. Why?!* The article had something to do with Lorraine Glass and her disappearance, but why would he go to that class? What could it possibly accomplish?

After Dunya disappeared and Samo vanished from room 227, Monty recalls making a resolution to tell his best friends about the secrets he had uncovered. But who could he have told? Those best friends were Samo and Dunya, and they had been gone. *Was it Monica? No! I didn't tell Monica for another week or two. I remember when that happened, at the library.*

And then there was the matter of the shattering glass. That's the strangest part of all. All quarter long, windows would explode at the strangest moments, inexplicably. Thinking back on it, he can draw connections to the activity of the turbines–Lorraine Glass' disappearance three years before–and the massive shattering of last Friday. But *what* had caused it? In his memory, it seemed spontaneous.

Monty turns the facts over in his head, and then he turns them over again and again. But two plus two never equals four. He thought that he had uncovered all of the secrets, but here's a huge one, and based on the way it stacks up, it isn't like there's something else he needed to notice but didn't. There is no clue that needs to be unearthed, or puzzle deciphered. No. This feels like a part of his brain–an important part–a part he cared about–has been carved out and discarded, and all of its insights, its power, its emotion, lost to him forever.

He doesn't realize it for a moment, but his face is wet.

Whatever has been lost, he realizes, is precious. But it's gone. That absence is one of the worst feelings Monty has ever known.

Putting his arm and elbow across his face to stifle the tears, which are coming on stronger and stranger, he curls himself into the sleeping bean shape of Monica at his side, to take comfort in her closeness and her warmth.

Goodbyes

Don't worry about missing your friends
at the end of Autumn Quarter.
You'll see them again, and it won't be long.
You'll take a short break,
but soon you'll be back and working harder than ever.

Saturday dawns.

The sun rises over a new dusting of snow, which makes the skeleton shapes of the Cradle even more stark and bleak by contrast.

Dunya hears a slight tapping at her door.

"I'm awake," she says, surprised at the lilt in her voice. *I've done it!* she thinks. *I've survived my first quarter of college!*

The door opens a crack. It's Monty, with Samo beside him.

"Can we come in?" Monty asks.

"Sure!" says Dunya. "Where's Monica?"

"Still sleeping," Monty mutters. They open the door and step inside.

"You leaving soon?" asks Samo.

"In about five minutes. I've got to get to the airport. I'm going to do everything I can to catch some sun in the next few weeks, since I know I'm not going to get any here."

"Yeah?" says Samo with a laugh. "The cold getting to you?"

"It's awful."

"Nah! This is nothing. You haven't seen nothing yet."

"I hope you're wrong. I hope global warming is right. At least this winter. But I'm going to see if my dad can drive us down to Tijuana for a week, and we can maybe ring in the New Year down there. What are your plans?"

"You mean *our* plans!" says Samo.

"Second person plural?" asks Dunya.

"Boom! No, but it's our plans, for real. Monty agreed to stay here in Arkaic over winter break. And Argosy, too. So we're just waiting for my Moms to come and pick us up. Right, Monty?"

But Monty is distracted. He's crossed Dunya's room and is examining the closed door that leads to the inner room.

"Monty?" asks Samo.

"I swear, I remember," says Monty, "I swear, being in that room. We *did* things in there. We were in there...a number of times."

"That doesn't make any sense," says Dunya. "Nobody lives in there."

"I know, right? But then why do I remem –" and a new thought occurs. "Dunya, why did you pick this room?"

"What do you mean?"

"No windows. You mean, you like being in here, without any kind of view? I think you would have picked the inner room if you didn't have a roommate."

"Hm," says Dunya, "yeah, that is weird. I don't know either. I would've liked –"

Monty has opened the door.

Inside is a room that feels still, watchful, haunted. There are books on a bookshelf, and an unmade bed, and piles of papers, and a closet full of scarves and shawls and bracelets and dresses, all with a sort of innocent exuberance, a half-cautious leap into color.

"Wow," says Samo, quiet as a breath.

"Wow is right," says Monty. He walks over to the bookshelf. "I remember shreds–ragged edges–I can't even say how–it's like something that I read has been erased. It's like I don't even know. But I know something. I've been here. I cleaned up a mess of broken glass here on the very first day of Orientation."

424

"But that doesn't make any sense," says Dunya, and she crosses to the desk and begins flipping through the loose papers there. "Some of these are dated from this term."

"Is it your handwriting?" asks Monty.

"No, it isn't."

"Hey, check this out," says Samo, picking up a manila envelope off the floor. "Now here's some spooky shit." He flips through it. "Someone did a first-rate stalker job on that vanished prof, Lorraine Glass. I mean we've got photographs here, and newspaper articles, and...and hand-written letters, it looks like. Monty, please tell me you put this together when you were homeworking up on that Sybil?"

Monty crosses over to Samo and examines the papers.

"No," he says. "I've never seen these before in my life."

"Oh," says Dunya.

Samo and Monty look up at her.

"What now?" Monty asks.

"Someone wrote a play," she says. "It looks like it was written by hand."

"Is it any good?" Samo asks, with a laugh.

"Yeah," says Dunya. "It's beautiful, actually. It's...from the first page, I can't help but think it's something I'd like to see performed someday."

"Really?" says Monty. "A play? Not typed up, written by hand?"

"Right, I know, but listen to this."

And Dunya begins to read, quietly but confidently, with her own sharp eyes, with a focusing of emotion.

QUASIMODO'S METAMORPHOSIS

I think a play in two acts
maybe three acts

Alphonse, Ada, Apollo and Glass all stand in a little brick room.

A student enters.

APOLLO: What would you like to say to those you are leaving behind?

STUDENT: I just want to say: Goodbye.

THE END

Made in the USA
Lexington, KY
07 September 2014